LINDA ANDERSON

WHEN *Night* FALLS

POCKET BOOKS
New York London Toronto Sydney Singapore

An *Original* Publication of POCKET BOOKS

POCKET BOOKS, a division of Simon & Schuster, Inc.
1230 Avenue of the Americas, New York, NY 10020

ISBN: 0-7434-1147-1

First Pocket Books printing October 2000

10 9 8 7 6 5 4 3 2 1

POCKET BOOKS and colophon are registered trademarks of Simon & Schuster, Inc.

Front cover illustration by Lisa Litwack; photo credits: © White/Packert/Image Bank; Corbis/Richard Hamilton Smith

Printed in the U.S.A.

Praise for Linda Anderson and *The Secrets of Sadie Maynard*

"This romantic mystery is full of plot twists and surprises and will delight readers who enjoy a good scare and plenty of action."

—*Booklist*

"An erotically suspenseful tale complete with a surprise villain, a gutsy heroine, and, of course, ghosts. Guaranteed to give you goosebumps!"

—*Library Journal*

"An intense drama spiced with intrigue."

—*Romantic Times*

"Linda Anderson has woven a suspenseful, tightly written plot that just pulls you along from the start. . . . The ending is great! You'll be on the edge of your seat until the very last pages of the book."

—*The Belles and Beaux of Romance*

"An outstanding romantic suspense novel that will haunt your heart and mind. . . . *The Secrets of Sadie Maynard* will have every reader spellbound by the characters, the bittersweet mix of love lost and love found, and the absorbing murder mystery."

—Bookbug on the Web

Also by Linda Anderson

The Secrets of Sadie Maynard*
Over the Moon

*Published by Pocket Books

For orders other than by individual consumers, Pocket Books grants a discount on the purchase of **10 or more** copies of single titles for special markets or premium use. For further details, please write to the Vice President of Special Markets, Pocket Books, 1230 Avenue of the Americas, 9th Floor, New York, NY 10020-1586.

For information on how individual consumers can place orders, please write to Mail Order Department, Simon & Schuster, Inc., 100 Front Street, Riverside, NJ 08075.

for my sisters, Joan and Kay, who remember

ACKNOWLEDGMENTS

A major portion of "thank you" goes to Linda Parr, who rescues me when I am in technical panic and saves my word processor from being dumped on the floor in disgust. Also, I am eternally indebted to members of my talented and caring writing group, Marcia King-Gamble, Debbie St. Amand, Marilyn Jordan, and Margaret Fraser. The theater knowledge comes from my own summer-stock days, many years ago, and from my talented daughter, Duffy Anderson. My attorney daughter, Melissa Anderson, and attorney-at-law Stephanie Mullins provided me with legal information. The hair debacle by the creek I owe to my creative hair stylist, Angie Viard. Any mistakes I have made are my own.

There is a kind and beautiful mountain village in North Carolina where I have spent the past thirty summers of my life. It is the village on which I have patterned High Falls. I will not say its name, but those who live there will recognize it. I have, of course, taken literary license in some descriptions and customs for the sake of the plot. God bless you, my mountain friends—you are the best neighbors a person could have.

There were times when finishing this book seemed illusive and difficult, and I'm deeply grateful for the understanding and encouragement of my agent, Karen Solem, and my editor, Caroline Tolley.

I wish it were possible to meet all of my faithful readers and the hardworking booksellers who sell my books. I would love to thank you in person for allowing me to share my storytelling with you, but all I can do is send you heartfelt gratitude. Thank you.

WHEN *Night* FALLS

PROLOGUE

He walked out of the prison gates without a backward glance.

The odors, the sickly green institutional paint on the walls, and the miserable moaning during the long nights would be forever imbedded in the seams of his patched-up soul. He stopped his slow deliberate pace to survey the moss-draped oak trees surrounding Raiford prison, then closed his eyes and took a deep breath. The north Florida air, though hot and thick, was free, and the blistering June sun on his face energized him.

From the prison bus he heard jeers and name-calling. They wanted him to hurry and board the bus into Starke. He flipped them a finger. Let 'em wait. He deserved this moment. He'd waited for deliverance ever since he'd stepped into his cell, and now that his attorney had engineered a pardon, he intended to savor every second of freedom.

The jeers and chants grew louder, but he ignored them. His eyes closed, he thought of the woman who'd prosecuted him for rape, assault, and kidnapping ten years ago. Her form and face were sharp and clear in his mind. He even caught the light fragrance of her signature perfume, as though she stood right in front of him. She didn't, of course, but he knew where she was and soon he would confront her. He'd dreamed of the confrontation every night for nine interminable years.

Sophisticated DNA testing, not available when he'd been accused, had cleared him, had proved that he'd never raped anyone. He'd only taken what was rightly his. Lannie Sullivan, and that other bitch, Susie Slater, were liars. The governor had signed his pardon yesterday.

"Come on, you dumb sumbitch! Looka him. His first day out de walls and he stands there like a fuckin' retard!"

He opened his eyes and grinned at the yelling, waving men, then ambled toward the dusty yellow bus. He was in no hurry. She was in North Carolina, a day's drive to the north. He'd get there in due time, but first he had things to take care of, errands to run, people to see. He knew she would still be there when he was ready. After all, he'd kept an eye on her for nine years. His idiot cousin had helped with that. Buster had gathered the information he'd needed to blackmail a villager into watching her in North Carolina. The man had reported to him once a month.

He would always know where she was and what she was doing.

He boarded the hot bus. It reeked of body odor and cigarette smoke. For a finite second, he missed the chill air-conditioning of the prison, but then laughed, sucking in a huge breath of freedom as he headed to the rear where he could be alone to dream his dreams. He tugged at the window until it gave with a reluctant squeal. A big blue-black June fly buzzed in and circled his head. He swatted it away and slouched down in the seat.

From his spotless shirt pocket he extracted yellowed newspaper articles his cousin Buster had sent him. He read them over again, and rubbed his thumb across her picture. He still loved her, but she would have to pay for the misery she'd brought him. She deserved the tragedy he read about. If she'd treated him properly, he would have been there to take care of things, to make sure there were control and order in her life.

After he'd punished her, she would understand that she was meant to spend the rest of her life with him. He folded the newspaper articles carefully and returned them to his pocket.

As the bus pulled away from the penitentiary, he stared out the window and saw her face again. He went over the plans he'd made and his excitement mounted.

The fly returned and whined at his ear. He caught it in his fist and held it for a moment, feeling its angry vibrations against his sweaty palm. He knew just how it felt, captured and helpless. He squeezed the bug slowly until the vibrations stopped, then dropped the lifeless thing on the littered bus floor. He took an immaculate white handkerchief from the pocket of his new khakis and scrubbed the sticky yellow residue from his hand, then folded it meticulously and returned it to his pocket.

He closed his eyes and again conjured up her face and her fragrance. Soon. Not now, but soon, he would see her.

ONE

Children drown silently.

The toddler reached for the ball and toppled softly into the pool. Her arms and legs flailed valiantly as she fought a desperate solitary battle to survive. She opened her mouth to cry out, but gulped water instead. Instinctively, she locked her jaws to stop the overwhelming rush of water from invading fragile lungs. Her blue eyes widened in heart-catching fear, and she had a moment of bewilderment at the betrayal of the mother who should have been there to keep her safe. She began to lose consciousness, and the irises of her eyes rolled back until only the whites showed. As the water closed over her ears, the pretty song of the bird nearby became a muffled trill and soon dissolved completely. It was the last sound she heard. All was quiet. Air seeped from her delicate nostrils and she sank until she drifted lifelessly, like a formless amoeba, along the bottom of the pool.

The red ball she'd reached for bobbed merrily on the crystal blue surface.

"Noooooo."

Lannie woke with the familiar cold sweat beading her hairline.

"Damn."

She sat up, drew up her knees, and wrapped her arms around them. Eyes still closed, forehead pressed hard against her knees, she rocked back and forth.

"Gracie, lacey, dancing daisy, makes her mom a happy lady." The singsong rhyme they'd made up jangled in her head.

"Dammit, dammit, dammit."

Lannie hadn't been there when her daughter Gracie drowned, but she knew this was how it happened. She'd suffered this vivid nightmare almost every night since Gracie's death three years ago.

But she deserved the nightmare. She deserved to suffer every damnation that came her way. She should have been there for Gracie.

A gruff bark, and then a soft whine made her smile. She stretched out a hand and found the wiry head of O'Bryan, the Irish wolfhound who had slept at her bedside for the last two years. The reassuring feel of his rough, warm coat soothed her.

"It's okay, Bry," she whispered into her knees. "Only twice this week. I'm getting better, huh?"

He whined again.

She lifted her head and laughed. "Okay, okay. I know it's time to get up."

Early June sunlight streamed through the square screened windows. The rustic one-room log cabin faced east. When she'd first arrived she'd resented the cheery intrusion of the sun first thing every morning and had kept the shutters closed, preferring the dimness. The sun picked up the golden hues of the log interior, carefully crafted more than one hundred years ago by men who knew how to build fireplaces that drew and structures that survived. And, though the nights were still cold high on this North Carolina mountain, she kept the shutters open now and welcomed the light.

Five minutes later she was following her morning routine: letting O'Bryan out, slipping on her soft moccasins, poking up the embers that remained in the fireplace from last night, making coffee in the old tin pot and placing it on the Coleman camp stove to boil, pulling on her threadbare jeans and blue and orange Florida Gator sweatshirt.

O'Bryan barked, and she opened the screened door to sit on the stone stoop with him. Coffee mug in hand, she surveyed the colorful scene before her. The only sounds this morning were the distant wheezy *cheee-up* of a pine siskin, and close-by, the energetic whir of a hummingbird.

She held her breath and froze as the ruby-throated hummingbird hovered over the vivid red Indian pinks growing wild next to the stoop. She could have reached out her hand and touched its tireless body. For a blessed, sacred moment she and the hummingbird existed alone together, and then the tiny bird took impatient flight.

This had been her solitary domain for two years. Though she suspected friends had an idea where she'd disappeared to, only three people knew for sure: her father, and her friend and former law partner, Nell Smathers, and Wilkie Talley. Just this spring she'd followed her father's suggestion that she get help to put in her garden, and she'd hired their former handyman and mountain caretaker, Wilkie.

Guilt and grief had kept her company here for a long time. She hadn't really begun to appreciate the isolated plateau until the last few months, and now woke up each morning looking forward to any gifts the mountain was offering up that day.

Waves of blue-green spruce and hemlock stretched before her for endless majestic miles. Budding mauve and deep-rose hardwoods blended their colors artfully with the evergreens. A dawn mist drifted, weaving lazy lavender ribbons haphazardly through the summits. The effect was ethereal and soothing.

June might be heading into early summer elsewhere, but here near the top of Haystack Mountain early spring flowers and trees still blossomed. Yellow dogtooth violets radiated over the ground all around her and disappeared into the sharply sloping treeline.

Bry's tail began to thump rhythmically.

"Yes, I don't know how you know, but yes, we're going into town today."

She tossed the dregs of her coffee onto the ground and stood up.

"Okay, you big brute, give me a few minutes to perform my pitiful beauty routine, and then we'll leave."

Inside the cabin, she washed her face, brushed her teeth, and drew a brush through her thick red hair. A quick glance in the small rectangular mirror that hung on the wall told her that she should, at least, tame her hair in some manner.

Where was the green ribbon she'd had a month ago? She rummaged in a drawer, found a worn shoestring, contemplated its use, but then discarded the notion. The crumpled ribbon, saved from a birthday present from her father, finally showed itself in the rear corner of the drawer. Quickly, she bunched the mass of hair into a ponytail and secured it with a rubber band and the ribbon. She had no idea what she looked like from the neck down and didn't care. Grabbing her shopping list, she left the cabin.

Bry waited for her beside the olive-drab Jeep parked at the rear of the cabin and across the creek. The 1950s army-issue jeep was perfect transportation for Bry. It had no top or sides, so he could spread his big body in just about any direction. He sprang in easily, and sprawled across the back seat, his head hanging over the side. They splashed through the shallow creek that ran near the cabin and tore down the mountain. Gears screaming, brakes straining and protesting noisily, they followed a barely discernible two-track path, sloshed recklessly through other knee-high streams, and finally emerged onto a rocky dirt road that led to the main highway three miles away.

As she approached the highway, the boulder-strewn, spine-shattering ride smoothed to a rocky crumble, and she shoved into fourth gear.

The Panoz AIV roadster's swift and powerful passage up the curling mountain highway pleased and matched the personality of its owner. Drum Rutledge pressed the accelerator, and a small smile lit his grim face at the immediate response of the small car. He didn't want to be here in the first place, so he took extra pleasure in the performance provided by the special-built roadster. He also had to admit that the cool bite of mountain air was a refreshing relief from the hot weather in Charlotte.

Other than the brisk invigorating air, he found no enjoyment in his first trip to High Falls in five years.

Two reasons brought him here today: one a business favor for a friend in New York, and the other in response to an urgent phone call from the caretaker of his summer house here. A violent storm, not unusual this high in the mountains this time of year, had caused extensive damage and the man wouldn't take responsibility for repairs until Drum inspected the lodge.

He chanced a quick glance at the passing terrain and realized he was probably passing some of his own land.

Usually a small, discreet dark-green sign anchored close to the ground, which said Rutledge Timber in pewter letters, marked the boundaries of his properties. But he'd let this area go untended and uninspected for a long time. So it wasn't surprising that he couldn't identify anything.

Rutledge Timber's enterprises were far-flung. He owned millions of acres of prime timber, lumber companies, and paper mills all over the world. Drum knew that Rutledge employees swore he knew every tree on every parcel, every lot line, the particular whine of every buzz saw that felled a tree, and every hand that planted a new tree to replace the old. But he'd ignored this land in North Carolina. He surmised that longtime employees knew why he didn't spend more time at the beautiful summer lodge that he'd once loved. Newer employees didn't even know it existed.

It was unlike him not to protect what was his, and not to keep a close watch on his investments, but Drum had a deep aversion for the place.

He shifted into fifth gear and swooped around a looping curve, loving the swift obedience of the small car. The mostly aluminum custom-made car had a low center of gravity so it hugged the road and handled well at high speeds. It was Saturday, and traffic was light at this time of the morning. The tourists hadn't found their way up the mountain yet. Except for pickups filled with locals on their way to construction sites and a few retirees wending their careful way to town to buy a newspaper at the convenience store, the looping, dangerous highway was his to conquer. He'd passed them all easily, smiling when the construction workers shook their fists at him.

He took the next curve on two wheels, but the joy he received in the skilled maneuver turned to fear and caught in his throat as a vehicle shot onto the highway from his right.

He stood on the brake and the clutch, downshifted, and swerved to his left. He caught the shoulder of the road, but corrected enough to stay half on the road and screeched to a halt, gravel flying. A jeep careened wildly across the road in front of him, bounced off a tree, then back onto the hard surface and to the center of the highway, rocking from side to side until it came to a complete standstill.

He remembered with alarm a lumbering old Cadillac he'd passed about a mile back. It would be coming around the curve any minute. They were all in danger.

Choking back his anger, he yelled at the driver of the jeep. "Move that piece of junk out of the middle of the road before we all get killed."

A huge brindled dog, thrown from the jeep when it hit the tree, stood protectively next to the vehicle barking at the driver. The woman raised her head, shook it as if to clear it, and looked around her.

Drum pulled onto the shoulder and shut off his motor. He leaped over the side of the Panoz and ran toward her. The Irish wolfhound turned its head, growled menacingly, and bared its teeth. Drum saw the fur on the dog's ridge rise, and he backed away a step.

"It's okay, sport. I have to get your mistress out of the middle of the road." He spoke calmly and softly, hoping the dog would back down. He loved dogs, and was good with them, but he knew this huge brute was deadly serious.

Drum heard the purr of the Cadillac coming toward them.

The wolfhound heard it also. The dog nudged roughly at the stunned woman's side, then gently took her wrist in his big mouth and pulled her from the jeep.

"Good dog," said Drum.

As the dog tugged the woman to the shoulder of the highway, Drum jumped into the decrepit contraption, stomped on the clutch, yanked protesting gears into place, and moved it onto the shoulder in front of his car as the Cadillac rounded the curve. As it passed, the elderly couple within gawked in curiosity.

Emergency over, Drum's anger surged again.

A redhead, a small bruise on her forehead, stood at stiff attention with her hands on her hips, glaring at him. The dog sat docile at her side.

"What the hell did you think you were doing?" she yelled at him. "You've got to be crazy, driving that fast on these mountain roads."

Every foul epithet he'd learned as a young lumberjack surged forth and threatened to erupt, but he fought to keep his cool.

"Look, lady, I'm the one who had the right-of-way, and I'll be damned if I'll apologize. You, and that dangerous thing you're driving, came out of nowhere. It's a blind curve, if you haven't noticed."

"Yeah, and you're the one who's blind," she spit back at him. "I've been using this road for years and this is the first time I've had any close calls."

"Has that contraption you're driving been registered lately? Do they even license jeeps like that anymore?"

She flushed guiltily, and he figured she was driving it illegally. She stuck her hands in the rear pockets of her ragged jeans and threw back her shoulders.

"You lowlanders with your fancy cars come racing through here like you own the place. Go back down to Atlanta, or Charlotte, or Charleston, or wherever the hell you came from, and stay there."

Strands of her red-gold hair had fallen into her face. She stuck out her lower lip and blew at them, but they fell back across her eyes, and she swatted at them impatiently, finally managing to tuck them behind an ear. Her toe tapped rapidly against the gravel. Her ragged Reeboks had holes in the toes and were wet, as were her jeans halfway to her knees.

"So, a redhead with the proverbial temper." He folded his arms and raked her over with his eyes. "What a shame. You look like you'd be nice to take home tonight."

He could have kicked himself. He hadn't said anything like that in years, but something about her infuriated him. He was angry enough at the close call they'd just had, and she was only fanning the flames.

She paled, and raised her hand as if to slap him, but drew back. "Why you . . . you . . ."

"Bastard?" he supplied.

"Among other things," she gasped. Her dusky gray eyes silvered as tears threatened, then dried quickly as she seemed to will them away.

Drum sucked in a quick breath. There was a mystical quality about her lovely eyes that drew him. The velvet-gray ovals were fringed by thick black lashes, but it was what the eyes portrayed that interested him. Behind the angry, defiant curtain of silver, he caught haunting shadows. He knew that look. He'd seen it before.

He took a new appraisal of the woman standing before him, and his curiosity grew. She looked like a derelict, a homeless creature of sorts. However, beneath the frayed jeans and grubby orange-and-blue sweatshirt, he noticed how regally she held herself. She was of average height, but stood tall, lifting her chin imperiously. The bulky sweatshirt camouflaged her chest, but torn, tight jeans revealed long slim legs.

He hated the brief tears he'd seen and knew he'd been acting like an ass.

"I'm sorry. My apologies. I shouldn't have said that. We're just lucky we didn't kill each other, but you should look before you shoot out of side roads like that. Where were you coming from anyway?"

She glanced across the highway at the dirt road she'd emerged from, and his eyes followed hers.

"None of your business."

Drum spotted a Rutledge Timber sign lying half-buried and askew in the weeds along the entrance to the dirt road.

His waning anger returned. This strange woman had been on his land. Of course, he knew people hiked and crossed the acreage from time to time as they did in the mountains, not realizing it was private land. That had never bothered him before.

"Maybe it is my business," he said, but decided not to pursue it. They weren't getting any friendlier, and he was wasting time, something he abhorred. He looked at his watch. "I have an appointment in town. Do you think you can get that excuse for a conveyance off the shoulder and onto the road, or should I do it for you?"

As she walked away from him, he couldn't help but notice she moved with the grace of a dancer, with an airy bounce, on the balls of her feet, toes turned slightly out. She gave him one last dirty look, ordered the dog into the jeep, and climbed in herself. Spitting gravel against his polished shoes, she roared off toward High Falls, the jeep's smelly exhaust coughing noxious fumes. What remained of the tattered canvas hanging from the rusted metal frame over her head flew in the wind like last year's football pennants.

Drum climbed back into the Panoz. Putting one hand on the body and the other on the center console, he slid his long body in under the wheel. He had planned on stopping by the lodge first to change into casual clothes, but wouldn't have time now. He needed to buy food and other essentials for the weekend before his ten o'clock appointment. Underneath this reasoning, he knew that he was simply putting off his arrival at the lodge.

Spencer Case, the director of the High Falls Summer Playhouse, had asked if they could meet at the theater at ten this morning. An ungodly hour for anyone in the theater, thought Drum. But from all he'd heard, Spencer Case wasn't your usual run-of-the-mill Broadway director, and this was summer theater.

Robert Keeting, his producer friend in New York, had coerced Drum into investing in the shows produced here this summer. He had done so gladly, happy to help an old friend and happy to give financial aid to a theater he'd enjoyed in earlier years here in High Falls. But, eventually, Keeting had called to say the summer fare "was in crisis," whatever that meant, and since Drum lived in North Carolina, would he please visit the theater and see if he could come up with some solutions.

He switched on the ignition and pulled back onto the highway with a heavy heart. The weekend had started badly, and he didn't expect it to get any better. It was only his ingrained sense of duty and friendship, and his determination to protect his investments that motivated him to press the accelerator and drive on into High Falls.

Spencer Case frowned at the newest sketches given to him by the set designer. The guy meant well, he thought, but he just wasn't hacking it. He sighed. Oh, what he wouldn't give right now for one of his eager, talented New York designers. *No grumbling, Spencer. This is something you wanted to do.*

He heard voices in the back of the theater, and looked from the brightly lit stage into the dimness of the house.

A tall man strode purposefully down the left aisle. He couldn't see his face, but the immaculate gleam of his shirt collar and cuffs shone blue-white in the darkness.

Spencer ran a hand over the top of his brush-cut, tugged at an earlobe, and sighed again.

"Here comes trouble," he said to his assistant.

Mae Nevins, who sat on the floor next to him, glanced up from the notes she was making.

"Who is it?"

"Robert Keeting's friend, Drummond Rutledge. He's an investor in this summer's shows. Lives in Charlotte. Got more money than God. Owns most of the timber in Virginia, North Carolina, and South Carolina. Keeting figured he'd be a good troubleshooter."

"Who's in trouble?"

"Keeting thinks we are. We're considered a show in crisis."

"What's that?"

Mae worked hard, and he was lucky to have her, but sometimes her lack of theater knowledge drove him up the wall.

"I'll tell you later."

Rutledge bounded up the stairs two at a time. His charcoal-gray suit was immaculate, trouser pleats knife sharp and bending at the correct angle on his polished loafers. But his sandy hair looked wind-blown, as if he'd stepped from the shower and forgotten to comb it and couldn't care less.

From a quick experienced once-over, Spencer decided this was not just a well-dressed, overly rich young man. The clothes were expensive and tasteful, but the ruggedly handsome face had been nicked here and there, and the nose looked as if it had been broken at least once. A short scar slashed through one eyebrow lifting it a derisive fraction. Football, rugby, fistfights? wondered Spencer.

"Spencer Case?"

"I am, and you're Drummond Rutledge."

"Yes." He gave Spencer a brief smile, a firm handshake, and a swift, charming Robert Redford smile, but his navy-blue eyes, so dark they were almost black, remained cold and unreadable. "I'm not going to beat around the bush here, Mr. Case. I know Keeting told you that I was just an investor interested in this summer's playbill because I have a home here. I suspect you know that I'm here for other reasons."

"Yes, I thought as much." Spencer had been prepared to dislike Drum Rutledge, but decided to withhold his opinion. The man might be brusque, but he was direct and to the point. "Robert doesn't like the dollars and cents picture coming from down here. You're really here to snoop around."

Anger sparked fleetingly from the dark eyes, but quickly faded. "I wouldn't call it snooping, but yes, I'll be hanging around for a few days. I'll try to stay out of your way. Maybe I can be more objective than you, spot some things that could help improve the operation."

God, they talk like this is a corporation, not a creative entity, Spencer thought.

"Perhaps, perhaps not. Maybe we'll always be just a struggling group, trying to put on an entertaining show for a few good audiences the old-fashioned way."

Rutledge said nothing for a moment. His frosty eyes pierced through the first layer of Spencer's outer defenses before Spencer had a chance to lock the gate. He knew he was being read by an expert, and he determined to watch his sarcastic tongue and his attitude from now on. Spencer might be a foot shorter, but he was twenty years older than this rich smart-ass, and he'd worked with all sorts of characters in and out of the theater.

Come on, Spencer. Don't let him hook your child.

"If you don't mind, I'm working on some plans here, and rehearsals start in a few minutes," Spencer continued. Yawning actors were straggling into the theater, and someone idly tickled a show tune from the piano. He spread his hand in an inclusive gesture, indicating the seats in the house. "Make yourself at home. We'll try to forget you're here."

Instead of heading for a seat in the dark theater, Rutledge stuck a hand in his trouser pocket and casually stooped to pick up a sheaf of set designs that lay on the floor.

"This what you're working on?"

"Yes."

The grim set of the man's jaw relaxed, and he loosened the square knot of his silk tie as he studied the first page of the design. His finger traced around a hinged joint on the blueprint, then lifted the first page to thumb swiftly through the rest of them. Spencer watched interest gather on the stern face.

"Who drew these?"

"Our technical supervisor." Spencer had given the man the courtesy of a title, but he was really little more than a local carpenter.

"I see. Any chance I could take a look at your shop?"

Spencer's heart sank. Any hope that this man was going to do a cursory inspection, stay for a couple of shows and then leave, were dispelled.

Mae Nevins said, "I'll be happy to show you around, Mr. Rutledge."

Spencer belatedly introduced the two, and his heart took another downward turn when he saw the glow on Mae's middle-aged face as she gaped in starry wonder at Drummond Rutledge. All he needed was an assistant with a crush on the man. Mae would be rendered absolutely useless. Nothing he could do about it.

He sighed. "Sure. Mae, take him to the shop, or wherever he wants to go. Let me know if you want to meet later, Rutledge. I've saved a seat for you for tonight's performance."

"Thanks," Rutledge said. "Do you have another set of these plans?"

"The head carpenter should be in the shop. He may have another set. These people aren't exactly professionals, Mr. Rutledge, but most of them have worked here before, either giving their time voluntarily or being paid a small pittance. I'd appreciate it if you didn't scare the piss out of them. If you have any concerns, please address them to me and not to my people."

"Certainly, Case. I'm not here to cause trouble."

Maybe not, thought Spencer, *but my old bones are telling me otherwise.* He watched as Mae, twittering non stop, led Rutledge backstage.

The ingenue for *Our Town,* who ordinarily avoided him like the plague, sidled up to him.

"God, who was the hunk, Spencer?"

"Just an interested visitor, Betsy," he growled. "Aren't you supposed to be learning lines?"

She skittered off like a frightened kitten.

Spencer wondered why Rutledge would be so interested in the building of the sets. He rubbed a hand over his face and tugged at his chin. One thing he knew for sure. With the arrival of Drummond Rutledge, the placid summer he'd hoped for was fading.

TWO

Lannie, still angry from her encounter with the arrogant lowlander, raced into the parking lot, braking sharply as she almost nicked a corner from the statue of Henry Bascom, founder of the town, and came to a screeching halt in front of the post office.

It was early in the season and parking spots were easy to find. Three weeks from now, after the Fourth, the lot would be filled with elaborate four-wheel drives and Mercedeses, hugging close to the locals pickups, modest Hondas, and Fords.

"Stay here, Bry," she ordered.

She hurried into the new square, red-brick post office High Falls residents were so proud of. Frankly, she preferred the old clapboard one, which sat between two big elms on Sally Street, and was now David's Tea Room. The former one had always felt like an old-fashioned general store, with people stopping to chat with one another, and then buy a few groceries from the postmistress, Mimi Tate. Ancient Mimi had been replaced when the new building opened last year.

She approached one of the two clerks on duty at the counter.

"Hi, Buck. General Delivery for Lanier Sullivan."

The man smiled at her and turned to check the general delivery box. The postal employees were local people and accustomed to her bimonthly visits. Buck knew her face, but she came so infrequently she always asked for her mail by name. Sometimes she was sure that town people from her younger summer years here recognized her, and respected her need for privacy and anonymity, though she'd never even asked.

The mountain folk were friendly, but closed mouthed and kept to themselves mostly. In the wintertime, High Falls was a sleepy village of twelve-hundred residents. She knew some were curious about the carelessly dressed woman with the huge dog who came to town infrequently and never made friends, but they never asked questions.

She felt someone looking at her. She turned to find a woman in tennis whites regarding her with unabashed curiosity. The woman looked away quickly. A Gucci racquet carrier was slung over one shoulder and enormous diamond studs sparkled on her tanned ear lobes. So, the country club circle had arrived, thought Lannie. She'd been a part of them once. Maybe the woman recognized her but couldn't reconcile her careless appearance with the Lannie Sullivan Ravenal she'd once known. Good. That was fine with her.

Lannie now viewed the tennis, golf, bridge-playing crowd with wonder.

How had she ever lived so blithely? How had she ever thought that losing a match might ruin her whole week? Had she been so conditioned to the status quo that she never noticed the misery of those around her? Dear God, she hoped not.

Surely, such people had suffered tragedies, too. Were they braver than her, stronger than her? The year after Gracie died, she thought she might be able to keep smiling, keep enduring the sympathetic looks, the well-meant, but torturous solicitous comments. She'd thought she might make it through. But then came the double whammy. Tom, the law-school sweetheart she'd loved and married, had left her, blaming her for their daughter's death.

The day the divorce papers came through, she wimped out. Ran away from Madison, Florida, to the mountains of her summer years and to the remote cabin her father had kept for secluded weekends.

She wanted to stick out her tongue at the curious woman, but turned back to Buck, who still sifted through a pile of mail.

Lannie knew it wasn't only her thrown-together mode of dress that interested the woman. High Falls people, locals and summerfolk, were accustomed to all sorts of dress, but not having a postal box was almost social annihilation. Postal boxes were a sign of having been a longtime summer resident of High Falls, and the lower the box number the higher your status. Families who had been coming to the small town for one hundred summers or more had the lowest numbers.

Around the corner, a box numbered 277 belonged to Lannie's father, Judge Wexford Sullivan of Madison. More than two years ago, in line with her complete rejection of life and polite society, when she'd begun her self-imposed exile, she'd opted not to use the box or anything connected with her former life here in High Falls. She seldom encountered people from that country-club life, but when she did she simply turned and headed in the opposite direction.

She doubted if they would recognize her unmanicured appearance anyway.

"Here you go, Miz Sullivan." Buck handed her a large envelope and several smaller ones.

Inside the large envelope were odds and ends of legal notices and business correspondence, which Nell forwarded to her every month and a tearful note from Mausie, the family housekeeper begging her to come home.

At first, many friends had tried to keep in touch, but her decision to hide from everything, including intrusive relationships, had kept her from corresponding with anyone.

Nell had been the only one who'd persisted, until finally, last winter, Lannie had answered one of her letters. They'd written to each other ever since. Lannie tossed the envelopes into the jeep, saving them to read later over a cup of tea.

"Let's go, Bry."

He leaped from the jeep and followed her down the hill to Main Street. They passed Mary's White Cottage Antiques, the Christmas-All-Year Store, and the Gem Shop (N.C. rubies, sapphires, and opals, polished and unpolished).

Emerald saddlebacks and mountain peaks rimmed High Falls, giving the impression of a cozily cupped toy Swiss village, white-spired churches and quaint log buildings included. Though the influx of developers, Yankees, and weekend tourist buses annoyed her no end, Lannie still loved the look and feel of the crisp little village.

They turned the corner onto Main Street, and Bry whined. Until a year ago, an ice cream store had been there, and Lannie had always treated him to an ice cream cone. Now a real estate office filled the space, one of many that dotted the town. Real estate offices competed with as many churches for available space in the rapidly growing town.

The Victory Methodist Church steeple bell chimed ten o'clock.

Lannie usually made only three stops when she was in High Falls: the post office, the grocery store, and Longfellow Books. Sometimes a visit to the General Store was necessary if she needed hardware supplies. This morning she headed for the bookstore, leaving hardware and groceries until last.

Bry's ears perked, and she knew he recognized Longfellow's bow window filled with the latest best-sellers and standard classics, and the hunter-green striped awning that covered the entrance. Knowing he wasn't allowed inside, he lay on the sidewalk, head between paws, and prepared to enjoy the *ooohs, aaahs,* and scratches between the ears he would receive from passersby.

The bell over the door tinkled as Lannie entered the book-jammed store. John Lamb, proud proprietor and knowledgeable literary source, looked up from a pile of regional literature he'd lovingly stacked near the front. The one luxury Lannie allowed herself was books, and her visits to the shop had eventually evolved into discussions with John about the literary merits of various books and authors. He was the only friend she'd permitted herself to make.

"Well, hello," he said, as she wound her way through a narrow aisle. "I thought yesterday that it must be about time for a visit from you. Wow! Did you take some of Uncle Pouty's Spring Syrup, good for all that ails you, or do you have a fever?"

"Why? Do I look sick?" Lannie asked, alarmed.

"No. On the contrary. You're a beautiful woman, Lannie, but you usually come in here, shoulders bent, face closed, body all buttoned up like storm shutters during a hurricane. This morning you're all lit up, color in your cheeks and a lift in your walk."

Lannie laughed. "Must be spring fever."

She realized then that her anger at the close encounter with the stranger was the first surge of honest, uninhibited emotion she'd allowed herself since she'd been in North Carolina. She started to tell John about the rude man she'd met, but hesitated. She wanted to forget the man and the effect he'd had on her. Besides, she would sound like a woman chattering about unimportant things, when all she really wanted was a spirited discussion of books, new and old.

"Whatever it is, you should take a dose of it every morning. Where did you get the bump on your forehead?"

Her hand flew to her forehead. "Oh, well, I didn't know I had one. Must have been the tree limb I ran into when I was hiking this morning."

"Have you given any more thought to what I suggested the last time you were here?"

"What was that?"

"Volunteer work. It's time you ventured out from your hermitage, Lannie Sullivan. I saw a notice on the community bulletin board begging for help at the theater."

"Whew, you're as bad as my former law partner, Nell. She says it's time for me to start living again. I'm living as I want, John. In peace and solitude. No one to bother me. No fears, tears, or stress. All I need are a few good books, a long walk every day with Bry, and I've started a garden that I enjoy tremendously."

"If you were seventy years old and had most of your life lived, I would say that sounded like a blessed and ideal existence. But you're only thirty-two, Lannie. You have a lifetime ahead of you."

"I know you mean well, but I'm doing just fine." She watched a frown mar his pudgy face, and his intelligent eyes shone with concern for her. "Really, I'm fine."

"Okay, if you say so."

"John, one of the reasons I've welcomed your friendship is your nonjudgmental attitude. You've allowed me to be who and what I am without questions or advice. So, please, don't start playing wise counselor now."

"Right," he said, then smiled. "Must be habit. My children are out of school for the summer, and I'm called upon to referee many a discordant conversation."

John Lamb had arrived in High Falls ten years ago to start living his dream. Other than seeing a diploma certifying a master's degree in English from Dartmouth, Lannie knew little about him. He talked of children she had never seen and a wife who taught school down the mountain. She knew the town had been slow to accept this overweight, balding, quickwitted Yankee, because she remembered his arrival and the opening of the bookstore, a long-awaited, much-needed enterprise.

John Lamb had worked hard, had prospered, had joined the right church, and had finally become a respected member of the community.

They talked about the Lamb children, the town's continuing struggle to balance the efforts of environmentalists and developers, and the latest best-sellers. She bought paperbacks by Alice Hoffman, Anna Quindlen, and Anne Rivers Siddons, and *Divine Secrets of the Ya-Ya Sisterhood*, by Rebecca Wells, and then left. It was Saturday, and the town would soon be crowded with weekenders. She wanted to be back on her mountain before the weekly traffic jam ensued on the looping one-way street through the center of town.

On her way to the General Store for gardening supplies, she glanced at the shingled bell tower of the former school building, which stood on the crest of a hill directly behind Main Street and peeked above the rooflines. Local and summer residents had worked together to convert the school into a theater fifty years ago. Energy burned in her this morning. It wouldn't hurt to just walk up and take a look inside the theater, see what they needed.

Why not?

She took a shortcut through an alley that ran past Thelma's Bakery. Fresh-baked bread and cinnamon roll aromas made her mouth water. This was one thing that hadn't changed since she was a child running through the alley to catch a ride on the fire truck. Thelma Howell wasn't a fine French baker, but she made the best sticky buns in the world.

Bry stopped and gazed longingly through the window.

"Nope. Sorry, bud. Maybe later."

The rest of the brown-shingled building came into view as she turned the corner and walked up the incline to the theater. White shutters, paint peeling, framed the front windows. Beneath the hip-style roof, and across the broad length of white fascia above the vestibule, a large sign read High Falls Summer Playhouse.

She walked past a glass-enclosed display case that held discolored handbills from last summer and a freshly typed one listing this summer's schedule. Playing at the moment was a comedy, *You Can't Take It with You*. Listed for the rest of the summer were a drama, *Our Town*, and two musicals, *Oklahoma!* and *A Chorus Line*, which was scheduled to be the last production of the season. The playhouse closed the week after Labor Day.

Fairly standard summer-theater fare, she thought. *Our Town* was a bit heavy, but no doubt High Falls theatergoers were intelligent and knowledgeable. *Oklahoma!* would be playing during the Fourth of July weekend, which was good scheduling. Someone knew what they were doing.

An orange posterboard, hastily lettered and taped to

the outside of the display case, said, VOLUNTEERS NEEDED FOR PAINTING OF SETS, COSTUME PREP, OFFICE WORK, ETC. PLEASE! STEP INSIDE THE LOBBY AND SIGN UP, OR ASK FOR MAE NEVINS. Summer stock was hard work, performing one production while you rehearsed for the next. It was something she could get lost in.

Filled with trepidation, Lannie set her chin and climbed the shallow stone steps, worn into smooth hollows in the center from years of use, to the wide verandah.

"Wait here, Bry."

In the lobby, a faded red oriental carpet partially covered worn floorboards, and a table held yellow handbills. The ticket window, a small opening in the wall with a grill, had a piece of cardboard covering it. The cardboard said OPEN AT NOON EVERYDAY. A large bulletin board had notices thumbtacked haphazardly all over it.

She searched for a sign-up sheet, but couldn't find one. *Good. An indication that I wasn't meant to do this.* With relief, she turned to leave, but encountered a pleasant-faced woman coming from the direction of the house.

"Good morning. Can I help you?"

The woman was a High Falls native. Lannie could tell from her mountain twang. *Can't* became *Cain't,* and *thank you* became *thenk yew,* and so forth. This woman's accent was soft, though, indicating she'd been in the outside world and had had some formal education. Lannie recognized her then as the librarian who'd run the library so efficiently when Lannie was a teenager.

"Oh, well . . . John Lamb said you needed some help up here, and I thought . . . but I can't find a sign-up sheet, so I guess you've gotten all the volunteers you needed."

"Darn it. Someone has walked away with that thing again. It has phone numbers on it, and people take it into the office to copy them." She extended her hand and introduced herself. "I'm Mae Nevins, and we desperately need more volunteers."

Lannie cleared her throat. *God, help me do this.*

She heard music coming from the auditorium. A piano rapped out "Everything's Up to Date in Kansas City," and feet pounded in rhythm on the stage. Someone yelled, "God, no. Angie, you've got two left feet and no brain. Let's start again." Rehearsals had begun for *Oklahoma!*. Her heart tripped a beat at the familiar sound, and she knew she was hooked.

"Okay. I've worked in theaters before. What can I do?"

"Are you afraid of getting dirty or getting paint on you?"

Lannie laughed. "No, I've painted many a flat, if that's what you're talking about."

"Good. That's the first thing we'll assign you to. *Oklahoma!* starts in ten days, and we're no way near ready. Come into the office and we'll get you signed up."

In the small office off the lobby, Mae Nevins searched for the sign-up sheet and finally found it beneath a pile of bills.

"Now, if you'll just write your name, phone number, local address, and times you can work, we'll be all set."

"My name is Lannie Sullivan. I don't have a phone or an address other than General Delivery, and I can only give you one morning a week."

Disappointment spread over Mae Nevins' face. "Oh, well, that's okay. Maybe you can work in more time later. Can you start this morning?"

"No, but I'll be here tomorrow morning."

"Great."

"Just one thing. Can my dog come with me?"

"Sure." The woman laughed. "When has anyone in High Falls ever turned away a dog?"

° ° °

As Lannie walked away, Mae looked after her thoughtfully. She was almost certain Lannie Sullivan had been one of the teenagers who had frequented the library when Mae ran it years ago. Sullivan? Sullivan? Of course, she's Judge Sullivan's daughter. Mae remembered her as a voracious and eclectic reader.

Hmmm, how interesting, thought Mae. She looks like a hippie refugee from the sixties. Not at all like the classy, colt-legged teenager she once was. And the Sullivans hadn't been here in years. After Mrs. Sullivan died, the judge and his daughter leased their spacious home on Satulah Mountain to an artist from Palm Beach.

Spencer entered the office, the perpetual frown on his face. She felt a blush creep over her breasts and up to her throat. Good heavens, was she going to do this all summer, everytime Spencer Case came near her?

You really have become a needy virginal old maid, Mae Nevins. First you get a crush on the big New York director, and then you get all flustered over the Rutledge fellow.

"Who was the good-looking redhead I just saw walking out the door? Someone with a willing pair of hands, I hope."

"Yes. She can only help one day a week, but I'll take anything I can get. This has been my lucky day. Two volunteers in one morning."

"Who was the other one?"

"Well, believe it or not, Drummond Rutledge."

"What?" Spencer ran his hand over his white brushcut, and the frown furrows that framed his mouth deepened. "You told him that was impossible, right? I can't have the man around here all the time."

Mae could see he was truly upset and she felt terrible.

"I couldn't say no, Mr. Case. You should see the way he handles a piece of wood, and the way the carpenters listened to his suggestions. He obviously knows his way around with a hammer and a plane, and you should have seen him with the table saw."

Spencer Case groaned and Mae felt worse.

"He said it would only be a few days," she hurried to reassure him. "Just until he made arrangements for repairs to his house here, then he had to get back to Charlotte. Gosh, I'm sorry but I couldn't say no, Mr. Case."

"You're right, that's okay, and will you *please* stop calling me Mr. Case? My name is Spencer, remember?"

Yes. Every night in my dreams.

"Yes, sir . . . I mean, yes, Spencer."

He smiled at her, a rare occurrence, and she thought she would melt.

"You afraid of me, Mae?"

"Ah, no, no, sir. Well, maybe a bit awestruck, I think."

"Don't be impressed by all the credits they hang behind my name. This is the way I started, you know. In a summer theater just like this one, in Maine."

"Yes, sir." She got brave. "Why *are* you here? We haven't had a director of your stature in a long time."

"Lots of reasons. If you want to know the truth, I just had two successive failures on the Great White Way, and I wanted to think about that. Mostly, though, I needed a change, and some peace and quiet. I don't know why, in God's name, I ever thought I would find it here, but I let Robert Keeting talk me into this." He sighed. "In short, I'm escaping."

He patted her arm, as if they were pals. At his touch, her knees quaked.

"But, we'll make this summer fun, even if it kills us, right, Mae?"

Unable to speak, she nodded her head weakly, feeling it wobble like a straw scarecrow.

° ° °

Drum cursed as he shifted gears and bumped and bounced the last few yards into the heavily forested drive that fronted his house.

What a damned fool, Drum.

The Panoz AIV had been a lot of fun on the sweep and swoop of the paved highway, but the rugged climb to the lodge had been a nightmare. What had he been thinking of? He hoped he hadn't ripped the lowslung undercarriage beyond repair. He should have brought his Land Rover or the Ford pickup.

Oh, well, he'd only be here for a few days. He'd just have to take it easy coming back and forth to the house.

Wilkie Talley, the caretaker, waited for him in front of the large log structure.

Built in 1906 by a wealthy Atlanta family, the rambling log-structured lodge boasted six fireplaces, two kitchens, and a ton of charm and atmosphere. Drum had bought the place ten years ago, modernized it, and added five thousand square feet of decks, which took in the panoramic views surrounding the property.

"Hey, thar, Mr. Rutledge," called Wilkie.

Drum shook hands with the gangling, gap-toothed man, and smiled. "Nice to see you, Wilkie. How ya been?"

"Right good, right good. Wife's in good shape, and the grandchildren are comin' along." He shoved his hands in the pockets of his loose-fitting, mud-splotched overalls. "Sorry, you had to make this trip."

"That's okay. It's time I checked on things anyway."

Drum tilted his head back and searched for the sunlight through the tops of the majestic trees that protected this side of the house. The bastion of dark-green firs and pines had always been a source of comfort. He inhaled deeply, drawing in the fresh, cool, pine scent like a bee sucks nectar.

Except for the hushed whispering of the evergreens, which he was sure were discreetly discussing his belated return, the clearing held a hallowed silence. The forest had always been a balm to his soul, and this particular spot had always been special.

Despite the heartache that had kept him from returning all these years, he had missed the place like a sailor misses the sea. There had never been a struggle for direction here or futile wondering about the meaning of his life and what he should be doing about it. The forest was his natural element, where he was happiest, where he woke up in the morning and felt his spirit lift to the sky.

Wilkie was talking to him.

"Cain't see nothin' on this side, Mr. Rutledge. Most of the ruin is on the cliff side."

"Do we have to go inside to see the damage?"

"No, sir, no, sir. The main kitchen was hit bad, but you'll see that when we look at the big deck."

Relief melted through Drum. He wanted to be alone when he entered the house. He grabbed his duffel bag from the passenger seat of the car, ran up the steps and placed it on the stone porch, then followed Wilkie through the trees and over several wood decks, to the panoramic-view side of the house.

Drum caught his breath as they walked across the deck overlooking hundreds of miles of mountains. His favorite view in the whole world. He forced his attention back to Wilkie Talley.

"Damn."

"Yes, sir, pretty bad ain't it?"

A huge red oak had crashed through the roof of the house and into the main kitchen.

"I got most of it cut away already, and you kin see I covered the holes with plywood and canvas so yer kitchen won't get wet and full of bugs. A mama bear and her cubs was sniffin' around the other day, too. You shore don't want them messin' around inside."

"Looks like I'm going to have to rebuild this whole corner. Were any of the appliances damaged?"

"Yes, sir. You'll see when you go inside."

"Okay. What else, Wilkie?"

"Same thing on the north corner. Ain't the main bedroom, but one of them other, huh, whatchacallit, guest bedrooms."

They toured the perimeters of the house, discussing the damage the nasty storm had wrought last week.

"Okay, Wilkie. I'll decide what I want to do and give you a call. I assume the phone is in working order."

"Yep. I had the water and electricity turned on for you, and Miz Chambers comes in once a month to dust things and make shore no field mice have nested. She put fresh sheets on your bed and took the dust covers off the furniture. I stacked you some firewood."

"Thank you. I'll talk to you on Monday."

Wilkie left, and Drum retrieved from the car the few supplies he'd bought and approached the front door of the lodge. He placed the groceries at his feet, then fiddled nervously with the key in his pocket.

The massive door loomed threateningly before him as he marshalled his courage. Finally, he inserted the key, shoved the heavy door open, and entered.

He ventured a few steps forward, dropped his duffle bag on the floor, and took a deep breath. Absent of a presence all these years, the house slumbered. The air was dense with stillness. Everything seemed to be as he had left it, and yet different. Had the leather sofa in front of the cavernous fireplace always been so big? Had the brass lamps near the front windows always caught the filtered forest sunlight so?

He wished that Mrs. Chambers had left everything covered. He could have walked through without seeing anything. As it was, he had the feeling that if he took one more step into the interior he would give the house life, that it would start living again, have life, breathe.

And all the pain would come back.

He shifted the grocery sack in his arm, closed his eyes, opened them, and walked toward the kitchen, glancing neither right nor left.

One glance inside the once immaculate, efficient, chef-happy kitchen told him it was out of use until repaired.

"Just as well. I always preferred the smaller one anyway."

The sound of his voice startled him and, just as he'd feared, the house began to breathe again. As he walked to the galley kitchen near the master bedroom, the dignified grandfather clock in the hallway began to tick and sounds of laughter and a child's voice echoed around him.

"Go away," he whispered.

He deposited his groceries in the galley kitchen and continued the short distance to the master bedroom.

Heart beating fast, he entered the bedroom with eyes open, ready for whatever assailed him. He'd forgotten the breathtaking effect of the scenic views from the expansive windows. He'd also forgotten that he'd never been quite comfortable in this room. Too feminine for his taste, but beautiful and soothing in shades of mauve and moss green.

"What a coward you are, Drum Rutledge," he said aloud, and the sound of his voice echoed throughout the room. "Doesn't hurt too bad, does it? You can exist here okay for a few days."

He grinned, proud of himself, and turned to bring his duffel from the entrance hall.

His heart stopped in his throat. After the tragedy, Mrs. Chambers had been instructed to put all personal photographs in the storage closet. She'd forgotten one, or left it out on purpose.

A large silver-framed photo of Ann-Marie and Chip stared at him from the dresser.

THREE

"Whooo-eee, honey, you sure ain't forgot a thing. Still the best dancer in three counties. I thought you'd be mad at me, you know, after I told on you and all."

"Hell, no, doll face, I never get mad." *I just get even,* Jeb thought. He whirled her around the one-room swamp shack she lived in, the music blaring so loud the walls vibrated. "Couldn't wait to see you again."

"You ain't going to get rough with me the way you did before, are you? I was in the hospital for a week."

Freddie Cannon's "Tallahassee Lassie" thumped and twanged from Susie's cheap boom box.

"Naw, you know that was an accident, Susie. Never could figure why you was so bent on sayin' I raped you. Thought you liked me."

Susie's body had lumped up in the years he'd spent in prison. She wore one of those short, skimpy nylon dresses from K-Mart, which was much too small for her and showed everything. He pressed her sweating body close to his. Every fold of her stomach, her hips, and her cellulite-dimpled thighs rolled and gyrated against him. In spite of his promise to keep himself clean until he located his girl in North Carolina and in spite of the beery smell of the poor excuse for a woman in his arms, he knew he would fuck her before he finished tonight. It had been too long. He needed a woman.

"I do like you," she said. "I always thought you and me were alike. You know, kinda hangin' around the edges of all them fancy people in town, waitin' for somebody to notice us."

Fury caught hard in his brain, making pink stars burst fast and painful behind his eyes, but he held the fury back, saving it for later.

"Not me, honey. I never hung around waitin' for nobody. I was always in there with the important people."

"But you come to see me first when you got out, didn't you?"

"Yep. Come to find out why you said I raped you, when all along I just thought we was havin' some fun." The stupid woman hadn't answered him yet.

"Because you *did* rape me. We was drunk and you took advantage of me. When I was in the hospital, that prosecuting attorney, Lannie Sullivan, said I should tell what happened so you would go to prison and not hurt anyone else. I was hurtin' so bad, I figured she was right."

When she said Lannie's name, the sound of it got all mixed up and swirled around and around with the pink rage in the back of his brain. Lannie, Lannie, Lannie. Waiting for me.

He couldn't wait any longer,. He sucked Susie Slater's lipsticked mouth into his and dug his fingers into her crotch. She squealed with delight, but the squeals soon turned into whimpers of fear as he squeezed harder and harder and bit down on her bottom lip. Blood gushed onto his immaculate white shirt and he didn't like that.

"Oh, Susie, you shouldn't have bled on me. I like my shirts spotless."

She screamed and tried to twist out of his arms. He held her fast. "Shut up, Susie, or I'll kill you this time. Should have the last time. I've never killed anyone before. Maybe you'll be the first."

He held her by the neck and threw her on the bed. She scrambled to get away from him, but the slippery orange sateen spread she'd won at a local carnival slid her off the bed and onto the floor.

He put his foot on her chest, then bent over to grab a hank of her hair and jerk her head up. The terror in her mascaraed eyes excited him beyond belief. He took her by the throat and choked the air out of her until she went limp. He didn't want her dead, just controllable.

He fucked her then.

An hour later, he stared at her alcohol ravaged face as it floated in the murky water of the swamp. Her dirty-blond hair drifted on the water and got stuck in her gaping mouth. The fear reflected in her eyes sent a thrill over his spine and into his scrotum, replacing the anger that usually raged in scarlet waves throughout his body.

"Sorry, Susie. But you're better off where you're going. Jesus loves everyone, even sinners like you."

He heaved the cinder-block he had tied to her neck into the water and sucked on his beer as he watched it pull her to the mucky bottom. The whites of her eyes were the last thing he saw, and he relived the enormous excitement that shook him when he finally felt life leave her.

This was a never-to-be-forgotten power he'd just discovered and treasured; a way to dominate those who he cared about who didn't understand his need for control.

But Lannie would understand. He would explain it all to her, and she would apologize for everything.

FOUR

Lannie lavished bright yellow paint on the flat depicting Aunt Eller's farmhouse. The light she worked under was barely sufficient, but sunlight streaming through the big barn-like rear doors of the theater helped. Like headlights, the yellow beams pierced the dim backstage area with welcome precision. Except for the stage, none of the nooks and crannies of the old playhouse were well lit.

Bry had sniffed around the area that she worked in, inspected the entire perimeter of the building, and decided they were going to be all right in this strange new place. He'd lain beside her for a while, but woke up to go exploring. When she'd last checked, she'd found him sleeping in the jeep, which was parked in the shade of an enormous oak tree.

From the stage behind her came an occasional snatch of music, and from the carpenter shop just outside the open doors she heard someone whistling while they hammered. The pleasant sound floated in with the light breeze and sunlight. Church bells rang in the distance. She decided Sunday morning was the perfect time to be here, to initiate her first emergence into a more normal way of life. Most of the other volunteers were in church, so she wouldn't be stared at, or asked a lot of friendly but intrusive questions.

The smell of paint began to bother her, while the sunshine and sounds from outside begged that she take a break. She deposited her paintbrush in a can of murky water, wiped her hands on a rag, and stepped outside. Arms folded, one foot propped against the shingled building behind her, she leaned back and closed her eyes. The sun showered her with its healing rays, and she bathed in it like an old hound dog after a long cold winter.

The hammering began again and she opened her eyes to glance through the wide open doors of the carpenter shop adjacent to the theater. Who was the other person brave enough to work on Sunday morning, tempting the disapproval of the churchgoing townspeople and the condescending amusement of the country club crowd who were on the golf course? Curious, she walked across the graveled drive to get a better look.

A solitary man, shirtless, with his back to her, worked on a sizable sheet of plywood. Probably going to be a tree, or maybe a bench, or maybe the interior of Judd's shack. In the spirit of trying to make a new beginning, the reason she was here in the first place this morning, she started to say hello, but suddenly turned shy. He seemed intent on his task. She meant to turn away then, but something about the way he worked caught her.

His hands caressed the sheet of plywood with subtle reverence. She knew immediately that he'd worked with finer wood, and she knew instinctively that those fingers were talented in more ways than one. His hand moved slowly, intimately, sliding with sure knowledge across the grain. A slanting stripe of sun shone on his shoulders and arms, and Lannie wished she were an artist. She wished for the talent, and a palette of oils, and a clean canvas to capture plaited ligaments and tendons moving in healthy harmony. Fascinated, she stared at his sinewy biceps, polished with perspiration and bursting with horsepower.

He bent to pick up a saw, then hefted a two-by-four onto the worktable. She noticed how the tanned, muscled back narrowed and met slim hips in faded jeans. He drew the saw back and forth a few strokes. His firm shoulder muscles rolled and moved like a well-oiled machine. The energy and insight he put into every motion made her feel good.

She had a notion that he was invincible, capable of holding the world on those expansive shoulders, like Atlas. Embarrassed now, but unable to stop herself, she found herself taking measure of his whole body. Long-legged, he stood with his feet planted wide, as if he were rooted to the earth. The carpenter emanated heat, strength, and an aura of fierce independence.

Lannie found she'd been holding her breath. She exhaled, but her next breath came shallow and shaky, and her chest quivered with gossamer excitement. She recognized the budding of attraction that had been too long put away and wondered at herself.

Her eyes traveled back to his shoulders, and she noticed that his sandy hair, though neat over his ears, was longer and untamed in the back. It clung in damp clusters to his sweaty neck.

He began to whistle again, startling her. How long had she been standing here admiring this man? She backed quietly away, and returned to her painting job.

She tried to concentrate on the flat in front of her, but found herself searching for the title of the tune the carpenter whistled. Yes, she knew it. "But Not for Me." A lovely tune, with not very happy lyrics. Interesting, she thought, a lusty carpenter with a taste for Gershwin.

"Well, and why shouldn't he? Who am I," she chastised herself, "the world's snobby music expert on who should know what?"

She finished the porch railing on Aunt Eller's house and moved to the next section.

Wait a minute. This doesn't look right, she thought. *There shouldn't be a window here. Wonder if someone made a mistake when they sketched this in?*

She thought she'd better check with someone before she finished the flat.

Lannie doubted if Mae Nevins knew either, but there was no one else to ask for the moment. No one was here except Mae, Spencer Case, and some of the cast, all of whom were on stage rehearsing. She would try to find someone who was unoccupied. She knew better than to ask Spencer Case. She'd already learned he had a short fuse. She suspected his bark was worse than his bite, and that he was just a grumbly ol' lovable bear of a man, but she wasn't ready to test her theory.

She picked her way through backstage darkness, haphazardly stored flats, and scattered props. The stamp of syncopated feet hitting the floor got louder as she neared the stage, and then entered the wings.

She indulged herself for a few minutes, watching the young dancers prance and step through "Everything's Up to Date in Kansas City." A girl upstage kicked with the wrong foot and seemed to have no sense of rhythm. The whole company appeared listless. No energy. Lannie yearned to get out there and restart them, show them how to master some of the steps they struggled with. But she wasn't here to dance. She was here to paint.

She searched for Spencer Case and Mae Nevins and found them in the hall, four or five rows back. She took a seat directly behind them, but waited for the appropriate time to speak. Spencer Case called a break. Lannie put a hand on Mae's shoulder, and was about to ask her question when a claxon of a voice sounded from the rear of the theater.

Her hand stilled on Mae's shoulder, her whole body froze.

Oh, God. She would know that woman's voice anywhere, and so would anyone else who played golf in North Carolina, Alabama, Georgia, and all points southeast. *Beezy Bowdon of the Mobile Bowdons, the Fortune 500 Bowdons.*

Lannie had known that eventually someone from her other life would discover where she was, would disturb her careful retreat from the world, particularly since she'd just decided to cautiously reenter. But why did it have to be Beezy, whose forked tongue was laced with sugared malice?

"Spensah Case, why weren't you at my cocktail pahty last night?"

Beezy's voice had none of the lovely southern lilt that Lannie's mother had had. Her voice rang stridently of Alabama red clay, and the overbearing self-importance of too much money. Richer than Bill Gates and tackier than a small-town two-bit carnival on Saturday night, Beezy was a longtime member of the High Falls Summer Playhouse Board of Directors.

"You friggin' well better have a good excuse, sugah. The guvnor came just to meet you."

Beezy was halfway down the aisle. Lannie saw Spencer's eyes close in resignation.

I have to get out of here, she thought. *I can't face Beezy right now. I'm not ready.*

She stood, sidestepped out into the aisle, walked swiftly to the stage, and up the stairs into the wings.

"Hi, Beezy," said Spencer. Lannie imagined him rising to greet the old harridan. "Sorry I couldn't make it. Some young actors arrived last night, and I had to stick around to make sure they were taken care of."

"Thought Mae Nevins was supposed to do all of that for you. That's what we hired her for. Oh, there you are. Hello, Mae," she said with an insulting dismissive tone.

"Well, she is, but she was busy at the printers working on new programs."

"Don't desert me again, sugah. I put a shitload of money into this place every year, and you could at least get that sexy ass of yours to my pahties. Now, I want to meet your new actors. You know I like havin' them at my pahties. Especially the good-lookin' ones. They dress up a shindig. Who's that tall boy up there, the one with the droopy lips? He looks absolutely delicious."

"Uh, well, he's only sixteen, Beezy. He's from Atlanta, and his parents have rented a place here for the summer. He's got bit parts in two productions."

Lannie heard their voices move closer. Beezy was coming onstage.

Lannie wanted to run, but someone had turned off all the lights backstage. Probably one of the young kids. She fumbled around until she found several flats layered vertically against the wall. She edged between two of them. Flaccid canvas with flaking paint billowed against her face. Her nose started to itch, and she sneezed.

Behind her a man said, "God bless you."

She jumped with alarm. Someone was in here with her.

The man moved, and the canvas behind her shook. He stood between her flat and the next one.

His voice came again. "Are you the idiot who turned off the lights?"

"I certainly am not," she whispered.

"My apologies." He edged around the end of the flat and joined her. "Come on, let's get out of here."

"This is my first day. I'm not familiar with the backstage area, and I don't want to go onstage, so I'll just stay here, thank you, until the lights come on," she whispered again, wishing he would keep his voice down.

"Ridiculous. Why are you whispering? Are you hiding? Oh, Christ, you're one of the teens playing some game," he said, and his voice softened. "It's not safe back here, you know. It's pitch black. Come on, give me your hand and I'll get us out of here without anyone seeing you."

He stood next to her now. She smelled wood shavings and faint musky male aftershave and knew right away it must be the carpenter. A moist bare arm brushed her arm, and he found her hand.

"I want to stay right here, and I'm not a kid," she hissed, wishing he'd go away.

"Sure you are, but don't be afraid. I'll stay with you until the lights come on."

Lannie jerked her hand out of his, but his brawny presence filled the small space they were confined to. Again, she felt excitement flutter in her chest, and this time it wiggled down into her stomach. Sexual tension. Not difficult to identify.

Damn.

Beezy's strident voice sounded from the stage.

"Wonduhful, wonduhful group of youngsters you've got here, Spensah. I'm sure they perform superbly, especially this handsome young man." She giggled shrilly.

"Oh, Christ, Beezy Bowden, the scourge of every golf course between here and Atlanta," muttered the carpenter. "Come on, kid. I'm getting out of here, and you're going with me. I'm not leaving you here alone."

Lannie felt momentary surprise that he would know Beezy.

He fumbled for her hand, found it, and pulled her along the length of the canvas. She didn't know which was worse, potential discovery by Beezy Bowden, or her growing discomfort in the overpowering company of the carpenter. The only way to be rid of both annoyances was to follow him out of the maze of sets, so she followed as they bumped blindly along.

Beezy's voice receded when they neared the area where Lannie had been painting. The carpenter kept her hand in his as he headed toward the loading area and big back doors, then out into the bright sunlight.

"Thank you," she said. "Now if you'll excuse me—"

"You," he declared, "the female idiot with the jeep."

"You, the reckless bozo with the fancy sports car," she bit out.

He dropped her hand as if it blistered him and glared at her. She noticed his hair, shorter in front than it was on his neck, stood straight up over his forehead in funny little wet tufts, as if he'd shoved his hands through it while he was working.

"What in God's name were you doing pretending to be a kid?"

"I wasn't, you imbecile. You assumed what you wanted to assume, probably a habit of yours, like running down other cars at your leisure."

His eyes narrowed. She knew he was angry, but continued goading him.

"They ought to put a big danger sign on the front of your car. I'm sure everyone would be safer. You're a menace. Mothers should warn their children of your impending arrival."

His hard dark-blue eyes lit up, and she felt their heat

physically, as if silvery-blue and red sparks needled and scorched her. *Maybe put a "danger" sign on his body, too,* she thought. She stepped back, away from his disturbing effect on her, and wondered what she'd said that had finally gotten to him.

"I won't dignify that tirade. You have a mean temper, lady," he said, and his eyes raked over her again as they had on the highway. "And obviously you don't know the meaning of good manners, or you would have thanked me for getting you out of whatever predicament you were in backstage."

"I could have gotten out of there by myself, but no, you had to be the big macho-man protector. What are you doing here anyway?"

Something about this man brought out the fight in her, a part of her that had been nonexistent for the last three years. Her father had always said her fighting spirit came from the Sullivan Irish in her.

He lifted an eyebrow. A small smile curved his lips, then disappeared. "I could ask you the same question, but I see you must work here. Do you own any clean clothes, by the way? Yesterday you were covered with mud and water. Today you look like a painter's dropcloth. Did you know your face is speckled with yellow paint, and your nose is blue?"

Her hand flew to her nose, and she wondered if she looked as embarrassed as she felt.

"Did you know you have wood shavings in your hair?" she shot back.

His small smile returned and widened into a rakish grin. Her heart literally shook at the sight. He laughed, and she found herself laughing, too.

Their laughter dwindled, and he stuck out his hand, "Drum."

"Lannie," she said as she shook his hand. "Uh, I'm sorry I lost my temper."

"Same here. You also have a purple bump the size of an olive on your forehead," he said with concern, and reached out as if to touch it, but dropped his hand quickly. "Do you have a headache?"

"No, I'm fine. The bump is the only wound from yesterday's mishap."

"That's good."

"I have to get back to work."

"Yeah, me too. Looks like your lights are on now."

She turned and walked toward the playhouse, but couldn't resist a glance over her shoulder before entering. He'd made no attempt to move in the direction of the carpenter shop. He stood watching her, bare shoulders braced back and his hands stuck in the rear pockets of his jeans.

She jerked her head around, and quickened her pace into the playhouse and away from the disturbing look in his eyes.

Lannie could never decide which was her favorite part of the day here on top of Haystack Mountain; early morning when the lavender mist played indolently through the treetops that spread before her, or now, at twilight when the sun had sprinkled gold dust on the peaked ridges.

She sat on her stoop watching Bry chase squirrels in the lengthening shadows and sipped a wine cooler. She'd only recently allowed herself such small pleasures. Wine coolers weren't something she would have enjoyed in Madison, Florida, but they were safe. Her skin still glowed from the scrubbing she'd given herself in the creek. She rubbed her nose, hoping she'd removed all the blue paint. Her mirror wasn't that great, and the light was faint in the cabin at this time of day.

What must that stranger, the carpenter, think of her? And what did she care anyway? Never before had she worried about what others thought. Why would she begin now?

Nell had always said, "Lannie, you're the world's freest spirit. You don't give a damn what anyone thinks. Wish I could be like you."

Dearest Nell. Nell had her own carefree nature, always laughing, always encouraging, always loving. She thought of Nell's letter, and her law partner's request for a visit.

Lannie, I know you're still licking your wounds, and that's fine, but it's time to begin living again, at least a little bit. I know your strength and your courage. I can't believe the brainiest, most opinionated female in law school is going to let all her talent go to waste. I can't believe you're going to spend the rest of your life up there contemplating your navel.

I'm driving to Washington next week and would love to stop by for a short visit. Please say yes. I know your accommodations are sparse, but I don't mind roughing it. Come on. Say hello to the world again by saying yes.

Well, why not? Volunteering at the playhouse had been a big test. Except for her encounter with the carpenter, she'd passed with an average grade. But the disturbing presence of the carpenter, Drum, and his effect on her didn't bode well for future encounters. Her face heated at the thought of his arm brushing hers in the darkness and how she'd reacted. She would avoid him.

Yes. Being with Nell seemed a natural next step. She would go to town tomorrow and call her.

* * *

"Thank you, Mr. Rutledge. We're right pleased to have your business. We'll start first thing tomorrow morning."

"Good, Lester. You don't mind if I poke my nose into what you're doing now and then, do you?"

Lester Hall's family had been building houses in High Falls for fifty years or more. Drum knew better than to hire one of the newer construction companies that had established themselves here. They were well-qualified, but the work would be finished faster by mountain people. It wasn't that native High Falls subcontractors weren't unfailingly polite or didn't respond to the newer companies, but phone calls and requests for service from the "johnny-come-latelies " somehow always ended up at the bottom of the mountaineers' lists.

" 'Course not. I can tell from some of the cabinet work you did in the house that you're a darned good carpenter."

"He'll do a right nice job fer you, Mr. Rutledge," said Wilkie Talley. He hiked up his overalls and spat a stream of tobacco over the deck rail. "You kin be sure of that."

"Well, since his grandfather helped build this house years ago, it seems only right that Lester work on it now."

After he bid goodbye to Wilkie and Lester, he grabbed a cold beer and returned to the wide deck overlooking ridges and ridges of mountains. A lavender glow lingered in the darkening sky, and here and there glints of gold from the disappearing sun clung to scattered purple peaks.

He'd only been here two days, and though he'd avoided this place he'd once loved so well, Drum recognized the old magic working on him. He'd needed a respite from the tough schedule he imposed upon himself, but never thought he'd find it here. There was so much pain here, too much he didn't want to remember.

This had always been a family place, but Ann-Marie

had placed herself beyond his reach, and Chip was gone forever.

Don't start feeling sorry for yourself, Drum. Don't start down that path again.

He shook his head to clear it, then threw it back to suck half the beer in one swallow.

Using his hands at the theater today had been immensely therapeutic. Even working with cheap plywood had revived the sense of satisfaction he'd always received when creating something. He could kill two birds with one stone at the theater: He could get an idea of what their operation problems were and have some fun in the carpenter shop at the same time. He wanted to keep an eye on the repair work here at the house, too, so spending two weeks in High Falls, instead of the three days he'd originally planned, began to look attractive.

The pain didn't beat at him as he'd been afraid it would, but the master bedroom had been too much for him so he'd moved into one of the guest rooms. Maybe he could handle all of this and leave having achieved more than he'd imagined when he'd headed for the mountains.

He remembered another reason for a longer stay. Two thousand of the surrounding acres belonged to him, except one twenty-acre out-parcel on top of Haystack. Everytime he looked at a plat of the land, the red-outlined rectangular space right in the center of his acreage bugged the hell out of him. It wasn't that he was greedy for the twenty acres, it was his need for everything to be neat and in order, easily managed.

The out-parcel had always been an irritant. The previous owners of his lodge had given it to a young lawyer fifty years ago in exchange for legal work. Drum had tried to purchase it from him, but the man had turned him down, saying, "No amount of money could persuade me to give it up. My daughter loves the place."

The twenty acres belong with the rest of my land, and I intend to have it sooner or later. I think "sooner" has come.

The lavender and gold had faded, and the sky turned a soft smoky gray . . . like the redhead's eyes. His groin had tingled and heated swiftly at the sight of the lissome movement of her legs and the subtle bounce of her small, but nicely rounded derriere as she'd walked away from him. The memory bothered him. She'd lit a fire that he really didn't want kindled right now.

But he grinned, remembering her blue nose.

FIVE

Jeb turned off his reading light and shadows fell around him. He grinned with satisfaction. From Interstate 10, just west of Tallahassee, the faint hum of traffic filtered through his shuttered window, but he'd become accustomed to the sound. It was almost comforting. Better than angry voices, the constant shuffle of shoes, and the clang of cafeteria trays at the prison.

The room he'd rented a week ago suited him just fine. With explicit instructions from him, his computer-whiz cousin had invested his small nest egg for him, and he was in good shape financially. For a price, the landlord had been happy to oblige his requests for a new air conditioner, a scrubbing of the room, and removal of all wall decorations. The stupid psychiatrist at Raiford had said his need for cleanliness was another indication of an obsessive personality.

"Dickhead. Didn't know his ass from a hole in the ground." He could still hear the man's slimy, whiny voice and mimed it. "Rehabilitate your vengeful nature, Jeb, or it'll get you in trouble. You're smart. With an IQ of 150 you have an advantage over most people, and you should make good use of it."

Yeah, yeah, yeah. He'd heard it all before.

Little did the stupid doctor know that he'd attended those psychiatric sessions in the cool, quiet office to catch a break from the continuous clamor of prison life.

It was simple. He was starting a new life, and the immaculate bare walls symbolized a blank slate, a fresh beginning with Lannie. All that hung on the pretty yellow walls now was a picture of Jesus praying at Gethsemene.

He had a few arrangements to make, and a few more weeks to make them, before he traveled on to see his girl. Maybe at first she wouldn't like his being around again, but she'd get used to it. And soon she'd be begging forgiveness for convicting him of something he hadn't done. She just didn't understand, but he would help her understand. When he was in control, they would get to know each other better than before. She would admit she'd been wrong, and they would live the rest of their lives together.

No one would ignore him, or boss him around, or laugh at him then.

It was important that he surprise her though, that she not know he was coming, because she believed all the garbage they'd testified to at the trial, and she wouldn't take kindly to his being back in her life. But she'd always liked surprises. Some of the best jobs he'd ever worked had been waiting tables at surprise parties they'd given her, for birthdays and graduations. He'd even been to her college graduation celebration. All those tony snobs had ignored him, but she'd touched his hand and thanked him. Susie had been right about that, but he would never have admitted it to her.

He turned on the light again and returned his focus to the book he held in his lap. Only one of many books he'd devoured on the subject he'd been studying, this one was his favorite—*Surviving in the Wild: With Jesus*. He knew it almost by heart now. He closed it with reverence and put it on his bedside table. His spy in High Falls had told him Lannie was out in the mountains somewhere hard to reach, and he had to be prepared for anything.

Time for his push-ups. With a proud smile he lowered himself to the floor and began the nightly ritual he'd begun years ago. He pumped his powerful body up and down. Giving himself no rest, he pushed on to a count of five hundred. Breathing easily, but perspiring, he rested a moment on the floor, happy for the expensive air-conditioning unit that kept the room ice cold.

He got to his feet, flexing rock-hard muscles in his arms, and admired his physique in the mirror. The pimples he'd suffered with when he was a teenager were gone and so was the prison pallor. He looked tan and fit. His jet black hair had grown out of the institutional cut he'd been forced to wear for years and was combed straight back from his high, domed forehead. He wouldn't be happy until it flowed down his back. Next week would bring a transformation of his glossy black hair, and he hated that, but it couldn't be helped. Oh, well, the new color would grow out eventually.

He picked up the green contact lens that he'd bought today. With precision he went through the drill again, inserting them carefully just like the man had told him. When he looked in the mirror again, he giggled at the green eyes staring back at him.

"Ain't so bad. In fact, they are fuckin' sexy. Maybe I'll keep them."

He added the steel-rimmed glasses and thought they made him look more dignified. Taller, maybe.

There was nothing he could do about his nose. He'd always hated the large blunt blob of his nose and blamed it for the way girls treated him in high school. Someday he would have it modeled into proper shape, something more like Brad Pitt's. But his money wouldn't stretch that far right now. The ugly blob had been broken twice at Raiford, so it was hardly recognizable anyway. His nose was just a flat piece of shapeless flesh on his face.

Prison jocks had teased him about his nose and about his shortness. But that hadn't stopped them from fucking him. The pain and humiliation of those first violent attacks flashed back at him in lurid detail. He quaked with rage, shaking until his bare heels lifted and tapped the floor with a dull tattoo. He'd worked out at the prison gym until he was exhausted, his malice for them growing with the bulge of his muscles. When he was able to fight them off, he indulged in and relished bullying and fucking the same men who'd sodomized him. Soon, he controlled his entire cell block, and the other prisoners toadied to his every wish, as Lannie would someday.

Bedtime. He had to be up early in the morning. He was taking his cousin Buster fishing tomorrow, and he looked forward to it with great pleasure. Buster had been good for two things: using his computer skills to get him out of prison, and to dig up the information on his contact in High Falls. His usefulness was over.

He stripped off his jockey shorts and slipped beneath the covers. He slid down until his entire head was covered, a childhood habit he'd never been able to break, his way of believing he could evade the nightly visits of his mother with her probing finger and tongue. He cowered and shook but eventually succeeded in reminding himself that the slut deserted him long ago. Then he held his breath, knowing the night sounds would come next, and they did. He kicked his feet against the mattress and squeezed the pillow to his ears, warding off the dreaded night sounds he'd hated during his years in prison.

A free man, remember? You're a free man.

Flashes of hot resentful anger threatened his new-found calm. He forced himself to breathe in and out rhythmically and thought of Susie Slater and the earth-shaking power he now possessed.

Finally, he saw the face of his obsession, the face of the one he lived for, the face that would save him, the face he'd fallen asleep with every night since sixth grade.

He fell asleep with a smile on his face.

Buster liked to fish. Jeb and Buster had coped with the misery of their childhood by escaping to the swamp or river to fish.

Not that his cousin ever knew he was having a miserable childhood. Buster was an idiot. He was mentally deficient, except for processing data and operating computers.

At the behest and with the help of his welfare worker, and much to the relief of Buster's mother, his exceptional brilliance in these areas had secured him a part-time job at Florida's state criminology lab. It was here, after weekly detailed phone calls from him in prison, that Buster finally understood what he wanted and knew enough about DNA to tamper with Jeb's file and transfer the results to another case.

Lannie Sullivan, though a sharp attorney, had made one fatal mistake in presenting the state's case. Unsure that the DNA evidence, a new technology at the time of Jeb's arrest, would hold up in court, Lannie hadn't used it. Buster's later switch of Jeb's semen sample and DNA records went undetected and got Jeb pardoned.

Buster sat across from him now, a delirious grin on his clueless face.

"How ya' doin' Buster ol' buddy? We're havin' a good time, ain't we, just like when we were young?"

Buster nodded. "Yeah." Looking at Jeb, he tilted his head back and forth like a seesaw. "Your eyes sure do look funny."

"Never mind my eyes. You told anyone what you did for me in Tallahassee, Buster?"

Buster jerked on his line and brought it in, a frown marring the happy face. He looked at the dangling empty hook, then dropped it back in the water without any bait.

"Answer me, Buster? Did you tell anyone about the computer at work, and the changes you made?"

"Naw, I don't think so."

"Did you tell anyone about the information you got for me on those people who live in High Falls, North Carolina?"

"Naw, I don't think so."

"But you aren't sure, are you?"

"Naw, I don't think so."

"Looka there, Buster, that big ol' fish just wiggled off your hook and is hurryin' off home. Your mama going to be real unhappy if you don't bring fish for dinner."

Buster frowned, looking confused.

"Where's the fish? Where is it?"

"Well, right there by the bow of the boat. See, turn around and look real good. See, lean down real close to the water."

Buster, ever the obliging idiot, and worried about his mama's fish, hung over the bow of the boat.

One good shove of his foot against Buster's bottom pushed him into the warm, muddy brown water. Buster struggled for a while, and his fat hands plopped helplessly, making the water slurp against the aluminum boat.

"Shhh, Buster. You're going to scare away the fish."

The sounds of his unintelligible squeals finally stopped, and the surface regained its smooth face.

"Sorry, cousin, we had some good times, but you should have learned how to swim."

Jeb started up the small motor and moved to another part of the lake. He fixed a mullet on his hook and dropped it in, watching it fade from view toward the bottom.

He glanced around him. Good location for fishing. Shady, out of sight, and away from Buster. He didn't want to be hooking Buster's belt, or an eye or ear, and then pull him up thinking he was a grouper.

Buster wouldn't be much good for eatin'.

SIX

Lannie heard a groan and laughed.

"Get with it, Nell," she said. "Weeding a garden every day makes for a beautiful bod and a glowing complexion, and just think of all the fresh veggies I'm going to be eating in August. Eat veggies every day and you'll be a glowing bride."

"Trust me, love. I'll take my anemic grocery store lettuce anyday," Nell said and groaned again. "You know I'm allergic to hard work. Now I know why you let me visit after all this time. You needed cheap labor."

Lannie laughed again and rested for a moment, leaning on the long handle of her hoe. Affection rushed through her as she watched sturdy little Nell squat to yank another weed from the potato patch. Her friend's short blond bob swung over her cheek, hiding round blue eyes and a pug nose. Not until she'd seen Nell again did she realize how much she'd missed the cheerful chatter and staunch loyalty of her childhood friend.

After graduation from the University of Florida, they journeyed to New York together; Nell to study law at Columbia, and Lannie to study dance at Juilliard. Two years later, disappointed and heartbroken, she'd had to admit that she didn't have the supreme talent required to dance with the American Ballet Theater, a longtime dream, or even any of the minor dance troupes around the country. She would never be anything but a teacher or perhaps a choreographer.

Her decision to study law with Nell at Columbia had seemed a stopgap measure at the time, something to please her father, and a way to make a living until she decided what she really wanted to do with the rest of her life.

She'd found to her surprise that she liked the law and went home to set up a practice with Nell.

She'd also done a short stint as an assistant state's attorney, but found she didn't like prosecuting cases for the State of Florida. The tough elderly state's attorney had begged her to stay with him, said she had the brightest mind and toughest litigating style he'd ever seen. Her father had been so proud of her, but after a year she opted out. Her forte had been in family law, adoption, divorces, wills, what she called the "human" part of law.

"Ah, no, no, don't pull that one. That's a carrot top."

"They all look alike to me," grumbled Nell.

Lannie squinted, shading her eyes to look into the cloudless sapphire sky. The sun was midway over the horizon. Must be almost ten o'clock. A pine-scented breeze flirted around them, cooling the light sheen of perspiration on her bare shoulders and brow.

"Come on. One more row, and then we'll take a break."

"Okay. Whoops. I think I pulled something I shouldn't. What is this?"

Nell held a large purplish misshapen lump in her palm.

"Looks like one of the seed potatoes I planted, but it must have come from a bad gene pool. Must have been rotten to begin with."

Nell began to laugh.

"What's so funny?"

"Does it remind you of anyone?"

"No."

"Look. It's a face. The big bump is a nose, these smushed in spaces are eyes and the yellow pits are acne." She fell back in the dirt, and her peals of laughter echoed across the mountain top. "It reminds me of Jeb Bassert, and how he used to stand and stare up at your bedroom window, his ol' wall-eyed bass eyes all watery."

Lannie tried not to laugh. Jeb Bassert brought back an assortment of memories, some she preferred not to think about. But Nell's infectious laughter triggered her own, as it always had, and she laughed too.

"Oh, Nell, you were always so bad to Jeb."

"Lordy, Lannie, it was hard not to be. You were the only one who was ever nice to him." She paused. "And then you were the one who sent him to prison. The irony of it all."

But she couldn't be serious for long. Another chortle broke from her, and she laughed so hard tears rolled down her cheeks. "Remember the time he waited on our table at the club, and he got so nervous when he brought your ice cream sundae that he tripped and it fell in Tom's lap. I'll never forget all that fudge sauce rolling down Tom's cream linen pant leg into his shoe, and jerky Jeb trying to rub it off and making more of a mess."

Lannie sobered quickly. "Yes, Tom's first visit to Madison and his initiation into Madison's eccentricities. He wasn't very pleased. Swore like hell at Jeb, until Dad quietly told him to shut up. Dad never did like Tom after that. I should have had a clue then what a rat I was about to marry."

Nell sat up and wiped the tears from her eyes. A streak of mud stretched across her nose to her ear.

"I'm sorry. I didn't mean to bring up bad times." She stood up and wiped the dirt off her rear end. "But I wouldn't feel bad about falling for Tom Ravenal. Any girl would have. He wined and dined you in New York, then took you home to Atlanta to meet all the Coca-Cola Ravenals, and danced you around all their plantations. Honey, you were the belle of the ball."

"Yes, but I should have known," Lannie said softly, staring out across the mountain peaks.

"If you hadn't married Tom, you never would have had Gracie," returned Nell, just as softly.

"No, I wouldn't have, and that's unthinkable." Her throat clogged and a single tear coursed down her face. She wiped it away impatiently. "Thought there weren't anymore of *those* left."

Nell moved to hug her, but Lannie held up her hand to stop her. "I'm okay, really I am. When I first got here, I couldn't cry. When the tears finally came, I thought I'd never stop crying. It went on for months. My eyes got irritated. The skin on my face broke into a rash. Poor Bry. Weeping into his coat became a daily ritual. He began to lick my face dry, like I was one of his puppies."

"You should have let me, or someone, be with you."

"No, I needed to work it out by myself. And I've done a pretty good job of it. I still blame myself for not being there, for spending too much time at the office and away from Gracie, but I'm hoping I'll finally come to terms with that, too."

"Lannie, you feel that way because Tom accused you, said it was your fault for not being a stay-at-home mom. He was wrong and you know it. You spent more time with Gracie than most nonworking mothers, and Mrs. Halliday was a wonderful nanny when you weren't there. Gracie's death was an *accident*. It could have happened in any family."

"I keep telling myself that." She smiled weakly. "Maybe someday I'll believe it. Come on. Let's take a break. I've made some sun tea."

On their walk to the creek, Nell said, "Speaking of Jeb Bassert reminded me of something I should have told you when I first got here. That gossipy old lady who lives next to the Basserts' old place swears she saw Jeb sneaking out of his house a few weeks ago."

"Nonsense. She's ninety years old, and her eyesight has never been good anyway. He's not up for parole for three years, and if he had escaped, the state would tell us."

"There's a rumor going around the courthouse that his attorney had some DNA testing done, but I can't find the shifty sleazebag. He's disappeared. When I called the state testing lab they said such information was confidential and couldn't be released, not even to prosecuting attorneys, and certainly not to attorneys like Lannie Sullivan who had gone back into private practice."

"Call and see if he's still at Raiford."

"I've been so busy with wedding plans and new clients that I didn't have time, and then I forgot about it until now. I'll get it taken care of it when I get back to Madison. I'll sure be glad when you come home and start being a lawyer again."

"Don't worry about Jeb, Nell. It's not you he's angry with. It's me he threatened, and if he's looking for me, he'll never find me up here. Some of the best woodsmen in North Carolina get lost trying to locate the top of Haystack."

Lannie shrugged it off, trying to show Nell she wasn't worried about the rumor of Jeb's release. Apprehension sanded her spine when she recalled the hot hate in Jeb's eyes, and his shouted threat as they'd led him away from the Madison County Courthouse in shackles and chains.

"I'll be out someday, Lannie, and I'll come for you. You can count on it. I thought you was my friend. It ain't nice to treat old friends like this, Lannie Sullivan. You'll be *real* sorry. I'll find you . . . I'll find you . . . "

His rage had shaken her then, as it did now. Until the tragedy of Gracie's death, Jeb's shouted warning had been an infrequent, but horrifying nightmare. Losing Gracie had chased away the bully's threat. She concentrated on steadying the tremor in her hands as she showed Nell the most effective way to clean herself off in the creek.

As they washed themselves off, Nell shivered and shook her head in wonder. "I don't know how you've done this for two years. How in God's name did you do this in the wintertime? This water is ice cold now. I can't imagine what it is in December."

"Freezing. When it wasn't frozen solid, I managed to wash in it twice a week. Thank God, I had well water to drink most of the time. When the well froze, I chipped ice from the creek and carried it into the cabin to melt."

Nell slicked her hair back with wet hands and gave Lannie a hard look.

"All this hardship living is a form of punishment isn't it, Lanier Grace Sullivan?"

Considering her answer, Lannie didn't reply right away. From a tree branch nearby, she retrieved a clean towel for each of them, tossed one to Nell, and then scrubbed her face dry.

"Yes, I have finally realized that it is, or was. Self-punishment. I felt like I deserved to go to jail, or something, just like we sent people to prison for wrongdoing. I wanted to die, but didn't have the courage to kill myself."

"You wouldn't let any of us help you."

"I know, but I knew if I was going to recover I had to

do it on my own, or I'd never be strong again. When I ran away, I just wanted solitude, I wanted to find some peace, some answers. The harsh living conditions here at the cabin supplied little of that in the beginning, but I relished every scratch or bruise I received, every hunger pang when food supplies ran low, every freezing day and night, every discomfort, every miserable moment that came my way. I reveled in it."

She led the way back up the wooded slope to the cabin.

"Self-flagellation," stated Nell quietly.

"Yes, it was."

Nell sat on the stoop next to her as they drank their tea. Bry lay next to them, dozing in the warm morning sun, his long tail twitching now and then in the green grass as he dreamed dog dreams.

"Still feel that way?"

Lannie smiled. "No. I'm better now. I woke up one morning grumbling because the fire had gone out and I didn't have enough wood to rekindle it properly. I had to go outside in the snow, knock ice off the tarpaulin covering the wood pile, and then carry a load into the cabin. I was so angry with myself. The discomforts began to bother me. Looking back, I see now that that was the beginning of recovery. At about the same time, I stopped dreaming of Gracie every night."

"I'm so glad, love. You don't want to die anymore, do you?"

"No, I don't. I've accepted Gracie's death, but not the way she died. I still haven't achieved the peace I yearn for. Maybe none of us do."

"Maybe." Nell squeezed her hand. "I'm proud of you. You're a survivor. I wouldn't have done it the way you did. I would have wallowed in everyone's sympathy and clung to every pitiful hug, or look, or word. I couldn't have survived here, not only the hardships, but the isolation. God, Lannie, it's beautiful here, but, Lordy, you are really by yourself."

"It's been good for me, but I'm happy that my first trip off the mountain will be for your wedding in October. Seems kind of symbolic."

Nell's face glowed. "Yes, it does. A new beginning for both of us. Wait till you meet Hartley. You'll love him. I wish you'd go to Washington with me tomorrow. You could meet him, and help me look for a wedding gown, and a maid of honor dress for you."

"I'm not ready to leave the mountain yet."

"Well, at least you've made a move in the right direction by volunteering at the playhouse."

"Yes, I'm looking forward to going tomorrow."

"But you should be doing more than painting sets. You're a first-class choreographer. Why don't you ask if you can help?"

Lannie smiled. "You know me too well, Nellie, me girl. My feet are itching to get in there and straighten out a few things, but I've been away from civilization and polite company for so long that I'm shy. Also, I don't want to call any attention to myself. I just want to be anonymous."

She didn't mention the brawny carpenter she wanted to avoid, the stranger who had stirred up dormant physical sensations she hadn't felt since she was a sex-crazed teenager.

Nell hooted. "You? Shy? Anonymous? The girl who led the charge onto the field at the Sugar Bowl when we won the national championship? The girl who danced an Irish jig on top of the bar at every O'Hara's, O'Grogan's, and O'Hearn's in New York, red hair flying, and as your father says in his delightful brogue, 'a-yellin' at the top of her voice'? All that joy is still there, Lannie."

"No, it's gone, the pleasure for living is returning, but not the joy. It's gone forever."

"I hope not." Nell frowned. "Your father worries about you being up here all by yourself. He thinks you've been here long enough. Before he left for Ireland, he told me he wants you to move over to the big house on Satulah Mountain."

"I know. Since Mummy died, he worries more about everything. I've tried to reassure him, but it doesn't help. I remind him of the weekends we spent here when I was a child, camping, and just hanging out, and that we were safe then. I remind him that Wilkie Talley checks on me from time to time. Wilkie chops my wood for me, and he dug the garden. And, of course, I have Bry." She reached down to smooth the wiry hair on his powerful neck. "There aren't many people or animals who would mess with an Irish wolfhound. Besides, Nell, me girl, I haven't seen hide nor hair of anyone since I've been here. A bear sometimes, deer, foxes and their babies, but I'm much more interested in them than they are in me."

"But what if you got sick or something?"

"Not me. If I can survive the last two years, I can survive anything."

Spencer Case slumped further down into his seat. He pressed his fists to his temples trying to will away the headache he felt coming on. He sat by himself in the rear of the darkened theater, ordinarily his favorite place to be during rehearsals. Wrapped in darkness while looking into the light and magic created on stage never failed to enchant him. But this morning the enchantment had turned to dust and disillusionment.

This retreat of his into the hinterlands, which had been planned to restart his fifty-eight-year old doldrums, was turning into a disaster. He felt worse than he did after his two recent disastrous Broadway flops. What in the name of God had he been thinking of to let Robert Keeting talk him into this? He should have gone to Maine and spent his time fishing.

He closed his eyes, but he still heard the leading man singing off-key, and the graceless tromping of the out-of-step dancers. With every misstep, he winced, shuddered, and squeezed his eyes tighter.

Before these last few years, he'd always been able to pull order out of chaos. Chaos was almost a given in the beginning of any theatrical production, but a good director or producer saw the problems and solved them. Spencer recognized the problems here, but he didn't know how to solve them.

He wondered for a moment if the playhouse was haunted, as rumor suggested, and if he'd been hexed with a curse that some witch of an actress had cast upon the place years ago.

Come, come, come Spencer, my man, you're making excuses for yourself. You're getting carried away by your love of the dramatic and the mysterious.

A fluttering movement in the next seat startled him, but the idea of ghosts and goblins vanished quickly when he caught the scent of Mae Nevin's ladylike cologne. He kept his eyes closed, hoping she would go away. He liked the woman, but she was so afraid of him that she made him nervous.

"Do you have a headache, Mr. Case?" she asked timidly.

"Call me Spence, or Spencer, remember, Mae? And yes, I do have a headache."

"Oh, dear. I'll get you something right away."

"Sure, sure." Maybe she would go away and never come back. No, he wouldn't be so lucky.

She hurried up the aisle, and Spencer sat up to face the beastly confusion on the stage.

"Okay," he yelled. "Let's take a break. Young tenor, please go somewhere and run the scales a few times, preferably into a tape recorder so you can hear yourself. And Mr. Patton, who calls himself a dancemaster, would you for Christ's sake pull your group together? They look like a herd of cattle blundering through cowshit."

Vince Patton set his hands on his hips and wiggled his bottom.

"Well, well, well, aren't we in a foul mood this morning, Spencer," said prissy Vince. "We must have had something sour for breakfast or else we wouldn't be casting our sour self on the rest of us, would we? Come my darlings, let's go catch one of those divine cappuccinos at the new coffee shop down the hill."

Vince Patton minced off the stage, his dancers following dispiritedly. Spencer wished he'd mince himself back to New York.

Robert's brainstorm had seemed good when they'd discussed it last winter. He wanted Spencer to train a group of promising young actors through summer stock until they were good enough to come to New York and work as an ensemble doing revivals Off Broadway. It would give Spencer an opportunity to relax, stand back, and look at his New York work from afar, see the reasons Keeting's last two shows had failed. It would also season young actors whom Keeting had had an eye on for a while, but hadn't been able to use in New York productions.

The premise wasn't working. The talent was there, but the energy wasn't.

"Here you go, Mr. . . . uh, Spencer. I brought you some Tylenol and some Advil. I didn't know which you preferred."

"At this point, I'll take anything." Mae handed him a

glass of water and he swallowed three Tylenol. "Now, if you've got a pill to cure vapid toneless voices, foundering feet, and a cocky, know-it-all, pissant of a choreographer, I'll take a summer's supply."

"I'm sorry things aren't going well. I'm sure they'll get better before opening night."

"I don't think so, Mae." He sighed. "*You Can't Take It with You* isn't doing too bad, but we're not filling the house. I didn't see Drum Rutledge laughing real hard when he watched the play last night. We've got other investors, but if he pulls his money out we'll be in seriously poor shape. High Falls people can't keep this place going by themselves anymore. They need outside money. Second time he's come. Curious, especially since he wasn't enthralled with the show."

"Second time who has come? Drum Rutledge?"

"Yeah."

"He seemed to be looking for someone," said Mae. "He asked me twice if all the volunteers were listed in the program, and I said yes. By the way, you should go back to see what's happening in the carpenter shop. Now there's a place that's showing big improvement. It will make you feel better."

"I doubt it, Mae, I doubt it." He knew he was being grumpy, but he couldn't help it. That was his middle name. Grumpy.

She smiled her sweet smile, and said, "Why don't you give it a try?"

"Okay. Believe I will." He patted her arm, and said, "Thanks, Mae."

She shivered at his touch. Christ, he'd have to be careful about touching her.

Women. He'd never understand them. He'd sworn off them forever after Julia Jane left him.

He moved off toward the carpenter shop with relief.

° ° °

Drum gave a final twist to the cross-head screw, securing it firmly to the two-by-four that would become a support for one of the heavier flats. He kept a watchful eye on the young actor who worked across the room from him on another part of the frame. Each of the apprentice actors was required to spend an allotted amount of time building sets and sewing costumes. He had just instructed the seventeen-year-old boy on how to use a saw. The kid seemed to be doing okay. Drum didn't see any blood yet.

Saturday always brought volunteers from town, and summer people, so the shop hummed with activity.

Spencer Case shambled in and rested his butt against a sawhorse, both hands deep in the pockets of his roomy painter's pants. Drum nodded to him and went on with his work. He fitted another screw to the wood and turned the handle of the Phillips screwdriver. What he wouldn't give for an electric screwdriver, but the playhouse couldn't afford expensive tools. He'd bring one from the lodge or buy one on Monday. Couldn't buy one tomorrow.

Tomorrow was Sunday. In High Falls everything closed on Sunday, except the Superette on one end of town and the Quick Shop at the other end, both of which sold the big city newspapers the summer people demanded.

Sunday. He wondered if the redhead would be here.

"Hey, Drum, whattaya figure we do with this here extra joint?" asked one of the locals, Heck Howell. "Looks like it's supposed to go on that corner, but we sure as hell can't find a place fer it. Can't see it on the blueprint nowhere."

"Be right with you, Heck. Soon as I finish this I'm going to take a break."

"Yeah. Sounds like a good idea. Maybe we will, too."

The hammering stopped as the men left to have a Coke or a beer outside in the cool pine-scented shade.

Spencer, hands still in pockets, shoved off from the

sawhorse and walked slowly around the shop looking at the work in progress. The shop was empty now, except for Drum, Spencer, and the young apprentice.

"Doing good there, Jason, doing good," Spencer said to the young man. "Learn your lines yet?"

"Y-y-yes, sir."

"Good, good."

He returned to stand next to Drum.

"Did I put you in charge out here?"

"No."

"Well, it looks like you are, and I just did."

"I don't want any responsibility, Spencer. I'm leaving in a few days."

Spencer rubbed his chin, tugged his ear lobe, and closed his eyes. When he opened them his clear blue eyes said volumes.

"You're a natural leader, Rutledge, and you obviously know your way around a carpenter shop. You've gotten more accomplished in a week than we did in the previous month. I know you're a busy man, but I need help here and you have a vested interest. How about giving me a couple more weeks?"

The more Drum saw of Spencer Case, the more he liked him.

"To tell you the truth, I've been considering a longer stay. My house out on Haystack is going through some serious renovation and I want to keep an eye on that. Let me give it some thought."

"Good, good. You came to see what was wrong with the operation here at the theater, and you've become part of the solution. I just realized I need the same sort of energy and direction in the acting group." He stopped, scratched his chin, and said in his slow manner of speaking. "I used to have it. I could inject anything I wanted into a production, but I don't seem to have it anymore."

Surprised, Drum realized Spencer Case had just partially bared his soul, and he felt sorry for the man, but knew Spencer wouldn't appreciate sympathy. He also wondered if the New York director might be looking for a friend. He worked another screw into the wood and chose his next words carefully.

"I think we all go through times like that. Sometimes you have to just step back and let things go for a while. Seems to give you a fresh perspective."

"Yeah, well, anyway," Spencer said, and cleared his throat. Obviously embarrassed now that he'd revealed some of the tender soul beneath the gruff exterior, he changed the subject. "How did you become so skilled in woodwork? Hobby?"

"No. I grew up in the Northwest. Washington and Oregon. My father died when I was a boy. I helped support my mother and me by lumberjacking. Lied about my age and got my first job when I was thirteen."

"Rough life for a kid."

"It was, but I was a tough kid. You had to be to survive in that environment."

"How did you get to this part of the country?"

"I'd fallen in love with wood, hardwood, any kind of wood, and what you could do with it. Wanted to learn how to make furniture. Only one place for that. Here in North Carolina. Got a scholarship to Duke, apprenticed myself to several craftsmen, and worked my way through college making furniture on the side. Don't get to do enough of it these days."

"You can work to your heart's content around here. Hope you'll give it some serious thought." He glanced at the old battered Timex on his wrist. "Gotta go. I gave the kids an hour. See you tomorrow?"

"Yes, I'll be here."

Oh, yes, I'll be here. I've been waiting for Sunday

morning all week. If the redhead isn't here tomorrow, I'm going to track her down.

Shocked at his thoughts, he bit the inside of his cheek, then afraid he would throw the screwdriver in frustration, he placed it carefully on the work table.

You don't need or want another woman in your life, Drum Rutledge. The last one was not a good idea. Take charge of your senses. Leave High Falls before you get in serious trouble.

SEVEN

Nell waved goodbye as she drove her perky red Miata out of the parking lot of All Saint's Episcopal Church. Dispirited, Lannie watched until the car was out of sight. Nell had provided the first fun and laughter Lannie had experienced in three years. She missed her already.

She turned to walk back to the jeep and Bry, but paused to admire the English garden that encircled the steepled stone church. Like a kid with a stick, she ran her hand along the white picket fence that bordered the pastel garden. Lannie had noticed loving parishioners tending the restful flowerbeds through spring and summer months.

But no one worked early this Sunday morning. The small parking area was empty. Episcopalians didn't feel the need to get to church as early as the Baptists. Across the street the faithful already moved in and out of the solid-looking, square, red-brick Baptist church.

A mother with two children in hand hurried toward a side door of the church. A three year old in a frilly pink dress lagged behind her, fascinated with her feet and the shadow the morning sun cast from her small body onto the concrete.

Turn around, Lannie wanted to call to the mother. *Watch her, keep her in sight always, please. She's too far away. You'll lose her, you'll lose her. Turn around.*

Lannie started to cross the street, running to extend her hand to the child. The child giggled at a cat who played with a frayed tennis ball beneath a tree. At the sound, the mother turned and called to her.

"Hurry up, Barbara Jean. We'll be late for Sunday school."

Barbara Jean's chubby legs hurried to catch up with her mother.

Lannie halted, halfway between heartache and recovery. Would she never heal? Would the sight of a child always hurt? Would mothers who took their children for granted always offend her?

A gentle hand on her shoulder startled her.

John Lamb smiled at her. Dressed in jeans and carrying gardening gear, he'd come prepared to work in the Episcopal garden.

"Lannie, how nice to see you. What are you doing in town?"

"I could ask you the same thing. I didn't know you liked gardening."

He surprised her by blushing. If she didn't know him better, she could have sworn he looked embarrassed.

"Eh, well, I'm just taking my friend Ellery Smith's place this morning. Now it's your turn. Why are you here?"

"I just brought my friend Nell to her car. She visited with me a few days. I'm on my way to the playhouse."

"Aha, you're really making progress. A visitor was invited into your bower on the mountain, and you're working at the theater. I'm proud of you."

"So am I, John. Gotta go."

She hated her abrupt manner, but she had to hurry to

the playhouse right now, or she would chicken out and bolt back up Haystack to the safety of the cabin, the creek, and her own garden.

"Got a new shipment of books in. Come and take a look."

"I will," she said. "See you later, John. I've got to get going."

"Surely, you've got time for a few good books. We can go to the shop right now. Won't take a minute."

"Next time I come to town, John."

"But these are some of your favorite authors," he tempted. "Auel, Oates, Hoffman. I had you in mind when I ordered them."

Was it her imagination or was John Lamb anxious to get her into his shop? She'd never been alone with John in the bookstore before. For some odd reason, the thought made her uncomfortable. Sometimes he could be a little pushy, which irritated her.

"Sorry, I've work waiting for me at the playhouse."

"Okay. See you soon, I hope." He squeezed her arm and she shivered with distaste. She reminded herself that he was just being friendly, but she hurried to the jeep with relief.

Minutes later she parked beneath the big oak that Bry loved and walked swiftly toward the theater.

She stopped for a minute to admire the lovely old brown-shingled building sitting in the tall oaks and evergreens. It was in ragged condition, shingles missing here and there, dusty windows, a couple of shutters hanging askew, but it stood with dignity, reminding the viewer of better yesteryears.

Why then, she wondered, did she sometimes shiver with apprehension at some unseen menace she felt as she worked?

She brushed away the intrusive, annoying thought and moved on.

With studied nonchalance, she avoided glancing through the open doors of the carpenter shop, which were just opposite the big barn-like rear stage doors. Bry followed, warily surveying everything around them, as he always did. Satisfied that they were secure, he settled in the sunny entryway with a contented sigh.

Maybe the carpenter won't be here today, thought Lannie.

She heard music and tapping feet from the stage, and smiled.

Mae had left her a note with instructions from the set designer. It said if Lannie had any questions she should ask Drum, who worked in the shop.

Lannie shivered. She would get along just fine without any help, thank you.

She finished painting a tree that had been left for her to do and set it outside in the sun to dry. Someone new played the piano this morning. The beat came back to her stronger and clearer than it had last Sunday. As she painted a fence on the canvas flat leaning against the wall in front of her, her feet began to move in time to the music.

"The Farmer and the Cowhand" steps came naturally to her because she'd done them so many times through high school and college productions. Someone yelled, loud and angry. "Oh, for pissy sakes, Jimmy Hardy, you've got the feet of a g.d. elephant. You summer interns are going to kill me, just frigging kill me. Step out of line and let Joanna work with you."

Lannie couldn't resist. She deposited her brush in a bucket of water and walked to the wings.

The piano started thumping again. She stood out of sight and watched the dance troupe struggle through the number. A young dark-haired girl about eleven years old stepped on the heels of the dancer in front of her, garnering a nasty backward look from the injured party. The eleven year old valiantly continued on for a few more steps while tears of frustration ran down her cheeks. Finally, she gave up, and stumbled back into a protecting fold of curtain, bumping into Lannie.

"Oh," she gave a squeal, then covered her mouth quickly. "I'm sorry. I'm *so* awkward."

Lannie's instinct was to draw the broken-hearted girl into her arms, but she resisted her maternal summons, and said, "No, you aren't, darlin'. You just need a little attention and lots of practice. I'd be happy to show you the steps. Would you like that?"

"Oh, yes, ma'am. Would you?"

"I'd love to. It's too dark here. Come with me. We'll find some sunshine."

Bry raised his head and lifted his ears when he heard them coming. He watched the girl following Lannie, then got up to sniff her. Bry was almost as tall as the girl and she recoiled, drawing her arms close to her body as Bry inspected her.

"It's okay. He won't hurt you."

Bry licked the child on her cheek and ambled back to his napping spot in the sun.

"What's your name?" Lannie asked.

"Daisy." She wiped away the remaining tears on her cheeks, and Bry's saliva.

"Hi, Daisy. I'm Lannie. I promise I'll have you dancing in no time. Who knows, you might be so good that he'll put you centerstage."

Daisy sniffed and gave a wan smile. "I don't care about that. I just don't want to embarrass my grandmother. She volunteered me."

They stood in a sunny patch just inside the open doors. "We can't hear the beat as well here, but we'll hum as we go, okay?"

Daisy nodded.

Lannie instructed her in some basic steps first, a buck and wing, and the standard soft shoe. She caught on fairly quickly, so Lannie knew she was capable of doing the steps required for "The Farmer and the Cowhand." She took her by the hand and they kicked and twirled together.

Bry growled and moved quietly out of his sheltered shade into the sunshine. Startled, Lannie threw him a hurried glance and wondered what had put him on alert. He lay down closer to her. Positioning himself out of his mistress's way, but close enough to reach her in one leap, Bry watched her efforts with Daisy. Must be nothing dangerous or he would be in a quivering stance, hair raised, teeth bared.

Lannie forgot about him and lost herself in the little girl and the dancing. "Use that toe. Reach. Reach. Reach for the sky. Now, heel down and up again."

Daisy giggled. "This is fun."

"Okay, remember to spot yourself. Pick out an object in front of you and use it for a target. On every round-about, pin your eye on your target. Okay, do it by yourself now."

Lannie sang as Daisy danced. Halfway through, she said, "No, stop, darlin'. You're doing a half turn instead of a whole turn." She gave her a hug. "Let's do it again."

They were both perspiring liberally. Lannie paused to remove her sweatshirt and welcomed the coolness and freedom the tank top beneath gave her.

The eleven year old worked earnestly. She wasn't the most graceful dancer Lannie had ever seen, but she tried until she'd mastered several of the steps Vince Patton had choreographed for the number.

Bry growled again and Lannie surfaced from the concentrated attention she'd given the child. He stood and sniffed the sir, his ears braced forward. She had a strong, uncomfortable feeling of being watched. She glanced around, saw nothing amiss, then looked at her watch.

"Come, Bry. It's okay. I don't see anything." She rubbed his back. "I think you're so accustomed to our mountain quiet that any strange noises here in town make you nervous."

She continued to soothe him, but glanced at her watch.

"Oh, Lord, Daisy. We've been working for an hour. They'll be looking for you, and I'm way behind in my painting chores."

The child gave her a big hug. "Thanks, Lannie. Can we do this again tomorrow?"

Lannie returned the hug, sucking it in, treasuring the little girl's arms around her neck. Tears came to her eyes. "Sure, we'll do it again, but I won't be here until next Sunday."

"Oh, please, come tomorrow. I'm in another scene and can't do any of the steps right. Mr. Patton hates me."

"No, honey, I'm sure he doesn't hate you. Some people just aren't very patient."

"*Please* come again this week," she begged. "I'm not ready for the opening next week, and my friend Jennifer isn't either."

"I'll think about it. Now you go back up front. They must be missing you."

"No. No one misses me much. My mom is in Paris at art school, and my dad plays golf all the time."

"Oh, I'm sure they miss you. I would if you were my little girl."

A summer child, thought Lannie, *and not having the fun that I had growing up here in the summertime.*

"It's okay. I don't miss them either," said Daisy, her chin lifting defiantly.

"I haven't seen a rehearsal schedule. When is the next rehearsal for your scenes?"

"Tomorrow morning, and Wednesday, I think."

"Tell you what. I'll come tomorrow if you'll promise me something. Have you been to the Nature Center next to Sargent Creek on Lower Lake Road?"

"No. My grandmother says it's full of bugs, snakes, and mountain things I wouldn't like."

"I'll come tomorrow and Wednesday if you promise to walk over there and spend an hour or two after rehearsal today. Your friend Jennifer would probably like it, too."

Daisy grinned. "Okay."

"It's a deal then. I'll quiz you tomorrow on what you learned at the center and what you liked the most," teased Lannie.

The grin on Daisy's face widened. "I'll pass the quiz."

An irritated voice called from the stage area. "Daisy, where the hell are you?"

"Scoot now. I'll see you tomorrow."

Daisy disappeared in the backstage shadows. Lannie, feeling guilty about the unfinished flat, hurried to rescue her paintbrush from the can of water, and returned to work on the gray fence. Bry walked to the door of the carpenter shop and sniffed, then circulated the whole compound worriedly, stopping at a grove of evergreens near the building. Finding nothing, he ambled back to his shade tree and went back to sleep.

The man slid hurriedly from his hiding place in the small grove of evergreens that hugged a corner of the playhouse. He glanced up and down the street to make sure he wouldn't be seen when he emerged, then stepped out to saunter casually down the hill, a satisfied smile on his face.

Keeping Lannie Sullivan under surveillance was serving two purposes, he thought. First, he knew where she was most of the time when she was in town, which was a great pleasure. Secondly, there was the delicious chance of seeing her naked or half-dressed in some manner. He didn't know how he would accomplish that, but he would find a way.

He'd been so good until now. Lannie and her nosy prison friend had changed all that. *But surely I deserve a little fun after all this time.* Yes, he thought, as he gave himself permission to indulge in his dirty secret.

The dog was going to be a big problem. He frowned and hunched his shoulders with displeasure. Sucking furiously at his teeth, he searched for an answer.

By the time he reached Main Street, he had one.

Drum inhaled sharply, still trying to draw a breath without shaking, still trying to deflate the rocky bulge that threatened to pop the grommets on the fly of his jeans.

He swung the hammer and caught the edge of his thumb, drawing blood.

"Godammit." He sucked it furiously, the iron taste of blood tainting his mouth.

He couldn't get her out of his mind.

He'd heard Lannie as she'd instructed the young girl and had been drawn to the door to watch. He'd meant to step into the sunlit grassy drive between the two buildings to see better, but the dog had growled, probably trying to alert his mistress that a nosy, horny carpenter was watching. Drum had stepped back into the recess of the shop.

At first he'd kept his presence quiet because he hadn't wanted to disrupt the intense concentration both child and teacher were giving to the dance lesson. Then he'd become enchanted with the scene before him: the lonely young girl so obviously enjoying the attention; the lovely smiling woman, her vibrant red hair flashing in circles as she whirled and twirled so gracefully. Entranced, he'd forgotten his work and, like an overheated fan guzzles beer at a July baseball game, had devoured the sight of a dancing Lannie.

Even now, the swirl and sway of her vibrant hair flashed shining red through his mind. A piece of yellow yarn had flown loose from her ponytail, and the gleaming hair had tumbled down her back.

Then she'd removed her sweatshirt and tossed her head impatiently to get the hair out of her eyes. The vibrantly alive red mass had swooped over her shoulders to hang down her back again. That's when the heat began to rise in his groin.

She'd spun and kicked and the ripple of supple muscles on her thighs had made his heart beat faster.

The flesh on his arms had lifted with goosebumps.

The fallen yellow yarn from her hair still lay in the grass, forgotten. He wanted to retrieve it and return it to her, but knew the gesture might be a dangerous one, perhaps the beginning of something he didn't want to begin. If he looked from the corner of his eye, he could see it lying there like a mesmerizing golden snake.

"Dammit."

Jesus, this was only the third time he'd seen her and he lusted like a bull over a ripe cow.

He threw his hammer on the table in front of him. Again he tried to control his breathing, tried to ease the tension that distended every muscle and every nerve until he felt as if his skin would burst, and every pore would spew his lust throughout the shop.

He walked to the cooler in the corner with deliberate concentration, counting every step.

One, two, three, four, five. Lift the top. Six. Find a Coke. He rummaged through the ice, found a Coke. Seven. Pull the tab. Eight. Take a drink. He sucked eagerly at the refreshing coolness, enjoying the bite as it slaked his thirst and took the taste of blood from his dry mouth. Nine. Walk back to worktable. Ten. Pick up hammer and get back to work.

He gripped the hammer, but heard Lannie's voice as she talked with Mae Nevins, and his fist shook.

Mae called to him. "Drum, could you come over here for a minute? I have a volunteer who needs some help."

He grabbed his blue workshirt, jammed his arms in the sleeves, and buttoned it, then glanced down to make sure the tails covered the hard bulge in his jeans.

He walked over to the playhouse with his heart in his mouth.

Mae and Lannie stood before an old canvas surveying it with concern. Lannie had her hands on her hips. She avoided looking at him, which was fine with him.

"What's the problem?" he asked.

"They've sketched a barn on this canvas, but the frame holding it looks too weak to hold up. It's really shaky. Lannie wondered if it didn't need some new supports before she started covering it with paint."

"I'll take a look at it, but let's pull it outside where we can see better."

"Okay," said Mae. She pointed to the costumes hanging over her shoulder. "I've got to deliver these dresses to the girls so they can be fitted. I'll leave you two alone if you don't mind."

He did mind, but couldn't say so. "No, you go ahead."

Lannie offered to help him, but the flat was small enough for him to handle by himself. Outside, he studied the old wooden supports with minute concentration, trying to ignore the faint fragrance of her as she stood next to him. It wasn't perfume that arose from her, which made sense for this wild hippie kind of woman. But there floated around her the fresh, brisk aroma of soap and something else he couldn't define, which was pleasant and alluring.

She ran her hand over a section of the canvas, feeling it for imperfections. Her shoulders and arms glistened with a faint sheen of perspiration. She chuckled softly and asked, "What would you guess? Put together in the nineteen forties or fifties?"

"Nineteen forties probably." He let himself look directly at her, and smiled. "Played any hide-and-seek lately?"

"No," she laughed.

Her small breasts swelled over the edge of her canary-colored tank top when she laughed and his heart did double-time. She must have seen his glance because a pink line zipped along the tips of her cheekbones then disappeared, and her breasts rose and fell as she breathed faster. So, he wasn't the only one affected by this insane madness.

He lowered his gaze and bent from the waist to inspect the canvas again, but could not control himself and glanced sideways at her breasts again, which were now eye level.

Jesus.

Her nipples had stiffened and extended until they poked hard against the pliable cotton of her top. The urge to take one of them in his mouth and suck until she screamed for mercy almost undid him. He forced his eyes downward, but encountered a strip of pale creamy skin showing between the bottom of her top and the denim of her jeans.

He ran a finger down the splintered wood, but ached to run it beneath the band of her jeans at her waist to feel the softness of her skin.

Drum stood up quickly, and tried to speak. He couldn't.

Her silver eyes were smoky with warmth but filled with uncertainty.

"Your nose is green today," he finally said. It broke the tension.

She grabbed at her nose, and laughed. "It depends on the day of the week. Tomorrow it might be purple. You don't have wood shavings in your hair this morning, but you've got sawdust in your ear."

"Earmark of a good carpenter," he said. He cleared his throat. "I saw you with the young girl. You're good. Good with children, and you dance like a professional."

Maybe that's why she hung around the theater, he thought. Maybe she was a chorus girl, or what did they call them in the theater, a "gypsy"? Went from one dancing job to the next.

"I've had professional training. Well, I'd better get back to work."

"Yeah, me, too. I leave at noon everyday to work on my own house."

Mae returned. "Lannie, I noticed you with Daisy. Would you be willing to work with the children? Vince doesn't have any patience with them. He just yells. Last week he had them all in tears."

Drum watched her struggle for an answer. It seemed as if she wanted to say yes, but was afraid to.

She said with hesitance, "I told Daisy I would come tomorrow and Wednesday, but I don't know about coming on a permanent basis. Let me think about it."

"We really need help around here, and you seem to know your way around a theater." Mae was almost begging now. Silently Drum urged her on, hoping Lannie would assent to coming more often. Mae frowned. "And you should see the costume mess in the attic. Gosh, I could use an army up there, too. If I didn't have to run home and dress for church, I'd take you up there right now."

"I'm a terrible seamstress, but I'm good at organizing. Let's see how it goes with Daisy when I come in tomorrow," Lannie replied. Drum could see the interest mounting in her face. "If I can be of help with the choreography, I'd be happy to stay an extra hour afterwards to help organize costumes."

Mae's face shone with hope. "I'll make sure it's okay with Mr. Case and with Vince. Uh, I hate to even ask you, but I know they will want to know. Have you had any training in dance?"

Oh, for Christ's sake, Mae, what difference does it make? Don't make it hard for her to say yes. Make it easy.

"Yes, most of my childhood and teen years, and then at Juilliard."

He saw the amazed look on Mae Nevins's face and wondered if his looked the same way.

Mae cleared her throat, "Oh, Juilliard . . . well, uh, I'm sure they won't have any objections then."

"See you tomorrow. I'll bring my lunch." She glanced at her watch. "I'm afraid I have to leave now. I want to hoe my potatoes before it gets too hot this afternoon. Bry, come."

She avoided Drum's gaze, but lifted a hand in farewell to both of them as she walked toward the jeep.

Mae Nevins gave Drum a quizzical look and though they exchanged no words he imagined she wondered the same thing he did: Who was this shabbily dressed beautiful woman, who had studied at Juilliard and hoed potatoes somewhere in the maze of mountains around High Falls?

Drum walked slowly back into the carpenter shop and began to sweep up the shavings he'd left on the floor. The morning seemed dreary, though the sun still shone high in a cloudless sky. He'd be happy to get back to the lodge this afternoon. He was designing built-in walnut cabinets for his library. Woodwork always soothed his demons.

Thinking of the conversation that had just taken place, it occurred to Drum that Mae was taking care of some problems he'd already identified and had intended to put in the evaluation he would fax to Keeting in New York. He'd caught part of an *Oklahoma!* rehearsal last week, and it hadn't taken him long to realize that the dance troupe lacked precision and spunk. There were few smiling faces and even fewer dancers who looked as if they cared whether they were there or not.

Maybe Lannie, who became more and more interesting each time he saw her, could inspire the lackluster group.

The costuming he'd seen when he attended *You Can't Take It with You* last week had been abominable, too—suits and shirts unpressed, dresses with hems hanging at erratic lengths, terrible colors. Ordinarily he paid scant attention to such things. His schedule was hectic so he didn't get to the theater often, but when he did, he expected the best, especially a Keeting–Spencer Case production.

The performances had been as listless and uninspiring as the costuming. If he didn't have money invested in this show and others, he'd have gotten up and walked out. Yes, this was summer stock, not Broadway, but people were paying good money to watch actors who seemed to care little about providing their audience with entertainment. Mae Nevins could take care of improving costumes and find someone to work with the dancers, and Drum could work with set designers and carpenters, but only Spencer Case could give this group the life it needed. He was beginning to like the gruff New York director, so he hated reporting that to Keeting.

What had happened to the inspired brilliance he'd seen in so many of Spencer Case's earlier productions? Maybe he would find out in the next few weeks, for he'd decided to stay awhile. He hoped the decision he'd made this morning had more to do with the playhouse and its problems than with his intense attraction to the redhead.

Though he'd forced himself to come to High Falls, he now found himself enjoying working with his hands again and realized he'd needed a break from maintaining his far-flung timber empire. His corporation required constant surveillance, but he thrived on jousting with other business barons. He'd always loved competing on any level, scholastically, in the board room, and on the rugby field. If he worked hard enough, the business he'd built continued to grow. At the same time, the even larger need to bury his grief and loneliness was subjugated.

This morning, he'd called his secretary in Charlotte and had outright canceled several appointments and had reassigned other appointments and conferences to his staff and members of his board of directors. For the first time in five years he would be free of schedules, airports, conference calls, and confrontational board meetings.

The camping trip on Chip's fifth birthday was the last time he'd had a vacation. He should have taken Chip camping more often. As he propped the broom in a corner, he winced at the pain that sliced through him. He squeezed his eyes tight against unfamiliar tears that welled and swallowed hard. Strange. First time he'd had that sensation in a long time.

Maybe I've made a mistake. Maybe being in High Falls is wrong. Or maybe feelings stirred up by the redhead have loosened other emotions as well.

Action was what he needed, and he gunned the Panoz AIV roadster out of the driveway and toward his mountain. He would take a tough hike this afternoon, to the twenty acre out-parcel he felt was rightly his. The rugged climb to the top of Haystack should sap some of his anger at himself and his thoughts.

EIGHT

Spencer Case walked away from the playhouse with relief and headed down the steep hill toward Main Street. All the years of his adult life had been spent happily inside of a theater somewhere in the world. But he couldn't wait to get away from the High Falls Playhouse this morning. He was having problems with the talented, but inexperienced young troupe, and the decrepit old school building, with all of its dark corners and crannie holes, gave him the creeps.

What in hell had gone wrong? How had everything turned to crud so fast?

He'd been so wedded to the theater that friends said this was the reason he was a bachelor. He'd never married. Didn't have time for the investment marriage required in time and attention. There had been women from time to time, but no one kept his continual interest and excitement except "Lady Temptress Theater," his coined expression for his life's work.

Only one woman had come close to keeping him happy. Julia Jane Howard. The toast of Broadway for thirty years and his lover for the last fifteen. She'd presented him with an ultimatum three years ago. Either he married her, or she would marry young Brad Alcott, Hollywood's newest hot star. Though twenty years younger than Julia Jane, Brad had worshipped at her feet since he'd appeared with her in a revival of *Camelot*. Spencer had ignored her ultimatum, thinking she would never marry the young pup.

How could I have been so stupid?

Holy crapola. Is that what's wrong with me? Do I miss Julia Jane that much? Hell, no.

He'd always been proud of his independence, of his solitary life free of encumberments and mushy relationships. Close relationships usually caused more heartache than joy.

He stopped to admire the garden in back of town hall. He didn't know anything about gardening. Had never had time for that, either. But he knew the weather here in High Falls must be good for such things.

His work at the playhouse might be depressing for the time being, but he liked the mountain village with its diverse citizenry, and he especially enjoyed the climate. The days were soothingly warm, and nights and mornings were cool, almost cold sometimes. He rented a small apartment behind the theater, where he enjoyed a fire in the fireplace every evening and slept under a blanket every night.

He ducked through the alley, past Thelma's Bakery, and in the rear door of Longfellow's. John Lamb defied the town's unspoken law that said no business should be conducted until one o'clock on Sundays, which gave all the town's good citizens an opportunity to attend church. The front door of the book shop was closed and shuttered, but favorite customers knew the back door was always unlocked and visitors were welcome.

Spencer drew himself a mug of coffee from the large urn near the door, selected a fat, sugary doughnut from an adjacent platter, and wandered down a book-filled aisle to find John.

The bookstore owner sat on the floor in the middle of a stack of science fiction paperbacks.

"Hey, Spencer," John said. "How're things at the playhouse? Sorry, I couldn't make the board meeting on Thursday. The season is fast shifting into high gear. I'm busy all week now, not just on weekends."

Spencer sat on a box of unopened books and ate his doughnut as he watched John sort books. In the two months he'd been here, he'd found John had a sympathetic ear and an intellect that equaled any of those he'd matched wits with in New York.

"Yeah, well, we need you at those meetings, John. When you're not there, Beezy pretty much takes over. She's driving me bananas."

"I know." John smiled, and sighed. "Same thing happens every summer. I'll try to get some of the stronger board members to start going again. No one likes attending when she's there."

"Thanks. I'd really appreciate that." He brushed powdered sugar from his shirt, ruing the growing girth of his stomach, which caught every dropped crumb. He sighed, and sipped the hot coffee. "I don't have a vote, or power or anything, but there are things that cry for attention. Those old red velvet seats, for one thing. I know there's sentimental attachment to them, saved out of some historic old theater in Atlanta and brought up here, but, for Christ's sake, my ass sank so far down in one of them that it touched the floor. How's an audience going to enjoy a show if they're in pain?"

John eyed him with amusement. "You're an old grouch this morning. Anything wrong?"

"I'm chopping and no chips are flying. I can't get anything to jell at the playhouse. Scares the shit out of me. Never happened before. Kind of like writer's block, I guess."

"What you need is a good woman, Spencer Case. Someone who will pillow your head on her bosom and listen to all your grumpy gripes."

"A woman is the last thing I want. Always telling you what to wear and what to eat. Spending all your money. Talking too much. They drive me crazy."

John said, "Ahhh, but the look of them, the feel of them, the smell of them. Nothing like them, huh?"

Spencer thought John almost lurid in his description, but said nothing. He got up to get another doughnut and met Mae Nevins coming through the back door.

"Well, good afternoon, Spencer. I had no idea you were here."

"Good morning, Mae. What are you doing here? Thought you'd be in church." Oh, great, Spencer. The woman was already scared to death of him. He should be nicer to her.

"I was. Church just let out. I came to pick up a book I ordered."

Spencer contemplated leaving, but instead picked up a doughnut and headed back to John. Mae poured herself coffee and followed him.

He could have poured the coffee for her, he thought. That would have been a nice thing.

He shrugged his shoulders, retrieved his seat on the box of books, and listened to John and Mae.

"You're looking mighty fetching this morning, Mae," said John.

She blushed. "Thank you, John. Tell me where my book is and I'll get it."

Spencer figured John was just being polite, but he took a second look at Mae anyway. She was pretty, in a small-town way. Her short, light-brown hair waved softly about her round face. Her eyes were cornflower blue and more kind than they were beautiful.

"No, you sit on the box next to Spencer there and enjoy your coffee," said John. "I'll get the book."

Spencer made room for her. She was a small woman, so she didn't take up much space, but a fold of the skirt of her pink dress fell lightly over his knee. He wanted to get up, move around, but didn't want to appear unfriendly, so stayed where he was.

He couldn't think of a damned thing to say to this woman he worked with almost every day, except theater stuff, which he didn't want to talk about.

Geez, he wished she wasn't so afraid of him. Though he still carried the mannerisms and speech patterns of his humble beginnings in New England, he'd long since become accustomed to the fast life of Manhattan and sophisticated theater people. He'd realized early on that his gruffness and plain-speaking ways gave him a unique persona in the Broadway crowd and added to his eccentric reputation. He was different, he was honest, he was brilliant Spencer Case, and he enjoyed that.

But here he sat next to a nice lady, feeling out of place, stripped of persona, any reputation to hide behind, and it made him extremely uncomfortable.

He cleared his throat. "Ah, any problems I should know about?"

"We need a handyman, that's for sure. The steps to the attic need repairing, and so do a lot of things." She frowned. "And the kids say they've seen someone lurking about the theater."

Spencer laughed. "They would. It's their dramatic nature."

"No, I think this is more than imagination. They say he hides in the shadows and is good at disappearing if someone gets close."

"Bunch of baloney."

John returned with her book. "What's a bunch of baloney?"

"The kids say we have a ghost," Spencer told John.

"No, he's not a ghost. He's a real person," said Mae.

Damned nervous woman didn't know what she was talking about. Summer interns always had jokes going on.

"Hmm, interesting, " said John. Casting Spencer an arch smile, he changed the subject. "How's my friend Lannie doing, Mae?"

"Oh, do you know Lannie?" Mae asked.

"Yes. I encouraged her to volunteer."

"She's great, and I think I can persuade her to do more, but I need to discuss it with Spencer." She looked at Spencer and smiled hopefully. "She's a wonderful dancer and good with the children. Do you think Vince would mind if she worked with some of them?"

"Knowing Vince, he'd probably hate it. Has she any credentials, any training?" he asked, and retrieved his coffee cup from the floor. The coffee was tepid. He needed a new cup, but felt trapped in the close confines of her skirt and John crouching in front of them. But he had to admit he enjoyed the faint fragrance of lilacs that drifted around her. Maybe John was right. Maybe he did need a woman to talk to.

"Yes. Lannie is a Juilliard graduate."

"That lady from the hills went to Juilliard? What the hell is she doing here? Hell, yes. We'll give her a try, but I'd like to watch her while she works next time she comes in. Know anything else about her?"

"Not really. She's your friend, John. Who is she?"

John hesitated, then said, "Well, Lannie's more than she seems. She's had a few rough years, but is recovering. Trust me when I tell you that you're getting a gem of a volunteer. She needs you as much as you need her."

"Good," said Mae. "If we had more volunteers like Lannie Sullivan and Drum Rutledge we'd have that place orderly in no time."

"Drummond Rutledge is helping?" John seemed startled, and worried. "I knew he hired Lester Hall to repair his lodge on Haystack. I haven't seen him moving around town, but then he never did much. He and his wife and son always kept to themselves. Everyone said the wife was a little queer, shy, and retiring."

"Well, I don't know about all that," said Spencer, "but, he's doing a damn fine job supervising the shop volunteers and getting the sets in shape. When he arrived, I thought he was just another rich investor poking his nose into something he knew nothing about. I was wrong. Says very little and keeps to himself. Hope he stays around for a while."

"Me, too," said Mae, and blushed again.

Holy crapola. She's got a crush on Rutledge, and she's afraid of me. Maybe this woman is too emotional to be working around a theater, where emotions run high anyway. I better keep an eye on her, make sure she's stable enough to do her work.

John frowned. "Rutledge has a reputation as a womanizer. Not misbehaving with any ingenues, is he?"

"Nope. They give a lot of excuses for visiting the shop to take a gander at him, but he's not interested."

The grandfather clock at the front of the store chimed one o'clock.

"Excuse me," said John, as he walked down the aisle. "Time to open up."

Mae drank the last of her coffee. "Well, this has been nice, but I have to go home and feed my cat."

Spencer smiled. Of course, she'd have a cat. Old maids always had cats.

Mae put on her gloves and got to her feet, and the heavy book in her lap fell on Spencer's foot.

"Ouch," he bellowed.

"Oh, dear. I'm sorry." She bent to pick up the book at the same time he did, and their heads banged together.

"Ohhh," she wailed, and held her forehead as tears welled in her eyes. A red knot rose on her pale forehead.

Spencer stood up quickly, and said, "Well, dammit to hell, I'm sorry. Are you okay?"

She smiled, and his heart did something it hadn't done in years. It flipped over like a chef flips a pancake on a hot griddle. "Sure."

He felt terrible. "I'll walk you home."

"Okay."

Aww, geez, now what have I gotten myself into?

Drum came to a halt in a grove of virgin eastern hemlock. The long climb had been rugged, but his hours on the rugby field and in the gym kept him in shape. His breathing was a little fast, but even and easy. The steepest, most difficult section of the trek to the out-parcel lay just ahead.

He stopped to admire the forest around him. Moments like these made him realize that despite all the energy he put into his business and into sports, he was half dead most of the time. He tried to fill the hollow hole in his heart with hard work or physical pleasures, or sometimes, on rare occasions when he felt desperate, even alcohol, but nothing filled him completely.

His young years as a lumberjack in the northwest had

fostered a deep respect and love for forestland, its beauty, its diversity, and the gifts it provided for the human race. High above him the green feathery canopy of the hemlocks spread majestically. Ahead, a grove of smooth-barked birch showed palely through the dimness of the cool forest.

He ran his hand over the deeply ridged brown-black bark of the massive hemlock beside him, then gazed up into the feathery emerald-needled umbrella overhead, and felt alive again. Forests held dignity, tranquility, and a power that kept him in touch with his own spirit, reminding him that he still lived and that there was much to be enjoyed in spite of the sadness that ate at him always.

The Great Smokies and the Blue Ridge Mountains contained probably the best preserved temperate deciduous woodland in the world. Amazingly, about one hundred thousand acres were virgin timber. Some species, the hemlocks, Carolina silverbell, Fraser magnolia, and northern red oak reached record size. The two thousand acres that surrounded his lodge had been kept inviolate, and except for the out-parcel, undisturbed for hundreds of years.

That's the way he intended to keep it. The acreage that didn't belong to him had been a burr in his gut for a long time.

He didn't like the idea of someone spoiling the pristine nature of the overall acreage. The chance of someone tearing down the old Joe Webb cabin, which sat in the center of the clearing, and putting an aluminum recreational vehicle on top of the mountain appalled him.

Logging companies such as his always got a bad rap, but he was a conservationist at heart, and though he made his living off the land, he also revered its gifts. Rutledge Timber always replanted more than they cut, and they replaced with adolescent trees. Tiny seedlings took too long to reach maturity and had a lower survival rate than the older trees.

None of the land owned by his companies would ever be used or sold for second-home or resort development. He had a running battle with some of his board because of his refusal to make greater profits by selling out to huge global real estate firms. He was rich enough, and so were they.

A sharp snuffling grunt from above drew his attention.

Up the slope he saw a black bear and her two cubs. The cubs were about four months old, gangling, cute, and inquisitive. He'd learned early that bears were never to be trusted. But generally, in the summertime, they found enough to eat, and if left alone weren't dangerous. He stepped sideways and stood quietly beside the trunk of the protecting hemlock.

He was sure the mother bear knew he was there, but so far she hadn't displayed any bad temper or hostile behavior. He knew from experience that she probably just wanted to pass by without hindrance. Alert, but not concerned, he stood silently and watched.

She grunted to the cubs, and he imagined she was telling them to stay put. She started down the grade in front of her, sliding on moldy leaves as she came, and slid right past Drum, a mere twenty feet away. He held his breath when she landed on a level clearing not far from him. She grunted again, as if giving permission, and the two awkward cubs came sliding after her, tumbling and turning like giggling two-year-old toddlers.

Delighted at the unexpected meeting, and the show put on by the lively cubs, Drum watched as the three of them continued down the incline.

When they'd disappeared from sight, he continued up the mountain.

An hour later he crossed the creek that transversed the land he headed toward. Soon, he saw the roof of the cabin that had sat there for almost a hundred years and sighed with relief. At least the Sullivan family had left the historic structure intact. In fact, he doubted if they ever came to the property. He knew they owned a large home on Satulah Mountain.

He headed toward the cabin site, hoping the land remained undisturbed.

A menacing guttural growl stopped him in his tracks. The hair rose on the back of his neck. Had the mother bear changed her mind, decided he was a threat, and followed him? No, that wasn't likely.

The growl became a snarl and grew in volume and ferociousness. The clearing was now in sight, and he took two cautious steps forward.

A huge dog, an Irish wolfhound, stepped out of the shadowy trees to confront him.

Drum held his breath. The dog looked like the friendly hound that belonged to the redhead, but the resemblance stopped there. This dog's teeth were bared, and there was nothing friendly about the mean, deepening growl in its throat. The dog's anger grew with each dangerous second.

He stretched his hand out to the dog and murmured soothing phrases. "It's okay, pal. I'm not going to hurt you. It's okay."

The calming words had no effect. The dog braced its feet and leaned forward in an attack mode, anxious to leap on his prey.

Drum braced himself.

He tried again to pacify the dog.

"Settle down, buddy. I'm not here to hurt you," he murmured softly.

"Stay, Bry. Down." The grim voice came from behind him.

He whirled to find the woman named Lannie aiming a 12-gauge shotgun at him.

She stood with her feet wide apart, the shotgun at her hip, but leveled squarely at him. Her hair had loosened from the ragged blue yarn that held it and strayed disheveled about her flushed face. A streak of brown earth crossed one cheek. Her usually smoky eyes were silver bright with anger.

She bristled with hostility and anger whistled through him like hot summer wind.

"Bry is not accustomed to intruders. He'll sit there until I release him, but if you take one more step into the clearing, I can assure you he'll be on you in a flash. And in case he misses his mark, which is highly unlikely, I'm damned good with this Remington."

"So this is where you hoe your potatoes," said Drum. "Should have known you'd be somewhere you're not supposed to be. You're trespassing."

"No, sir. You walked onto my land about five minutes ago. Now kindly turn around and walk away. Pretend you never found your way here."

"Sorry, I can't do that, and I'm going to have to inform Judge Sullivan that you're squatting on his land."

She hooted with laughter, letting the gun relax in her hand, and the muzzle point toward the ground. Drum drew a sigh of relief, but wondered what on earth she found so funny. He threw a quick glance at the dog. The once menacing animal now lay on the ground, but alert and looking up at him with liquid brown eyes.

The redhead laughed until tears ran down her cheeks. The tears mapped muddy white ribbons on her dirty face.

"Oh, the judge would love that," she got out, then whooped again.

He had an urge to shake her, but she finally stopped

laughing and wiped her face with a tissue she dug from the pocket of her jean shorts. In spite of his anger, a smile tugged at his mouth as she unknowingly turned the muddy streak into a brown mess that smeared her cheek and nose.

"You know the judge?" he asked. "You have his permission to be here?"

What had he happened upon? A secret love nest of the prestigious Judge Wexford Sullivan? He didn't want to think so, and tried to squelch his sudden disappointment in this infuriating redhead who stood before him smiling in delight.

"My father has a devilish sense of humor. He would get a huge kick out of the image of me squatting on his land."

"You're a Sullivan?" asked Drum incredulously.

"Lanier Grace Sullivan."

"But the judge has only one daughter. If I remember correctly, she's an attorney in Madison, Florida."

"That's me," she said flippantly. But her face sobered, and she raised the shotgun to her hip again. "Actually, however, the land belongs to me now, not my father. He gave it to me for Christmas last year. If you doubt my word, check the transferred deed at the county courthouse in Franklin."

Drum took a moment to absorb this interesting information. Irritated with himself, he found that even through his anger and hostility, he wanted this unkempt woman who stood so confidently and brazenly before him. The lust that had shaken him this morning at the playhouse brewed as strong now as it had then.

Her long legs were lightly tanned, as if she'd worked bare-legged in the garden before. They were lithe, the calf muscles subtly defined, as with most dancers. Her cut-offs were loose at the waist, hanging around her hips, showing a great deal of milk-white skin between the band and a brief sheer white cotton tank top. She wore no bra, and prominent dark rosy nipples thrust against the material.

They glared at each other.

Bry rose to his feet, and twisted his head from side to side to give them both a good look. He pawed the earth nervously, and Drum knew the dog had homed in on the dangerous currents sizzling between the two of them.

"Down, Bry. I'll take care of this." She hefted the shotgun up a notch. "We've never had visitors before. This region of Haystack is almost unreachable. How did you get here, Mr. Carpenter? You might have happened upon a faint trail had you driven the dirt road part way, but there's no way you could have climbed here."

"Put the shotgun away and I'll tell you."

"Tell me, and then I'll put it way," she said. Drum heard a stubborn note in her voice.

"If you'd paid attention earlier, instead of being so hostile, you'd remember that I said I owned the surrounding acreage. I know every inch of this land."

"Hah! Likely story. It's all Rutledge Timber land."

"*Privately* owned Rutledge land."

He saw understanding light her frowning face.

"Oh, sorry. My turn to be obtuse. Your name is Drum. Must be short for Drummond Rutledge." Her words scorched with dislike. "Mr. Moneybags himself."

He watched with interest and relief as she efficiently ejected all the shells from the Remington onto the ground, and then let the gun rest in the crook of her arm.

She was mollified, but not happy. Angrily, she jabbed her other hand into a pocket, and with the weight of her hand, the waistband of her shorts fell below her belly button.

° ° °

Lannie's fury at this man's unwelcome intrusion hadn't lessened any.

She was startled at her fierce reaction to Drum's appearance. Was she still clinging tenaciously to the isolation she'd used as a protection against reality and all it had to offer? She hated guns. The one she held belonged to her father. He used it to hunt with when he came to the cabin. The weapon hung heavy in her hand now, but she had grabbed it immediately, and would have used it without hesitation. She knew that with a certainty that disturbed her.

"Just exactly why did you come, Mr. Rutledge? No one knows I'm here and that's the way I like it. You're not welcome."

"I apologize, Miss Sullivan, or should it be Ravenal? If I remember correctly, the last time I spoke to your father about buying this land, you were married to one of the Atlanta Ravenals."

Her heart tightened at the mention of his buying her land, and she said coldly, "I'm no longer married, Mr. Rutledge. I use my maiden name, and I'm not interested in selling my land."

In spite of her anger at this intrusion of her private domain, and her fear at the thought of losing it, his physical influence on her grew as it always did in his presence. It was as if he'd invaded not only her land, but her body and her soul. Every recess, every private niche of her felt entered and explored.

She hated it, but couldn't help but notice his feral grace as he walked lazily toward her.

He moved casually, but Lannie sensed that he didn't feel lazy or casual. Here was a man who was restrained, clearly conscious of his strengths, but with the power to keep them tightly leashed. She knew instinctively that he was a man of deep emotions who kept them strictly disciplined.

He stopped in front of her, hands planted squarely on his lean hips.

"Could we stop being angry with each other, and go back to being Lannie and Drum, the two playhouse volunteers?"

"Why? So we can get cozy and you can talk me into selling you my land? I don't think so, Mr. Drummond Rutledge. My father told me of your generous offers through the years. He wasn't interested then, and I'm not interested now."

The seams of his worn-soft jeans were bleached white, and the yielding cloth molded and cupped the bulge of his crotch.

Her body tensed, and her muscles coiled tightly.

"Why?"

"This is my refuge, my . . ." Wait a minute. What was she doing? Revealing her intimate feelings to anyone but her father or Nell was something she never did. "Never mind why, Drummond Rutledge. Just know that there's no way in hell that I'm going to sell you this land. What on God's earth would make you want it anyway? I'm not bothering you or anyone. In fact, no one even knows I exist here except three other people, and I'd appreciate it if you would keep the information to yourself."

"Why?" he asked again.

A ray of sun caught a streak of gold in his light-brown hair, and she noticed the shadow of a day's growth of beard on his squared jaws. He hadn't shaved this morning. The pulse beat in her throat quickened, and the corners of her mouth tingled.

Damn. There seemed to be no controlling his effect on her, and she hated that. This man was dangerous to her.

"It's none of your business, but let's just say I like my privacy and let it go at that."

"Okay. I respect that. I'm kind of the same way."

"Fine. Then we understand each other."

"And I promise to keep you and your retreat a secret if you'll forget about this afternoon and we can be just Lannie and Drum again."

He painted her body with a look of such obvious admiration, her insides knotted with a honeyed ache and her heart hurried so fast that she found it hard to breathe.

She knew she should say no, but before she could speak, he continued.

"I take that back. No conditions. I'll keep your secret."

She had been looking forward to tomorrow morning. The thought of working with Daisy at the theater had given her more pleasure than she'd had in three years. Should she give up that pleasure because her desire for this man had spooked her?

No.

I'm more of a woman than that. I'm stronger than that.

"Thank you," she said coldly. "Goodbye, and please don't come again."

"Certainly won't. Wouldn't think of it," he said with insouciance and gave her a casual salute as he turned to leave.

Bry rose to watch vigilantly until Drum Rutledge disappeared into the treeline.

Lannie ran her hand soothingly over the dog's head, and said, "It's okay, Bry. It's all over. We're fine, and it's okay."

But deep in the pit of her stomach, she knew that it wasn't.

NINE

The boots Jeb wore were thick and protective, but the wet swampland he stood in penetrated them anyway. His socks were damp. He'd become accustomed to discomfort in the past week. That was the reason he'd come to Apalachicola. Prison had toughened him, but he needed sharpened skills in woodland survival, and this camp in north Florida was the foremost in the country.

Woodland survival training turned momma's boys into real men, and besides it enhanced his feelings of superiority and security. He would not need everything he'd been taught in this Florida camp, but he'd come primarily for the rigorous rifle course. He could now match his rifleman's score with the best.

Dawn broke uneasily. Patches of pale gray marked the sky around him. No-see-ums stabbed through the mud and black grease he'd spread on his face and hands. He let them bite, not moving an inch from his hiding place behind the slash pine. A dark creature moved sluggishly around his feet. The cotton rat searched for insects or maybe the eggs of a ground nesting bird. He hated the ugly thing. He hated all ugly things, but he let the rat hunt, not moving a muscle, even when the rat mounted his foot and stood on hind feet to nose around the top of his boot.

Ignoring the rat, he waited patiently for his human prey. Prison had taught him infinite patience.

He wished the two men in the palmetto thicket behind him would shut up. The secret militia camp had been recommended by Jesus survivalists, and he had come for serious training, not for social discourse. He agreed with what they were saying, but sometimes the men here were filled with more talk than they were action.

"Shit, I'm tellin' it like it is, Joe," one man said. "I'm fed up with the way the government intrudes more and more into our lives. Hell, I don't want nobody, but nobody, sayin' my kid can't say prayers in school or makin' laws about who can have babies and who can't."

These men were playing soldier. He wasn't playing. He was here to ensure his readiness to find Lannie, to convince her that she'd made a mistake, and that she belonged to him. He knew she was in High Falls, but not in the big fancy country-club house. He'd followed the Sullivans there one summer, so he knew exactly where that house was, and where Lannie's room was, just as he knew the Florida house like the back of his hand.

The decision to come here had solidified when his contact in High Falls had informed him that he couldn't pinpoint Lannie's location, but knew she was in the highest reaches of the mountains and that it would take supreme survival skills to search for her undetected in the rough western North Carolina ridges.

He would be prepared. He was leaving nothing to chance. His next stop was a mountain camp near Franklin, North Carolina, then on to High Falls.

A figure crawled furtively through the saw palmetto

hammock two hundred yards in front of him. His Model 70 Winchester flashed its blank load through the dim dawn, and hit the target. A bright splash of orange covered the back of the ghillie concealment suit the man wore. The man yelled, "Son-of-a-bitch! Damned good direct hit for someone. Who connected?"

He didn't answer. He didn't need for anyone to know how good he'd gotten with the rifle, and he didn't need praise or recognition. He hadn't come here for that.

One of the men behind him whispered to his buddy, "Shit, Clay, there ain't no one around but us, and I sure didn't see the son-of-a bitch. Where the hell is he?"

He smiled. Under his breath, he muttered the motto of the sniper camp, "Happiness is a good kill."

He secured his rifle, melted into the shadows, and lowered himself to the ground. On his belly, he slithered like a snake through the mud to dry ground.

Back at camp, he gingerly removed his boots, and massaged the scarred bottom of his feet. The thick, ugly burn scars were a daily reminder of his drunken father's favorite method of punishment. His mother had long since run away with a circus roustabout when his father discovered the pleasure he derived from correcting his son's behavior by holding the boy's feet over the burners on the electric stove.

The pain, and the rancid memories it brought, receded with thoughts of Lannie. He bathed his feet, powdered them, and slipped on soft socks.

Sighing with relief, he found a quiet area away from the activity, and lay under a slash pine to light a cigarette and contemplate the brightening morning sky. He was coming into his supremacy. He could feel it as sure as a flaming queen knows he's going to get fucked in prison. All the fumbling uncertainty, all the feelings of inferiority he'd felt when he was young were gone.

He was "king of the hill," and he would prove it to Lannie.

He'd hated Tom Ravenal for taking Lannie away from him. He still hated Tom Ravenal. Maybe someday he'd make Ravenal suffer for the unhappiness he'd caused, especially for the pain he'd caused Lannie. He knew Ravenal blamed Lannie for the death of the baby, Gracie.

When he'd been in Madison to take care of Buster he'd made a nocturnal visit to Sullivan's Rest, as he always did. A convenient overhang of thick ivy near the kitchen window provided perfect protective covering for spying. He'd heard Old Mausie and Big Billy talking. They'd talked of the times Ravenal had yelled at Lannie and told her she spent too much time at her law offices and not enough time with the baby.

Old Mausie said that was why the Ravenals had divorced and Lannie had run away. Someday he would make Ravenal suffer for hurting his woman.

Yeah, he'd heard a lot on his visits under the ivy. If the two old people had any idea the precious information he'd gathered, and to what use he would put it to, they'd fall on their knees to God prayin' for forgiveness for their gossipy ways.

He took a deep drag off the cigarette, held it, then blew it out forcefully. Overhead, he saw Lannie's face form in the hot blue sky, the sun's ruby streaks across the huge expanse were locks of her hair, and he imagined the fiery feel of them in his fist as he made love to her.

It was sad, what had happened to Gracie, but the baby should have been his anyway. Lannie's next child would be his.

What was that childish tune again, the one Mausie sang tearfully to Big Billy every time they talked about little Gracie? Something about "Gracie, lacy, dancing daisy."

He pinched the smoldering end of the cigarette between his thumb and forefinger and dashed it to the ground.

Eagerly he thought of tomorrow's destination. He was returning to Madison one more time before traveling on to High Falls. Time for more spying on Mausie and Big Billy, and he wanted to visit Nell Smathers. It was time for he and Nell to get reacquainted for several reasons.

The next afternoon he stood in the deep shadows of a live oak, one of the many that circled Sullivan's Rest, Lannie's home in Madison. He couldn't count the hours he'd spent in his youth in this very spot, watching Lannie through her upstairs bedroom window as she brushed her hair.

It was too dangerous to get any closer to the house today. Big Billy was working outside behind the house, and Mausie was entertaining cousins in the kitchen.

Sullivan's Rest hadn't changed. The large rosy-bricked house only grew lovelier through the years, as did all the old houses in this slow-moving southern town. Dark-green ivy climbed its walls and draped portions of the wide, white painted veranda, which wrapped three-quarters of the house. He wondered what kid trimmed the ivy now. He used to be the one who cut and controlled the growth of the glossy vine.

That's how he located exactly which window was Lannie's bedroom window. He'd taken a long time to trim that day. The Sullivans had gone to the beach. Old Mausie, the cook, was in the kitchen baking sweet potato pudding and country ham. He imagined he could smell it right now, the salty tang of the ham mixing with the sweet brown sugar and cinnamon of the pudding. His mouth watered today at just the thought of it. Big Billy, the caretaker, had been polishing Judge Sullivan's ancient Cord in the old carriage house at a far corner of the spacious grounds, so no one was paying him any attention. People never had paid him any mind then, but they did now.

He was making sure of that.

He'd stood on the porch roof and peered in the room at his leisure that special day so long ago, memorizing which wall her bed stood against, memorizing the placement of her toilet articles on her antique cherry-wood dressing table, memorizing the number of pillows on her bed and imagining the one she tucked between her legs every night.

She'd evidently tossed her bra and panties on the bed while she changed into her bathing suit. They were the only articles out of place in the white, green, and coral room. Lannie was usually very neat, so he was certain she'd left them there for him to see.

He'd tried the window, but it was locked. He remembered his frustration, and how he'd finally been forced to leave because of his mounting lust. He'd climbed hurriedly off the porch roof and retreated to this spot under the tree where he'd jacked off.

Lannie didn't know it, but he had just marked the grounds of Sullivan's Rest as his. His seed on her soil made Lannie his forever.

Big Billy had caught him around the grounds several times when he wasn't supposed to be there, but Jeb had always had a ready explanation. He'd told the old black man he'd been searching for a key he'd lost the last time he'd cut the grass, or he was checking to see if Big Billy needed anything done, or he was on his way to the house to see if Mausie needed errands run.

He was older now and smarter. He'd never get caught again.

He'd stored many memories of the house and its lovely occupant: Lannie in her short white tennis skirt running across the lawn to jump in someone's car, her tan legs flashing in the sunlight; Lannie, Nell, and their friends on the side porch, dancing to music blasting so loud and hard that it made his heart jump as he hid in the tree branches and watched; Lannie playing her ukulele, and all of them singing gospel music and old songs Mausie had taught her; Lannie, before she could drive, climbing into the boxy Buick Big Billy drove, with her ballet bag slung over her shoulder; Lannie with Nell, before either of them had a learner's permit, sneaking the Buick down the drive late at night when they were supposed to be having an "overnight."

Nell had seen him hiding in the tree once and pointed him out to Lannie. Lannie had waved at him, but Nell had made an awful face, sticking out her tongue and laughing, then yelling at him, "Shame, shame, shame on you, Jeb Bassert. Mind your manners."

He still burned with embarrassment at the memory, and swiftly remembered to turn the embarrassment into anger and hate. Anger and hate were powerful.

Reluctantly, he turned away from the peaceful visage of the house and the memories it held for him, good and bad. Ah, well, he'd be in Madison awhile. He had important things to do here. He would come back and visit often. He would probably even enter the house one night so he could catch a whiff of her.

Just one whiff of her, one tiny whiff of her perfume, her sheets, anything to hold him until he was with her again.

When they were together, there would be no Tom Ravenals or any other man who would distract her. She would finally admit that she belonged with him. Something he'd known since sixth grade.

After she said she was sorry, he would make her his for always.

At the hotel later that night, he knelt by the bed to say

his prayers, confident that Jesus was listening. "Friend Jesus, lead me to her. She knows we just need to talk things through. Then she'll remember all the things we shared when we were young. Thank you for taking care of my beautiful girl while I was locked up. Thank you for taking her baby up there with you. It saves me from having to get rid of it myself. You knew I wouldn't like another man's baby in our lives. She made a big mistake marrying Ravenal and having his baby. She should have been having *my* baby, but we'll take care of all that."

He was angry at Jesus, though. He'd discovered Nell Smathers wasn't in Madison, and he blamed Jesus for messing up his plans. He'd planned on pinpointing Lannie's exact location in the mountains by going through Nell's mail, but she was out of town, her office was closed, and the mail was being held at the post office. He'd broken into her law office, but found nothing that would tell him what he needed to know.

For long horrible minutes rage shook his body until the mattress he rested his elbows on shook, too. He grit his teeth until they ached and tears formed under his closed lids. Finally, the cold rage lessened, and he stored it away in its proper compartment and resumed praying.

"You know I don't like my plans messed with, Jesus. Play with me from now on. I'll find her whether you help me or not. Amen."

TEN

The toddler reached for the ball and tumbled . . . her wheat-blond hair floated on the surface of the water, then dampened and clung to her diminutive head . . . blue eyes widened in fear. . . .

Lannie woke up shivering. She should have been there for Gracie. *If I'd been home that afternoon, Gracie would be with me right now.*

"Lacey Gracie, dancing daisy, makes her mom a happy lady. Gracie, lacey, dancing daisy, makes . . ."

No, no, no. Not tonight.

But it wasn't night, it was morning, thank God, and very early. The sun's early light had just begun to slip through narrow breaches in the cabin walls to the east.

She sat up, trembling. The vast sack of pain and grief that dwelled within her throbbed like a bellows. Swiftly, she yanked the drawstring that drew it closed, cutting off its supply of blood, and tears, and emotion.

Bry, ever alert at her bedside, sat up, too, his big body rising swiftly at her movement.

"Good morning, my beloved friend," she said.

A gurgled rumble, similar to a contented cat's purr,

came from somewhere in his throat. It was his way of communicating with her, and she gave his thick, strong column of a neck a long hug.

"Well, Bry, it's been two weeks since I've had the nightmare. I think getting involved at the theater has helped, don't you?"

He rumbled again.

"Which reminds me, I've got work to do in the playhouse attic this morning, and Daisy and Jennifer promised to be there early to help organize the prop room. So we better get cracking."

An hour later, she stood in the windowless costume storage attic, which stretched the entire length of the playhouse. Row after row of musty costumes extended before her into murky cavernous depths at the far end.

Fifty years of costumes from every imaginable musical, drama, and comedy ever performed, and some not so imaginable, hung in haphazard fashion in the huge rectangular room. Sporadic efforts at organizing resulted in period clothes hanging from the rafters: pantaloons, crinolines, breeches, frock coats. Roaring Twenties' apparel, flapper shifts, white trousers, and striped blazers were supposed to be in the corner against the wall. But any attempt at organization or cataloging periods and sizes had been given up long ago.

Lannie yanked at the string from the bare lightbulb that hung over her head and flicked on her flashlight to head down one of the gloomy aisles.

It was no wonder that the teen apprentices didn't like coming up here. *No question it is spooky,* she thought. In their need for drama in their lives, the teens had created several hideous drooling creatures who lived up here. The worst specter they had fabricated was a vampire named Gavin, who skulked along the aisles in various costumes sniffing for small children to drink blood from. They scared the younger children to death with their stories, but Lannie suspected they scared themselves, too, because none of them liked doing costumes. "Doing costumes" meant searching the attic for whatever the director or costume mistress wanted.

The rumor of a man skulking in the shadows of the theater made her edgy, too, but she was sure the talk was just more nonsense like vampire Gavin. She laughed, making fun of herself, but the nervous laugh sounded eerie in the gloom of the shadowy cavernous room. Glancing swiftly into the shadows around her, she hurried down the long aisle.

As Mae had said, they really needed a costume mistress. Several women, local and summer, had offered their sewing skills, and dutifully appeared two evenings a week to cut patterns, or repair, or alter a voluminous dress to fit someone. But no one wanted the responsibility of planning the costuming for an entire show, much less hiring on for the whole summer, and Lannie couldn't do much here except put the attic into a semblance of order. Nell had always said her legal files were the neatest she'd ever seen.

She was here now at Mae's request, searching for gingham farmhouse dresses for Aunt Eller, Laurie, and Ado Annie.

Squeaking and rustling over her head startled her, but then remembered the mice Mae had told her nested in the top hats. She glanced at the shelves lining the walls from floor to ceiling to her left, imagining mother and father mice, and children, all snug and comfy in one of Fred Astaire's elegant top hats.

But, like the teens, even she was not immune to anxious feelings here, and she didn't like mice. She moved to the next aisle and, directing the flashlight before her, pushed her way through a rack of yellowing bridal gowns to find herself in the midst of the gingham dresses.

Good, because this was not a great way to spend a morning. She'd rather be in the cheery prop room.

Another bare lightbulb dangled above and she pulled the string, chasing any possible specters away.

Hurriedly, she flipped through the hanging dresses and found several that might do. She gathered them in her arms and made her way back through the maze of costumes, quickly jerking the strings on the two overhead lights as she passed beneath.

She'd promised Mae that she'd spend some time up here, but she dreaded it.

Carefully, she made her way down the rickety steps.

Someone's going to break their neck on this staircase, she thought. She made a mental note to bring the subject up with Mae or Spencer Case. Hey, Lannie, she cautioned herself. *You're only a volunteer, not Miss Take-Charge-and-Fix-it,* like you were in your old life.

Odd, she thought. When had she started thinking of her life in Madison as mother of Gracie, and Nell's law partner, as her *old* life? Was today her new life or had she just begun an exploration of new beginnings?

As she delivered the costumes to Mae and headed for the prop room, she wondered at the revelations she just experienced.

In the prop room, she knelt in the middle of twenty or so lamps, trying to sort them by period. Daisy and Jennifer hadn't arrived yet, which didn't surprise her. Spencer Case had held the entire *Oklahoma!* cast past midnight last night, hoping to instill some spark into the mediocre rehearsal. The two preadolescents were probably still sleeping.

The prop room was a small shed attached to the carpenter shop, with a door to the shop, and another door that opened to the outside area leading to the theater building.

A shadow fell across the floor as someone tall passed the outside door, then returned to fill the doorway, blocking the sunlight. Her heart tripped faster, and she dared to look up, hoping it was he and yet afraid that it was.

Drum stood there, a mug of coffee in one hand, a toolbox in the other.

"Good morning," he said pleasantly.

"Good morning."

"You're here early."

"Yes, well, with opening night this weekend, these props are still not . . . some of the people who were supposed to help never showed up and . . . uh . . . Daisy and Jennifer will be along shortly."

This was the longest sentence she'd addressed to him since their confrontation at the cabin last week.

Their encounters had been brief, polite, and awkward. She had tried to avoid him in every way she could.

If Drum was in the carpenter shop, she made sure she was in "Gavin's Garret," the apprentice's label for the costume attic. If he was onstage, she was backstage. She'd considered not coming to the theater at all anymore, afraid of her tumultuous feelings when she was close to Drum. But her hunger for human contact and communication indicated an important forward step in healing, and so she had allowed herself to be drawn into the working life of the summer playhouse. She couldn't permit her passing attraction for this man to halt her yearning for healing.

She was sure the seismic sizzle resonating between herself and Drum Rutledge would die a natural death. After all, it had been three years since she'd slept with a man. Any attractive man might have turned her on. Tom hadn't touched her after Gracie died. He'd always been a hasty lover anyway. He would grind away at her like she was a piece of meat, mutter a few grunts, and after he'd satisfied himself, fall asleep.

Drum cleared his throat.

"Look, Lannie Sullivan, I'm not some con man who's going to steal your land away from you," Drum said gruffly. "I've tried to apologize for the intrusion on your privacy, but you haven't let me near you. People can say what they want about me, and I frankly don't care what they think. But one thing they know. I'm honest. I'm not going to tell you I don't want your land, because I do. I'm hoping someday you'll seriously consider selling. You can't live up there by yourself forever."

The resurgence of anger she'd felt last week as she'd aimed the rifle at him was swift, and without thinking, she shot back, "I'll live there forever if I want. And *you* look, Mr. Drummond Rutledge, I'm not going to sell, so just forget it and leave me alone."

"Certainly. I wouldn't think of bothering you again." He paused, and she hoped he would go away. Her quick anger had faded, and had been replaced with a rapid rhythmic pulsation in her throat. "But I was hoping, since you seem to be here almost every day now, that we could be civil to each other. You run every time you see me."

Indignant now, she said, "I don't run when I see you. I'm not afraid of anything, and I don't run from anyone."

What a total-ass lie, Lanier Grace Sullivan. You've been running and hiding for the last two years.

"I see." His eyebrows lifted as he sipped his coffee and stared at her. His navy-blue eyes reflected amusement at her furious denial, and the faint white furrows that bracketed his firm mouth deepened. "Well, I hope your two young ones turn up soon. That set doesn't look anywhere near complete."

"They'll be here."

He saluted her with his mug and left.

Lannie sighed with relief and tried to still her fast beating heart, tried to stem the trembling of her inner thighs, but her legs weakened. She sank back on her haunches to the floor like wilted lettuce, knocking over several lamps in the process, and landed on her butt next to an old portable record player. The lamps clattered and tinkled, and she held her breath, praying none of them broke, and also hoping Drum's curiosity wouldn't bring him to investigate the noise.

She glanced at the door that stood open between the connecting rooms and wished that it were closed. But if she closed it, he would know it was because she didn't want to be reminded of his presence. The decision wasn't hers to make at the moment anyway. Her legs wouldn't have cooperated even if she'd ordered them to.

She heard him moving around and whistling. An old Chris Conner tune, "Angel Eyes." She remembered wondering how a rough-and-ready mountain carpenter could be acquainted with sophisticated jazz. The expensive sports car should have been a clue. She'd been so besotted with him that she'd only begun to recognize the air of authority he carried with him, and the respect paid to him by the men who worked with him next door.

Daisy appeared, Jennifer at her side, chattering about boys. They came through the door in a rush and looked mystified at not seeing her right away. Lannie busied herself dusting the record player.

"Lannie? Oh, there you are."

"Hey, girls." She stood, brushing dust from her hands, and smiled.

"Who was the utter creep looking in the window?"

"Have no idea what you're talking about. I've been sitting on the floor and wouldn't have seen anyone anyway."

"Some guy was watching you and . . ."

They broke into giggles, and covered their mouths with their hands.

"What's so funny?"

"He was feeling his . . . you know . . . where his zipper is," said Daisy, her face crimson with embarrassment.

"Are you positive?"

"Well, we were still on the hill in the street, but that's sure what it looked like."

Lannie forced herself to walk casually toward the door. She wanted to run, but was afraid she would frighten the girls. She looked around, but saw no one. "Where is he now?"

"Bry got up and moved toward him, and he walked into the back door of the playhouse."

"I think the older interns have got you imagining all sorts of things. He was probably just an interested visitor, or maybe a tourist, trying to see what was stored in this room," she said, but alarm bells rang all through her, setting her nerves on alert.

Nell's news of Jeb Bassert leaped to mind, and she wondered for one horror-filled second if he could be in High Falls.

"What did the man look like? Was he short, tall, dark, light?"

"Like we said, Lannie, we couldn't see too well. I just know he wasn't short."

Couldn't have been, Jeb, then, thought Lannie. She wasn't even sure Jeb was out of prison. She would call Raiford prison today.

"What were you doing on the floor?"

"Tinkering with an old record player."

"What's a record player?" asked Jennifer.

Surprised for a moment, Lannie then smiled and said, "Well, before there were tape players and compact discs, there were records. Your parents would know about them. Maybe I'll have time to show you how it works later, but right now we have to sort these lamps, then look for a pail, or lunch box of some kind for Laurie in the picnic scene."

They worked happily for a couple of hours, dusting, washing, polishing assorted items, and Lannie forgot about the man the girls had seen, but she could tell the girls were getting bored as their conversation got listless and quiet.

"Are you still going to classes at the Nature Center?" she asked.

"Yeah, I like it," said Jennifer. "We went for a hike up the Rhododendron Trail, and found purple-flowering raspberry. The Latin name is *Rubus odoa* . . . something or other. Anyway, it's this real pretty purple plant, and the cool thing is that early settlers used the berry for making jam and jelly. I never thought much about what I put on my toast in the morning, but now I realize things like that weren't taken for granted by the pioneers."

"Daisy, how about you? Are you learning anything interesting, or are you going because I asked you to?"

Daisy didn't answer. Lannie, extracting a buggy whip from assorted objects stacked in the corner, turned to see Daisy biting her lip.

"What's the matter?"

Tears welled in the girl's eyes. "I love it there, Lannie. I love the frogs, and the bugs, and the hiking, and the stories the leader tells about early days in the mountains. But . . ."

"But what?"

"Grandmother says that stuff isn't important, and she signed me up for golf lessons. The lessons are the same time as classes at the center."

Lannie's Irish temper began to rise, but she reminded herself that she had no business interfering in Daisy's life. Spending summers here as a child and teenager, she'd had golf lessons at the club, too, but her parents had always encouraged her participation in mountain activities. Learning the flora and fauna of the ancient land, learning the ebb and flow of the seasons, the eccentricity of the Smokies and Blue Ridge Mountains versus those of other mountain areas such as the Rockies, had made her feel part of the land, and had created a connection between her and the native mountain people.

She tried to keep the anger from her voice as she asked, "Do you want me to speak with your grandmother? Maybe she would listen to me."

Pleased with her simple but engrossing projects at the playhouse, Lannie didn't want to get involved with the country club crowd. She preferred that none of her old friends there know she was in the vicinity. But for Daisy she would give it a try.

"No, please don't," replied Daisy nervously.

"Yeah, trust us. You'll only make it worse," said Jennifer direfully.

"Well, we'll think of something." Lannie took one glance at Daisy's forlorn face, and decided she'd better change the subject. "Did you have a good time at Cindy's birthday party?"

They giggled and blushed.

"Super," they said in unison.

"Aha, there must have been some cute boys there."

"Oh, gee, Lannie, you should see Chad Bingham. He's thirteen, and absolutely to die for," sighed Daisy.

"Yeah, he and the sailing buddy he brought with him from Charleston, Nick Woodhall. Everyone has a crush on both of them," said Jennifer. "But they only paid attention to the girls who could dance. They wouldn't even look at us."

"But your dancing has improved so much since we started working last week."

"Lannie," said Daisy, with a certain amount of disgust in her voice, "that's not the same as swing dancing and slow dancing."

"Of course not." She smacked her head with her hand and laughed. "I'm such a big ol' dumb older person."

"No, you're not. You're cool."

"Hey, it's close to lunch and time for a break. Let's get a Coke, and, if you want, I'll teach you some slow dancing."

The two young girls looked at each other skeptically. How could a grown-up know anything about *real* dancing?

"Eh, sure," said Daisy, "but what will we use for music?"

"Well," Lannie's eye caught the record player, "we'll see if we can find records for the record player."

They shrugged their shoulders, and said "Okay."

"Jennifer, go next door and get Cokes." There was no way she was going in the carpenter shop herself. "Daisy, you help me look for some records."

Beneath a pile of rag rugs they found a cardboard box with a stack of black 78s.

Lannie lifted them from the box and sat them carefully on the floor. She went through them and found they were all Elvis Presley records.

"Oh, I love Elvis Presley," said Daisy. "My Aunt Pooch has all his CDs."

"Great. Let's see. We could use 'Blue Suede Shoes' for the fast dancing, and 'Are You Lonesome Tonight' for the slow."

Jennifer came back with three Cokes, which they drank

while Lannie cleaned off the player and the records, and cleared a space for them to dance.

Lannie quickly devised a combination of "swing" dancing and jive that fit the fast pace of "Blue Suede Shoes."

They picked it up easily, as Lannie had suspected they would, but they were more curious about "slow dancing."

"Can we slow dance now? How do you hold a boy around the neck, I mean, isn't it embarrassing?" asked Daisy.

"Definitely not embarrassing. It's fun. And you're not clutching him around the neck. He should be holding and guiding you with one hand fixed firmly at your waist and the other holding your hand. He guides where you go."

"But your bodies are touching," said, Jennifer giggling. "God, I'd just die if Chad Bingham felt my body against his."

"No, you wouldn't. Your bodies don't have to touch, but they usually do. It's very nice, if you pay attention to your dancing instead of worrying about your bodies. Let's give it a try."

She showed Daisy how to approach the boy partner, how to place her hand gently around his neck, and how to accept his hand.

Jennifer placed the phonograph arm on the record and Elvis Presley's "Are You Lonesome Tonight" came softly from the speaker. Daisy faltered at first, but Lannie did a slow one-two-three, one-two-three with her until she found the beat and finally began to move with Lannie.

Stiff at first, Daisy finally relaxed and Lannie rested her cheek on Daisy's head, moist with perspiration from the exertion of the fast dancing.

A flash of remembrance almost stopped her in her tracks. She kept moving, but the bruise around her heart pinched until she could scarcely breathe.

Daisy's sweet head reminded her of Gracie's, moist and heavy against her shoulder as she'd held her one night. The baby had been feverish from a lingering cold. Mother and daughter had rocked late into the night, Lannie soothing golden curls away from Gracie's face each time she woke up, giving her cool water to drink, humming and singing until the fever-soaked head rested on her aching shoulder again.

She flinched away from the recollection and drew a sharp breath, wanting to be finished with the dancing and the warm camaraderie with the girls. As much as she enjoyed being with them, their presence reminded her too much of what could have been. Gracie would have been five now, but someday she would have been eleven, like Daisy, and Lannie would have taught her to dance. They would have whirled around on the porch at Sullivan's Rest, where her mother had taught her to dance.

"Okay, that's enough. You need to find Mae Nevins so you can make sure your costumes are in shape for opening night."

She watched them as they ran into the theater, envying them their youth and all the possibilities ahead of them, but not the heartaches they were sure to experience. How did you prepare someone for the cruelties that life served up from time to time? People said life wasn't fair, but she'd never believed that. Still didn't. She felt that life was unfair *sometimes*. The shocker was how unprepared you are for those hard times, how excruciating and destroying the pain was, and how you think you'll never survive. How you want to go away and hide, like a sick animal, until you die, at peace at last.

She didn't want to die anymore, but there was a time when it had seemed the easiest solution.

Bry brushed against her waist reminding her it was time

for lunch, but the hard memory of Gracie had left her sad and unwilling to face anyone.

"I know, boy. In a minute. I'll dust and stack these records, then we'll go sit under your tree and eat the sandwiches I brought."

Bry loped back outside and she reached for the top record. One of her Presley favorites. "Always Loving You." Well, it wouldn't hurt to have some music while she worked.

The theater complex sat quiet in the bright midday heat. No breeze today either. Unusual heat for High Falls, but even in High Falls summer held a few uncomfortable hot days. Most of the cast and crew had probably scattered for lunch. An occasional voice could be heard from the theater, and she heard the faint tinkling of a piano as someone played "chopsticks," but there were no sounds from the carpenter shop next door.

The bell in the Episcopal Church steeple chimed twelve o'clock.

She put the needle on the old record, and waited for Presley's velvety sensual voice. Smiling at the memories it brought, she ignored the work she'd intended to do, closed her eyes, wrapped her arms around her body, and swayed to the rhythm. Recalling happy times on the porch at Sullivan's Rest; Jimmy Smathers doing his Mick Jagger imitation, Lucy and Nell teasing him, sweet songs sung to the chords of her mellow uke. Good days . . .

"It's more fun with a partner."

Shocked at the sound of his voice, her eyes popped open. Drum stood leaning against the door frame, thumbs hooked in the waist of his jeans, watching her.

She flushed, feeling the color rise across her shoulders and into her face. Rarely at a loss for words, Lannie found herself speechless. Finally, she found her tongue.

"I thought everyone had gone, I . . ."

Their eyes met, neither of them looking away this time. He walked toward her, and there was no mistaking the intent in his eyes. They were rich with desire, and the deep blue darkened with each step he took.

The arm of the record player gyrated back and forth, the needle scratching across the barren center. He bent over and replaced the needle to begin the music again, then stood to gaze at her with a dare in his eyes. She wanted to look away, but couldn't. They were centered in a kinetic field that she couldn't break through even if she'd wanted to.

He reached for her, and the spiraling warmth low in her stomach was sweet, yet disturbing. For a moment, her body tensed, the muscles protesting and instinctively protecting, but then she went to him as though she'd known this moment would come. She leaned into his body with a need that denied reason, thought, or caution.

Bry's soft growl came from the door. From the corner of her eye, she saw the dog watching, uncertain, but alert. With a motion of her hand, he left, but deposited himself right outside.

With Presley's soft, summer song, his seductive voice, and the subtle pressure of Drum's firm arms, she yielded easily against his lean length. He danced them lazily around the small circle she had cleared. The rhythmic rock of his warm body as he moved them around spun sensation after sensation through her until her frame shook with tension.

"Shhhh, it's okay," he murmured huskily. "We're okay."

The sound of his voice in her ear staggered her, and a grinding, glorious need ignited in the pit of her stomach.

Somewhere in the distance, someone laughed, a bird whistled a lethargic melody, and church bells chimed faintly with an old hymn, but it all sounded and receded hazily for Lannie. The light aroma of Thelma's freshly baked bread traveled up the hill, drifted through the complex and away.

"Look at me," he whispered. She turned her head and looked directly into his eyes, and he must have found what he searched for because he lowered his head to brush his lips across hers.

The taste of him hummed through her like a vibrating tuning fork, and with a small sound, she moved even closer to him. Her lips parted, sweet and molten, and she sank into his languorous, invading intimacy. The feel of his mouth, soft, moist, deep and warm, so good, oh, God, so good. The intimacy spread through her like wildfire, to the roots of her hair and the soles of her feet. She was lost in adagio kisses that left her loose-jointed and heavy-limbed.

He drew her closer, and she inhaled the scent of fresh-sawed wood, his musky aftershave, and the aromatic cigar he'd stuck in his shirt pocket. Her halter top caught and clung to the dampness of his soft chambray shirt. Through the worn fabric she felt the ripple and pull of his chest muscles as his breathing quickened. They stood locked together, their bodies swaying to the music in a private primal cadence all their own.

Responding with violent yearnings that frightened yet thrilled her, she drew a quivering breath. He left her mouth for a moment and placed downy kisses along her jaw line and up to her ear. She drew another breath, hoping to gain some equilibrium, but found it hopeless as the feel of his lips on her cheek spun her back into a surge of terrible wanting.

"I don't know you," she managed to whisper. "We don't know each other . . . I . . ."

"Yes, we do. We've both known since I found you hiding back stage the night the lights were out that this was inevitable." He ran a finger under her halter strap, then lightly down her throat to her breastbone, and she shivered with shock and delight. "But, if you want me to go away, I will."

"No, it's just, I . . ."

"Shh, don't talk."

He pulled her hard against him and everything shut down. Nothing existed for her except this man and the feel of his mouth and his hands upon her. Lannie knew that despite where they were, despite the conflict between them, despite everything, if Drum wanted to take her right there on the prop room floor, she would have let him, and the thought shocked her.

She thought she heard the needle gyrating on the completed recording, but lost her senses again as he lazily inserted his knee between her thighs. The traitorous thighs gave easily. She squirmed with delicious agony as he pressed higher and higher, until she was straddling his hard knee and wanting more, wanting it to push hard where she ached and needed the most. She groaned, and he laced his fingers through her tumbling hair, and locked her head in his hands as he sucked her tongue into the heat of his mouth.

She squirmed hard against his rocky erection, which threatened to split apart the grommets on his supple jeans, and welcomed the pressure against her tenderness.

She had a moment to wonder what Drum must think of her quick response to his advances, but then didn't care. This was sweet heaven, and she wanted to stay here forever.

Drum, lost in the wonder of Lannie Sullivan, breathed her in like a bee sucks nectar. He wanted all of her. He wanted time. God, he wanted time to just stand with his nose in her flaming hair and breathe in the light fragrance of flowery soap and brisk clean creek water. He wanted to lick the tiny beads of perspiration that dotted the bridge of her nose, and crossed the ridge of her shoulders. He wanted to play with her fingers, stroke the silkiness of her buttocks, and feel the tautness of her nipples between his teeth, wanted to hear the shattering intake of her breath as he entered her.

His arousal was sharp, hard, mindless. *Jesus, he wanted her.*

Someone called his name. He didn't care. Let them call.

She pushed against him weakly.

"Drum, I think Spence is looking for you," she said shakily.

"Let him look," he said against her ear.

"Drum, we can't do this," she protested.

"I know." He pulled away from her reluctantly, and brushed away some wayward tendrils that clung to her flushed face. "You're beautiful."

Spencer's voice came louder this time. He was in the carpenter shop.

"Drum? You here?"

"Yeah. I'll be right there, Spence." He tilted Lannie's chin against his fist, and surveyed her face carefully, but his gaze came back to bore into her eyes. "Are you okay?"

"Yes," she said. But he worried that he'd gone too far, that he'd upset her.

"Are you sure?"

"Yes. Please, let's just go on about our day. You just forget I'm here, that this happened. Bry is waiting for me. I, ahh, I think we'll go home after we eat our lunch."

"Sure," he said, wanting to take her quivering embarrassed body into his arms again. A thousand questions to ask her. How long had she lived on the top of Haystack? Why did she hide herself away? What had caused the wounded look in her silver eyes?

Self-consciously, she straightened her halter strap, gathered more of the shining tendrils into the topknot on her head, and walked swiftly out into the sunlight. His eyes followed her hungrily.

Yes, he wanted her. He wanted her no matter what the cost, and the cost would be great.

ELEVEN

Thirty minutes until the curtain went up, but to Spencer every agonizing minute seemed like a year. He stood at the rear of the hall, trying to look unobtrusive. He sidestepped behind one of the artificial potted palms Mae had salted around the theater, hoping it would hide him, and poked a line of sight between the plastic leaves. He hated opening nights—the tension, the chaos backstage. His reward was the creation onstage, and the joy it brought to the audience. This gnawing pain in his stomach would go away as soon as the curtain went up. At least he hoped it would.

Was it an uprising of his old ulcer or was it fear that made his stomach hurt and his hands sweat?

He ducked as a local hired hand sat another plastic palm next to him and the drooping branches scratched roughly along the back of his neck.

"Hey, look out thar, buddy, I almost busted yore head."

Spencer smiled weakly and waved the man along. "I'm fine. Don't bother about me."

What did Mae think she was doing with all these trees anyway? They looked ridiculous. He hated real palms, and artificial ones only added insult to injury. Palm trees belonged in Florida, not in North Carolina.

He hoped Keeting, and the entourage he'd brought with him, would remember that this was summer theater and ignore the obvious amateur attempts at big city sophistication. Much hung in the balance with tonight's production. If Keeting and his crowd didn't like it, Keeting could pull his money out and encourage other investors to do the same. This was only the time-worn *Oklahoma!*, done by semiprofessionals, but Keeting had high hopes for this young acting ensemble they had put together. The New York producer had encouraged Spencer to come to the North Carolina mountains to direct the group knowing they would be in good hands and expecting the move would help his old friend out of the doldrums.

Well, so far, none of Keeting's or Spencer's expectations had come to pass. Spencer's mouth watered when he thought of the new musical Keeting wanted to begin work on in the fall. God, how he'd love to sink his teeth into it. He knew that he could direct the new show if Keeting thought he'd regained some of his magic here in the mountains of North Carolina.

The orchestra began tuning up, and instead of the big, brassy "OOOOOOklahoma" that he'd tried to wring out of them, they were uncertain and wavery in the first run-through. Spencer wanted to plug his ears with his thumbs, but knew he couldn't. Aw, geez, what was he doing here anyway? After the last Broadway failure, and Julia Jane's defection, he should have just crept away to his little farm in Maine and retired.

The allure of "Lady Temptress Theater" held him fast, however, even as he stood here with an aching belly, perspiring so heavily that his shirt collar felt wringing wet. He ran a finger around the inside of his collar and loosened his tie. He was accustomed to Julia Jane's cool, calm presence and, for the first time, admitted to himself how much he missed her.

Briefly, he let himself speculate if her departure might have had anything to do with his failures. No. No. Impossible. He had never needed the soft, gentle web a woman could weave around a male.

He was just plain scared to death.

A small, soft hand slipped into his and he jumped.

Mae Nevins stood next to him. How long had she been standing there?

"Oh, hi."

"Hi," she said, and smiled and squeezed his hand. "Sorry, didn't mean to startle you. Just thought you could use some company."

"Yeah, well, no, I'm fine." He cleared his throat. "I'm used to this, you know."

"I'm sure. But it's always nice to share important occasions with someone."

He didn't know what to say. Her hand holding his made him uncomfortable. Hot. Hot, the fragile hand with its birdlike bones felt hot, yet she seemed calm and composed. He hoped she wasn't sick. He'd seen her sneaking pills sometimes and suspected they were for angina.

Please, Mae, don't get sick, don't leave me. Okay, I hate to admit it, but I need you. He'd come to rely on her more and more, but for the moment he wished she'd go away.

"How are things backstage?" he asked, hoping she would take the hint.

"Frantic, but they're pulling things together. I have to go right back there, but I wanted you to know I'm thinking of you, and I know everyone will love it."

He turned to look at her. Was she really not that observant about the listless production or was she the eternal Pollyanna?

The fluffy white stand-up collar of her frilly blouse covered her neck to her chin. Accustomed to the deep décolletage of first nighters in New York, Spencer shocked himself by wondering what Mae Nevins looked like beneath all those ruffles and bows.

"They probably need you backstage," he said. She blushed bright red and let go of his hand. He could have kicked himself.

"You're right. I must go. I'm saying a prayer for all of us this evening."

"Yeah, well prayers don't help an opening night. A top-notch performance is the only thing that makes an opening night memorable and successful."

Her face paled, and then kind of melted into odd red streaks until she almost looked striped. *Good God, Spencer, this is a nice little woman, and you persist in taking your nerves out on her. How boorish can you be?* Pretty boorish, he decided.

She stiffened her shoulders, and said, "I'll pray anyway."

"Sure."

She marched away from him, and he sighed with relief. But with her absence came a vague emptiness. He missed the warmth of her hand and the feel of her by his side. Despite her small-town cheeriness, and his big-city boorishness, Mae had made him feel better. For the first time since he'd entered the High Falls Playhouse two months ago, hope inexplicably flared in him. Maybe he should get to know Mae better. He couldn't have Julia Jane, so, why not? He thought of the lyrics from *Finnegan's Rainbow*, "When I'm not near the girl I love, I love the girl I'm near."

The orchestra geared up again, and the sound held

more of the brassiness he'd asked for. He wiped his wet palms on his trousers and began to breathe easier. Maybe this wouldn't be a total disaster.

"Coo-ool, Lannie. This is so exciting," said Daisy.

Lannie smiled, her own heart picking up a beat or two. Opening nights always provided drama and excitement.

She and Daisy were peeking through holes in the curtain to watch the house fill up.

"Oh, look there's my grandmother," said Daisy, and her voice lost some of its excitement as worry entered it.

"Where?"

"There, about halfway down on the left aisle. She has on a shiny gold dress."

Lannie's view was blocked by people searching for their seats, but she noticed a contingent of what were obviously New Yorkers streaming down the aisle. Mostly in black—the men in Zegna suits, and the women in Chanel or St. John ensembles—they stuck out like solemn pallbearers at a festive spring wedding. Spencer Case wasn't among them. She wondered if Keeting and his crowd intimidated him, but immediately dismissed the thought. She'd gotten to know Spencer enough to suspect that, though he was essentially a shy man, he was intimidated by no one.

The flurry of activity behind her grew. The technical crew shoved flats around, carried fences and furniture, and hustled to fly a replica of the "Surrey with the Fringe on Top" out of sight.

"Shit, Buddy, that ain't the way he wanted it hung," said a stagehand.

"Only place we've got to store it, asshole."

Lannie wanted to place her hands over Daisy's ears, but knew the child had been around the theater enough this summer to have heard it all before.

Someone tapped her on the shoulder. It was Jennifer. "Lannie, would you button the back of my dress for me? They're short a helper in the costume room."

"Sure, sweetheart."

Jennifer and Daisy both had been made up, their faces laden with a base cover, rosy red blush on the cheeks, and a bit of mascara around their anxious, but eager, eyes. Jennifer's long hair was combed back and hung in neat braids down her back, and Daisy's was bunched, caught, and pinned into a cascade of curls. Hopefully, from the audience, they would look like healthy, All-American farm girls from the early 1900s.

They had rejected the false eyelashes worn by some of the other girls.

Daisy had taken them off quickly. "These are dorky, Lannie. I feel like I've got black spider legs glued to my eyes."

The steady hum of voices from the audience grew louder as the house filled.

Daisy still peeked through the hole in the faded-red curtain. "Oh, wonderful! Grandmother's parading all over, like she owns the place. It's s-o-o-o embarrassing. Now she's talking to those important looking people in the ninth row. They must be the people from New York. She's having a party at our house tonight in their honor."

A horrid thought entered Lannie's mind. She returned to her slit in the curtain and searched for a woman dressed in shiny gold.

There she stood, big bosomed, loud-voiced, talking to a Chaplanesque figure of a man with the New York crowd.

"Is that your grandmother talking to the short man with the cane in the black suit?"

"That's her. And she doesn't talk, she blasts. Isn't she the most embarrassing person you ever saw? I could just die. I really could."

Beezy Bowden was Daisy's grandmother. With this knowledge, many of Daisy's problems with her family became quite clear.

The short, dapper man must be Robert Keeting. Drum had to be sitting nearby. She'd avoided looking for him, but finally could not overcome the great desire to find him somewhere in the socializing crowd. It didn't take her long. She located him almost immediately, as if she'd always known exactly where he was, but had saved the treat for the last moment, like dessert.

He sat quietly reading a playbill in a seat not far from Keeting's. Was this the Charlotte, North Carolina, Drum, or the New York Drum? Probably both. This was the Drummond Rutledge image most of his friends knew, she thought.

She'd heard of Rutledge Timber all of her adult life, but had always thought of Drummond Rutledge as a portly, balding old man. She knew better now, of course. This cool, polished, sophisticated man wearing an immaculate navy-blue blazer, with crisp white shirt, collar open and without tie, certainly wasn't the brawny, perspiring, hard-bodied carpenter who had kissed her yesterday. His light-brown hair was slicked wetly back, which made it look darker than the tousled gold-streaked thatch she'd ached to thread her fingers through yesterday.

The memory of his strong mouth capturing her tongue intruded, and she found it impossible to tear her eyes away from him. The woman seated next to him, a lovely, and elegant brunette in a summery, off-the-shoulder black cocktail dress leaned over and whispered in his ear. He threw his head back and laughed, a big, full sound that she heard even over the rumble of the crowd and the nervous backstage chatter.

Who was she, this confident woman who seemed to know Drum so well?

He patted her on the arm and whispered something back. She laughed. They were obviously together. Damn. Who was she? A business associate, his sister, the woman in his life? Why had she thought there wouldn't be a woman in his life? Wishful thinking? Opening-night butterflies fluttering in her stomach turned into buzzing bees, dive-bombing around her insides.

For the first time, she felt like the messy, forlorn hippie she must appear to be to others. She felt like a poor relative invited to a grand party where she didn't belong. She felt like an unwanted Victorian urchin peeking through windows at the big "swells" and their rich lives, and she hated herself.

"Lannie, my switch is coming loose. Could you fix it?"

She released the supporting fold of grimy curtain, and bringing herself back into focus, turned to help Daisy. Vince rushed by, looking harassed, fussing at his dancers, his thinning hair flying askew, his pink ballet tights wet with nervous perspiration. He gave Daisy a look of exasperation, smiled weakly at Lannie and hurried on.

"Of course, but do you really think you need the switch? Your hair is so nice and thick and lovely," said Lannie.

"Yeah, but I want it to look longer."

"Okay, sweet pea. Whatever you say."

She repinned the black extension onto the crown of Daisy's head, and tried to weave it into the rest of the child's hair. Her hands lingered for a moment in the warm, silky strands, imagining what Gracie's would have been like at age five. Thick and wavy, like hers, but blond like her father. The familiar sick thickness began to gather in her throat.

No. She coughed.

The lights flickered and dimmed, and Daisy said, "Lannie, is my hair okay? They're ready to start."

"Yes, yes. It's perfect. Break a leg, kiddo. I'll be around if you need me."

Lannie kissed her on the cheek, and Daisy ran backstage as Mae hurried toward her looking wan and exhausted.

"Lannie, I really need help, but it's way above and beyond the call of duty. Maggie has lost the sash on her dress, Martin is short a shoe, size eleven, and we can't find the peddler's top hat. Would you mind running up to Gavin's garret—oh, Lord, listen to me talking like the kids—anyway, would you run up there and see what you can find?"

"Sure. Be back as soon as I can."

"Take a flashlight," Mae reminded.

"Right."

Nearby, someone whistled an aimless tune, and she shivered with apprehension. No whistling inside the theater was an old superstition held sacred by the acting profession. One could whistle in the prop room, or the design shop, or anywhere if it was outside the theater building proper, but never near the stage or in a dressing room.

Whistling brought bad luck.

She glanced around her, but actors rushed back and forth, Kent stood across the backstage area, Jack Edwards, the new man hired to keep the theater clean, swept debris near the wings. Neither of them were whistling. Mae had disappeared somewhere. She shivered again, but determinedly shook off her feelings of foreboding.

Minutes later, she climbed the narrow steps to the attic, flashlight beam traveling in front of her. She had to admit that she didn't relish going up there any more than the kids did.

She opened the door, reached for the switch, which provided a feeble yellow light, and headed for the shoe section first. That was the only item of apparel they'd managed to keep in one area through the years. Quickly, she rummaged through a pile of farmhand brogans and found a pair of mildewed size eleven and a half that might fit Martin, the tall young leading man. They would have to do.

Gathering her full peasant skirt in front of her, she threaded her way down a dark aisle toward shelves on the far murky side of the crowded musty place, hoping to find a top hat. A mouse skittered along the floor in front of her, and she shivered.

Gavin, I know you're a figment of the kids' imaginations, but just in case you aren't, I hope you're not thirsty for the taste of a redhead's blood.

She had to laugh at herself. The sound of her quick laughter in the sepulchral stillness of the place sounded bizarre, yet somehow comforting. A bat whizzed close to her head, and she ducked, forcing another laugh.

"God, Lannie, you're worse than the kids."

Her laughter and the sound of her voice alerted the little beasties who lived here that a foreign entity had invaded their space, and the attic grew even more still as they drew back into their hidey holes and nests.

Absolutely silly, but she felt as if someone was watching her. "Silly, Lannie, silly," she muttered to herself, then yelled out in a joking voice, "Hey, I need some help, Gavin. Show me where the perfect top hat is."

She shook her head, ashamed of her nerves, but this time unable to completely rid herself of the notion that she wasn't alone. She tried to convince herself that it was the complete silence up here, and the rows and rows of costumes that had clothed so many characters through the years. Naturally, she would feel the energy of all those personalities.

Hurrying and humming tunelessly, she flashed her

shaking beam here and there, praying for a top hat. She found a shelf of hats right in front of her and flipped through them. Her heart skipped a beat when she realized she was now humming the Elvis song she and Drum had danced to yesterday, "Always Loving You." She bit her lip, and tried to put the memory of the burning kiss out of her mind.

She located a moth-eaten top hat, and turned to search for the sash. As luck would have it, the farm dresses were right behind her. Maggie's dress was blue-and-pink plaid. Her beam played through the dresses until she found a blue sash that would have to do for tonight.

With relief, she left the attic with her bounty. Her hands full and unable to hold the handrail, Lannie knew her hasty flight down the dark rickety steps wasn't the wisest idea in the world, but she couldn't wait to get away from the attic, and Mae needed these things right away. Her dancers' feet found the way until she neared the bottom. She missed a short tread and tumbled down the last four steps, skinning an elbow and turning an ankle.

"Dammit."

She sat crookedly, one leg on the bottom step and the other folded awkwardly beneath her, her skirt flared about her. Her treasures from the attic were spilled helter-skelter.

Gingerly, she drew her extended leg beneath her, gathered everything together, and sat on the bottom step.

A young intern hurried by.

"Jimmy? Would you please find Mae and give these things to her?"

"Is that you, Lannie? It's so dark back here. Are you okay?"

"I'm fine. Just resting. Hurry now. Mae's waiting for them."

She knew from experience that this wasn't a serious

sprain, but it sure hurt like hell. She just needed to sit here for a few minutes and massage her ankle. Some of her sue-happy former clients would have filed a lawsuit by now, claiming the theater was at fault for injuries rendered because of neglect to the property. With the thought came the certainty that she didn't want to go back to the law when she was finished with her mountain withdrawal.

She wanted to work with children, wanted to be close to them in some manner. The idea surprised her and brought a flash of pure happiness. *A step forward, Lannie, my girl. Making plans for the future is a positive step forward.*

Despite her determination not to think of him the rest of the night, she wondered what Drum Rutledge was doing out front and massaged her ankle harder.

Drum tried not to squirm in the sagging seat. The production, so far, had been passable. Better than dress rehearsal, but far below Spencer Case standards. He was proud of the sets, and the crew who had worked with him. Some fine tuning was needed here and there, but generally, for a summer playhouse, the sets were superior. He wasn't so sure that Keeting was going to find the cast's performance stellar, however.

He glanced over at Emily Appleby to see how she was faring. She caught his glance and raised an eyebrow. He knew she wondered and worried as he did. His best friend, "Hatch" Appleby, unable to come until tomorrow, had sent his wife, Emily, on from Charlotte. Hatch was a business partner and a rugby pal, and the Applebys had stuck with him through thick and thin, had even invested in this little out-of-the-way show with him. Emily had been a good friend to Ann-Marie. His wife had few friends and had never allowed anyone to get really close to her, but Emily had managed to partially penetrate Ann-Marie's fantasy world.

Ann-Marie wouldn't have liked this evening. She had been happiest when they were alone together, reading poetry to each other in their library, dancing on the terrace at sunset, having dinner in a quiet corner at some superb restaurant. Ann-Marie, a fragile soul always in need of tending, and Drum had done the tending. His heart wrenched and then righted itself.

Emily patted his arm and whispered. "It'll get better. They have first-night jitters."

"Yeah. Right." Why did he care so much? It was a minor investment, done as a favor for Keeting. Somehow he'd gotten emotionally involved.

But he knew there was no "somehow" about it. He knew why he'd become attached to High Falls Summer Playhouse, and the people within it. He'd looked for her all evening. Lannie had to be here. He'd heard Daisy begging her to come, so she must be here.

He'd observed her patience with the children, her kindness to Mae and Spencer, her care with the work she did, whether she was painting a set, polishing a prop, or sewing a flounce on a dress. He knew her well enough to know she wouldn't have disappointed Daisy.

He leaned over and said quietly to Emily, "Excuse me. There's something I forgot to do backstage. I'll be back soon."

He rose from his aisle seat, and Robert Keeting, seated directly behind him, grabbed his arm as he passed.

"Only rats leave a sinking ship, Drum."

"I'll be back soon. Something I forgot to do." He gave Keeting his most reassuring smile, and then lied through his teeth. "It'll be better, Robert. They need to tuck a few more performances under their belt."

"You promised to go with us to the Bowden woman's

party. You know these people and the way things work here. Don't desert me, Rutledge."

"I won't. Be right back."

He looked in the prop room first, but it was empty. Cautiously, he stepped into the high-ceilinged backstage area. Actors, in various stages of dress or undress, lounged around in the dim shadows waiting for their turn onstage, or scurried in and out of the brightly lit makeup room for repairs. Panting dancers dripped with perspiration from their recent exertion onstage, and the place reeked with perfume and body odor.

"Hey, Drum," greeted one of his set builders. "Thought you'd be sitting out front tonight."

"I am. I forgot to tell Lannie Sullivan something. Have you seen her?"

"No, but I saw Mae talking to her a while ago. I think Mae sent her up to Gavin's."

Drum circumvented several large flats and bulky shipping boxes and made his way to a far corner where steps led to the costume storage. The white of Lannie's blouse was a bright blurb in the gloom of the stairwell.

He heard her muttering before he reached her. "Dammit, dammit, dammit."

"Lannie, what's the matter? Are you okay?"

"I will be. Just a small sprain. I should have known better. Should have taken one of the kids with me. Couldn't carry it all. What are you doing back here?"

He could tell from her voice that she was hurting, and it made him angry.

"This goddamned building is dangerous. I can't believe Mae sent you up there at night."

"Mae was in a jam, and I don't think she even thought about it. She's never been up there at night." She rubbed her ankle again.

"Where is Bry?"

"Bry has a bellyache. I hate to say it, Drum, but I'm beginning to suspect that someone here is poisoning him. He gets sick after every visit to the theater."

Drum frowned. "That's hard to believe. People in High Falls are nuts about dogs."

"I know, but . . . ohhhh, darn this ankle," she moaned.

From the stage came the girls' lilting voices as they sang the dreamy refrain of "Out of My Dreams."

"Here, let me help. I'm pretty good with injured ankles."

"No, no, you need to go back to your . . . to your friends out front."

He ignored her suggestion and knelt in front of her.

Her delicate ankle fit easily within the circle of his thumb and forefinger.

"Where does it hurt?" he asked softly.

"There, near the bone," she said shyly.

He removed her sandal and gently rubbed the tender area around her bone and down her heel, then carefully applied pressure to the ankle. He massaged it, enjoying the feel of her slender foot in his hand.

"Oh, that feels so good, Drum." She gave a little sigh. "You must have done this before. You'll never know how much a dancer loves a good massage."

"I'm at your service, fair lady."

"But you really should join the audience out front."

"Be quiet," he ordered, and continued his steady rubbing.

His fingers moved upwards, kneading her calf with sure strokes. Her legs were strong, with long, healthy muscles, and the skin silky and sleek. The leg he massaged warmed to his touch.

He took a deep breath. The urge to have more of her had beat at him for days, and with the soft sleekness of her skin beneath his fingers, his groin tightened.

"Feeling better?"

"Yes, much."

"Good. Next time take someone with you or don't go."

This was dangerous, this urge to explore the rest of her. He forced himself to replace her shoe. His long legs wouldn't allow him to sit on the bottom step with her, so he sat on the step above her, close enough to feel her shoulder brushing his arm, and close enough to breathe in the scent of her, clean, maybe a lilac soap, maybe a faint mustiness from the costume room, definitely an evergreen fragrance in her hair. Her shampoo, perhaps?

"Lannie, about yesterday, I want to apologize—"

She interrupted, whispering. "No, please, don't. I wanted that as much as you did."

They sat silently, listening to the music onstage. He knew he should return to Emily, but couldn't bring himself to leave Lannie.

Then he felt her hand searching for his, like a child lost in the dark who needed reassurance, and his heart leapt with the implication.

He gave her hand a comforting squeeze, and they sat quiet until he couldn't stand it a moment longer. He wanted, no, needed, to taste. He found her chin in the dark, and turned it up toward him to brush her lips with his. She resisted at first, but then her lips responded as they had yesterday, shyly, then eagerly, hungrily. The rush of heat that hit him, shocked him. He was intoxicated, drunk with the sensation of Lannie.

She moved closer, her breasts against his ribs. The edge of the step behind them cut into his hip. He ignored it, and pulling her up by the shoulders, settled her on the step beside him, gathering her in his arms. She yielded against him. His hand moved beneath the hem of her full skirt and found the soft vulnerable spot behind her knee. Caressing the downy skin, he bent to place a kiss on her kneecap, but soon sought her lips again. Her mouth was so warm and gentle, yet her lower lip pulsed against his as if her heartbeat had jumped to her mouth.

Hotness swamped him, and the dull ache in his gut got heavier, threatening to overcome him. Her hand stroked the back of his neck, and he headed in a direction that he knew he shouldn't. He found her breasts and pushed away the elastic gathering of her low-cut blouse, and the top of her bra, to cup one breast in his palm.

Her breath quickened on his cheek.

He took his time as his mouth slid down her silky neck, over the pulse-beat in the hollow of her throat, all the way down to brush his tongue across one quivering nipple. The nipple took on a life of its own, as her lower lip had, and grew taut and heated against his tongue. Swiftly, he drew it between his teeth and sucked hungrily.

Her hand gripped the back of his neck, and she choked back a moan. Flames leaped wild and fierce in him, almost consuming him in the desire to know more of her, more and more, and more.

Lannie said something. What did she say? His ears roared with the sounds of his heart, his breathing, and the flames that burned almost out of control. What did she say?

"We . . . can't. No, no . . . I . . . not here."

Drum knew that she was right. What had he been thinking? He hadn't been thinking. He'd acted like a mindless rutting pig.

He covered her breasts reluctantly and hugged her to him, trying to catch his breath, trying to will away a monstrous hard-on.

"You're right," he murmured. "God, Lannie, let's not pretend any longer. This is ridiculous . . ."

The house lights turned up, and lights sprang on all over the backstage area. The first act was over.

He brushed the hair off her flushed face and started to make a joke about being caught in the act, but thought better of it. This wasn't a laughing matter, this feeling of uncontrollable lust, and it grew every time he thought of her or saw her.

"Just like a couple of teenagers," she said, flushed with embarrassment.

She attempted a casualness that he knew she didn't feel. Her chest moved rapidly up and down, and her hands trembled as she tightened the elastic that bunched her hair on top of her head.

"I don't think so, Lannie," he said, and reached for her hand.

She ignored his gesture, and stood up. He saw her wince with pain. "I have to help Mae, Drum. Enjoy the rest of the evening."

"I'll see you at Beezy Bowden's party later."

A full smile came from her then, filled with delight.

"Hardly. I wasn't invited. The party is only for visiting muckety-mucks, like you and the New York crowd. But I wouldn't have gone even if I'd been invited."

"Why?"

"Because I . . ." The haunted look he'd notice before, entered her eyes. "I'm not ready for . . ." She stopped again.

"Ready for what?" he prompted, wanting to kiss away the sadness in her eyes and wondering what she meant about "not being ready."

She forced a laugh. "I didn't bring my party dress down from the cabin. Next time, maybe. See you around, Drum."

She walked away, favoring her right ankle, but he knew she walked away with the same sense of incompletion that he felt.

As he walked back out front to join Emily, he knew he had hard decisions to make soon. Would his mounting craving for Lannie fog his thinking? Lannie Sullivan was not the kind of woman who gave of herself casually. In fact, he wondered if she'd ever really given herself fully to anyone. He sensed in her a hunger as deep as his.

Things were worth whatever you were willing to pay for them.

"Lannie, where are you going?" called Mae. "I thought you were going to help the youngsters change costumes during intermission?"

"I'm sorry, Mae. I'm suddenly not feeling well. Mrs. Chafin said she'd fill in for me."

She hurried out before Mae could question her again or see her face. Her face must be stamped with guilt, like a child with his hand caught in the cookie jar. Mae was saying something about a rugby match tomorrow, and Lannie remembered that Drum had organized a charity game to raise money for the theater. Well, Lannie Sullivan wouldn't be there. Lannie Sullivan had embarrassed herself enough to last a lifetime. She and Drum had acted like two hormonal teenagers.

Shaken from her second sexual encounter with Drum in as many days, she climbed in her jeep and leaned her head against the back of the seat to get a peek at peaceful stars through the tattered canvas top. When her heart had slowed to its regular beat, and her skin stopped its tingling, she took a deep breath, switched on her ignition and headed toward her mountain.

She missed Bry. It was the first time she'd been without him in three years. He'd been off his feed lately, vomiting, and not eating. It worried her, and though he'd tried to jump in the jeep to come with her, she'd ordered him back to the cabin.

Later, sitting on her cabin stoop with a cup of tea, she reviewed the night with mixed emotions.

The drive up the mountain had been harrowing. What had she been thinking of when she'd told Daisy she would come tonight? She never went off the mountain after dark and had forgotten that only one headlight on the jeep worked, so finding her way up the rocky, twisting, almost nonexistent road had been frightening.

Foolish. She'd never do it again. One good thing, though. The drive had taken so much concentration that it had taken her mind off Drum Rutledge and her mindless attraction for him.

Once safely at the cabin, she sank with relief on the top step. Bry, moaning with happiness at her return, nudged her elbow and she took his big brindled head in her lap. He seemed to feel much better. She knew he was bewildered that she'd left him at home this evening. Well, she'd never do that again either.

A half-moon balanced on the peak of Blackface Mountain to her right. The moon and stars were her sisters. How many nights had she sat here with only Bry and the moon for company? They kept away the loneliness that hung close within her and around her lately, its presence almost a physical entity. The irony of it all. Before, when pain had been her constant companion, her friend, her very own possession, she'd never felt lonely. The pain had filled her.

She counted the stars and yearned for unaccountable things, until, like a wayward balloon, she let herself go and bobbed throughout the universe's dark density until she reached her sister moon. There she floated on a silvery lake and took in the vastness and wonder of the sky and all its shining mysteries.

The catlike meow of a long-eared owl brought her back

to earth. As she listened, the lost and lonely sound turned into a soft low hoot.

"Must be breeding time. That's the only time you hear the long-ear." She laughed. "Maybe that's what's wrong with me, Bry. Maybe it's my breeding time, too."

She sighed and fondled the dog's ears.

"I'm tired of nourishing my own soul, Bry. Do you think maybe I'm tired of being alone?"

TWELVE

Flags and red, white, and blue banners flew from every light pole and hung in the window of every shop. Customers streamed in and out of Jill's Gourmet Feasts and Teas as Lannie passed by. The place filled Lannie with nostalgia. She missed Hap's Diner, which for forty years had occupied the nook where Jill did business now.

Hap's place had a wood-plank floor and a lunch counter with stools and meatloaf, mashed potatoes, and gravy to die for. Her father used to take her there for early morning breakfasts, which had been sausage, eggs, grits, and biscuits rich with melted butter and honey. Thick, rich, creamy milkshakes, tuna salad sandwiches made with real mayonnaise, and western omelets chockful of ham had been available any time of the day or night.

Since she'd begun helping at the theater, she'd eaten a hurried snack at Jill's a few times and liked the scones, clotted cream, and moist blueberry bagels Jill offered, but she'd rather have a meal from Hap's Diner any day.

She'd spent every summer of her growing up years in High Falls, and though she admitted the town fathers had done well preserving the integrity of the little village as it grew into a trendy summer place, she missed the things that had made it home.

She walked on up the hill toward the ballfield and heard the shouting crowd attending the rugby match. Local people might not understand the game, but they would give it a good try because everyone was in a holiday mood, locals, summer people, and weekenders. The annual fireworks display would be held tonight on the ballfield where the rugby match was being played now.

The town was so busy with a variety of Fourth of July events that few tickets had been sold for the matinee at the playhouse this afternoon, so it had been canceled. The evening performance was sold out. Great. Maybe Spencer Case would cheer up.

The town fathers should thank Drum for organizing this rugby match, she thought, and her heart skipped a beat as she approached the field. She had tried to keep away from the game, but the tug to watch Drum play had been irresistible.

Ordinarily, the High Falls Flyers softball team played the Grandfather Mountain team every Fourth of July, but Grandfather Mountain had canceled at the last minute, and the Flyers hadn't been successful in finding another team. Drum had come to the rescue and volunteered to set up a rugby match to take the place of the softball game. He'd told all of his friends who were coming for the opening last night to bring their rugby gear with them. Then he'd had an opposing team from Jacksonville flown in by helicopter. The proceeds from the game would go to the theater.

She stood at the edge of the bleachers and looked for a place to sit. She saw Spencer Case sitting near, but apart from, Keeting and his entourage from New York. Spence was not a part of their party-making. He sat hunched over, his arms folded and resting on his thighs, talking to no one, not even Mae, who sat nearby with an anxious expression on her face. A battered canvas hat, which had seen better days, and which Lannie suspected was his fishing hat, rested on his ears, hiding any expression on his face.

If she had to guess, she'd guess that Keeting had expressed displeasure at the performance last night. It was obvious that Spence had not invited, nor did he want her sitting next to him. Ordinarily she would have left him alone and found herself a solitary seat high in the bleachers, but she wanted to talk to him about hiring extra hands at the playhouse. Spence was recognized by most people in High Falls now, and people would notice her presence beside him. She ran the risk of someone from her younger years discovering her, but it was time for her to come out of hiding. The theater had been a good halfway house. Working backstage at the theater, she'd been hidden from the general public.

There was space for Bry near Spencer, too.

Determinedly, she pulled her billed cap further down her forehead, fastened her ponytail more firmly through the gap in the back, and with one finger, pushed her big black sunglasses tighter against the bridge of her nose.

"Oh, Lannie, dear, how nice to see you," called Mae. She looked tired, and Lannie felt guilty. She's doing too much, thought Lannie.

"Hi, Mae. Do you mind if I fill this space between you and Spence?"

"No," said Mae with a small smile. "Maybe you can cheer him up. I wasn't able to."

As she sat down next to Spencer, he said, "Ummph."

Bry settled down on the other side of him.

She grinned, "Is that supposed to be 'hello,' Spence?"

"Yep."

The crowd uttered a collective intake of breath and let it out in a big sigh. Lannie glanced quickly at the field, which she'd been trying to ignore, and saw several players carrying another off the field.

"That's not Drum, is it?" she asked before she could stop herself.

She felt Spence's quick interested glance at her before he answered, "No, but he's plenty battered, too. You know anything about rugby?"

"Some. Fifteen players on each team. Each half is divided into forty minutes, and they change ends of the field at half-time. There are no substitutes, so if someone gets hurt, they play shorthanded. The players try to get the ball over the goal line, but can't pass it forward. They can only kick it or run it forward. The ball is similar to a football, only blunter on the ends."

"Pretty good for a dame. You must have seen a game or two."

"Yes, when I lived in New York."

Unable to wrench her eyes from the field now, she searched for Drum, but the players moved so fast and furious, she wasn't sure.

"Which one is Drum?" she asked, almost biting her tongue to keep from asking, but the question came anyway.

"His team is wearing the dark green jerseys and white shorts. He's the bloodiest one."

Even from here she could see the well-defined shoulder muscles straining against the wet jersey. His hair was dark with sweat and stood straight up, held off his forehead by a dark band of some kind. His nose was bleeding, and there was a purplish bruise on one cheek.

On the sidelines a player vomited, wiped his mouth, and then headed back into the game. Drum patted him on the back and then charged down the field again.

"Rough game, isn't it? Do you like it?" she asked, interested in a male perspective of what she perceived as a merciless battlefield.

"Ummph. If you like a game where rich guys from North Carolina and Florida kill each other, I guess it's okay. Players tell me it's almost more a religion than a game. There's fierce team spirit involved. You have something you want to talk to me about?"

"Yes. I almost broke my neck on the attic stairs last night, Spence. I know Mae hired Jack Edwards to keep things clean and in order, and he's made a difference, but we need someone to repair things. Also, we need help getting that attic cleaned up and organized."

"Well, forget about help in the attic. Mae has begged people to work up there, and everyone turns her down. Local people say its haunted, and outsiders say we can't pay enough to get them to spend a day in the dark and dust."

"Do you suppose Drum would assign one of his carpenters the repair job?"

He cleared his throat and gave her another significant glance. "Drum's way ahead of you. He had a crew up there before dawn this morning and worked right along with them until time for the game. You've got yourself some new steps, lady."

Spence watched Lannie's face pale and then flush with pink, leaving a stripe of bright coral across her cheekbones. He didn't know what had happened last night, but obviously Drum had been highly motivated to put in a new staircase, and in a hurry.

Spence tore his eyes away from Lannie and tried to concentrate on the gory game, but he recognized his rapid pulse and the catch in his throat as envy, envy for what might have been and never would be. The passion and burning light he'd seen in Drum's eyes as they'd discussed the staircase late last night had brought to mind a white knight eager to rescue the damsel in distress. The quick flush of emotion and excitement on Lannie's face just now told the whole tale.

He glanced at Lannie again. She'd forgotten he was there. Her gaze was riveted on the playing field. It almost hurt to see the excitement on her face, to see the yearning forward slant of her body, to watch the rapid rise and fall of her chest. Her hands clenched in fists as the thud of bodies hitting the ground sounded again.

Without thinking, he reached over and squeezed her clenched fists for a moment.

She jumped, startled out of her fierce concentration.

"Oh, whew, well, I really get involved in a game, don't I?" She flushed again, this time with embarrassment, and looked pointedly at her watch. "I've got to get on up to the playhouse. It's hard to tell in what condition the interns left the set last night. See you later, Spence."

She tugged at the ends of the knot that tied her blue chambray shirt at her waist, a self-conscious gesture assuring herself it was in place, and then waved goodbye as she descended the bleachers with agility. Her flowery peasant skirt fluttered behind her like a streamer, which Bry followed.

"Goodbye, Lannie," Spence whispered. "How I envy you."

God, how he'd love to feel that way again. He missed feeling that way about someone.

Mae moved closer, bravely filling the space Lannie had just vacated. Her perfume smelled good.

Mae was a huge help and an efficient assistant, but much to his dismay and surprise, he'd begun to see her as a desirable woman. Suddenly, it seemed okay. She could never replace Julia Jane. No one ever would, but he had to move on. Mae offered comfort and caring and a soft love he'd never known.

He smiled, and gave her knee a tentative pat. A bright flush rushed across her face and shoulders. Tenderness he thought he'd never feel again welled up in him.

Maybe if he could manage being nicer to her once in a while, she would overcome her shyness. He would get to know her better. Who knows, he thought? The passion Lannie and Drum felt might never be his again, but Mae might be interested in a companionable relationship with a bit of romance.

I've been putting my personal life on hold. What personal life, he wondered? *I've never really had one.*

The hell with Keeting. I'm doing the best I can. Somehow, I'll overcome these abysmal failures and come up with a solution.

"Spencer, have you noticed that Drum seems inordinately interested in Lannie?"

"What man wouldn't be? She's a beautiful woman and an exceptionally vibrant one."

Mae hesitated then. He knew she hated gossip as much as he did. "Do you know Drum's background?"

"It's none of my business or anyone else's."

"John Lamb told me that Drum is married. Maybe Lannie doesn't know. She's been out of touch for a long while. Don't you think someone should tell her?"

"They're both consenting adults. I expect she already knows. His friends in North Carolina and points south seem to, as do most of his New York crowd. That's where I heard it, from Keeting."

"She just doesn't seem the kind of person, who would, you know . . . play around."

I don't think she is, but I'd bet she's a woman who loves to the highest degree, giving all, and blast the damn consequences.

Drum's adrenaline had pumped high since the first hard shot he'd gotten at the beginning of the game. Someone gave him the ball. He tossed it laterally to Hatch. They careened into a jumble of players and ground forward until the ball was flicked away.

The blood from his nose flowed steadily into his mouth. He licked his lips to clear them and tasted the peculiar, but familiar taste of iron. If all sports were about war, then rugby was an eighteenth-century epic of bayonet charges and hand-to-hand fighting. To the rugby player it was a hymn, it was poetry, it was violence and creativity in motion with rules.

Abruptly, he lay pinned to the earth, the ball lying close-by, and a huge Neanderthal from Jacksonville churned through the mayhem, his cleats pounding the earth like a train engine. Drum knew his head would take a direct hit. Hatch cut through low and fast, blurring as he passed over Drum and knocked the guy on his ass. Hatch jerked Drum up off the turf. He gave Drum a happy grin, exposing a chipped tooth. His old college buddy hated wearing his mouth piece, the only piece of protective equipment worn by the players, so his dental bill mounted every year. Hatch, with a well-deserved reputation as the best litigation lawyer in North Carolina, attacked on the field as fiercely as he attacked in the courtroom.

Time to put the ball in play again. They formed a scrimmage, his teammates linking arms and shoulders and shoving hard against the Jacksonville scrum. The ball popped out and into play. Drum charged forward, clods of earth flying, and the whole scene, blue sky, fellow players, and clamoring crowd whipped by at an implausible speed, sometimes blurry, sometimes focused razor-sharp.

The ball skipped on the grass. He grabbed it, swung behind a moving wall of players and darted over the goal line for a touch-in. They were ahead now and with not enough time for Jacksonville to score again.

His heart soared with jubilation. "Butch" Cassiday, vice-president of Rutledge Timber operations, slapped him on the back, and yelled "Good show, boss" as the noisy melee continued. Butch, who already sported a crooked "rugby" nose, looked like he'd broken it again, but the elation in his eyes mitigated any discomfort he might be in.

The loyalty and camaraderie of rugby teams was legendary, and none more so than after this game. Members of both teams sat or lay on the ground together, perspiring, groaning, grinning, drinking beer and belching ceremoniously, and slapping one another on the back. Their knees were skinned, their faces streaked with dirt and perspiration, and some of them bled from busted noses, lips, or foreheads. A player from Jacksonville with a pulled hamstring groaned one minute, but laughed the next as he recapped the game with a buddy.

Drum sat quietly next to Hatch, drinking water from the cooler Emily always provided. Hatch was a recovering alcoholic and Drum had made it a point years ago not to drink around him, though his friend protested mightily.

Drum's lungs still heaved, but every breath inhaled and exhaled victory. A glorious, if fleeting, feeling, he thought.

Had Lannie been here today? It was a miracle to him that he'd gone an entire afternoon without thinking of her, without wanting her. But wasn't that why he played rugby . . . to exorcise all the pain, all the grief and memories? He'd learned to play at Duke, and he considered the game one of the most important elements of his education. It had certainly served him well through the years, and now it soothed his craving for forbidden fruit, if only for a few hours.

Lannie Sullivan was forbidden fruit for him, he knew this as well as he knew that his lungs begged for more air.

"You're known as a remote, distant SOB, but I've never seen you so quiet after a victory. You're usually celebrating harder than anyone. Emily said you seemed different somehow. Anything the matter, friend?" asked Hatch, who lay on his back on the turf beside him.

"Not really. Just sorting some things out."

"You said you were going to be here for a week. It's been over a month. It's got to be damned lonely here, Drum, without Ann-Marie and Chip. Why don't you come back to Charlotte with us? Helicopter's leaving in a half hour."

"No, believe it or not, I'm enjoying helping at the playhouse, and getting a big kick out of working with the construction crew at the lodge. I think I'm chasing away ghosts that needed chasing. I've also installed a small office at the lodge. Got all the latest in communication systems, faxes, you name it, so business isn't suffering."

"Okay. Frankly, I'm happy to see you turning the burners down some. You work too damned hard. But let us know if you need us."

"I will." He heaved himself up from the grass. "I'll say goodbye to everyone, and then I'm going to the playhouse. Left some of my tools there that I need at the house."

After the helicopter left, carrying the team members away, Drum climbed the hill to the theater, his cleats tapping against the pavement. Sounds of the little town celebrating the Fourth were all around him. His body still sang with adrenaline and victory.

The fire truck came slowly down the street with its bell clanging and filled with children waving small flags and eating hot dogs. Their chins were dotted with mustard and ketchup, and Drum was filled with nostalgia for his own childhood, but mostly for Chip's small hand in his.

That last Fourth of July they had spent here in High Falls, and had walked up this hill just as the fire truck passed, as it did now. This was one of the reasons he'd wanted to be back in Charlotte before now. But he was glad he'd stayed, and finally gave in to the vivid memory the fire truck had revived.

He felt the gentle tug of his son's hand. "Hey, Dad, can I ride the fire truck?"

"Sure, sport." They had waved it down, and Drum had lifted the five year old aboard. His face etched with excitement, Chip had waved happily at his dad as the truck bore the animated children away down the street.

Later that day, Chip had tried whittling a stick the way he'd seen Wilkie Talley do, but the knife had slipped and he'd gotten a deep cut on his palm. Ann-Marie had fainted when she'd seen the blood, and Drum had rushed his son to the hospital by himself. In the emergency room, his chin thrust up bravely, Chip had held tight to Drum's finger as the doctor put in the stitches. Drum remembered the child's small choked cry, the feel of the little hand squeezing his finger, and even remembered the sound of the thread being pulled through the wound.

The poignant memory hurt, but all he had left were memories, so he took the pain with gratitude.

This had been a good day. It would have been even better, he thought, if the beating he'd taken on the field had lessened any of his obsessive sexual attraction for Lannie Sullivan, but it hadn't.

° ° °

Lannie hurried to place the props needed on the set for the first act tonight. She wanted to start home before dark. Bry lay on the stage nearby. She kept him close to her now.

The theater was quiet. A teenager composed a rhythm and blues piece on the piano in the pit. Kent, the stage manager Spencer had just hired, worked on the lighting board and changed the moods onstage as the lights went up and down. She moved Aunt Eller's bench into place, set a wicker laundry basket near it, then stood back to survey her work on the stage. Everything looked ready.

Late afternoon sun cast shadows on the barn-red building that held the carpenter shop and prop room. Bry headed for the jeep and his favorite sleeping place in the shade of the big oak, but she directed him to stay outside her open door. She could keep an eye on him there. Make sure he didn't eat anything he shouldn't. They wouldn't be here long. Only a few things to do, and they could leave.

Hands shaking, she tried to still her churning stomach. *Oh, God please stop this. I've never felt like this before.* She picked up an ironstone milk pitcher then put it back down carefully, afraid she might drop it.

Her stomach had started this craziness during the rugby match. She'd left the game early, hoping the sick yearning feeling would disappear once she stopped watching Drum. But she couldn't get him out of her mind. The powerful churning wouldn't stop. Tears of frustration pressured her eyes. She'd be damned if she'd cry.

No matter how hard she tried, impressions of Drum and the game kept returning. As the summer breeze flapped the flags beneath a clean blue mountain sky the players gave all that they had to give, and the crowd voiced their pleasure. The fullness of life in all its grandeur had been played upon that field today. All the wanting and giving, all the glory and stomp and shout of life wanting to be lived had been exposed and enjoyed, and Drum had participated fully, fiercely. Or was it just *her* perception that he'd been a major portion of the celebration?

Drum had been tough, unyielding, merciless, and she hadn't been able to take her eyes off him. The knots in her belly had grown tighter and tighter as she'd watched.

Two members of the Rutledge Timber Board of Directors had sat within hearing distance at the game. One of them had commented, "The old man is as hard as nails at the game as he is in business. Gives no quarter and expects none, and cares nothing about destroying an opponent." The other man agreed. They were twenty years older than Drum, yet called him "the old man." It was plain they considered him their leader and though their words seemed damning they were said with respect and a certain awed fondness.

In the carpenter shop next door, someone whistled a soulful Willie Nelson song, "Stay a Little Longer" as he swept woodshavings from the floor. It wasn't Drum. He'd still been at the field when she left. She wished she could slow the rapid beating of her heart to the unhurried rhythmic whish of the whistler's broom against the floor. Sunbeams lanced through the open window, highlighting a corner stacked with books. On the top of a bureau, glass perfume decanters flashed violet, red, and yellow.

The earlier breeze had died, and the small room was warm.

In the act of moving a standing Chinese black-lacquered screen to its assigned place, her hands stilled. She knew he was somewhere near. She turned slowly.

Drum blocked the outside doorway. He stood there, his hair plastered wetly onto his forehead, an eye blackening, dried blood on his upper lip, like a wounded warrior returned home for his reward. His damp green jersey clung to his muscled chest, then drooped carelessly over the top of his white shorts.

Bry rose to his feet, a faint rumble in his throat, but Drum rubbed the dog's head affectionately and indicated he should lay back down. Bry obeyed with a grateful sigh.

Drum's eyes traveled the length of her, and she knew what he wanted, her whole body knew what he wanted, every sense she possessed knew, and trembled with apprehension and terrible, terrible wanting.

She gripped the edge of the screen. Whatever he'd come back to fetch in the shop was forgotten.

He advanced toward her, the cleats on his shoes tapping dully on the wooden floor. As he drew close, his presence stormed her senses, and she couldn't have moved or said a word even if she'd wanted to.

He framed her face in his hands. His midnight blue eyes burned and burrowed into hers, as his thumb trailed lazily over her cheek and traced around her trembling mouth.

Parched dry with aching want, Lannie was afraid where this would take them, but the ache was too hard, too hot, too urgent to put aside, and she couldn't have even had she the willpower of a saint.

He kissed her softly. His lips were warm, rough, and dry, from thirst after the game. She circled them with her tongue, wetting them smooth. Tasting his dried blood, she absorbed the tang of him into her and wanted more. She felt the rippling response of his body as their soft kiss raged out of control.

The kiss became a hot, feverish hunger between them, a sucking, needing exchange. She could scarcely breathe and heard Drum breathing hard. He smelled of musky perspiration and grass.

Next door, the man stopped whistling and she wondered briefly if he could hear them. In the distance a single firecracker popped.

Were the two of them crazy? Someone would walk in on them, would discover them feeding on each other's bodies like animals in heat. Common sense caught her for a moment, and she murmured, "No, not here" against his lips.

"Too late, Lannie, too late," he whispered hoarsely in her ear, and all sound faded away as Drum took over her senses.

His mouth closed over hers again, and they consumed each other. Drunk with desire, each fueled the other's passion. He pushed her back against the wall. She was grateful for the solid wall at her back, for her watery limbs threatened to drop her to the floor at any time.

He unbuttoned her blouse rapidly, but too slowly for her. She fumbled to help him, ripping buttons off in the chase to be free. He slipped her bra straps over her shoulders, and pulled it down to her waist. Licking at her nipples hungrily, he moaned softly. Wanting the feel of his bare skin against her breasts, she slipped her hands beneath his jersey.

Oh, God, she loved the feel of his chest beneath her hands, the muscles smooth and taut, and the layer of bristly hair matted with perspiration. She realized now that she'd wanted to explore this sensual surface since she'd watched him at work that first time.

He placed fervid kisses across her shoulders and raised her skirt searching out the tenderness between her thighs. One finger slid intimately into the slit of her soft folds. Wild pleasure burst through her and a shocking need to scream, cry, and drive hard again and again against the finger. He plunged further, recklessly now. She choked back the cries, swallowed them until the knot in her belly drew tighter and tighter and begged to be loosened.

His hand stroked her swollen softness, as his mouth worked eagerly, wetly at her breasts until the twin peaks were hot with rigid agony. She whimpered. Swiftly he moved from her breasts and caught her jaws with his free hand. He held fast as he pursed her lips and sucked a kiss from deep within her.

Her nails scratched down his back and caught in the band of his rugby shorts. She wanted them off. She wanted him inside of her. His hands left her for a frantic second as he helped her yank the shorts off, and he kicked them aside.

Unwilling to wait while she struggled with her skirt, he lifted it again, raised it above her hips, and stripped her panties from her. He skimmed both hands beneath her buttocks, slid her up the wall, and pushed his fingers into her cleft to hold her in place. He pressed her hard against the wall, his erection hot and unyielding against her bare belly. A soft groan escaped him and vibrated in her ear.

He drew back, his eyes black with passion, as he stared almost mindlessly into her eyes.

"Yes," she whimpered, "please, Drum." She pulled him back to her, clasped her arms desperately around his shoulders and held tight.

His arms tensed. He lifted higher, shifted his arms, and opened her fully. He drove into her with a primal moan that set her senses spinning out of control. He locked inside of her, hot, hard, and full.

She cried out. He absorbed her cries with his mouth as he drove hard and deep. A kaleidoscope of sensations staggered her with heat and light and racking emotion. She bucked frantically against him, wanting more and more and more, wanting this to never end, yet reaching for the glorious release.

Suddenly, she arched and the light and color burst and exploded into a vibrant rainbow. *Oh, God, let me live this again and again and again.*

Drum shuddered violently. His fingers dug deep into her buttocks as he seized her to him, and his seed flooded and filled her, spread hot over her, and spilled warmly down her legs.

Spent, and fighting for breath, he lowered her feet to the floor, and she dropped her head weakly onto his shoulder. They held each other, exhausted. She stroked his back, as if soothing a tired child, and kissed him beneath his ear.

"Lannie, Lannie, Lannie," he whispered. "How wonderful you are."

She shivered with delight at his soft words and, satiated, settled into his gentle embrace.

"Drum, what have we done?" she whispered back.

He laughed quietly. "I'm not sure, but I think we just made mad, passionate love. We've wanted to get at each other since the get-go. We just did."

Still breathing hard, he kissed her bare breasts once more, then tenderly pulled the bra up to cover them and buttoned her blouse. Minus its top buttons, the sheer fabric lay loose, falling askew and revealing a tempting portion of her chest down to the swelling of one breast. He kissed the softness again, and traced a dangerous path of butterfly kisses up her neck to her mouth.

Incredibly, she felt the swirling, twirling, sexual tension begin to mount again.

Voices engaged in conversation could be heard just outside the window. Reality emerged with a start.

"No-o-o-o, Drum, we can't," she whispered. "Dear God, we're crazy. Anyone could have walked in and caught us."

"Would you have changed anything if you could have?" he asked, and bent to grab his shorts and pull them on.

"No, but . . ." She felt shy now, the import of what they'd recklessly engaged in just hitting her. "I . . . uh, I've never done anything like this before."

"Well, if it makes you feel any better, neither have I." He laughed, delight joining the shine of victory in his eyes. "I usually like making love in a nice comfortable bed."

"We weren't making love, we were engaging in lust."

"Maybe." There were questions in his eyes and something else she couldn't identify. Confusion, perhaps. "But next time we'll choose a better place."

Next time? Was this a jet she'd boarded, a super force from which she couldn't detach?

The prop room had dimmed with shadows of a fast coming dusk.

She ignored his last remark and stood erect, pushed her shoulders back into a dancer's stance of good posture, and straightened her clothes. He smoothed a strand of her hair into place and kissed her temple.

"I have to go," she said shakily. "I need to get up the mountain before it gets dark."

"I'll follow you, make sure you get home safely."

The thought of him at the cabin disturbed her. Why? Because he wanted her land? No, she decided. It was because she was afraid of what would happen if she took him there, afraid of another encounter like this, and afraid of him invading her refuge.

"No, I'll be fine," she said firmly. "Drum, let's just pretend we're strangers who will never meet again, like seat mates on a plane who carry on intense conversations, and then part forever."

An amused smile crooked up one corner of his mouth.

"Sure, Lannie, we can give that a try." He raked a

tanned hand through his disheveled hair, and she caught her breath at the spasm of wanting that caught in her stomach. Dammit. "But I don't think it will work."

"Why?"

"Because we're not strangers, never have been. Because no matter how we try to avoid it, we'll always meet again."

THIRTEEN

Mae sniffed and wrinkled her nose. Someone was smoking, or had been smoking. Alarmed, she glanced around her. No one in sight. The lull before the storm. It was late afternoon, always a quiet time between rehearsals and the evening performance.

She was by herself in the main building, waiting for a truck to pick up the potted palms she'd rented to make the theater more festive for opening night of *Oklahoma!* last week.

Mae, never one to let an idle moment go by, wandered the backstage area picking up debris left behind by the young interns. She wished the truck would come. They'd been promising for days, but then wouldn't show. A stern phone call to the manager of the trucking company had gained her a pick-up date for this afternoon. She ached for a nap. She was tired. Lannie hadn't been here since the day of the rugby game, and Mae really missed her. She hadn't realized how much she'd come to rely on Lannie.

Why had she stopped coming? Mae had a strong suspicion it had something to do with Drum. What a shame.

She sniffed again. There was no mistaking the smoke.

In the faint light filtering from the stage, she saw layers of blue haze drifting in midair around the big black curtain.

She knelt to pick up two crushed butts. They were at her feet next to the excess curtain length piled on the floor.

"Those darn teenagers," she said. She hated to blame everything on the young kids, but members of the veteran acting troupe knew better.

No Smoking signs hung everywhere, but someone obviously ignored them.

It was strange, though. She'd never had trouble with this before. She thought then of the new stagehand she'd hired, Jack Edwards. He'd smelled like cigarettes when he'd come to inquire about a job. He hadn't smoked in her presence, but at the end of the interview she had emphasized the rule about not smoking backstage.

Of course, Kent Shaw smoked, too, but he knew better than to smoke inside the theater.

She turned to head out front to the office. Her heel caught in the heap of curtain and she stumbled. She grabbed at the thick hanging to break her fall and felt something solid in its fold.

Suddenly, everything went black as she was twirled and wrapped in the heavy velvet folds of curtain. For a moment she heard the harsh breathing of whoever trapped her. She tried to scream, but the dusty material flat against her mouth refused to give. She would smother if not released soon. Around and around she was rolled, her arms and legs useless. A mummy entombed in endless weighty black musty velvet.

Heart pounding with fear, she tried to breathe, but couldn't get any air. Searing pain wrapped her chest, drawing tighter and tighter. *I'm having a heart attack. Please, God. Save me.*

The band squeezed, squeezed, squeezed. Surely her

chest would explode with the pressure. She faded in and out and knew she hadn't long to live.

Abruptly, the steel vise that enfolded her, let go. Tears running down her cheeks, she sank to her knees in the relaxed folds of curtain.

Carefully, she pushed with her feet and arms until she found an opening and fresh air hit her face. She crawled from the black mound, weak and shaking, only to be jerked back up again and rolled tight and tighter and tighter.

As Mae lost consciousness she thought she heard a nervous giggle, then a soft laugh. Someone laughed as she died? *How odd,* she thought.

Mae had stumbled upon Jeb's hiding place as he watched the young female actors undress in the makeup room. His spy had told him of the best vantage places for girl-watching. The man had evidently had a good time keeping an eye on Lannie and other females in the theater.

Can't be discovered this early in the game, thought Jeb. He'd meant to just get Mae all tangled up in the curtain so he would have time to get away, but her quick breathing and moans of fear as he'd twisted her around had excited him.

He'd released her reluctantly, but when he heard her gulp for fresh air, he couldn't let go of the thrill of power that surged through him. The impulse to smother the life out of her was easy to give in to. He'd yanked her back into the curtain with exhilaration, lost in the wonder of this newfound power he so enjoyed.

As he felt life leave her, he almost blacked out with pleasure.

He dropped her limp body at his feet and a new thought hit him. Maybe he could make this a game. He'd strangled Susie, drowned Buster, and smothered Mae. Finding new ways to "off" people might be fun.

In the meantime, except for discovering where her cabin was, he had Lannie in sight most of the time. He wished that he could let her know he was here, but she still thought of him as a rapist. That's why he'd taken pains to disguise himself. He wanted to surprise her.

FOURTEEN

Holy crapola, Daisy. Will you please turn that thing down?"

"Yes, sir," Daisy said, a crestfallen look on her young face.

Aww, geez, Spencer, what have you gone and done now, spoiled the kid's picnic?

Daisy and her friends took their boom boxes to the other end of the meadow. A softball game, organized by stage manager, Kent Shaw, occupied the center of the sunny meadow. John Lamb, and other board members, played with cast and crew. A girl squealed as she rounded third base and her teammates cheered her on, her orange shirt a pleasing contrast against the lush green grass. In the shade of a big hemlock, a young couple nestled in each other's arms. Spencer wondered sourly if pine needles bit into their ass and if ants crawled up their legs. If so, their discomfort didn't seem to bother them.

Though the sky was bright and sunny, the air was cool and invigorating. Reminded him of summers in Maine.

He scooped his plastic fork into the mysterious mess on his paper plate and shoved in another mouthful of beans, trying not to grimace. This syrupy southern version of baked beans made his teeth ache. He much preferred his sainted mother's staunch Boston beans.

He sighed and for the first time in his life came up with the absurd notion that he was lonely. He missed Mae, really missed her, not just the invaluable aid she'd given to him, but he missed her calm and cheerful presence.

The news of her sudden death from an apparent heart attack had stunned the whole community and spread a definite pall throughout the theater. Her funeral, at Victory Methodist Church, had been filled to capacity with mourners showing respect for the solitary woman who for years had moved quietly, but lovingly, throughout their town, only giving and never expecting anything in return.

Spencer had been shocked at the depth of his grief. He missed her in many ways and realized that his growing romantic notions of Mae had improved his outlook on everything, including his attitude toward his work here in High Falls. Now he'd plunged back into the doldrums. Here he was alone again.

The corny suggestions she had made, such as getting the cast and crew together socially away from the theater once in a while, had really helped the espirit de corps. This Sunday morning picnic had been her latest brainstorm, and his grudgingly growing affection for her hadn't let him tell her he hated picnics.

The cast knew the picnic had been Mae's idea, and they worked even harder to have a good time. After a while, they forgot to work at it, and found themselves really enjoying the fresh air and sunshine.

Spence's idea of a picnic was sitting around a campfire late at night with his pals, eating their freshly caught fish. Now that was the ticket, not this silly dancing in the mountain meadow sort of Shakespearean folderol.

Yes, Mae's suggestions, her careful attention to detail at the theater, and her gathering of volunteers had helped tremendously. Lannie's innovative dance style, and her insistence on excellence had made a huge difference in the dancers' attitudes, too. Even that little twit, Vince, had to admit that he valued Lannie's assistance.

Kent Shaw sat down cross-legged on the blanket across from Spencer, a can of Miller Lite in his hand. Spencer had bitten the bullet and asked the board for extra money for a stage manager. Though he knew of him only by reputation, he'd recruited Kent from a touring show in Atlanta. The man had arrived the week before *Oklahoma!* opened. Though he kept to himself much of the time, he was a cheerful chap and knew the workings of theater and production. He did a great job and had made a difference, also.

Kent took a swig of his beer, then scratched at the unshaven stubble on his pointed chin.

"Hate to give you any headaches on a beautiful day like this, but I've been wondering what happened to the Sullivan broad. Man, she's like uptown. Class all the way, and the dancers really miss her."

"I don't know where she is, but I need her, too. She appeared the day of Mae's funeral, and then disappeared again. She hasn't been around for more than a week."

"She stopped coming without any explanation," said Kent, running his fingers distractedly through his disheveled platinum hair. Spence wondered if it was bleached and dyed. "I asked Daisy if she knew anything, but she hasn't heard from her either. No one has any idea where she lives, and she doesn't have a phone. Lannie and Rutledge are friendly, but when I asked him about her, he got huffy and said he didn't know."

"Well, hells bells, people don't just disappear." Then again, who knows? Maybe they did here in these vast mountains.

"Closing night is in two weeks. Maybe she'll show up when she realizes *Our Town* is rehearsing. As soon as it opens, rehearsals for *A Chorus Line* will begin and I really need Lannie," said Kent. "By the way, I heard Drum Rutledge has invited everyone to a party at his lodge when *Chorus Line* closes Labor Day weekend."

"Yep. End of our season, too. One of Mae's brainstorms. Said everyone should celebrate together—cast, crew, volunteers, and board of directors. Some people aren't comfortable at a country club, so she talked Drum into volunteering his place."

"He's a pain-in-the-ass lately," said Kent. "I'm surprised he said yes."

Spence amazed himself by defending Drum. "He hasn't always been that way. You haven't been here long enough to make any judgments." Shaw made a face at Spence's slight reprimand. "Mae talked him into it. Told him it was silly to do all that remodeling on his lodge, and then leave it empty."

He wondered again how such a dainty, quiet, unassuming woman had gotten so much done. No one else would have had the nerve to try and persuade Drum Rutledge to do anything.

"Doesn't he live way up in the boonies somewhere?" asked Kent.

"Yeah. We're on his land now, but his lodge is higher up. About a thirty-minute hike from here, I understand."

Kent frowned, "Sounds like a bitchin' place to get to for a party."

Daisy had returned, her knee bleeding.

"Mr. Case, do you have any Band-aids? I scraped my knee climbing a tree."

"Sorry, Daisy, I don't carry supplies with me." But Mae would have, he thought. Guilt filled him, as he noticed the glistening tears she fought not to release. "Here, let me see if I have anything."

As he searched his pockets, Kent whipped out an immaculate white handkerchief and gave it to the child. She sat on the blanket to press it against her injured knee.

"Thanks, Mr. Shaw."

"That's okay. Just make sure it's clean before you return it. As I was saying, how do they expect people to get to Rutledge's party? I don't have no four-wheel drive."

"I have no idea." Mae had arranged all that and hadn't told him what she planned. "You've got a whole month to worry about it. In the meantime, we've got two shows to do."

"I know how guests will get there. My grandmother told me," said Daisy. "They'll be picked up at the theater and taken up the mountain by jeep and other four-wheel drives. Grandmother says receiving an invitation to the party has become the 'in' thing of the summer season. She says everyone is wearing suits and cocktail dresses. Wish I could go."

Spencer groaned. "Aww, geez, what a crock. You mean I have to go to my own closing night party, up a mountain in a Ford Explorer or such, dressed in a suit?"

Daisy blushed, afraid she'd joined an adult conversation without invitation, and obviously afraid of him, thought Spencer. "I guess so, sir," she muttered.

Mae would have comforted her. He patted her on the head. "How's the knee?"

"Much better. Here's your hanky, Mr. Shaw."

Kent Shaw recoiled from the bloody square of white linen. Spencer thought he was teasing the kid, but his next words changed that notion.

"Hey, kid. I told you. I want it back clean."

Daisy blushed again and jumped up. "Oh, right, I forgot. Jennifer's waiting for me." She stuffed the square into the pocket of her shorts and ran toward the softball game.

Spencer wished Kent would go away, too. For the first time in ages, he didn't want to think about "Lady Temptress Theater." He wanted to think about Mae, and what might have been, and maybe dream a bit of Julia Jane.

"Think I'll close my eyes for a while," he said to the man.

He lay back on the blanket and closed his eyes, hoping Shaw would take the hint. He heard the man get up and leave.

And soon, he'd drifted off to finer places and dreamed of Mae smoothing her gentle hand across his aching forehead, while a magical Julia Jane did the can-can on a stage in front of him.

Drum ran his hand over the burled walnut cabinet. Lester Hall's construction company had done a good job refinishing the wall units in his office. He sipped his coffee, repositioned an antique rocker in its corner, and looked around.

"Good job, Lester. Looks like you're going to finish ahead of schedule."

"Yep, well, only because you've been such a big help, Mr. Rutledge. The specs you drew were easy to follow, and you've gotten our lumber here real quick like. The weather has cooperated, too."

"When do you think the kitchen will be finished?"

"In time for your party."

Drum frowned. "It's not my party, but it's what Mae Nevins wanted, and whatever Mae wanted is fine with me. Keep up the good work, Lester. I have to return to Charlotte soon, before they forget who the boss is. Having an office here is great, but my physical presence seems to galvanize them. It's good to know that I can trust you to put the finishing touches on everything while I'm gone."

He wandered through the remainder of the house, inspecting the renovations. Hall's company had done a fine job. Drum was pleased. Mae Nevins had been right, though. How had she known that the house, though perfect in every way and structurally sound again, was empty? It was a mountain lodge in every sense of the word, with heavy rough-hewn beams overhead, immense stone fireplaces in the living room and kitchen, and wide-planked pegged floors, but the place lacked life. He knew it and he knew why.

He'd removed every picture reminding him of Ann-Marie and Chip. He'd instructed the housekeeper to give away every piece of clothing, every toy, every book, every personal item that had belonged to either of them. The pictures and other things that he'd been unable to part with had been stored in a closet.

When grief overtook him, when he thirsted for Chip or the bruises from his immature worship of Ann-Marie became more than he could handle, he would unlock the closet and wallow in moments of self-indulgent pity. Eventually the feel of Chip's rough, ratty old baseball or the filmy scarf Ann-Marie had worn when they first met brought more pain than they did pleasure and he would lock the door again.

He walked outside to look for Wilkie Talley, and found him planting a bed of hosta lilies next to the rear deck.

"Hey, thar, Mr. Rutledge. Beautiful day, ain't it?"

"Sure is, Wilkie, sure is," he said, and took a moment to gratefully survey the endless expanse of green mountain ridges that spread before him. The morning sun spotted the eastern slopes with jumbo splotches of hard gold.

"I heered them actin' people is having a picnic on your lower meadow. Why ain't you thar?"

Drum didn't answer. He knelt to examine a struggling dahlia bed near the hostas. He preferred the lush natural effect of native plants, but allowed several beds of bright annuals and perennials near the house. Beneath the lofty evergreens that circled the outer perimeters of the lodge, stubborn native purple rhododendrons and vivid pink mountain laurel still bloomed, hugging the ground with thorny tenacity.

"Hadn't thought much about it, Wilkie."

Mae had talked him into the picnic, and the closing night party. He hadn't the heart to turn her down, and now he was determined to go all out, making the party a memorial for Mae.

He knew he should be returning to Charlotte. The repairs to the house were almost complete, and the crew he'd trained at the theater were doing well enough to build the *Chorus Line* sets by themselves.

But he delayed, and he knew why he delayed. Lannie. The party gave him an excuse to stay longer.

He'd been a bear to work with, so no one would think it strange if he didn't show at the picnic. Lannie's absence from the playhouse was driving him crazy. He snapped at his coworkers and could scarcely grind out a civil response to anyone. The idea of confronting her at her cabin worked at him constantly, but he knew his appearance there would spook her even more. She'd revealed little of herself, but he sensed that she'd kept to herself the past few years to recover from an emotional pain of some sort. The few conversations they'd had as they'd worked side-by-side on a few occasions, and before they'd given into the powerful lust that drove them together, indicated that her volunteering at the playhouse was her first venture back into the civilized world.

It was obvious that Lannie wanted to be left alone, but

he knew one thing for certain. He wouldn't go back to Charlotte without seeing her again. If that meant storming her cabin, so be it.

He'd fought a battle with himself all morning about the picnic. He wasn't in the mood for making merry in a meadow. Would there be much merrymaking anyway? Mae's sudden death had shaken all of them. The only reason to go was the possibility that Lannie might show.

"Maybe I will go, Wilkie."

"Probably do ya good, Mr. Rutledge. You been lookin' mighty pale and peaked lately."

An hour later, Drum followed the barely discernible path that led to the meadow Ann-Marie had always liked. As he negotiated the seldom traveled trail, startled birds were flushed from their lofts and crannies. A dusky-gold pine warbler flurried from a hemlock, skimmed a pearly patch of mountain mint, and lit in a dogwood tree.

Drum tried to enjoy the beauty he walked through; the strands of orange, red, and pink July wildflowers that played in sunny spots along the shaded path, the liquid trill of the warbler, the brilliant strips of azure sky that showed through the lofty treetops. But he found his efforts failing.

He felt like a dog who couldn't scratch the itch on its back, and rolls, rubs, and gyrates frantically upside down on the earth. The strong desire to see Lannie affected every movement he made, every thought he had, and every plan that he tried to make. Lannie was like warming your hands on a cold night, like oxygen in your lungs at the end of a race, like the deep, rich color in red wine held to a sunbeam. The pull to finish what the two of them had started was so hot and strong that he knew it would eventually defeat him, no matter how desperately he resisted playing it out.

Halfway to the meadow, he heard the roar of Crystal Falls. Behind the waterfall, the walls and floors of its cave were striped with veins of crystals. Ann-Marie had called it a magic place, and Chip had loved the occasional rainbows that reflected through the interior and danced vicariously through the powerful rush of water.

They hadn't visited there nearly enough. All the adventuring and sharing they could have done was past capturing now. Regret and guilt hit him hard, as they always did, but he willed the draining emotions away, tamped them down into the hidden, soft part of his heart that he guarded zealously.

The air around him grew cooler, and spray from the falls sparkled pink, blue, and silver all around him. He sat on a boulder next to the first great deluge of water and watched the dramatic show that nature produced here eternally. Something about the beautiful setting before him bothered him. On closer perusal, he realized it was color, where color shouldn't be, near the entrance to the cave. He got up and walked closer.

A pair of cut-offs and a T-shirt had been tossed on a rock. Dainty lace-edged silk panties had slipped to the wet grass below.

He recognized the pastel green shirt. The clothes belonged to Lannie.

His heart beat faster. He looked around, but couldn't see her.

"Lannie?"

No answer. The clamor of the water covered his voice. She had to be in the cave. Why had she removed her clothes? If she'd slipped between the water drop and the rock wall, she would have gotten damp, but not drenched. A large white towel hung from a tree branch nearby.

Showering. Lannie must be showering.

Not stopping to think, he sat on the rock and unlaced his boots, then shed his shirt. He maneuvered his body through the narrow opening, catching his breath at the coldness of the spray as it hit his chest.

He spotted her immediately. Lannie stood in the center of the most gentle fall. Her head tilted back, eyes closed, she let the water sluice down her skin. She raised her arms and turned around and around, then, sliding her hand beneath her armpits, down over her tummy, and between her legs, she soaped her body.

He knew he should let her know he was there, but he was entranced with every graceful movement she made and couldn't bear to see an end to her sensual ritual.

She threw her head back again. In its wetness, her long hair had lost its vivid redness and had turned into burnished auburn that clung darkly to the curve of her back all the way to her buttocks. He drew a sharp breath as she soaped between her thighs and delved into her bushy mound. He thought he would go mad. The erection he'd felt coming grew hot and hard until it threatened to burst through his damp jeans.

How should he alert her to his presence without frightening her? Maybe he should just slip away and never let her know he'd seen her showering.

The threatening snarl behind him made his hair stand on end. He knew it was Bry. Bry knew him as a friend, but Drum was where he shouldn't be as far as Bry was concerned. The dog wouldn't back away unless Lannie ordered him to.

His dilemma was solved when Lannie opened her eyes and looked straight at him. Shock and fear widened her eyes, and she screamed. He couldn't hear the scream, but saw her mouth open wide and then close when she realized it was him. Bry moved close behind him, and Drum felt the dog's feral breath on the bare skin at his waist.

Embarrassed and frowning, Lannie tried to cover her breasts and mound by making an X of her arms and hands.

But then she surprised him by dropping her arms to her sides as if she'd changed her mind. With a flick of the wrist, she signaled Bry to back off, and Drum knew the dog had gone.

Lannie stood boldly before him and proudly challenged him to view her in her entirety. And he did. She didn't move an inch as his eyes moved over her.

Drum took his time appreciating the lovely body he'd so thoroughly ravished against the wall, but had never felt or seen in its entirety. Like a connoisseur, he studied, appraised, and appreciated the beauty of her form. Molded by years of dance, and refined even more by tough work at her mountain retreat, Lannie's slim, lithe body was breathtaking. The water streamed over her, making glistening pathways into secret places he longed to explore himself.

Neither of them moved, but he noticed a pale coral flush color her breasts, spread over the graceful column of her neck, and travel to highlight her cheekbones. Her nipples tightened and lengthened, and he groaned.

She lifted her chin even higher, but closed her eyes. When she opened them, he saw they were bright with challenge. He stripped off his jeans and walked into the water drop, covering the distance between them in a dream, hardly noticing the slippery rocks he trod. Usually a cold shower dampened his enthusiasm for sex, and he'd taken many of them the last seven years, but this fierce, hard, incessant wanting would not fade or go away. He felt cold on the outside, but hot on the inside with a fever that threatened to consume him.

He drew the firm length of her naked body against him. Breathing quietly against her mouth, he pressured her slick buttocks until her wet pubic hair tangled with his thick erection. Holding her close with one hand against her bottom, he explored and searched her body with the other, getting to know the lithe limbs, the precious dimples, and secret hollows he had lost so much sleep over. He cupped her breasts, kneading gently, and she began to shake uncontrollably. He kissed each breast and she cried out.

He found her lips again and drew her tongue into his mouth, wishing she could melt into him, become one with him, wishing he could carry this excitement, adoration, and wonder with him always.

Lannie closed her eyes and wished herself a part of Drum. Pinwheels of crystal color whirled behind her wet lids, blue, silver, and gold. Were they reflections from the water and glittering walls of the cave or were they swirls of magic dust tossed willy-nilly over two crazed, enchanted lovers? They lit up the cave, her body, and Drum's hands as he hungrily found each private part of her.

The falls roared in her ears, but she didn't need to hear, only feel, only enjoy, only give up the fight.

She put her arms around his wide, slippery shoulders, and found him firm and strong. Like an encompassing bulwark, he blocked out the water, and even the noise. With great relief she let herself slip into the slow pull of his seductive mouth. Her groin, heavy and throbbing, ached with wanting. She'd never wanted anything or anyone the way she wanted Drum Rutledge at this moment. His kiss became urgent and demanding.

He took her hand and pulled her out of the hard-driving shower and into the dryer portion of the cave. The air was pleasantly warm against her cold, but feverish, skin. He held her tight by the wrist and stared as if starved for the sight of her. With obvious appreciation and blazing hunger, his perusal swept her long legs down to her toes and back up again, pausing for a moment at her thick thatch of hair. Lannie's knees weakened and her heart beat furiously.

He drew her back to him. Nerves jumped and jingled everywhere he touched or kissed.

"I've been going crazy," he whispered hoarsely, warm against her ear. "Do you have any idea how much I want you, how many minutes of the day I spend trying to get you out of my goddamned mind? Where have you been?"

She shook her head, unable to speak.

Her breasts touched his chest, and the extended needy nipples reached achingly to mingle with his mat of wet hair. With trembling hand, she smoothed his dripping hair away from his face. He caught her lips with his again, and her mouth opened to receive his tongue. Their gentleness ended as the flames leapt high and fierce between them. On a tide of wild, frenzied lust they kissed, nibbled, and sucked at each other until they were breathless.

Lannie's knees buckled and they dropped to the moss-covered floor together. Drum took a tender nipple in his mouth and sucked hard, gathering all the breast in his mouth that he could until Lannie moaned with the exquisite sensation.

"Yes," she whispered, not knowing if he heard her over the roar of the water, but she urged him on anyway. "Harder, harder. The other one now, please."

He moved to the other breast and the sensation was repeated stronger and wilder. The heavy tug and pull in her stomach became incessant. Loose-jointed with passion, Lannie only wanted Drum against her, around her, inside her. She wanted the masculine smell of him, the sound of his harsh breathing, the feel of his hot large solidness wrapped around her forever.

The beat of her pulse matched the pound of the falls as it cascaded over the craggy cliffs and fell on the rocks sixty feet below. Was it the enchantment of this magic cave, the spell of the glorious summer morning, or an ancient primal mating call that created this time of scalding passion? Or was it simply Drum Rutledge and his supreme masculinity that had driven her across the line of common sense?

Lannie didn't stop to think or wonder. She heard nothing but the thunder of the falls and their soft cries, smelled nothing but Drum's muskiness and the clean mountain water that dripped from him, felt nothing but his electric touch, and the heat of his skin and the fine coppery hair on his chest and legs. All of her senses were drugged, immersed, and enveloped with this dynamic sensual man who drove her daft with the slightest touch.

The bumpy rock surface beneath their moss-covered bed poked her back and hips at odd places, but lost in the world of Drum, she hardly noticed. He sucked and tongued her navel until her womb contracted sensuously.

She grabbed his neck and brought his face close to her, licking the stubble on his chin, nipping at his lips, running her fingers through his wet hair. Then she explored the hardness of his buttocks and the muscles in his strong thighs.

"Take it, Lannie, hold it," he said roughly.

She slipped her hand between them and caught his engorged, throbbing maleness. It was hot and thick and sleek. She ran her fingertips up and down its length and Drum's whole body stiffened. He placed his hand over her stroking fingers and swiftly removed them from his penis.

"No, stop . . . I thought I could . . ." he grimaced. "I'll come all over you . . . Christ . . . do you want me—?"

"Yes," she interrupted with a gut-wrenching sob. "Yes."

He spread her legs with his knee, and she rose to receive him. He hovered for a moment at the swollen lips of her privateness, positioned the thick head of his shaft, then pushed into her. He moved slowly at first, as if savoring what was to come, but it drove her crazy. He kissed her breasts, then her lips, then her shoulders, and quick ecstasies of pleasure joined the hot ache that yearned for completion.

He drove harder and harder. "Look at me, Lannie," he ordered harshly.

She opened her eyes. His head, the square belligerent jaw, the strong mouth, the wet hair pasted against his tanned forehead, blocked out the roof of the cave. She looked into the dusky blue eyes above her without shame. They were inflamed with desire and an almost unholy quest for victory. The skin around one of them was still a yellowish-purple, a reminder of the shiner he'd gotten in the rugby game.

She had a moment to wonder if her eyes mirrored his, and then he plunged in and out fast and hard and she wondered no more. Lost in intoxicated joy, Lannie disappeared into a realm reserved for those who have learned to give and receive without thought.

Lannie could have sworn the triangle between her legs glowed, and she burst through, screaming with joyous release. Drum bellowed, and his hot seed pumped into her. The precious liquid seemed to be never-ending, and spread in her bushy mound and over her shaking thighs.

Drum slowed down, going in and out gently, then lowered himself carefully on top of her.

"Are you okay?"

She nodded and smiled. Filled with out-of-the-world bliss, Lannie had never been more "okay."

She hugged him tight against her and kissed and nuzzled his ear.

He slipped off of her and hugged her to his side.

"Ouch," he said. "I thought the moss would be softer than this. Christ, I'm sorry, Lannie. I should have—"

She placed a finger on his lips. "Shhh. I never felt a thing. All I wanted was you."

"Well, we certainly took care of that, didn't we?" He chuckled. "But let's get the hell out of here."

Drum swept her up in his arms and carried her out of the cave. He whipped the white towel from the tree and headed toward a sunny patch of turf above the falls.

He kissed her hair, and Lannie felt his grin against her cheek. "How often do you shower in my falls, Lannie Sullivan?" he asked her.

"Two or three times a week. I'm trespassing, aren't I?"

"Yes, and I might have to ask for special favors if you continue breaking the law."

"I feel like I should be slung over your shoulder instead of carried in your arms," laughed Lannie. "After all, we just made love in a cave."

He laughed, dropped the towel, and lowered her to the ground. She helped him spread out the large beach towel. "We do seem to make love in odd places. Be careful, madam, you never know where next we may meet."

"We're destined to be out-of-the way lovers, Drum," she said and caught a worried look fleeting across his face.

They lay in each other's arms. The sun warmed her bare body, and Lannie felt deliciously tired and content. Like two characters from a *Midsummer Night's Dream* revelry, they lay nude and unembarrassed beneath the azure sky. The mountain wrapped around them with a wild tenderness. Bry appeared, gave them both a faceful of happy licks, then deposited himself in the shade of a maple tree.

"No, I would hate that. We're more than out-of-the-way lovers," he said soberly. "I wish things were diff—" He stopped and started again. What had he been about to say?

"Why didn't you come to the playhouse last week?" he asked. "I almost went crazy. I'd decided to give you a few more days, then I was going to come to the cabin."

She sighed. "I was afraid, Drum. I *am* afraid of you, afraid of how I feel when I'm with you, afraid of even feeling again."

"Stop running from me, Sullivan. I'll find you no matter where you are. It's obvious that the stars are conspiring to upset any well-laid plans either of us previously had."

"This is just another summer romance, Drum."

He was quiet for a long time. She nestled into his chest, burying her nose in the fast-drying mat on his chest. He caressed her back, running his palm softly up and down her spine.

"Maybe, maybe not." He hesitated, as if making a decision. "You're so alive, Lannie. So vibrant and giving. Do you want to tell me what drove you to the cabin, and why you hide yourself away?"

Her heart stopped and started again with a thud. It was her turn to be quiet. She wondered if she could tell him of Gracie. Was she strong enough now? Yes. She could do this. She must do this or be forever stricken at the memory of her little girl, and Gracie deserved better than that. Gracie deserved to live again through her mother's words and actions, through everything she did.

"Yes, I think I would like to tell you." This was hard. So hard. Most people that she knew, knew about Gracie. She rarely had to talk about her. The only person she'd mentioned Gracie to in the last two years had been John Lamb. "I had a child who drowned. Her name was Gracie."

She told him then of her marriage, of Tom Ravenal, of the sleepy Floridian town of Madison, the thriving law practice she and Nell had built, the pride when she'd been appointed an assistant state's attorney, the subsequent discovery that she hated prosecuting cases that she felt should never have been brought to trial.

"So after a year of working for the state, I returned to private practice with Nell. Gracie was the icing on the cake. She brought such joy to all of us—me and Tom, my father, and Nell. Gracie and I had a special bond. She was only two years old when she . . . had to go. How do you explain a mother's love for a happy, loving, daughter? Mothers and daughters . . . I . . ." she struggled now.

He tightened his hold on her and she knew genuine loving comfort for the first time in years.

"I thought I could do it all. I wasn't enjoying the assistant state's attorney post, because I found I didn't enjoy prosecuting people. I'd just sent a childhood friend to prison for rape. It broke my heart when all the evidence showed he was truly guilty. The affection in his eyes turned to hate, and his threats to come after me someday, not so uncommon in such cases, upset me more than they should have."

She shivered and he drew her even closer.

"So when I found out I was pregnant," she continued, "I resigned, but I thought I could still practice law, keep a marriage going, and raise a child, too. Thousands of women do, and do it successfully. I stayed at home with her for eighteen months, then began working in the office part-time. Mausie was getting too old to run after Gracie, so I hired a wonderful local woman, Nancy Carrington, to take care of her."

She paused, searching for the words that were easiest to say.

"Tom didn't like any of it. He insisted that I stay at home full-time, but I attributed his attitude to a growing desire on his part to control everything I did. Turned out that he was right."

Threatening tears tightened her throat, and she coughed. She stopped, then started again.

"One early June afternoon, Big Billy planted young rose bushes. Gracie was there. She loved Big Billy. I had given her a new red ball that morning, and while he worked, he rolled the ball back and forth across the lawn to her. Nancy sat in a chair nearby, reading, but keeping an eye on Gracie. Somehow—and no one is quite sure what happened—except that Big Billy went to the shed to get a spade, and Nancy thought Gracie was with him. Big Billy thought she was with Nancy. We think she must have followed him part way, and then veered off to the pool area, around the corner.

"The pool was fenced, and Gracie knew how to swim. I taught her when she was a year old. She loved it. Someone had left the fence gate open, and she evidently wandered in, lost her ball in the water, and reached to get it."

It got tougher and tougher as she continued, but she was determined to finish without breaking down. This was the first time she'd told anyone the complete story.

"We don't know why she didn't swim, probably because the water was still so cold, and she wasn't used to that, and also because she fell in awkwardly and swallowed a lot of water before she righted herself, or maybe she tried to swim and couldn't make it to the steps. In my nightmare, she . . ." She stopped and gripped his shoulders. "She was without supervision for only a few minutes, but by the time they found her . . . it was too late."

Drum lifted her head from his chest, kissed her firmly on the mouth, and tucked her head beneath his chin again.

"Tom blamed me. It eventually drove us apart. He filed for divorce, and I came up here." Almost finished, she swallowed hard. "I'd spent a year in Madison discovering how exhausting insincerity is. I was wearing a mask.

People were so kind, so caring, so indulgent, and I hated it. I smiled until my jaws ached, and I pretended I was recovering when all the time I was disintegrating. I know everyone thinks I ran away, but I knew I needed to recover in my own way."

"And have you?" Drum asked softly.

"Somewhat. The first year in the cabin, I woke up when dawn broke, when everything is still and the day hadn't decided what it was going to be. Morning after morning, my first moment of awareness was a sick clutch of fear and grief in my stomach. It stayed with me through the morning until I'd worked myself weary chopping wood, carrying water, and all the other chores you do to survive in a primitive cabin. I thought that clutch, that horrible pit of panic, would never dissipate, that I would live with it the rest of my life."

"I know," he whispered against her hair.

How could he know, how could he possibly know?

"But the mornings aren't as rough anymore, and I'm learning how freeing a simple life can be. I've learned that I have to heal and nourish my own soul, that no one else can do it for me. In the process, I can feel Gracie growing closer again."

"Tom is wrong. It wasn't your fault," said Drum. "Sometimes life just plain rips us up, and it's damned hard to put yourself back together. Remember this, though, Lannie. When we isolate ourselves, we deny ourselves the love and nurture of family and friends, and we cheat them of the wisdom of *our* spirits."

He spoke with such certainty. Lannie wondered if he knew tragedy personally. She realized again that she knew little of Drum's personal life. There must have been women. Had there been a wife at one time or children? If so, why didn't he talk about them?

She was afraid to ask. At first she'd been afraid to let go of her emotions, afraid to let go and be free again. But after this morning, she realized a renewal burgeoned in her, and she clung to it desperately. She didn't want to know anything more about Drum right now. She might not like what she heard. She just wanted to cling to his comfort, his caring, and his strong physical presence.

Not now. Later, she would ask later.

Let me have these moments, God. These selfish moments of not caring, these selfish moments of complete pleasure. Forgive me, but let me know them awhile longer before real life intrudes again.

"Drum, I feel so sad about Mae. Did anyone know she had heart problems?"

"Only her doctor." He rubbed his cheek across the top of her head.

She hesitating, wondering if she should voice her disquieting doubts, but knew instinctively she could trust Drum to keep them to himself.

"I think it's very odd, the way they found her sort of crumpled in the folds of the curtain."

"So do I. It's suspicious, but I haven't said anything because I can't come up with any cogent explanation. It's probably as the doctor said. She stumbled, fell into the folds, and it scared her so that her heart flared up."

"Maybe."

"Let's not borrow trouble where there isn't any."

"Right. Is it bad at the theater without her?"

"Yes, it is. They need you there, Lannie. Spence is tearing his hair out trying to do the job of two people. They miss you. I miss you."

"I've been terribly selfish. I'll be there tomorrow morning bright and early. I can't fill Mae's shoes. They are unfillable. But I can help."

He brought her to him in a quick, rough embrace, and she felt his sigh of relief against her temple, "Thank God."

"You missed me that much, huh?"

"Yeah, I did," he whispered, and kissed her ear. "Lannie, I'm sorry, but I have to return to Charlotte for a few days. My secretary, and my board, have made it quite clear that my physical presence is needed once in a while. I'll be back at the end of the week. How do you feel about county fairs?"

"Never miss the one in Madison."

"There's one in Franklin next weekend. Will you go with me? We'll go down the mountain, eat cotton candy, listen to Willie Nelson, and generally have a good time."

"I would love that. Going back to the theater without Mae there is going to be hard. Having something to look forward to will help."

"That's what I thought."

"Getting to know me pretty well, huh?"

"There are things I just sense, as if I've always known you, always lo . . . always wanted you."

"I know." She wondered if he was about to say the word "love," but she dismissed the thought in a hurry. Too enormous to think about. "It's scary, Drum, wanting you so."

"I feel the same way, but let's take the ride, sweetheart. Let's take the ride and see what happens."

Yes, yes, let's do. I'm so tired of being sad and hopeless and alone. I'm ready for a ride with you, Drum, no matter where it ends.

FIFTEEN

The hours of their beautiful summer day at the county fair slid by like beads on a golden chain. Beyond the mountain peaks, the sunset glowed honey and pink in a dark purple sky. Wind fingers combed her hair as the Ferris wheel took them around and around. Drum's arm rested across her shoulder and she nestled safe and secure at his side, cupped close and snug beneath his arm.

The huge wheel swept them down again, and Lannie's swift intake of air at the thrill to her tummy made Drum laugh. Their laughter had intertwined all afternoon, his big and free, hers delighted and amazed.

The wheel stopped to take on new passengers below. Their car sat at the top and swung gently back and forth. Instead of rocking it to tease her, as many males would have done, Drum sat quietly as they listened to the voices of the fair below.

"The whole world could see if I kissed you up here," he said.

"And I wouldn't care a bit. You've been stealing kisses all day, sir. I'd be hugely disappointed if you stopped now."

His arm tightened around her and he dipped his head to tickle her mouth with teasing softness, and then caught her lips in his and brought her closer to him. Swinging free and easy high in the deep purple sky, his searing kiss sealed what Lannie had been feeling all day. Drum was more than a summer romance, more than a lusty liaison, or a passing sexual attraction. Drum, and the depth of her feelings for him, was love. Love as she'd never known it before.

As soon as she'd allowed the thought passage through her pleasure-drugged mind, she snagged it and packed it away, afraid to even think or consider such a thing ever again.

Be happy for *now,* Lannie, her mother used to tell her. And that she could do, for she was happiest at this moment than she'd ever been in her entire life.

Drum released her, and she sighed.

"I never want to get off. Let's just go round and round and round," she said.

"Yeah, I feel the same way." He smiled. "But I think all the hot dogs, corn dogs, and cotton candy we ate would eventually rebel."

Lannie felt suspended in a magic fairyland as below them, lights of the different exhibits, booths, and rides began to come on, twinkling like a mother lode of silver against the darkening earth, and above them the first stars spread and dotted the dome of sky to meet the horizon.

"Doesn't get much better than this, does it?" asked Drum.

Tears popped to her eyes, and she whispered, "No."

Why did she feel that she had to hang on to this moment so desperately? *Now, Lannie, enjoy the now.* She lifted her head from his shoulder and kissed his square chin, then his strong jaw. He hugged her to him, as if he understood her sudden apprehension that this glow of happiness and rightness couldn't last.

"We're okay, sweetheart. In fact, we're perfect. Reach out, gather a few stars, put my name on the brightest, and fold it into your heart to keep forever."

"I already have," she murmured against his chest, wondering how he would interpret her response, and almost hoped he hadn't heard her.

Drum had heard her, and his heart leaped to touch Orion burning bright in the hemisphere. The feelings that had played and built with him all day rushed forth. He thought he would drown from the staggering force of ensuing emotion.

He loved Lannie Sullivan. There was no doubt, question, or misgiving in his soul or heart. He knew he loved her as he'd never loved anyone, and for a moment he reveled in the flood of delirious emotion. But following close on the heels of this liberating perception, was the dogged knowledge that never left him, the knowledge that tagged him everywhere he went and in everything he achieved.

He didn't deserve love. Never again. He'd treated love with cavalier attitude once, hadn't given it the respect and consideration it required, and he'd lost it. He didn't deserve to love or be loved ever again. He'd had his chance and screwed it up royally.

He should leave Lannie now. Leave her before real damage was done. The wheel began to slowly lower them as the carnie loaded new passengers swing by swing, and Drum clutched her tighter to him.

"Hey, I can't breathe," she laughed against his chest.

"Sorry," he said, and kissed the top of her head before he released her.

"You two going round again? I think that makes ten

times," said the carnie man, a look of resignation on his unshaven face.

"Thanks, but we've had enough. We'll see you next year."

"Yeah, sure," said the carnie.

"You haven't won anything for me yet," Lannie teased Drum, as they walked away. "You have to do that, you know, or we won't have really been to a county fair."

"My thoughts exactly. The softball booth ahead looks like fun."

"I noticed it before, and I've already picked out a ghastly orange pig that I love."

"Uh-oh, the pressure mounts."

"Three tries, mister," pitched the game operator. "Knock down the Eiffel Tower three times in a row, and the lady takes away the beautiful orange pig."

Twenty-five tries later, they walked away from the booth, and Lannie carried the garish orange pig with her.

"Tired?" he asked.

"Wonderfully so. Let's go home, Drum."

He loved the sound of it. *Let's go home, Drum. Let's go home, Drum.*

Where was home? Home was where Lannie was.

"Come to the top of the mountain. Spend the night with me,"she said.

"It would be easier to get to the lodge than to the cabin."

"I know, but I want to sleep under the stars tonight."

"Yes," he agreed, "it's a perfect night for that."

Blinking red and green lights from a game tent flicked on and off across her lovely face. Her smoky gray eyes caught enough light to tell him what he wanted to know. For a brief, shared flaring instant, they recognized that this day had sealed an understanding, and an emotion so precious and of such portent that neither wanted to speak of it, afraid of breaking the spell. And on his part, thought Drum, afraid to say words he had no right to say.

Jeb, his stomach churning as he followed them, slipped behind the softball booth, bent over, and threw up all the junk food he'd eaten earlier.

He tore off the straw hat he wore and the red plastic sunglasses, and swiped angrily at his mouth.

Jesus fuckin' Christ! If he'd had to ride that damn Ferris wheel around one more time, he would have vomited all over Lannie and Drum, and he wished he had. He'd never liked carnival rides anyway, and the nausea had begun to build after the second or third time around. He should have just gotten off and watched them from the ground, but wanted to get as close as possible, and riding in the bucket behind them was the best way.

As it was, he'd gotten sicker and sicker, not only from the motion of the swinging buckets, but from watching Drum and Lannie kiss, and watching Drum put his hands all over her. It made him madder and madder, and sicker and sicker.

Oh, Lannie, you need to be taught a lesson or two. Just wait until we're by ourselves.

He stood up, and wished for a cool drink to quench his thirst and clean his mouth. A refreshment booth was nearby. He hurried to it, keeping an eye on them all the time. They hadn't been out of his sight since they'd left High Falls earlier in the day. Following them down the mountain to Franklin had been simple. Vehicles seldom passed one another on the twisting drive, so having the same cars behind you all the way down to the valley was common. He'd let a Chevy ride between him and Drum's Land Rover.

Here at the fair, the two of them had been so absorbed with each other that they noticed little of the people around them.

The biting coldness of the Coke revived him, cutting through the film of sickness in his mouth, and down his throat and filling him with the caffeine he needed to keep him alert. He knew he was a caffeine junkie, but he figured it was better than being a drunk like his old man. He swished the Coke around in his mouth and spit it out, pretending that he spat into Drum's face.

What a fool Drum Rutledge was. Did he really think he would impress her by winning a stuffed animal? The princess deserved jewels around her slim white neck, and furs on her back, and Jeb would give them all to her one day soon.

First they would spend time alone together, getting to know each other again. She would remember what a loyal follower he had been. When the others had been having fun on her big porch in Madison, he had been planting flowers for Big Billy. When others had danced her laughing around the floor at the country club, Jeb had kept the party table clean and the refreshments coming. While Tom Ravenal had fucked a girl from Atlanta in the men's locker room at the club during Lannie's wedding reception, Jeb had carried more chilled champagne from the bar.

Yessirree bob, Jeb Bassert knew the important things. The Bible said Martha made Jesus comfortable and showed Him respect. Mary just wanted to sit at His feet and listen to His words. Jesus told Martha that she shouldn't be mad at Mary for not helping her serve food and such, but he'd bet a beer that ol' Jesus liked the food and wine more than having his dirty feet washed by a dumb bitch.

They were leaving. Jeb watched as Drum made sure Lannie had her seat belt fastened correctly and then climbed into the driver's seat of the Land Rover. His rented Ford Explorer was parked four spaces away. He let them move out on Highway 64, and then followed a good distance behind, keeping their taillights in sight. He wasn't worried about losing them. There were only two ways up the mountain to High Falls: torturous, twisting Highway 64 or Buck Creek Road, which was a longer, but easier drive.

They took Highway 64 and Jeb imagined it was because Drum wanted to get home quick, wanted to get into Lannie's panties as soon as possible. The thought made him hot all over, hot with anger at the idea of Drum Rutledge invading his territory, and hot with wanting Lannie.

He imagined what it would be like when he stood naked in front of her and she admired his new honed-down, muscled physique. The years of working out at the prison gym, and the month of demanding conditions at survivalists camps, here and in Florida, had made him super strong. He imagined her panting with desire, as he tore ferociously at her clothes until she was naked. He wanted to watch the fear mount in her eyes as his "hungry Jack" got bigger and bigger. He almost ran off the road with his mounting lust.

He wished he could stop and jack off, but he'd lose the Land Rover.

With mounting misery, he drove on. After he'd made sure Drum and Lannie were returning to Haystack, he waited for an open stretch and then passed them. He raced ahead as fast as the twisting road would allow and headed for the turn-off to Drum's lodge and Lannie's cabin.

Drum's place had been easy to find. He'd followed Drum one day last week, just as he had Lannie. They both used the same turn-off from the main highway. Later that night, he'd crept up the old logging path by foot and followed it to the Rutledge lodge, but trying to find Lannie's cabin had been futile. He knew it was further up the mountain somewhere. He'd found faint traces of trails leading from a Y in the Rutledge road, but they'd all petered off into nothing. None of them had led to him to Lannie.

A trip to the courthouse in Franklin and a search through dusty records showed the Sullivan place on an old deed right smack in the middle of Rutledge property, about twenty acres on top of Haystack.

A return daytime trip to Haystack while Drum and Lannie were at the theater had yielded nothing. The cabin seemed mysteriously hidden in the mists at the summit of the mountain. Not finding it infuriated him.

Tonight he would hide his car in the woods near the Y and follow Drum's Land Rover on foot, hoping they went to the cabin. The Land Rover would have slow going up the hazardous mountain side, and Jeb was fast and sure-footed. He had no concerns about following them no matter where they went on that damned protective mountain.

Outside the cabin, with the scent of pine needles enchanting them and the dark mysterious fir forest a semicircle behind them, they lay on their backs and watched the stars. There are times like now, thought Lannie, when we know somewhere deep within us, that what is happening is heaven, the heaven that God talks about.

Filled with gentleness, and kissed by heaven, she knew this day and night would live with her forever after, from now through eternity.

Drum kissed her temple. "Warm enough?"

"Yes. Thank you for bringing me such gifts of caring, Drum, physical and spiritual," she whispered. "I'll never forget this night of lovemaking on top of Haystack."

"Neither will I, sweetheart. I never realized how much of myself I had to give, and how much of myself I *wanted* to give until tonight. Sounds corny, but you've got all of me, beautiful."

Lannie's body still radiated with sensuous warmth and complete release. She'd given over to him completely and not cared. She knew that made her very vulnerable, but that wasn't important anymore. She was free and easy and flew somewhere above, winging her way from star to star with carefree abandon.

"Me, too." What had they just done? Tried to express love for the other without saying the words? How silly. They were two grown-ups. But that's okay, she thought. The three words, I love you, are too important to toss around carelessly. She was ready to say them, but obviously Drum wasn't. She could wait.

In the bowl of ebony sky over them, stars spread in glorious chill-bright profusion. She snuggled close to his side as he pointed out the constellations he was familiar with.

Bry lay close to them. At first, he had scowled at Drum's appearance. Not accustomed to having anyone else on his mountain top except himself and Lannie, Bry had sulked, crawling hang-tailed to a nearby pine tree and hiding behind it. They had coaxed him out, and now he acted as if he *might* be okay.

He growled now and again and got up to prowl restlessly in the woods. Briefly, she wondered if the mother bear and her cubs Drum had spotted last week were near the cabin, but then forgot about the Irish wolfhound's unusual behavior as Drum's voice sounded husky and pleasing close to her ear.

". . . and see way up there near Aries, that's Pegasus. It looks like the Big Dipper, but if you study it you'll see it looks like a winged horse."

"Where is Pisces?"

"I'm not sure, but I think it's that small circle of stars near Pegasus."

"Lovely, just lovely," she murmured sleepily.

"Lannie, I have to go to Charlotte for a few days this week, and next. My board of directors is sulking, and so is my office staff. Seems the company is suffering from my prolonged absence. Will you come with me?"

"No, thanks, Drum. I'm not ready to come off my mountain yet, and I'm sure Charlotte isn't ready for my arrival in your life. You'll hurry back, won't you?"

"I'll be back for the weekend. I'll miss you like crazy, call you every day. When I get back, I won't let you out of my sight. The timing is terrible, but it can't be helped."

He gathered her up, quilt and all, took her inside, and slept with her enclosed in his arms in her narrow bed, Bry on the floor at their side.

Jeb ground his teeth in frustration as he crawled out of the brush he'd been forced to hide in. The damned horse of a dog wouldn't let him close enough to even see the whole cabin much less to see what Lannie and Drum were doing.

Everytime Jeb took a step closer, the dog growled and came into the woods to sniff out the smell that alerted him to Jeb's presence. Jeb had finally settled in a thorny patch of mountain laurel and kept his eye on the dark triangular peak of the cabin's roof.

He stood, scratching at his shoulders where bugs had bitten him. A light flickered in the distance. To his delight, he realized it was probably candlelight from a window. He would love to stay and get a peek through the window, but he couldn't. He didn't know how long Drum would be here, and he had to move the Explorer from its hiding place before dawn. Drum might be able to spot it in daylight.

In the meantime, he knew he could find his way back to the cabin because he'd marked a path as he'd followed the awkward Land Rover through the forest and through the brushy, obscure entrance onto Lannie's trail. He could watch Lannie at his leisure, and in full pleasure, something he'd fantasized about for years and years, and there would be no one like Big Billy to chase him off, except the damned dog.

His cohort here in High Falls had been poisoning the dog until Lannie started keeping an eye out for her pet.

The man had been useful in more ways than one, and it was time to get rid of the dog. He wanted Lannie to suffer before he surprised her with his presence. She would get so freaked out that she would welcome Jeb with open arms, a real man who could protect her, unlike Tom Ravenal or Drum Rutledge, who could never really know her as he did, what it was like to yank at her ponytail, or follow her home on her bike, or give her his only Oreo cookie from the pitiful lunch he brought to school everyday.

It was his turn to watch her as she undressed, and ate, and slept.

Lannie heard Drum leave just as dawn broke. He kissed her and tucked the blanket close to her chin.

"See you later, sweetheart. Take care of her, Bry," she heard him whisper.

SIXTEEN

Two weeks had passed since the enchanted night at the county fair. Lannie marveled at how time shortened or lengthened, raced or dragged, with Drum's presence. When he was in Charlotte the days almost ground to a stop. When he was with her in High Falls the days spun by at a dizzying pace.

For the second week in a row, he'd gone to Charlotte for a few days, but their weekend together lived shining and warm in her heart. He'd been gone only a few hours, yet she missed him like an evening rose misses its morning dew, as her mother used to say.

She'd arrived at the theater early and worked arduous hours in the prop room, then conducted a dance workshop for new interns. Exhausted, she left the theater early that afternoon to gather her mail and maybe find a good book to read while Drum was away.

The loafers' bench in the village groaned with the weight of too many men. Unlike the usual bench in ordinary small towns, this one contained more ice cream lickers than it did tobacco hawkers and spitters. It sat against an ivy-laden, rosy-brick wall between the ice cream store and Jacob's Antiques, shaded by a spreading sweet gum tree.

Lannie noted with amusement the difference between two local mountaineers wearing patched overalls who sat to themselves on one end of the bench and the tourist husbands dressed in seersucker trousers or coral and turquoise Bermuda shorts who took up the rest of the space. The "weekenders," or "day" people ate their ice cream and waited for their shopping wives to emerge from one of the boutiques that lined Main Street.

There had been a time when the horde of flatlanders who poured into High Falls in the summer would have annoyed her, but today they simply gave her reason to smile. She smiled about everything now, and the elderly men with their sagging paunches, bright colors, and dripping cones made her happy.

She picked up her mail in quick order and took it to her favorite place to read, a bench near the creek that ran through town. She sat cross-legged on the green wooden bench while Bry curled up in the grass at her feet

A child's laughter drew her attention to the shallow creek down the gentle incline in front of her. For the first time in years she allowed herself to enjoy the sight and sound of a child. Three children, she estimated their ages between seven and ten, waded in the bubbling clear water. The boy dipped a paper cup in the creek and tossed water at the two girls. The girls screamed and ran away, then turned back to laugh and kick water at him.

Bry lifted his rangy form and trotted to the edge of the creek with curiosity. He cocked his head with each movement they made, as if he'd like to play with them, but wasn't quite sure how. He'd never been around children, but Lannie knew he would be gentle with them.

Lannie watched, entranced, as if she'd never seen children play before. They knelt now, to inspect something in the water. The boy poked at it with a stick, then got brave and picked up a salamander. They placed it on a rock and watched it scoot off. They caught it again, and the boy gave it to the little girl with golden pigtails. She accepted it gingerly, then dropped it hastily in the creek.

Lannie could have spent the whole day watching them, but a voice called from the stone bridge above them.

"Becky Jean Bayard, Mary Lane, you are in super trouble," said the frowning mother. "Look at you. Y'all are soppin' wet, and we're supposed to be at Great-mom's in thirty minutes. And there's a huge vicious old dog watchin' you, probably going to bite you. Carter Lee, you're forever gettin' your precious cousins in trouble. Where's your mom, anyway? Ya'll get up here, lickety-split."

The chastened threesome climbed the bank and met the scolding mother on the bridge. Bry came back to lie at her feet, his head hanging with disappointment and embarrassment.

She rubbed between his ears. "That's okay, love. Someday you'll have your own children to play with. And don't pay any attention to the mean words that lady said. *I* know you're not old and vicious."

She picked up the first letter on her pile. It was postmarked Dublin, Ireland, and was from her father.

Peppered with the colorful phrases he used, the written words sounded as though he were there talking to her, and suddenly she missed him terribly. She'd been so selfishly lost in her own misery that she'd neglected him. His pleas for her to get professional guidance or to let him come and stay with her, had fallen on deaf ears. He'd finally given up. He wrote to her every month, always with a reminder that he loved her, and wanted her home when she felt she was ready.

Now she wanted her father next to her on this wooden

bench beside the gurgling brook. She wanted to share the news of loving Drum, to bury her head against his big, burly chest, and cry with happiness.

Hi Lannie Girl,

All's well here in Ireland. So well that I've decided to stay an extra month or two. I miss you like the dickens, I do. Remember our trip here with your mother when you were twelve? You met your Irish cousins, and we played some real golf, didn't we?

He went on to tell her about the awful wet weather, which every Irishman complained about, but loved. He told of her of visits to his sisters, and festivals he'd gone to, and favorite pubs where he'd downed a lager or two.

I may not be home till Christmas time, Lannie, girl. I've met a fine woman who's stirred my heart a bit. I want to stay awhile, Lannie, see how it works. I think your mother would approve. If everything goes well, I'll be bringing Mary Catherine home with me, and I'm hoping you'll be off your damned mountain by then. I love you with all my heart.

He'd signed it, "the Judge," which was her nickname for him and what everyone in Madison called him.

The news of another woman in his life took a while to absorb. The pages rested loosely in her lap as she thought about the bombshell her father had so casually dropped.

Wexford Sullivan, a bright, brash Irish boy studying law at Notre Dame on a scholarship, had met her southern-bred mother while visiting his college roommate in Madison. He'd fallen in love with Grace Whitney at first sight, and the road between Notre Dame, Indiana, and Sweet Briar, Virginia, burned with the tracks made by Wexford Sullivan's decrepit Ford convertible. It was 1960, and most of their generation was brewing a stew of excitement and changing the world with freedom movements, long-haired hippie defiance, and civil rights demonstrations, which would last for the next twenty years. But these two, the idealistic boy from Ireland and the girl brought up in the old-fashioned southern way with white gloves and deb teas, cared only for each other and lived in a world of romance and roses.

They had adored each other, and Lannie couldn't imagine her father loving anyone like he had her mother. Grace Sullivan's death from a heart attack, when Lannie was fifteen, had devastated both of them. She had thought that her father would never recover.

But love takes many guises, she chided herself. *Don't be so quick to worry. You might like this new woman in the judge's life.* At any rate, she decided she should be happy for him, as he would be happy for her when he found out about Drum.

Marriage had never entered her mind, but her father's news brought contemplation of whether Drum might want to marry her. Wonder upon wonders, what a delicious thought.

Yet marriage also brought thoughts of Tom Ravenal, disappointment, and heartbreak. Marriage would bring great changes. Drum would want to live in Charlotte where Rutledge Timber was headquartered. She couldn't imagine the bigness of Drum, his power and energy, contained forever in the smallness of High Falls, North Carolina, or Madison, Florida.

Bry got up to chase a butterfly and nearby someone

whistled idly. At the sound of the tune, her heart pounded with joy, and then changed to quick beats of anxiety.

Relax, everyone whistles. But not this tune. Not this tune that was so very personal for her. This tune meant something to her, and she identified it immediately. "Whiskey on a Sunday." One of her father's favorite Irish ditties. She could hear him now, singing under his breath as he studied judicial decisions in his den, "drinking buttermilk all week long, I wish in me heart it was Sunday, whiskey on a Sunday."

Somehow it was disturbing to hear it here in High Falls. There seemed an arrogant taunting in the whistler's jaunty rendition.

The whistle came again. She stood up abruptly, and the mail fell at her feet. At her quick movement, Bry loped back to her. Sensing her discomfort, he growled and the hair on the ridge of his neck stiffened. People strolled into the village on the arched bridge above them, and down the creek diners enjoyed a late lunch on a restaurant deck that hung over the water. Any of them could have whistled the Irish tune. Her father wasn't the only Irishman in the world.

Inhaling deeply, she soothed Bry, smoothing his coat, and rubbing his ears.

"It's okay, buddy. It's okay." But was it?

She counted to ten, gathered her mail together and sat back down.

Her breath coming in short jerks, she tried to calm down as she quickly sifted through the rest of her meager mail. There was a postcard from Mausie telling Lannie that she was going to Gainesville to visit her sister for a while.

A note from Nell she saved until last.

Hi redheaded recluse,

You're going to love your maid-of-honor dress. It's beautiful. Sapphire blue, off the shoulder, long, sophisticated. You'll need to buy shoes in High Falls and send them to me so I can have them dyed. It won't be long now. Can't wait to see you. I know you're not looking forward to the attention your presence will bring after such a long absence, but it's time you rejoined the world of the living, Lannie. I love you.

The letter from Nell erased the odd anxiety she'd felt on hearing the Irish ditty, restoring the joy of the morning. She headed for Longfellow's, her step light and easy.

Longfellow's bustled with activity. Two summer employees stood behind the counter ringing up sales, while toward the rear of the store John Lamb seemed to be in serious conversation with Kent Shaw, the stage manager Spencer had hired several weeks ago. Shaw hiked one shoulder and jerked his chin to the side to make a point in the conversation. Something about the movement reminded her of someone, but she couldn't think who.

As she perused the shelves, she recognized several people she knew from her former life here, but kept her head low and was grateful for the big black sunglasses she wore. She'd learned how to fade into the background and enjoyed the anonymity she'd grown accustomed to. She wasn't ready to give it up yet.

"Hey, Lannie. Why didn't you let me know you were here?"

He'd appeared so quietly that she whirled around in surprise. "Oh, hi, John. You were busy so I'm just meandering, looking at everything. You know how one meanders in a bookstore."

"Yep." He scanned her face. "Something has put a new

twinkle in your eye. You must really be enjoying your volunteer work at the playhouse."

"I am. I'm even coming to the party at Drum's lodge Labor Day weekend."

An odd look crossed his honest features and frown lines creased his forehead.

"Something wrong, John? I thought you'd be happy about my reentrance to the world."

"I am, Lannie. Just very surprised." A strained smile puffed his cheeks. "Come to think of it, most of my fun will be watching the surprise of the other guests when they see you."

"Oh, dear, do you really think anyone will be that interested in me?"

He hesitated, then said, "I think you have to consider it a strong possibility."

A tide of rebelliousness surged from deep within her, a powerful elixir she hadn't experienced in years. "Hey, you know what, John? I don't care. I'm going to have a good time. I'm even going to wear a cocktail dress."

John laughed. "You, in fancy dress? I don't believe it."

"I am. I'm going to phone Nell right now. She'll send me something from home."

He pumped his fist in the air. "Yeah, go for it, Lannie."

She paid for her books and headed for the public telephone on the outside wall next to Thelma's Bakery. Large clay pots of red geraniums lined the walkway, and Bry stopped to sniff every one. He also stopped to sniff the picnic lunch of two ladies who sat on a green bench, the only other occupants of the quiet bypass.

"Oh, my," said one lady, frozen with fear. "He's the biggest dog I ever saw. Will he bite?"

"No, he won't. He's just very nosy, and a beggar to boot. Come, Bry."

The dog settled himself next to the phone booth, but

she kept the door open so she could call to him in case he should find the ladies' lunches irresistible.

"Nell, darlin', it's Lannie."

"Lannie, Lannie. I'm glad you called. I have so much to tell you. Hartley just left to go back to Washington, and I miss him big time. I never ever thought I could be so happy. Can't wait until you fall in love again."

For a moment, Lannie contemplated sharing her miraculous news with Nell, but decided to wait until the weekend of the wedding. She didn't want to give such grand news to her best friend over the telephone.

Nell bubbled on, and Lannie reveled in her friend's happiness, but finally got a word in edgewise.

"Nell, would you do something for me?"

"For you, pal, anything, short of giving you Hartley."

"I'm going to a party, and I need something to wear."

"Oh, my God! You're going to a party. I don't believe it. What is going on with you? Something has happened, I can tell from your voice."

"You're right, something has, but I'll tell you when I see you. Do you remember the silk jumpsuit I wore to the Florida Bar party in Tallahassee?"

"The party where all the men drooled over you, and I thought Tom Ravenal was going to challenge one of them to a duel? Sure, I remember it."

"Mausie's gone to Gainesville so I need your help. You've got a key to the house, or Big Billy will let you in. Would you get the outfit for me, the shoes and jewelry that go with and send them to me?"

"Absolutely. By the way, I hate to inject bad news into this happy conversation, but remember when I told you Jeb Bassert might be out of prison? Well, he is. Can you believe the governor pardoned him because of a mix-up in the DNA evidence?"

Lannie was stunned. "That's impossible. He's guilty. I hated sending a childhood friend to prison, you know that, but I proved he was guilty. Has he turned up in Madison?"

"No, no one has seen hide nor hair of him. It was always overly important to him to be accepted by everyone, so I don't think he'd want to come back here as an ex-con, pardoned or not. I went to visit Susie Slater to make sure he hadn't been victimizing her again. There was a notice posted on her door that she moved to Wisconsin, but she left no forwarding address."

"If he isn't bothering anyone, maybe we have nothing to worry about."

There was a long pause. Finally, Nell said, "I don't know. Something about it stinks to me. Gives me the shivers every time I think of that hideous scene in the courtroom as they were dragging him away, and he was screaming at you. He swore he'd get out and come after you, Lannie."

Furious at the news that her well-researched case and guilty verdict had been wiped out with the signature of the governor, Lannie's mind raced with all sorts of scenarios.

"I think I would know if Jeb Bassert was in High Falls, Nell," she said wryly. "He hasn't shown himself so far, and if he is after me, which I doubt, he will never find the cabin."

The thought of Jeb Bassert and his stubby legs trying to make his way to the summit of Haystack amused her, but her smile was short. She continued, "However, I'm damned angry they've released him. I'll come there as soon as I can to do some nosing around, but I can't leave now. *Our Town* opens this week at the playhouse and rehearsals start for *Chorus Line*. We just lost a valued friend and employee, and they really need me. I'll come when the season's over, right after Labor Day."

"I'm happy you're coming. Maybe you'll stay around long enough to attend a few bridal showers, after all, the wedding is in October. You can just spend a whole nice big lovely wonderful month in Madison with me."

Lannie laughed. "We'll see." She hated the thought of being away from Drum for any length of time and knew deep in her heart that her newly discovered love and reawakening was another reason she would stay here until the season was over. "In the meantime, if you're in Tallahassee, visit the criminology lab, and ask a few questions of the DNA staffers."

"Good idea, though you know DNA evidence is not my area of expertise. All this talk of Jeb and law and cases makes me say that I'm hoping you'll come back and practice law with me someday."

"Maybe. Someday. Love you, Nellie, girl. 'Bye."

Jeb slid hurriedly out of the recessed doorway of Thelma's Bakery and was on his way down the lane before Lannie hung up.

Son-of-a-bitch. His plans for Nell had just moved from back burner to front. He'd thought she would be so occupied with her wedding that she wouldn't be interested in Jeb Bassert and his whereabouts. Now, it sounded as if she might ask questions at the criminology lab. But Nell wasn't as smart as Lannie and the important clinical DNA data would be beyond her. Science and math had been her worst subjects in school. Lannie had tutored her in both.

Lannie had prosecuted and convicted him, but she'd gone back into private practice with Nell right after his trial. He had always been jealous of Nell and her relationship with Lannie, and when Lannie had renewed the law partnership, Jeb hated Nell. He knew her almost as well as he knew Lannie. Nell would pay close attention to anything that had to do with her best friend, but she'd never catch the changes Buster had made in the DNA data. Lannie would, but Lannie had said she wasn't leaving here until after Labor Day.

However, he didn't want Nell investigating his release too closely. He would have to visit her before she got too nosy. Buster's tweaking of the DNA evidence wouldn't stand up under close scrutiny, so he needed to eliminate any threat to his freedom and his quest to have Lannie as his own.

He remembered Susie Slater and the thrill of his new power.

"Yeah, Nell, I'll bet you're a bigger bang than Susie."

His mouth watered at the prospect of Nell, but he couldn't find it in himself to go back to Madison just yet. He'd take a chance and stay here for a while because his lifelong dreams were coming true. He could watch Lannie at his leisure, with no interruptions from Big Billy or anyone.

Thanks to the night he'd followed Drum's Land Rover through the rough brush, he knew how to find Lannie's cabin now, and he wouldn't give up the precious glimpses he stole of her from his perch in the paw-paw tree near the cabin. He visited Lannie every night when Drum Rutledge was in Charlotte. His high-powered binoculars zeroed right in on her window, and on lucky nights, when she disrobed near the window, he watched her at leisure, lusting at every movement, lusting until his mouth drooled and his hard-on ached. It took immense willpower not to let her know he was there with her, but it wasn't time yet. The compulsion to taunt her, make her suffer, was stronger at the moment than the urge to announce his presence.

She'll be damned glad to see me when I finally make my move.

And he still hadn't decided how to take care of the monster dog on the big night when he announced his presence. Learning how to outwit Bry had become his favorite dangerous game.

Lannie laughed as Bry leaped from the jeep, over the creek, and up the bank into the clearing. Bry was always happy to be back on the mountain top. As she climbed the bank, she heard him tearing around and around in front of the cabin, barking with joy.

She entered the clearing, books and mail in hand, and headed toward the cabin door. Bry had stopped running. He stood silent, rigid and at attention, the fur on his neck and back rising into stiff bristles, his nose lifted at an angle. He'd caught a whiff of something he didn't like at all.

Lannie glanced around the clearing and took a quick look inside the open cabin door. Nothing amiss that she could see. She wondered what had spooked the dog.

"Come, Bry. There's nothing here. If Mrs. Bear and her children were here, they're long gone now. They can smell you just as well as you smell them."

But he wouldn't come to her. He prowled the perimeter of the clearing, sniffing, and peering into the forest.

Lannie deposited her books inside the cabin door and sat on the stoop.

"Come on, Bry. Everything's okay, really it is."

His behavior made her uneasy. She glanced around again. The last of the sun lowered behind a far mountain and a beam caught something shiny in the grass next to the stoop. It flashed, unfamiliar and out of place.

What on earth?

She bent over and picked up a small two-inch-square chrome picture frame. The cheap frame held a sepia photograph of her and Nell taken in one of those five-and-ten booths when they were in high school. If she remembered correctly, it had been taken on a school trip to Orlando.

How odd, she thought. Has this been here ever since Nell visited? Couldn't have been. *I would have seen it before now.* And this couldn't belong to Nell. She would never buy a frame like this. Nell would have put the photo in a silver frame. Only the best for Nell.

Shadows lengthened around the cabin, and Bry moaned, then howled long, high, and mournful, as if he knew something she didn't, as if to warn her, as if he had a premonition that bad things were coming.

She stood and peered hard through the dusk. Now she felt what Bry already knew. Someone had been here. But that's impossible. Only Drum and Wilkie Talley know their way here. Drum's in Charlotte, and Wilkie Talley doesn't even know Nell.

The picture had to be Nell's. It was the only logical explanation. Yet she felt as if something, or someone, had been here.

She urged Bry into the cabin. With great reluctance, he stopped his search of the perimeter and came with her. For the first time since she'd lived in the cabin, she reached to close and lock the door, something she never did throughout the lovely summer days. She'd always slept with door and two windows wide open.

No, I won't close the door. There's no one out there, she insisted to herself. Nell lost this weeks ago, and for whatever reason, it just surfaced. Bry smells an animal.

Every sound, and every movement or whisper of the surrounding trees and night life, once so soothing to her, seemed magnified and threatening as she tried to settle herself into sleep.

Is something out there?

Eventually, she drifted into fitful sleep.

SEVENTEEN

Lannie tried to ignore the silent telephone at her elbow. Drum usually called about this time because he knew she would be in the theater office.

She corrected changes in the contracts just returned to them by the new leading man from New York. She'd discussed the additions with the actor and his agent, and both had approved the pertinent clauses. Along with taking over many of Mae's duties, she had found herself doing legal work for the company. The High Falls Summer Playhouse board attorney had returned to his home in Charleston, South Carolina, for a month. When Spencer discovered Lannie had passed the bar in North Carolina years ago, he pressed her into service.

She tidied up the papers and checked her schedule. Time to collect the youngest interns for rehearsal. She missed Mae. Not just her physical presence, but her common sense, her calm manner in the chaotic life of the theater, and her injection of quiet humor and dignity into the most menial of volunteer chores.

Spencer stuck his head in the door, a perplexed look on his freckled countenance. "Hate to bother you,

Lannie, but two unhappy young ladies are asking for you. They can't find their costumes and swear the boys hid them."

Spencer had taken Mae's death harder than anyone. He was quieter, but had opened up more to Lannie, as if he needed to communicate, or share, with someone. They'd established a comfortable friendship of sorts in the last few weeks.

"Tell them I'm coming, Spence." She delayed, glancing again at the phone. "I have to file these contracts and then I'll be there."

Ring, damn you, ring. The rest of her day would be spent away from the office and the phone. The portable telephone covered only the office and the back lobby.

Heart heavy, and shocked at how much her day rose or fell on Drum's calls, she closed the file drawer and started out the door to solve a teenage feud.

The phone rang. Her hand trembled as she jumped to pick up the receiver.

"Hello, High Falls Summer Playhouse."

"Hi, beautiful."

"Hi, yourself."

"Miss me?"

"Too much," she said.

He hesitated a beat, "Yeah. Me, too," he said softly, and her heart soared into overtime.

They talked of his latest rugby game, and the big deal he had going in Moscow, and of her skirmishes with choreographer Vince, her new legal duties at the playhouse, and her vegetable garden.

Tamara, a voluptuous and whiny seventeen year old burst through the open door, her face flushed. "Lannie, please come. Tom Mitchell hung our tights for the first scene on one of the backdrops and flew them way up in the grid. We can't get to them, and everyone is laughing at us."

"I'll be right there, Tamara."

Drum said, "Sounds like you're needed."

"Yes, I have to go."

"I need you, too, Lannie."

"When will you be back?"

"Friday morning. I'll have all day to help the set people get ready for *Chorus Line* opening."

Could she live until then? Live until she was in his arms again? What had happened to her? Her soul had unfolded and found space for emotions other than grief, guilt, and unending sadness. Within her was a lovely room welcoming the warm, wonderful rush of Drum. Each time she talked with him the new room she'd discovered filled with glowing light and hope.

Close the door, Lannie, don't hope too much.

But there was no stopping the filling, and the rush, and the glow.

"Lannie, are you still there?"

"Yes."

"I can't wait to get there. I won't be coming back to Charlotte until after Labor Day, so we have two solid weeks to be together."

"Hurry. I miss you." How badly she wanted to say "I love you," but they'd never said the words to each other.

Tamara ran in again, and Lannie said a reluctant goodbye, her hand rubbing the receiver as if it was Drum's hand.

The last board member left, closing the massive mahogany doors behind him, and Drum drew a sigh of relief.

He flipped his pen down the table and watched it roll aimlessly down the long polished table. Aimless, that's how he felt at the moment.

The short trips to Charlotte had become mandatory, and he hated being away from Lannie. The company had done quite well without him for a few weeks, as long as he kept in touch by phone and computer. But as his staff had reminded him, Rutledge Timber *was* Drummond Rutledge. He was the fuel that made everything go, no matter how much talent he'd gathered around him, they'd said, and headquarters needed an infusion of energy.

Several days of meetings, decisions, and a walk-through of several operations had been completed, and now he gave in to the hunger he staved off every day. With great pleasure he recalled the phone call this morning.

The sound of Lannie's voice had kept him going all day.

Ravenous. He was so ravenous for Lannie, so hungry for the feel of her, and so desolate without the sound of her laughter and the whisper of her words, that he hurt. And the hurt was worse than any pain he'd suffered from downing trees as a youth or pummeling players in a rugby game.

He loosened his tie, unbuttoned his stiff white collar and tilted his plump-cushioned leather chair back with another sigh. He swiveled the chair so he could see the large oil portrait that hung on the paneled wall behind him. Chip's face laughed at him, full of mischief, and delight, and the wonder of being five years old with his whole life ahead of him.

The portrait of Ann-Marie, which he'd had painted at the same time, was another story. It hung over the fireplace at his home outside of Charlotte. He knew how he felt about Ann-Marie, but he worried that it wasn't right, and he felt guilty about it.

Lannie had never asked questions and that bothered him. He'd made up his mind that when he returned to High Falls he would talk to Lannie about Chip and Ann-

Marie. He hadn't hidden the facts of his marriage, but neither had he talked about it.

Guilty. Guilty by sin of omission.

He remembered his conversation with his friends the Appleby's last night at dinner.

"Please come and visit in High Falls again soon. Your trip there for opening night of *Oklahoma!* and the rugby game was too short." He'd held his breath, and then said as casually as he could manage. "And I'd like for you to meet Lannie."

A short silence ensued.

"Does Lannie know about Ann-Marie and Chip?" asked Emily.

Just like Emily. Spoken quietly, but directly to the point.

"I'm sure she does. How could she not? Everyone else seems to, at least they always remember it when I become involved with someone. I wish people would mind their own business."

"Sorry, Drum. but I think you're making a mistake by assuming that Lannie knows. If she's the sensitive, caring person you say she is, wouldn't she have mentioned them to you by now? Remember, she's been out of circulation for a long time, and she lived in the Florida panhandle, which is not an area our crowd, or many Carolinians, visit or socialize in."

"Haven't seen you this worked up over a woman since you met Ann-Marie," said Hatch, "and even then there wasn't this huge excitement, this energy."

Emily stuck to her original point. "No matter how much in love someone is, an intelligent person would soon notice that the object of their affections has spoken little of his past. I would think that might bother her."

"Who said anything about love?" He frowned, annoyed

with Emily. "Lannie must know that I'm married and the story of Ann-Marie and Chip. That's why she doesn't ask, because she's had her own tragedies and senses that I'm not ready to talk about mine. I think she's afraid to ask. Like me, she doesn't want to know anything more, doesn't want to risk disturbing what we've already found."

But he was afraid, too, afraid to change the course of things, afraid to burst the buoyant bubble that he and Lannie floated in, afraid it would all end. Maybe he shouldn't bring the whole thing up. Maybe, as his mother used to say, he should let sleeping dogs lie.

Why, with all this happiness he'd felt the past few weeks, why had the alarm bells begun to clang, why this sense of doom?

Ridiculous. He shoved himself out of the chair and hurried to meet Hatch for a rugby practice.

Spence stood in the wings and watched Lannie run the chorus line through its last exercise. Several dancers were here from a professional company in New York to spend a working vacation in the cool North Carolina mountains. The others were college and dance students from all over the south, eager for the opportunity to work with Vince Patton, and be part of a Case-Keeting production.

"Gee, Mr. Case, you think Grandmother will let me do that when I'm in college?"

Spencer looked down. On the floor, at his side, sat an enthralled Daisy Bowden, elbows on knees, her chin resting on her fists.

Good God, he missed Mae. What was he doing here in the wings when he should be out front? Doing his job *and* Mae's, he thought, answering his own question. He was ashamed that he had never really appreciated all that she had done. Now he found himself dealing with twelve-year-olds, and he'd hardly spoken to a child since *he* was twelve years old.

If deaths happened for a reason, he'd discovered one of the reasons for Mae's: so that he would develop patience and empathy. To survive here without her, he needed both of them. He was slowly and surely learning and feeling better about himself.

"Will your grandmother let you dance and do summer stock? I don't see why not, Daisy." But he thought of Beezy and grimaced. Poor kid. "You have to work hard, though. Everyone on that stage has earned the right to be there."

"I'll work hard, Mr. Case, I'll work real hard. I want to be just like Lannie."

Spencer doubted if awkward Daisy would ever possess Lannie's grace, but her enthusiasm shouldn't be discouraged. *Oklahoma!* became an easy drill for the young girl. And though Daisy didn't have a part in the present production of *Our Town*, and there were no parts for youngsters in *A Chorus Line*, she still came to the theater every day. Spencer and Lannie gave her jobs to do and errands to run. Much to his disgust, he'd promised Beezy that he would bring her granddaughter home tonight.

The big New York director chauffeuring a twelve-year-old intern home. What had his life come to?

Don't be so hard on yourself, Case. Beezy Bowden's money pays your salary.

The *Our Town* cast had a deserved night off. Taking advantage of the "dark" night, the stage manager, Kent, had called an unplanned rehearsal for *A Chorus Line*, which opened on Friday. What was supposed to have been a quick run-through had turned into a full-fledged workout. It was running late because Vince had walked off in a fit of anger, proclaiming his artistic disgust with the troupe. After some confusion, Kent had insisted that

Lannie leave the costume sorting she was doing in Gavin's Garret and take over.

Kent watched from the opposite wing. Spence noticed that Lannie drew most of his attention, and he didn't blame Kent.

A wave of warmth swept through him as she waved to him. He saluted her back.

"Where's Bry?" asked Daisy. "He's never far from Lannie, but I couldn't find him tonight."

"Lannie doesn't like to bring him anymore. Won't tell me why."

"Seems funny without him." Daisy sighed. "Look at the neat leg warmers, Mr. Case. Cool. I'll bet Lannie knows where I can get some."

Jumping Jesu, did all twelve year olds chatter on so?

But then Spence tried to imagine the scene from Daisy's twelve-year-old point of view: the colorful, rumpled leg-warmers covering the dancer's legs from ankle to knee, the body-hugging leotards and rehearsal togs, the girl's ponytails whipping and bouncing around with their movements, the fluent, rhythmic muscles of the boys, the occasional shout of triumph when a difficult maneuver became a success, when a toe reached for and found its highest point.

Ah, yes, the magic and romance of theater. Who would understand it better than he?

Daisy wouldn't notice the beads of perspiration on the heaving chests and shoulders, or the grimaces of pain on foreheads, or the puffing grunts of stress and strain. To Daisy it all looked romantic and exciting. But it was damned hard work.

The sight of Lannie would be enchanting for Daisy. The sight of Lannie these days would enchant anyone, and Spencer loved looking at her, too.

Lannie had always walked with perfect posture, back and shoulders erect, and had always had a dancers' bounce in her stride. Now there was a lovely lilt in her walk, as if she floated on air. Every dance movement was vigorous and spirited as if she'd been inflated with new life. The haunted sadness in her eyes had been replaced with light and hope. Her face was animated and expressive. She laughed a lot, and didn't hide herself away behind a flat or in the prop room.

Lannie looked and acted like a woman in love, thought Spence. Envy gnawed and cut through him and rutted deep within him where he didn't know he cared.

Love should be complete, accepting, and without question, and I've never been willing to give that much of myself.

"Mr. Case?"

The gruff voice behind him startled him out of his self-observations about love and Lannie. He turned to find the new handyman. Though grateful to have him around doing things that had been neglected for years, he found Jack Edwards a bit disconcerting. His green eyes never blinked, and he constantly ran his fingers through longish white hair. A nice man, he decided, but he took getting used to.

"Mr. Rutledge asked me to sand the rough spots off the new attic door. I did, but noticed the light is still on. I wondered if Miz Sullivan was going back up there or should I turn off the light myself?"

"You still here, Edwards? You should have gone home long ago. Is Mr. Rutledge paying you by the hour?"

"Don't you worry none, Mr. Case. I don't mind the extra hours. He's payin' real nice, and I like being around here. Used to do a little dancin' myself," he said. He whistled a few bars of "The Sidewalks of New York" and did an awkward buck and wing.

Daisy giggled, then smacked her hand over her mouth to cover her rudeness. The man smiled at her and patted her on the head.

"That's okay, missy. You can't hurt ol' Jack's feelin's none. Ol' Jack jest loves you."

"I expect Lannie left the light on because she hasn't finished what she was doing up there. Ordinarily Lannie goes home early, so she might finish her work up there tomorrow. You would have to ask her, but I don't want her bothered while she's onstage. Ask Kent."

"He's gone home. He told me to tell you. Well, I have to get goin'. Wife's expectin' me. I'll let Miz Sullivan take care of the attic light." He removed his raggedy straw Panama hat, tipped it, and replaced it on his white head. "Jest remember, ol' Jack loves ya. Good night."

He heard Lannie say, "Okay, gang," and he resumed his close inspection of rehearsal.

Onstage, Lannie wiped her face with the white towel that was draped across her neck, and called out to her dancers. "You were wonderful. I want you to go to sleep tonight remembering that you're using your body as a tool for expression. You're creating small stories you can't verbalize, but need to visualize. See you tomorrow. I'll be working with you, or Vince will. Good night."

That's the difference between Lannie and Vince, thought Spencer. Vince yells, screams, and mortifies his dancers. Lannie, though demanding and exacting, praises and encourages.

As the dancers disbursed, Lannie walked into the wings and Daisy jumped up to hug her.

"Hey, Daisy sweet pea, how are things going at the Nature Center?"

"Neat. I'm a Junior Advisor. They let me take the five and six year olds on short hikes around the center."

"And the golf lessons?"

"Pretty good. I'm liking those more than I thought I would. The neat thing is that I've learned to fit it all in, and still come to the playhouse. I'm having the best summer I've ever had, and all because of you."

Lannie smiled. "It's not because of me, pal. You're just growing up."

"Lannie, Edwards said you left the light on in the attic," said Spencer.

"Oh, I haven't finished up there. What time is it, Spence? Is it dark outside?"

"Yes, and I'm telling you to forget about the attic light and go on home."

Lannie never wore a watch. She lived by her own time and rhythms. She never stayed for the midnight rehearsals either or kept the dancers late when she rehearsed them. Spence assumed it was because she didn't like driving her decrepit jeep late at night.

"When I'm dancing, time slips away so fast. Do you mind if I leave now?"

"Of course not. Except for the chorus line, everyone escaped early tonight. You get on home. Let's go, Daisy. Your grandmother will be spitting nails."

Lannie watched them walk away, then sat on a chair to catch her breath.

"Well, there's no need for hurrying or worrying now anyway," she muttered to herself, patting her chest with the towel. "It's already dark. I'll just have to drive like a snail."

She closed her eyes and enjoyed the complete silence in the empty theater. The memory of Drum's voice humming in her ear through the telephone receiver this morning wrapped around her like a comforting blanket, bringing her the new sensations she found so satisfying and exciting.

She felt like a different person. She saw everything differently. All of her senses had been instilled with fresh light, fresh shapes, and new perceptions. How had she ever lived without the life-giving oxygen provided by Drum? Physically, she'd become a tuning fork, sensitive to the slightest sensation of sound and feeling around her. Spiritually, his power, his energy, his supremely confident outlook on life infused her with new hope and endless possibilities.

He wanted to wine and dine her and introduce her to his friends in Charlotte. Yes, that would happen eventually, but not now. She wanted their small, private world to remain inviolate for a while. She wanted to keep the egg intact, to keep the shell from breaking and from leaking out the special enchantment with which they were encased.

A faint click somewhere backstage interrupted her reverie. Her eyes popped open. Probably the hot water heater, she thought. *Get up, lazy bones, and get going.*

The jeep was parked out back. She had to turn off the house and stage lights before she could leave. The big light board wasn't complicated, and she soon found the correct switches and pulled them.

Behind her, the front part of the theater now lay in blackness. Faint light from backstage cast murky, odd-shaped caricatures onto the stage, and for a panicked moment she felt as if she wasn't alone. The ghost lamp was her only company. The ghostly floor lamp, a single bare light bulb without lamp shade, stood sentinel on the naked stage. Traditionally, it burned to keep away bad spirits and was never turned off in any theater, but it always kind of spooked Lannie.

Then she laughed at herself. She was worse than Daisy. She turned and looked into the black hole of the stage and the auditorium beyond.

"Hey, demons, look at me," she yelled in childlike defiance. "I'm chasing you all away. You can't catch me anymore. I'm done with you."

The blackness mocked her with its still emptiness, and she was reminded again of what a shadowy, haunting old playhouse of a theater it was. As she turned away from the black void to walk to the backstage area, she bumped against a curtain, and its curling movement changed all the shadowy mirages into dancing specters on stage around her.

She stood for a magic moment, imagining all the actors and dancers who had worked so hard through the years to create enchantment on these boards. They swirled and whirled around her, singing, dancing, loving, laughing, bringing joy, breaking hearts, having their own hearts broken. Instinct told her they still lived here. After everyone was gone, and the theater was dark and quiet, perhaps they staged their own shows, and entertained one another. Though the ghostly images spooked her a little, it was fun picturing them, and feeling them dance about her.

Oh, such whimsy, Lannie. Yeah, but it's the kind of whimsy you would have suggested to Gracie. Believe in the possibilities, child. Believe in things above and beyond what you see. How wonderful, Lannie girl, to be able to think about Gracie and to dream without crying.

She passed the steps to Gavin's Garret. The light she'd left on showed bleakly through the crack at the bottom of the door. It seemed silly to leave it on and, though she had no flashlight with her, the new steps and handrail Drum had built were safe. She climbed the stairs two at a time, stepped into the attic, and yanked the cord that dangled next to the door. The door swung shut behind her, and she jumped.

She groped her way to the door and stepped back out

on the small landing. Shock gripped her as she hugged the nearby railing.

The whole building sat in blackness. Not a light anywhere. She wondered if turning off the attic light had triggered an electrical malfunction to the entire system. She remembered Drum's advice to always carry a flashlight with her because the playhouse was an old building in need of massive repair and anything could happen. How careless, Lannie, she scolded herself, but she hadn't planned on staying so late.

The barn-like doors to the rear of the loading area backstage should be open. The doors weren't far from the bottom of the steps, and she knew her way there by heart. Holding the handrail tightly, she descended the stairs. She took each step with great precision, placing a foot firmly before feeling for the next.

Reaching the bottom, she took a deep breath, stretched her arms before her and searched for the wall. She found the rough stuccoed surface with relief and inched her way along its length, encountering obstacles along the way: packing boxes, a leaning flat, the wooden Indian the teens threw darts at, but she maneuvered safely around them all, and finally felt the big wooden doors beneath her hands.

The doors should be open, but they weren't. She pushed, but they held. She searched for the heavy iron bar that held it shut. It was gone.

She shoved hard again, but the door wouldn't give. Someone had barred it from the outside. They probably hadn't realized she was still inside.

Don't panic, Lannie. Somehow, you'll have to make your way through the auditorium to the lobby and the front door.

She turned and faced the vast blackness that lay between her and the safety of the front door, the office, and the telephone. There were no windows in the building, so there wasn't a glimmer of light anywhere. Her pulse raced as fear started building. She discerned vague shapes here and there, but nothing identifiable. Her worst impediments would be the jumble of sets, equipment, and props placed helter-skelter backstage.

Move, Lannie, move.

Relying on memory and instinct, she extended her arms and moved forward, and immediately stumbled over something on the floor. She righted herself before she fell. Something warm brushed her arm. It felt like body warmth, as if someone stood right next to her. Her heart pounded. *Don't be silly, Lannie.* Probably one of those old dress forms with a costume hanging on it. Her stumble had caused the costume to sway and brush against her. But would a costume have warmth to it?

She shook her head and inhaled deeply. The exhale came weak and shaky, and she coughed nervously. The small sound echoed eerily throughout the high-ceilinged area.

She studied the possibility of finding the light board and testing all the switches, but the route was dangerous in the dark.

Find the wall, Lannie, and go from there.

She made slow progress, but eventually picked her way around large and small objects to find the long wall that would guide her through backstage, the wings, the house, and then into the lobby. The rough surface of the wall felt reassuring and safe, and she moved successfully along, cautiously maneuvering around objects she encountered.

Suddenly, she remembered the ghost lamp. It should be on. Surely it would be lit.

Her heart leaped with hope and relief and she stopped to try to get her bearings once more. The clicking sound she'd heard earlier came again. It couldn't be the hot water heater. The water heater was in a closet on the opposite side of the building. This sounded like someone flipping the lid up and down on a cigarette lighter.

No. No. No one is in here with me. But no matter what she told herself, her body and her senses signaled that she was wrong. Alarm bells rang throughout her shaking frame, her knees tingled and threatened to give way at any time.

Ah, here, here were the wings. The ghost lamp was off, too. Of course, it wasn't Aladdin's magic lamp. It needed power, too. Damn.

She would have to leave the wall now, and find the wings and the steps to the auditorium. She ventured further into the darkness, sliding her feet along the floor so she wouldn't encounter a quick drop when she found the first step.

"Lacey Gracie, dancing daisy, makes her mom a happy lady."

The whispery chant came from behind her. She screamed with shock. Fear socked her chest and sucked her breath. Someone playing a joke, and not a funny joke.

"Who are you? This isn't funny. Turn on the lights."

Silence, but she heard someone breathing.

How would anyone know the childish chant she had made up for Gracie? Was she losing her mind? Maybe she sang it idly as she worked sometimes. Sure. That was it.

"I said this isn't funny. One of us could get hurt moving around in the dark. Turn the lights back on," she ordered. "I promise I won't tell Mr. Case or Kent."

A whistle came then, soft and low. "Someone to Watch Over Me." Her favorite song. But who would know that, and who disliked her enough to taunt her this way?

"Stop this, whoever you are," she said, but her voice came out weak and shaky, and she hated that. It showed her fear and her vulnerability, which gave her stalker more power. She'd be damned if she'd speak again.

But she couldn't control her trembling and was sick with fear. From the bottom of her feet to the crown of her head, she shook. She sank to her knees and crawled, searching frantically for the steps.

The presence with her felt malevolent, black and dense with hate.

A shoe shuffled on the stage nearby. How did the man see so well without a flashlight? The white towel she'd thrown haphazardly around her neck, slipped to the floor and lay there, a pale speck in the blackness. With mounting horror, she realized that the white shirt she wore must also make an easy target for the tormentor. Should she take it off?

First she had to find the stairs, get off the stage, where she felt trapped. If she could get down into the auditorium, she would have more space to move and hide, maybe even get to the office and the telephone. She remembered the emergency exit on the wall halfway between the stage and office and hurried faster.

Like a rat scrambling and scratching in the dark, her palms and fingers scooted along the floor picking up dust and splinters along the way, and then found—sudden emptiness. Her upper body zoomed forward, her nose smacked against the top step, and she almost fell face down into yawning space below.

The steps. Thank God. One victory.

She scooted on her butt down the stairs, found the solid floor, stood straight, and in a panic, ripped off the white shirt and threw it behind her.

Not knowing that she would be running a rehearsal today, she hadn't worn a bra. Standing there half-naked made her feel even more vulnerable, but she wouldn't be such an easy target now. The nipples on her breasts stiffened with the sudden exposure, and she heard the man suck in a quick breath.

Oh, God. He could still see her, and now she was without her shirt. Where was he? Had he followed her off the stage? Was he close?

A frightened whimper escaped her, and she clamped her mouth shut so tight that her teeth hurt and her jaws ached.

A soft laugh came from . . . where? Where was he?

Move, Lannie, move.

The long expanse of wall to the front of the building should be directly to her right. She headed for it, bumped into a row of seats along the way, corrected her direction, and finally connected with the solid wall.

Running and stumbling over her own feet, her slippery hand sliding along the plaster surface, she made her way up the aisle. Fear jangled and clamored through every cell of her body. Nauseous, an icy film of perspiration covered her skin, and she shivered uncontrollably.

Halfway up the aisle, she encountered the emergency exit. *Thank you, God.* Her eager hands searched for the release bar and pushed. Locked. Oh, dear God, it was locked, too.

Suddenly, the house lights came on, harsh, glaring, exposing, and she felt like one of those prisoners of war caught and unveiled helplessly in a spotlight against the fence as they tried to escape.

She whipped around, but saw no one.

"Where are you, you coward?" she yelled.

Her eyes searched frantically around the auditorium, to the stage, center aisle, and the half-concealed lobby. Nothing. No movement. No sense that anyone was there at all. She was alone. The stalker had turned on the lights and left her alone.

Nausea, which had threatened her stomach since the lights had first gone off, hit her full blast. The bile erupted violently. Lannie hung her head and vomited where she stood. Emptied, her nose bleeding from the fall against the steps, her throat sore from the vomiting, she stared at the mess she'd made on the threadbare burgundy carpet in front of her.

Exhausted, she sank against the wall, welcoming its support. Dear God in heaven what had just happened? Things like this didn't happen in High Falls. Stalkers, rapists, evil people didn't exist in this pristine place. Or they never had before.

Tears came now. They poured down her face unchecked, falling cool on her bare, hot shoulders. She let them drip, then stared at the vile mess on the floor in front of her. She would have to clean it up, and call . . . who?

Drum was in Charlotte. Call Spencer? He was driving Daisy out to the country club, and besides, could she trust Spencer? He was the last one to leave the building, and he'd been acting odd lately, not like himself at all since Mae's death. No, that was ridiculous. She refused to believe that grumpy, eccentric, but beloved Spence would do such a thing.

Wiping the tears from her face with her palms, she thought of the phone calls Spencer had made recently, which he obviously didn't want her to know about. If she came into the office while he was on the phone, he would turn his back and whisper into the phone and then hang up quickly. Instead of letting her pick up the mail, which she had done since Mae's death, Spence insisted he would go to the post office, and then went through the mail eagerly, as if he looked for something he didn't want her to see.

She leaned weakly against the precious supporting wall behind her while her mind shot everywhere with possibilities. Kent Shaw, the new stage manager or the handyman Jack Edwards or one of the volunteers from town?

No. She had to face it. This was some sickie who knew her, who knew her habits, who knew her fears. Why hadn't he stayed to do her harm? And who knew her that well in High Falls? No one.

Reluctantly, her mind reached back for the phone conversation with Nell. Jeb Bassert was out of prison. Could he have arrived in High Falls without her knowledge? Sure, but Jeb knew nothing about theaters, or lights. He wouldn't know a backstage from an arena, and Jeb seemed incapable of the hating evil she'd felt with her tonight. Until she'd prosecuted him for raping Susie Slater, Jeb had always seemed a clumsy, somewhat annoying, but innocuous admirer.

He's been in prison nine years, Lannie, she reminded herself. He could have stoked a heap of resentment and learned a lot about how bad people torture those they hate.

But I would know Jeb on sight. I would have seen him around, especially if he'd been in the theater.

She shook her head wearily and glanced once again around the deserted theater. Spotting her white shirt on the floor near the stage, she retrieved it and shakily slipped it over her head. Next, as if she needed physical activity to release her lingering fear and anxiety, she found supplies, mop, and fixed a bucket of hot water and soapy suds to clean up the mess she'd made when she'd vomited.

Finally, she sank thankfully into the chair in the office and lifted the phone to her ear. Thank God, a dial tone. She punched in the number of the town police. A recorded message informed her that, unless this was an emergency, would she please be kind enough to call back at seven the next morning. Was it an emergency, she asked herself? Not now. She knew instinctively that, whoever her stalker had been, he'd had only meant to frighten her, and he wouldn't be back tonight. She would talk to the police in the morning.

The High Falls constabulary were a laid-back bunch. Unaccustomed to major crime concerns, they took good behavior for granted, and except for the occasional jailing of a liquored-up mountaineer or a pot-smoking teenager, had little to do but play poker in the fire house with the volunteer fire department.

But she needed to talk to someone and dialed Drum's number in Charlotte. The signal rang over and over in her ear, then the answering service picked up. She couldn't relay to Drum what had just happened through a third party. "Hello, are you there, ma'am? Was there a message for Mr. Rutledge?"

"No, no. Just tell him Lannie called."

Huge disappointment filled her. Unable to hold her head up any longer, she dropped her forehead flat against the desk. With her nose pressed against the smudgy, ragged, green blotter, she sobbed tears of fright, release, and loneliness.

Finally, still shaken, but empty of tears and exhausted, she raised her head and blew her nose. It was probably just as well. Drum would be worried sick about her and too protective. She didn't want to be protected, and she didn't want her freedom restricted. She would tell him, but she would downplay the whole episode.

Trying to ignore haunting images created by light and shadow, she hurried through the lobby and out the front door. She commanded her knees to hold forth, to get her to the jeep, and to get her home.

She'd stopped bringing Bry because he'd been getting sick again, and the only way she knew how to really protect him was to keep him away from the mean-spirited dog hater who was trying to poison him. But she decided then and there that she would never go anywhere without him again. She would just have to keep a closer eye on him and what he ate. She had bought him for companionship, not protection, but he performed bodyguard duties instinctively.

Bry was her best friend. If anything ever happened to Bry, she knew she would just give up.

EIGHTEEN

Bry growled and lifted his head. He lay next to the door, one eye on her and the other on the open door that revealed the theater lobby. Her heart leaped several beats, and her fingers froze on the computer keys.

No, dammit, I will not live in fear.

Bry relaxed and so did she.

"Lannie! What are you doing here? I thought you'd be at the cabin."

Drum's voice, though imperative and angry, infused her with joy. She whirled around from the computer, where she was working on last-minute changes in the playbill for *Chorus Line*'s opening tomorrow night.

"Drum. You weren't supposed to be here until tomorrow."

She jumped from her chair, ready to fling herself into his arms, but stopped midway across the office, shocked at the look of him.

"What on earth is the matter? Are you sick? You look terrible. You're pale as a sheet."

He took two giant steps to meet her, and with one demanding reach of his arm, pulled her into his sheltering body and held her so close she found it hard to breathe.

"Thank God, you're okay," he said roughly. "Your phone call this morning scared the bejesus out of me."

"Yes, I'm fine, but you're scaring me a bit. You didn't have to rush here to rescue me. How did you get here so fast?"

Late afternoon light filtered through the slatted blinds on the office windows, casting narrow slanting shadows on the floor and across their bodies.

"The helicopter. Someone's driving my car up for me. You should have gone back to the cabin after you called me this morning." He set her away from him, holding her hard by the shoulders. "Let me get a good look at you."

His navy blue eyes, sharp with worry, inspected her keenly.

"Drum, he didn't touch me. I'm okay, really I am."

"He didn't touch you but he terrified you, and the next time he might not be able to resist touching you." His face grew even paler at the thought, and he drew her to him again. "You're coming to the lodge to stay with me. I don't want you alone one minute."

Just what I was afraid of. She smiled against his warm chest. "Thank you, kind sir, for your offer of protection, but I can take care of myself. After I called you, I talked with the town police, and with Spencer. The police are on the lookout for any known deviants who might be in the area, and Spencer insisted that they assign a deputy to the theater for the rest of the run. That's only two more weeks."

"Not good enough for me, sweetheart. I want you with me."

And, oh, how I want to be with you, but not for this reason, not on these terms.

She felt her stubbornness kick in, felt her well-earned fight for sovereignty, for freedom from emotional dependency swell up and muscle everything else out of the way. She pushed away from him and stepped back.

"No. I don't want anyone worrying about me. I don't want anyone watching out for me. I have Bry, and I'm safe at the cabin. If you care for me, Drum, you'll have to leave me alone."

A grim smile etched its way slowly across his set jaws. "Sorry, can't do that, sweetheart. If you won't stay with me, let me come to the cabin."

"No." As important as he had become in her life, she wasn't ready for permanent intrusion on her life with Bry on the mountain top. "I can't explain it to you, Drum, but I'm just not ready for that yet."

"Lannie, I wouldn't be moving in as a lover. I would be staying with you as a friend, for your safety."

"We'll be together a lot, Drum, as we have been all summer, but I haven't finished healing yet, and I need to do it on my own. I'm almost there, I'm almost well again, ready for another stab at life, but I need to *know* that I can survive by myself without anyone's help."

He sighed. "I can see you're determined. Okay, but you can be damned sure I'm not going to let you out of my sight for long. If you didn't have Bry there with you, I'd move in with you or carry you to the lodge bodily, in spite of your protests."

"It was just a passing stranger, Drum, curious about lights on at the playhouse late at night, I'm sure of it." She knew if she told Drum about Jeb Bassert he would really flip out. "The slime ball saw me there alone and decided to have a little fun."

He brought her to him again, and kissed her long and deeply, kissed her until her toes tingled and her knees turned to water, and she leaned against him weakly and gratefully. She demanded independence, but it was heaven knowing he was there for her anyway.

"Promise me you'll keep Bry with you always," he said into her hair.

"I will, I promise." He kissed her again, and when she finally got her breath, she laughed and asked, "We're not going to have one of our mad, impromptu sex scenes here in the office, are we?"

"I'm at your beck and call, madam," he smiled, murmuring the words against her lips.

"Ahem, excuse me. Sorry if I'm interrupting something, but I need to make a phone call." Spencer's gruff voice sounded from the office doorway.

Drum gave her a quick squeeze and turned to Spencer. "Come on in, Spence. I think the lady's ready to call it a day, and I'm planning a romantic dinner for two."

"Yeah, well, sounds good to me. Glad you're back, Drum. We're going to need you for *Chorus's* opening tomorrow night."

Lannie gathered her sweater and lunch bag, motioned to Bry, and said, "See you in the morning, Spence."

Except for voices from the ticket booth area, and an occasional shout of laughter from backstage, the building was quiet. Most everyone had gone home exhausted after a somewhat energetic dress rehearsal. *Chorus Line* was improving, thought Spence, and it just might save their season. It was improving and he knew why.

He remembered a day at the beginning of the summer when he'd yelled at all of them, "Go, leave, get out, forget about everything you've worked on this past week. Maybe you'll have some flash of brilliant insight as to why this production lacks energy. Maybe, by the grace of a charitable God, you'll come back ready to perform like the troupers you're supposed to be."

"Really, Spencer, must you be so sadistic? We're working our sweet asses off here, and your wee tiddly-widdly heart just doesn't appreciate it," Vince had replied.

Spence winced remembering how his fist had balled wanting to sock the impossible, cocky little twit. He'd wanted to fire Vince and put Lannie in charge, but thank God he hadn't. Lannie had added the verve and creativity that he'd been looking for, but with Mae's passing he'd needed Lannie as more than a choreographer, and despite his dislike for Vince, the guy did work hard.

His growing interest in Mae, his grief when she died, and his envy of Drum and Lannie, had made him realize how empty his life was and had given birth to his own epiphany. He'd finally acknowledged the awful emptiness in his gut, the kind of emptiness a gambler feels when he bets the whole pile and watches the dealer sweep it away.

One year after another, he'd built his life on his work, on Broadway, with all its glamour, joy, and heartaches, but in the end, it hadn't been enough. Watching Drum as he'd held Lannie just now, their passion burning like blazing light all around them, lighting up the room and the whole theater, Spence affirmed once again his own desires.

He'd felt that gigantic overwhelming passion only once in his life, when he was still young and fearless. The young actress, with whom he'd spent his first turbulent years in New York, went on to make a name for herself and left him for a screen idol in Hollywood. Julia Jane had rescued him, giving him physical satisfaction, a companionship based on shared friends and theater interests, and a lively intellect to bounce ideas off of.

He'd been taking himself too seriously this summer. Things had picked up after the picnic, but still weren't what they should be. Julia Jane had always said people had to have fun sometimes or life wasn't worth much. They needed laughter, energy, sparkle. Until recently, he'd been too introspective, felt too sorry for himself to think of anyone else.

But Julia Jane had left, too, with that pimply faced jerk who waited on her hand and foot. He'd shrugged off the notion that loneliness had anything to do with his failing directing abilities or that not having Julia Jane at his side had affected his work in any way . . . until now.

The great Spencer Case had finally caved in and admitted that he needed Julia Jane Howard. He'd heard that Julia Jane had discarded the young film idol in Hollywood. Spence had located her back in New York. They'd talked several times in the last few weeks. His decision to contact her had already made a noticeable difference in his attitude toward cast and crew. Everyone worked more cohesively and with more energy and desire. Rehearsals were jelling, and the present *Our Town* production had taken on the mystical quality it needed.

His hand hovered with indecision over the telephone, then dropped in his lap. He sank back in the desk chair and stared at the out-of-date black rotary phone. It stared back, mocking him, daring him to pick up the receiver.

The rest of his life depended on this call, on his persuasive abilities, on Julia Jane's true feelings for him. He needed her. Would she come?

He picked up the receiver.

"Daisy, this is a lot of fun, but I still think it's creepy up here. I feel like someone's watching us." Jennifer pulled a lacy white cotton camisole over her head, folded it neatly, and placed it on top of a growing pile.

"Don't be a total dork, Jennifer. Lannie says that whole Gavin's Garrett thing is nonsense. The older interns like to scare us. *Chorus Line* opens tomorrow, summer's almost over, and she needed help putting away all the costumes used in *Oklahoma!*, *Our Town*, and *You Can't Take It with You*."

"You didn't even ask her. You just got it in your head to come up here and do this so you could impress her."

"No. We're doing this because we love her. It was your idea to try on some of the costumes."

"Yeah, but now I feel weird." Jennifer shivered, and wrapped her arms around her bare chest. "Don't you feel it? Don't you feel eyes looking at you?"

"You're crazy, Jen. Here put your shirt back on if you're so self-conscious." Daisy tossed her friend a striped red T-shirt. Jennifer hugged it to her chest. "You know there's no one here. We walked down every aisle and poked our broom into everything."

"Okay, okay. I just feel funny, that's all."

"Ohhh, Jen, look. Laurie's wedding dress from *Oklahoma!* Don't you want to try it on?"

Jennifer dropped her T-shirt and squealed. "Oooo, yes, give it to me."

Daisy handed Jennifer the dress and worked her own pudgy twelve-year-old body out of the flapper sheath she wore. "Give me that dumpy old red bathing suit you put on the Twenties pile. Can you imagine our grandmothers wearing these things?"

The wedding dress had slipped rakishly over Jennifer's thin shoulders, the cap sleeves falling to cover her skinny elbows, and, like a balloon losing air, the bathing suit drooped awkwardly to Daisy's knees. They stared at each other, then broke into spontaneous giggles. The giggles turned into hooting laughter, and tears of fun ran down their cheeks.

It became a game then, the trying on of costumes, as each one tried to outdo the other in their choice of hilarious outfits. Everything else was forgotten.

∘ ∘ ∘

Oh, God, how had he gotten himself into such a position? He should never have let Jeb Bassert blackmail him. He should have just 'fessed up to his past and faced the consequences.

But his fear of exposure had made him weak, and he'd succumbed to Bassert's threats. Now here he was in an attic closet watching two nymphs dress and undress and getting the thrill of his life. At Bassert's request, he'd researched the history of the playhouse building's physical layout back to its days early in the century as the county high school.

When the deserted building was rescued in the 1940s and turned into the summer theater playhouse, the costume attic had been added. On the original plans he'd discovered a closet, presumably used as a sewing room for the wardrobe mistress. Through the years, as money and support for the theater program dwindled, funds for a wardrobe mistress became nonexistent, and the closet was filled with assorted unusable memorabilia. Eventually, the door was blocked and disappeared with a growing accumulation of costumes. Finally, all those living who ever knew the small room existed, died and the room was forgotten.

He and Bassert had searched for, and uncovered, the closet-like room together. Bassert had been elated at this small treasure laid in his lap. He suspected Bassert was excited because it gave him an opportunity to watch Lannie while she worked up here.

To satisfy his curiosity, he'd come back this afternoon when no one should have been around and inspected the closet. Sure enough, he found the space half emptied of junk and two rectangular spaces cut through the wall at eye level. A quick perusal through the apertures showed that Jeb had artfully cleared away costumes to expose the front of the attic where the girls now worked and another toward the center. The trick had been to keep the closet door covered. Jeb had done that by moving a rack of eighteenth-century male dress jackets in front of the door. He could come and go at will, the jackets swinging back into place after his entrance or exit.

The girls had come in as he'd been about to leave, and he'd stepped quietly back into the closet. The urge to watch them as they chattered and worked had been impossible to defeat. He hated Jeb Bassert, and the dirty compulsion Jeb's blackmail had encouraged him to give into once again, a compulsion he'd thought he had under control.

He sucked in his breath, as he watched Daisy yank the old bathing suit off her young body, her developing breasts bobbing gently with the effort.

The only thing Jeb hated about the mountains in western North Carolina was the cold weather. He knew the chill in the air was nothing compared to the bitter cold that winter would bring. He'd take the smothering Florida heat any day.

He'd adjusted to everything he'd encountered since he'd left prison in Florida, and he would adjust to the weather. His expertise in woodland survival was second to no one. He'd taken to it like a duck to water. He'd pit himself against any militia type he might encounter and come out the superior of any, even the reptilian dude sitting across from him

He used his teeth to tear off the last piece of roasted squirrel meat. Tasted like the thigh of a chicken. He liked it.

"Mighty good, mighty good," he said to the man across the fire. "Sure you don't want some?"

He held the bone up and waved it back and forth in front of the man's nose, taunting him with the meaty aroma.

The man's cold eyes never left Jeb. He rarely took his eyes off Jeb, but he couldn't speak because Jeb had stuffed his mouth with one of his discarded handkerchiefs.

They sat deep in a cave in a remote region of the mountains. Jeb had come upon the cave by accident yesterday, and exploring it, found that someone occupied the chilly cavern.

He'd hidden and watched the shelter entrance all afternoon. The occupant had returned to his hidey-hole cautiously, as he scouted the area for intruders. But he'd not spotted Jeb, which was a matter of high pride for Jeb. Instead of killing him on the spot, Jeb had come from behind, slipped a noose around his neck, knocked him out, and dragged him into the cave.

He'd bound his wrists and ankles with wire and propped him against a wall. The hairy, bearded man had wakened soon after. His anger-filled eyes had never left Jeb, as Jeb moved about the cave organizing his supplies in the space previously used by the other man.

Jeb tore another shred of meat from the squirrel carcass. He looked at the man and smiled.

"Very thoughtful of you. This cave is just what I need, and you've got it so well supplied that I don't have to go into High Falls for every little thing." It was a perfect location for him to camp while he watched Lannie. "Someone might get nosy, you know? Looks like you've been here for a while."

He stopped chewing and studied the glaring man. "I've seen your ugly face somewhere. A wanted poster in the post office? No."

He reached over and lifted the man's long, ratted, and

bushy beard. He dropped his squirrel in the fire and played with the beard for a moment, laughing as he looped it up around the man's ears, then tied a knot in it, and stuffed it into the man's mouth along with the cloth.

"Should shave more often, pig, and you should take a bath. You smell like a winter bear who's been messin' in a garbage pile. 'Course, I smell the same way when I smear bear shit all over me to fool that damn dog of Lannie's. Smart, that dog. He's almost caught me a couple of times, but I've learned to stay upwind of him. He knows something is around, but can't figure out where or what it is."

He kicked the man's ankle and delighted in the quick grimace of pain it produced. "Yep you should take a bath. Lannie's got a real nice place to shower. I've used the falls myself a time or two. I tell ya, dude, I wouldn't let you around my girl. Lannie ain't afraid of nothin', but she sure wouldn't like the way you smell. Phew, enough to make someone want to puke."

Suddenly, he thought he knew who the dude might be. "Yeah," he said, squinting his eyes. "Yeah. Maybe this will do it."

He yanked the handkerchief out of the man's mouth and began to hack at his beard with his knife. Blood dripped from the man's nicked cheeks and chin by the time Jeb had finished. Jeb ignored it and held the man's shoulder-length hair away from his face so he could get a good look.

"Yep." He grinned, hugely satisfied with himself. "I seen your picture in Jesus survivalist camps, Danny. Man, you are a big, numero uno hero there. Robbed a bunch of banks and sent a shitload of money to local militias. They really love it that you ain't been caught. They use you as an example. Be damned if they don't worship you."

He wiped his hands on his pants and picked up the squirrel to finish his meal.

"By God, I wish I could tell the world that Jeb Bassert caught the man the FBI, and every other goddamned law agency, has been huntin' for three years. Danny Kehoe, famous bank robber, and you killed a couple of bank guards, didn't you? You were the best until you met up with me."

A warm glow filled his crotch as he thought of Lannie. He tossed the stripped bone into a far corner, drew his legs up, and caught his knees with his arms. " 'Course I look different than I did when we was young, me and Lannie. My girl spent half the summer with me and never knew it. I want to surprise her. She'll get a kick out of how I fooled her. Lannie has always had a good sense of humor."

Red ants, as big as Jeb's pinkie nail, had found their way to the pile of squirrel bones, and Jeb watched them with great interest. "Look how organized them ants are. They got a good leader. Never leave anything to chance. Just like me. I finally found where Lannie is. Went to Franklin Courthouse and looked through deeds and titles. Took me two days, but I found it."

He moved the pile of greasy bones, dumping them into Danny Kehoe's angled lap, then took a bone and smeared its remains over the man's nicked, patchy cheeks. The ants changed course and marched toward Danny.

Jeb said nothing for a while, fascinated with the line of ants marching determinedly on Danny's awkwardly bound legs. Jeb wondered for a moment if he'd broken the man's ankles as he'd angled them to sit properly, but then forgot about it as a column of ants broke rank and followed the scent of grease up Danny's body to his face.

"I knew it was near Rutledge Timber land, 'cause I followed her that way one day and saw the sign at the dirt road."

The ants covered Danny's cheeks now, and Jeb saw the first flicker of pain and defeat in the man's glaring eyes. The warm glow in his crotch grew hot. Nothing turned him on as much as someone else's pain.

"Sorry about the ants. They like the taste of grease. I always say let nature have its way. Anyway, I found the Sullivan place on an old deed right square in the middle of Rutledge property, about twenty acres on top of Haystack. Then one night I followed them to her cabin. I wanted to kill him, but that would really have spooked her, and I want her off-guard for a while." A sudden thought caught him with alarm. "It really ain't that far from here. You ain't been spyin' on Lannie, have you?"

It seemed like the man wasn't listening now. Ants had crawled into his eyes. Jeb reached over and wiped them away. "Hey, pay attention. Nobody never paid attention to me until I went to prison. Now they sure sit up and take notice. You ain't been foolin' around with Lannie, have you? No, you ain't man enough."

The whites of Danny Kehoe's eyes had turned tomato red. He tried to close his lids, but it was useless. They were swelling, and soon would fit down over the mucous membrane anyway, trapping some of the ants between lid and pupil. The bottom half of his face crawled with them. In a feeding frenzy, they had filled in the white patches on his cheeks where Jeb had torn at the skin with his knife. What appeared to be a curly red beard was a mass of swarming ants. They'd eaten almost to the bone in a spot near Danny's chin.

The tormented man jerked and bucked in agony, and a thin whining wail came from somewhere inside of him.

"I think maybe I'll set you outside the cave for the time bein'. I don't want them things comin' after me when they're finished with you."

Gingerly, he hooked a finger in Kehoe's collar and yanked him to a spot near the cave's entrance.

When he had finished placing him just so against a tree trunk, he brushed his hands of ants, and said, "Sorry about this. I'm sure you coulda taught me a lot, but I can't trust no one, not even a Jesus survivalist's hero. It may take you a while to die, but I'll come back to give you a proper burial. I owe my survivalists buddies that much. Gotta go now. Gotta see what Lannie's doin' today."

NINETEEN

The great room in the lodge buzzed with theater talk, country club gossip, and High Falls hearsay. Drum was pleased with the successful mix of people. It was Labor Day weekend, the end of the summer playhouse season, and the closing of *Chorus Line.* A time for new beginnings, he thought. Certainly, the silent, empty, rough-hewn old lodge had come to life tonight.

Ann-Marie had never liked parties. Her fragile, angelic beauty, and quiet smile attracted attention most women would die for, but Ann-Marie was shy.

When they had married, he had thought that his love would bring her out of her shell, that she would blossom from the attention his friends gave her, but she was happiest when they were alone together. That was fine with him at the time. He understood her need for solitude, but he wondered now if her obsessive desire for only his company, and that of a few very close friends, would have stood the test of time.

"Hey, Rutledge, nice party. We never have gotten in that game of tennis."

Taylor Goddard slapped him on the back. Drum

refrained from cringing, not from the slap, but from Taylor's presence. He'd had to endure the vacuous man's over-friendly gestures in the carpenter shop weekly. *Be nice, Drum. He's been a faithful volunteer.*

"Yeah, well, all my extra time has been spent repairing this house."

"When are you going to get active at the club again?"

He'd never been "active" there. It was handy for an occasional game of golf or tennis. They had joined so Chip could use the swimming pool.

"I don't know that I will, Taylor. My work here is about done, and I have to get back to Charlotte."

He could tell the man was settling in for a long conversation about golf, tennis, and juicy scandals from the club, and he searched for an excuse to get away. Spencer Case sat in one of the leather wing chairs by the fireplace stoically smoking his pipe, his eyes closed.

"Nice to have you here, Taylor, but would you excuse me for a moment? I have to discuss something with Spencer."

Drum made his way through the crowd toward Spencer, glancing only once at his watch. Lannie had again promised to be here before dark. She had a few more minutes. Dusk was fading, and soon his guests would be on the deck admiring the sunset.

"Spencer, anything suspicious at the playhouse? Everything okay?"

Spencer opened his eyes, looked at him through a haze of blue smoke, and smiled. Spencer rarely smiled, but when he did his face lit up like a crinkly paper lantern. He'd seemed happier the last two weeks than he had all summer. Drum figured Spence's new attitude, and the improved performances of the entire cast and playhouse, were a direct result of two trips the crusty director had made to New York recently.

"Yep. Everything's cool, Drum. They pulled the town policeman away from us. I guess there have been some burglaries, and the chief needed him at one of the ritzy golf developments outside of town."

"I know, and I don't like it."

"The chief said *if* Lannie's story was true, the stalker was probably long gone."

"They don't believe her?"

"Nope. They think we theater folk a bit weird, you know."

"Damn. I can't be with her all the time, and I'm worried."

"Don't be. I really think the smarm-ball is gone."

"Okay, I'll try to have a good time tonight. Anything I can do for you, Spence?"

"Yeah, let me sit and enjoy my pipe, keep Beezy Bowden away from me, and don't say one word about *A Chorus Line.* I'll be damned if the thing wasn't a hit. I don't want to wake up in the morning and discover if I've been fooling myself."

"The men we hired helped smooth operations, and you seem to have a lot more oomph lately."

"Yeah, well, nothing would have gotten off-ground if it hadn't been for you and Lannie . . . and Mae, God rest her soul. As for me, yeah, I have a new source of energy." He grinned again, and Drum saw happiness in Spencer Case's face for the first time since he'd known him. "And Kent Shaw and Jack Edwards have been invaluable."

"Thanks for letting me borrow Jack Edwards for the evening. He's been a godsend helping Mrs. Chambers get the house ready."

"Hey, you're paying his salary at the playhouse, you can use him anytime you want. He's handy at just about anything."

Spencer's eyes widened as he looked at something behind Drum.

"Well, I'll be damned and double damned."

Drum turned. Lannie had just entered, with Bry two steps behind her. She hesitated for a second inside the doorway, but then, in a gesture he'd never seen before but sensed was second nature to her, she lifted her chin and stepped into room as if she owned it. As far as Drum was concerned, she did.

Lannie shimmered, cool and elegant. The easy flowing pant legs of her emerald silk cocktail pajamas rippled sensuously as she walked. Two wisps of the silky fabric covered her breasts in halter fashion, and were caught at the back of the neck with a rhinestone clasp. The long matching scarf, tied in soft folds around her waist, floated behind her like a lackey following with a banner.

With the huge dog at her side, Lannie looked like Diana, the huntress, goddess of the forest.

She spoke to Bry, motioning for him to go back out the double-doored entrance to stay outside. Bry refused, lying down right inside the doorway of the great room.

Chatter stopped and, except for isolated pockets of conversation, a wave of silence rolled across the great room. Her observers instinctively respected the dignity of this restrained redhead, and Drum knew they had no conception of the volcano that dwelled within. Lannie smiled, spoke to a few people, but her eyes combed the crowd. He knew she searched for him.

Comments sifted to him through the murmurs, as the fascinated crowd caught its collective breath.

"My God, it's Lannie Sullivan. God, she's as butt-bustin' gorgeous as ever."

"Do you believe this? I mean, she just appears all of a sudden like she's never been gone. Where the hell has she been, anyway?"

"Someone said she's been spotted around town once or

twice, or someone who looks like her but dresses like a derelict, and always has that hound with her."

"I saw Tom Ravenal in Atlanta last week. Honey, he looks like something my retriever dragged in. Since he left Lannie, he married again and divorced. Says that leavin' Lannie was the biggest mistake of his spoiled sorry life."

Stunned, Drum stared like everyone else.

Somehow, he'd thought that Lannie would look like she always had, wildly beautiful, but carelessly put together, her hair flying in disarray, her nose spotted with paint, her hands dusty and spotted with blood from pinpricks gotten while fitting costumes. Somehow he'd thought there would always be the paint to kiss off her nose, the hair to smooth back from her face, the hands to doctor with salve and Band-aids.

His mountain girl was not a mountain girl, but a woman of the world. This was the Juilliard graduate, the attorney with a Columbia University degree hanging on her law office wall, this was the daughter of Judge Wexford Sullivan of Madison, Florida. The pride he felt for her was shadowed for a moment with a twinge of regret. The other Lannie belonged only to him. This Lannie might turn her attentions from him to worldly interests and would certainly be wooed by other men. Their private world, their fragile bubble had been broken.

But he'd always known that their Eden wouldn't last forever, and here was Lannie, so beautiful, and so confident and glowing that he wanted to crow with a sense of ownership that he hadn't the right to feel . . . and he fell in love all over again.

This was Lannie the queen, from the emerald ribbon she'd woven through the French knot on the crown of her head to the fragile silk slippers she wore.

Yes, his guests had coaxed the lodge to life, but the

heart of it had now entered. He knew she belonged here like he knew he had ten fingers and ten toes. Lannie Sullivan belonged here. The hollow hole in his heart that he'd tried to fill with work, rugby, carpentry, and a woman from time to time began to fill.

"Well, as I live and breathe, child, where have you been? Ah been wonderin' if you let the Ravenals just chew you up and spit you out like sour grits." Beezy Bowden's claxon voice rang across the heads of the crowd. "Good God, I'll bet you're the good-lookin' redhead Taylor Goddard says he's been seein' at the playhouse."

Lannie blanched and faltered briefly, then lifted her chin higher and smiled at Beezy. Drum kicked himself for standing and staring at her like everyone else. He headed toward her, but someone came to her rescue before he could reach her. John Lamb appeared at her elbow, and her smile widened and lit up the room.

Drum could see that they were engaged in conversation, heads tilted toward each other, laughing. Jealousy surged through him so brutally and swiftly that his knees felt boneless. People spoke to him as he passed by them, but they seemed in a dream, nebulous and distant, their voices wavery and inconstant. His focus was on Lannie, and he knew without a doubt that she had become the most important thing in his life.

When he reached her, he heard John Lamb say, "I told you that you'd make an impact. It's been like Venus rising out of the east, or something."

Drum's jealousy grew. When had the bookseller and Lannie talked? Did they talk often? He knew it was foolish, and typical of a man who has just fallen madly in love, but he liked to imagine that she talked only to him.

Lannie laughed. "Hardly, John. I suppose their curiosity is well-taken, though. I do know most of them, and the last story they remember about me is Gracie's passing and Tom leaving me, and then I disappeared. Out of sight, out of mind."

Drum took her by the elbow, and said, "Not out of my sight or mind."

Lannie's eyes shone, and she touched his cheek, but dropped her hand immediately. "Hi, how was Charlotte?" she asked quietly.

His necessary middle-of-the-week days in Charlotte had become pure drudgery, and he wanted to say to her, "Terrible, I missed you till it hurt." But he couldn't. He said instead, "Just fine, but I'm happy to be back here."

He saw John Lamb frown, as if he disapproved of their conversation. *We're none of your goddamn business, bookseller,* thought Drum.

Beezy arrived before he could say anything, latched herself onto his arm, and kissed his cheek, giving his ear a good suck in the process. "Goddamn, Drum Rutledge, if you aren't the sexiest hunk of man in the entire state of North Carolina, I don't know who is. Someday I'm going to take you to bed and see if everything I hear is true."

Lannie paled and Drum wanted to kill Beezy. John Lamb's frown turned to an expression of deep concern, and he moved closer to Lannie. Drum gave her elbow a gentle squeeze and extracted himself from Beezy's grasp.

"Beezy," he said coldly. "Watch your nasty tongue, or you won't be invited again."

"Oh, lighten up, honey. But, I'm not kiddin.' I would like a taste of you before I get too old." Nearly as tall as he was, she gave his ear another lick of her tongue. He smelled her hennaed, tightly permed hair, and controlled a shudder. She turned her weasel brown eyes on Lannie. "Now I'm serious, Lanier Sullivan. You can't just disappear for years, and then crystallize in the midst of the biggest pahty High Falls will see all summer. It's Aunt Beezy's duty to spread the word that you're here again. So give, sugah. Where on this friggin' earth have you been?"

Drum knew that, despite Lannie's growing self-confidence, she still didn't want any intrusion on her solitary life at the cabin. He could lie quicker than she could.

"Lannie has rented a place in Franklin. She comes up the mountain to the playhouse several days a week for volunteer work."

"I do believe she can speak for herself, Drum."

"I certainly can, Beezy. I'm flattered you've noticed my absence. You're so busy with your golf, and bridge, and your board meetings. Daisy tells me you're hardly ever at home."

"Well, if that isn't rich," Beezy said. "Daisy has been talkin' all summer about the little things she does at the playhouse, and the lady who taught her how to dance, but I never paid much attention. But you should have let me know you were here. Your mother would have expected you to be part of the scene, sugah."

John Lamb insinuated himself halfway between Beezy and Lannie.

"Beezy, we need to talk about those theater seats for sale in Atlanta," he said. "Bill and Joan Berry said they'd be happy to donate money to the cause if you would match it. They're over in the corner. Let's go talk to them."

"Are you trying to shut me up, John Lamb?"

"Maybe. It wouldn't be the first time." He smiled. "But I'm serious about talking to the Berrys. We may never get another opportunity to find them together like this, and those seats go off the auction block this week."

"You go talk to them, I want to find out about Lannie, and why—"

"Go see the Berrys, Beezy," Drum interrupted, taking

charge of the situation. "The theater needs new seats. Lannie's coming with me."

"Now see here, Drummond Rutledge, I'm not accustomed to being ordered around."

Drum walked Lannie out of the circle the four of them had created, and John Lamb moved Beezy away toward a far corner of the large room.

"We'll talk later, Lannie," called Beezy over her shoulder.

Drum loved the feel of Lannie by his side, her gliding dancer's walk, the sigh of silk as she moved, the feather lightness of her arm resting on his, the hint of an expensive fragrance she'd never worn before.

If he'd been bewitched before by the beautiful mountain recluse, he was now spellbound by the fascinating creature who lit up the entire room. The desire to take her into his library right now, lock the door, romance her with a candlelight dinner in front of the fire, hold her in his arms as they danced to Gershwin, and then make love all night long was almost more than he could resist.

"Thanks for rescuing me," she said.

"John Lamb did most of the rescuing. You bowled me over just as you did everyone else."

"It's me, Drum, the same ol' Lannie. I just have on some new feathers."

She smiled up at him, and he wanted to grab her to him and ravish her right there in front of everyone.

"You are certifiably beautiful, Lannie Sullivan, and I'm finding it difficult sharing you with everyone else." He wanted to say, *You make a man proud, and though I treasure our private moments here on the mountain, I'm going to make sure the rest of North Carolina gets a look at you once in a while.*

He couldn't say those words, nor could he say the rest

of the things that burgeoned in his heart at the moment. He hadn't the right. Would he ever have the right? Guilt and despair rode him like twin horses whipping him down a long endless track.

" 'Deed, Lannie honey, you look as scrumptious as ever. Doesn't she, Daddy?" A big-haired blond with a piping voice, arm heavy with jingling gold bracelets, stepped in front of them, stopping their leisurely stroll through the crowd. She gave Lannie a saccharin-sweet smile, then turned her blue eyes on her Texas-tall husband next to her. "Now doesn't she, Daddy, doesn't she?"

"I don't need any coaxin', Carol Anne," said the man. "Lannie has always added flavor to anything she gave her attention to."

"Honey, Cabot and I were so sorry when we heard about Gracie. I swear, honey, those days when our babies were playin' by the pool seem like yesterday." Lannie stiffened. Drum drew her closer to him and tightened his hold on her arm reassuringly. "Gracie was three months younger than Jeannie, but Gracie could swim and Jeannie couldn't. Well, honey I was so jealous. 'Course now, Jeannie wins all the races at the club, and already has boys hangin' around. She's six goin' on sixteen, you know how that is."

"No, I don't know how that is, Carol Anne."

Cabot Carter had the grace to look embarrassed. "Carol Anne, we've said hello, now let's go out on the deck and have a taste of that delicious barbecue I smell."

"Well, now, Daddy, I haven't seen Lannie since her tragedy happened. Let me be. She should know how we all miss her at Junior League meetings, and she really needs to talk about Gracie. They say talkin' about bad things help them go away."

"I stopped going to Junior League years ago when Tom and I moved from Atlanta back to Madison, Carol Anne, but I'm glad to know you still miss me," said Lannie. Drum doubted if the insensitive woman caught the sarcasm, but he saw her husband wince.

"I'm hungry, Carol Anne," Cabot said. "Come with me."

"Comin', Daddy, comin'." As her husband hustled her off, Carol Anne called over her shoulder, "I'll find you later, Lannie, and we'll have a lil' ol' chat."

A tall, slim, white-haired woman approached, and Drum braced for whatever came next. He was surprised when Lannie's face lit up and she embraced the dignified woman. "Oh, Auntie Faye, it's so good to see you."

The two women hugged and Drum noticed tears in both pairs of eyes.

"Lanier, child, how proud your mother would be of you this evening."

"Thank you. I've thought of coming to see you often, but I wasn't ready."

"I suspected you were at the cabin, but I knew you needed your 'space' as you young people say."

"Drum, this is Faye Wickfort, my mother's dearest friend."

He recognized the Wickfort name, an old Charleston family. The Wickforts were major supporters of the High Falls Playhouse.

They shook hands. "I've heard of you, Mr. Rutledge. It was kind of you to host this lovely party."

Her words were spoken in a cultured southern lilt, but he heard the coldness in them and saw the concerned look she gave to his grip on Lannie's arm.

"I see Remington is waiting for me by the door," she continued. "I wasn't brave enough to drive myself up here. Please come to visit when you're ready. Lannie."

"I think perhaps the time has come. I'll be over next week," Lannie promised her. "Drum, I'll walk Auntie Faye to the door."

He pulled her close to him and didn't care what the whole world thought.

"Mingle as much as you think is proper, then meet me in the library in thirty minutes," he whispered in her ear.

"It will be the longest half hour of my life," she whispered back.

Spencer drew on his pipe, then exhaled slowly, letting the smoke drift around his head. If he blew enough of it, he reasoned, he might stay quietly hidden all evening.

Though he had to admit that watching the crowd was like watching a good play. Through the slits of his eyes he'd seen a pastiche of dramas take place, some expected, some surprising. He'd perfected the half-lidded eye routine when he was a drama student in college.

He'd taken the acting class as an easy way to fill out his schedule that semester. The explosive director had tolerated him. Rather than give the farm boy from upstate any direction, the man had simply ignored him. This suited Spencer just fine at first, but then he found himself caught in wonder at the way his fellow classmates created whole new personas for themselves, and how they told a variety of stories with their bodies and voices.

Pretending he was asleep, he would watch them through half-lidded eyes, memorizing their movements, registering the voice inflections that worked, the mannerisms that portrayed the most emotion, the natural spark that marked a gifted actor rather than a talented monkey aping others. Soon he found himself going to sleep at night plotting a stage crossing, puzzling over how Romeo could convey to the audience how much he loved Juliet without upstaging the actress playing her.

When the time came for Spencer to have a go at directing a short skit, as the course requirements dictated, the results stunned the professor and the class. Spencer Case received an A for the semester and went on to become a legend on Broadway.

He watched now as Lannie and Drum talked. They stood halfway across the room from him, but he felt their attraction toward each other as if he were a part of them. Lannie's urgent feelings were portrayed in her stance, in the subtle leaning of her body toward Drum. Drum's broad shoulders were hunched toward her, as if he wanted to protect her, exclude the people around them, and the hand he'd used to guide her around the great room subtly caressed her arm. The tug of their desire for each other was so palpable that Spencer feared everyone there would see it, be shocked by it, would want to interfere.

There were other points of energy in the crowd, and he focused next on Beezy Bowden, and shuddered.

Beezy monopolized a circle of women, but he knew the women were only camouflage for her broader array of interest. Her voice rang over softer syllabled southern accents, and even dominated the harder New York sounds. She stacked sentences like cordwood, strident, splinter-filled words, designed to catch her captive audience's lackey-like homage to her money and social position. All the while, *her* attention centered on Lannie and Drum. Beezy registered and judged, from the corner of her eye, every movement the couple made and every word they uttered. Her talent for keeping the women around her entertained without the barest hint that her watchfulness centered elsewhere awed Spencer.

What a nosy, interfering bitch she was.

Kent Shaw crossed his line of sight, heading toward the bar, a giggling ingenue on each arm. Shaw gave Lannie a good once-over as he passed her.

Shaw seemed a rather mysterious man, didn't mingle

much with others, and appeared and disappeared magically. Abracadabra, presto, Kent was there and then he was gone, into the bowels of the theater somewhere, always reappearing exactly when Spencer needed him. But he'd been highly recommended and had done a bang-up job.

His attention returned to Lannie. How could he help it? She made him want to be young again. He watched as she slipped quietly out of the room. Headed toward an assignation with Drum, he imagined, and he smiled. She made him miss Julia Jane desperately.

But Julia Jane would be here soon, he thought as a smile lit his face again.

Lannie wandered the library refuge with heightened fascination. She'd only been in the lodge a few times. She and Drum both preferred the spectacular beauty of the starlit mountaintop and the endless view outside the cabin. The romantic nights here at the lodge had been spent in the kitchen, cooking together, and then the bedroom.

Here, in this walnut-paneled, leather-luxuried room, Drum indulged his varied interests. Would their child be a collector of anything? Stamps, rocks, dolls, autographed baseballs, rugby stats? *Don't be foolish, Lannie Sullivan. You're not sure you're pregnant. You might just be nurturing an urgent wish.* But, in spite of her self-scolding, hope leaped for what she was positive grew within her at this very moment.

She hugged her secret knowledge to herself like a favorite blanket on a cold night.

"Thank you, God. Thank you for a gift I'm not sure I deserve, but one I shall take gladly. A February baby to brighten the gloom of winter, and bring with it the promise of spring and rebirth."

She wanted the time to be just right when she told him.

Tonight would be perfect. After everyone had gone home, and they were by themselves in front of a great, roaring fire, and they had made love, and he held her quietly, safely in his arms . . . then she would tell him.

She wasn't sure how he would react, but he had to be told. She hoped with all of her heart that he would be as elated as she was.

She thought for a moment about Madison and the questions and attention her pregnancy would create. Would she stay here in High Falls and raise this child or would she return to Madison? Drum would be an important part of this child's life, of that she was certain, and his decisions would give her a lot of answers. It suddenly struck her that Drum might want to marry her. Wonder upon wonders, what a delicious thought.

Her wonderful secret had completely displaced the fear that had haunted her since the stalking at the theater. Everything at the theater had been going like clockwork, no more incidents, no reports of strangers or odd happenings. As her fear gave way to mounting confidence and relief she allowed herself the joy of hope and expectancy.

She hadn't had her period for two months. At first, she had attributed it to her return to dance and its physical demands on her body. It wasn't unusual for a dancer, or a runner, to stop having menstrual periods from time to time. However, the physical stress required by her arduous work at the cabin had never stopped her flow.

If she was right, the conception took place the first time they'd made love. Someday she would tell her child how she'd been conceived in the prop room of a summer playhouse on the Fourth of July. Well, she wouldn't tell her it was against a wall, or how her mother and father had gone at each other like animals, but, oh, how glorious it had been and that that uncontrollable passion had grown into a beautiful love. How lucky the child would be to have parents who loved each other so much.

Don't be foolish, Lannie. Drum hasn't said he loves you.

So, that's okay. This baby will have all of my love and that will be enough. But in her heart she wanted Drum to love this child as much as she already did.

No, she had no medical proof that she was pregnant, but her body knew, her soul knew, and her heart sang with the knowledge. February, next February.

She stopped in front of a rack of canes on the wall. She noticed a humorous folk art cane with whittled figures on its shaft. Curious, she lifted a distinctive crutch-handled walking cane from the rack and stroked the smooth length of the cherry wood, enjoying the rich feel under her palm. Drum had carved this cane, loving every stroke and cut that he made as he created the beautiful work of art. She knew arthritis had hampered his mother's movements from early adulthood, and Drum had begun carving canes from the scraps of his cabinetry carpentry in an attempt to relieve his frustration at her pain, and as a way of helping and amusing her.

June Christy's moody "For All We Know" curled about the library, filling warmly lit corners and spaces with the poignancy of her smoky voice. Lannie hummed the blues song as she marveled at the cane collection.

On the wall next to the canes hung a silver-framed picture of a rugby team with Drum holding a trophy, his hair mussed, his shirt muddy, a trickle of blood on his chin, his eyes triumphant.

The lodge had a hand-hewn, rugged, masculine appeal to it, which she liked, but her eye searched again for personal touches in this most personal of rooms. Except for the cane collection, his large collection of jazz CDs, which were housed in a glass-encased shelf, the rugby picture, and a small portrait of an older gentle-faced woman, there were no indications of a life with connections. Unless the portrait was of his mother, there was no evidence of family, no pictures of parents, no snapshots of beach vacations, or college buddies, or old girlfriends.

Worry quivered beneath her joy, threatening to displace the excitement she felt at telling him about the child. Something was missing. She should know what it was. Was she deliberately tuning out trouble or was she simply nervous about how Drum would accept her news about the child? Maybe she should wait until the doctor confirmed her pregnancy. She should. She should. She should. But, oh how she wanted to share her joy with Drum.

The big fireplace beckoned with a friendly glow, and she went to warm her hands. The door clicked as it opened and closed, but she remained where she was, afraid if she turned to face him that her joy would show, and she would have to tell him before she was ready.

"Hello, my beautiful huntress." He put his arms around her waist, blew wisps of hair away from the nape of her neck, and placed small kisses on the bared skin, sending goosebumps up and down her spine. "I've missed you like hell the last few days. I don't ever want to be away from you that long again."

"How were things in the big city?"

"Good. Business is good, my house there is in good shape, my associates are doing well, we're making lots of money, flowers are blooming, rivers are running, birds are singing. Everything is good, good, good, but all I could think about was you. Did you bring your jammies?"

She laughed and wiggled around so she could fit into the circle of his hard arms and kiss him properly. "Yes, but they aren't sexy. They're just my old flannels."

"Sweetheart, we've never cared about what we were

wearing or where we were. As a matter of fact, I don't think I can wait. The sofa over there looks mighty enticing."

"Oh, no you don't, Drum Rutledge. This is the first time I've worn anything gorgeous in three years, and I'm not taking it off now."

"Which reminds me, how did you drive that certified junk heap with those dainty high heels on?" he asked, smiling. "I've been wondering ever since I saw you standing there so put together and so breathtakingly beautiful."

"Took my shoes off. Drove barefoot. I felt like Isadora Duncan and imagined my flying sash getting caught in my tires, but decided it wasn't my time to die," she laughed.

He crushed her against him, his lips tight against her ear.

"Don't even mention dying, do you hear?" The grim insistence in his voice frightened her. "You're here in my arms alive, living here and now. Never, never ever talk about dying."

He kissed her with an urgency that set her blood simmering. Demanding and rough, his mouth drew her into him, and turned her bones to cotton and her joints to water. His arms held her upright, and the width of his shoulders encompassed her entirely.

"Oh, excuse me. I didn't know anyone was in here." Beezy's unmistakable voice rudely invaded their private world. "I was lookin' for a phone. By the way, Drum, your man, Jack, is lookin' for you. Old Mrs. Berry broke a goblet and cut herself attemptin' to clean it up. You'd think people would have bettah sense, wouldn't you?"

Startled and embarrassed, Lannie tried to back away from Drum, but he kept her in his arms and turned to fix Beezy with an angry look that would have felled John Bunyan.

"Use the phone in the kitchen, Beezy, and tell Jack I'll be there in a minute."

Even Beezy Bowden couldn't have disobeyed Drum's flat order.

She raised her eyebrows, gave them a smirk of a smile, and backed out of the room.

"Sweetheart, I'm so sorry. I should have locked the door behind me." She gave his cheek a soft kiss, but saw a look of worry on his face. "I want to discuss something with you, and what just happened makes it even more important."

"What's wrong, Drum?"

"I'm not sure that anything is, and then again, everything might be wrong. Depends on you." He kissed her on the forehead. "Stay here. I'll see if Mrs. Berry is okay and be right back."

Drum hadn't been gone one minute before the door opened and Beezy slipped in. She locked the door behind her.

"What are you doing? Why did you lock the door?" asked Lannie.

Beezy crossed the floor between them with a triumphant bent to her body. She threw her head back and stared at Lannie with malevolent amusement on her sun-ravaged face.

"He'll never marry you, you know."

"What are you talking about? It was just a kiss."

"No, I've been watchin' the two of you all evening, and you don't even have to paw each other to see the hotness, sugah. Not that I blame you, of course. Drummond Rutledge is every woman's dream, and after that fartless wonder you were married to, Drum must be manna from heaven."

"Drum and I are none of your business, Beezy Bowden."

She felt her Irish temper rising and cautioned herself.

A chill of forewarning skipped along her spine, and as if to protect herself, she moved closer to the fireplace.

"I'm making it my business. I thought you were smarter than most, Lanier Sullivan. Your mother would have never approved."

"You are *not* my mother, thanks be to God."

"Yes, I thank God, too, because if I were your mother, I'd be ashamed of you. This might be the nineties, Lanier Sullivan, but havin' a blatant affair with a married man in front of the entire world is a tacky and cruel thing to do."

Lannie froze. She had a childish desire to clap her hands over her ears and run away as fast and as far as she could, but Beezy's voice continued relentlessly.

"Drummond Rutledge will never divorce his precious Ann-Marie."

TWENTY

The fire at Lannie's back seemed to flare up and blast through her, searing every sense she possessed, yet beads of ice formed on her shivering skin.

She tried to move her tongue, tried to appear normal. But she'd been felled and blown apart, and Beezy must have read the shock on her face.

The silence grew, as Beezy Bowden was quiet for the first time in her life.

"Sweet Jesus, you didn't know, did you?"

"Didn't know what, Beezy?" Lannie found her voice.

"Didn't know Drum is married. Most people know, honey, most people remember. Whew-ee, I'm sorry. I don't like being the bearer of bad tidings. But I'm surprised. Where have you been for the last seven years?"

"I haven't the slightest idea what you're talking about," Lannie said, struggling to hold on to her sanity and appear normal at the same time.

"Ann-Marie, Chip, the plane crash, her insanity." Beezy rushed on, as if she couldn't wait to get it all out at once, and through it all, Lannie could tell she enjoyed every spiteful word. "Their plane crashed on the way to Oregon.

The pilot died, and she was left alone with the five year old. She shot the poor child through the head. It was in newspapers all over the country."

Seven years ago. Where was she seven years ago? Married in April, Tom had taken her on a six month honeymoon to Europe. They hadn't returned until late September.

"No one condemns Drum, of course. In fact, we all wondered if he was going to be a monk the rest of his friggin' life. He'd always idolized Ann-Marie. Finally, he started dating once in a while, escorting someone to a charity ball and such. Then he had a long affair with one of those boring Beaufort women from Charleston. Since then, from what I've heard, he's had brief liaisons with several women, but they never last long."

Hoping this was a tale Beezy had made up from gossip, Lannie said, "How do you know these things for sure, Beezy? I know you get around, but you live in Birmingham and Drum lives in Charlotte."

"Sugah," Beezy replied, her voice filled with amazement, "Drum is a gorgeous tough hunk of man who owns a billion-dollar corporation. His picture is snapped wherever he goes, and the gossip columnists watch every twitch of his pinkie. He's on every southern mama's most eligible bachelor list."

"You just said he's married."

"He is, and he'll never divorce Ann-Marie, but there are always fools like you who think otherwise."

Beezy's grating voice bore on and on, and Lannie found she'd tuned it out. She didn't want to hear anymore. She just wanted horrid Beezy, with her hennaed hair, her purple acrylic nails, and her ten-carat diamonds to go away.

". . . . anyone who has ever dated him or slept with him knows there can never be anything serious. They say he puts a distance between them. Lets them know right away they're not going to get anywhere with him. It's become accepted behavior for Drum, and some people have even forgotten about Ann-Marie."

Ann-Marie, Ann-Marie, dear God, who is Ann-Marie?

"I haven't forgotten about Ann-Marie, Beezy," said a quiet voice behind them.

Beezy whirled, her gold taffeta dress rattling and swishing.

Drum stood just inside the door. They'd been so absorbed in Beezy's tense words, they hadn't heard the turn of his key in the lock.

He took full possession of the room. Every corner, every book-filled shelf, every chair, every inch of space, burned with his vitality and anger. He seemed enormous, and Lannie had never seen the steely, indomitable expression on his face before. Trappings of polite civilization had disappeared, and he looked like the tough lumberjack who'd survived a rough youth in the northwest.

"Oh, there you are, Drum," Beezy said sweetly, though Lannie detected a tremor in her whanging voice. "Lannie and I were just getting caught up on our lives."

"Sounded like you were getting caught up on *my* life." The furrows around his mouth and on his forehead deepened. "Get out, Beezy. Find your chauffeur and go home."

From force of habit, Beezy opened her mouth to make a stinging reply, but Drum's face tightened and the navy of his eyes turned black. Lannie sensed that if Beezy didn't leave immediately, Drum would physically toss her out.

Beezy smiled at Lannie, and her twenty-thousand-dollar crowns glimmered ludicrously in the reflected firelight. "Honestly, Lannie sugah, I can't imagine why the glorious man has his bowels in such a friggin' uproar, but I better get goin'."

As far as Lannie and Drum were concerned, she was already gone. Lannie, speechless, stared at Drum, praying for a denial of the tale told by Beezy. Drum advanced toward her, the anger in his face replaced with concern.

Her parched throat begged for water. She managed a couple of steps to a tea table nearby, and picked up a water pitcher. Her hand shook as she poured and the water came from the pitcher in stammering starts and stops, splashing out of the glass.

Drum covered her hand with his, and they poured the water together. He held the glass to her mouth, as a father would a child, and helped her drink.

"Ann-Marie and Chip are what I planned on talking to you about tonight. I'm sorry Beezy got to you first. Damn the bitch."

He put the glass on the table and took her in his arms. She stiffened at first, but then let her head rest on his shoulder. *For just a minute, God, let me rest here for just a minute, then I'll leave and never look back*.

"I thought you knew. Most people do. But you never mentioned it, never asked about either of them. I finally realized that anyone with your caring soul would have wanted to know how Ann-Marie was, and how I was feeling about that part of my life."

She pulled away from him so she could see his face.

"In the beginning, did you just assume that I was the kind of woman who would have wanton sex with a married man?"

"No, I never thought that. Oh, damn, Lannie, I'm so sorry. I wanted you so much that I never thought about anything except having you. I was consumed with a desire and passion I'd never experienced before. I still am, only it's moved beyond that. I can't think about anything but you."

Lannie admitted to herself that she'd felt the same way. She'd been so eaten up with the wild, earthy wanting of Drum that she'd never asked questions, never considered the consequences. The consequences, of course, she now carried within her. She pressed her hand against her flat stomach and knew it was growing with a child she wanted desperately.

It's okay, my baby. No matter what happens, you and I are together and I won't let anything happen to you. You hear me? We're going to be okay.

Drum saw her gesture. "Are you sick? You look pale. Here, sit down."

"No, no. I'm fine." Damn, she wished she could control her shaky voice. "Beezy was lying, right Drum? A mother wouldn't kill her son."

"No, Beezy told you the truth, she just didn't tell the whole truth." The lines on his face tightened again. She thought she'd never seen such pain.

"Drum, we can do this later."

"No, it's long past time when we should have talked about this. It's important that you understand." That was the understatement of the year, she thought.

He held her shoulders for a moment, then turned away from her to grip the stone mantel of the fireplace and stare into the fire. Somewhere along the way, he'd removed his dinner jacket. The cuffs of his gleaming white dress shirt were rolled to mid-arm, revealing bristly gold-burnished brown hair. In spite of her growing anger, she wanted to kiss his wrists, and feel his hands move the length of her spine. She sank gratefully into the comfort of an overstuffed tobacco-leather sofa, and listened.

"Maybe I'd better start at the beginning."

"That would be a good idea," she said dryly.

"I met Ann-Marie at Duke. She was in my Latin class.

She was the star pupil. I was the dumb one. Between working to earn money to supplement my scholarship, and the hours I needed for my furniture apprenticeships, I had little time to study. I should never have taken the class, but I had some notion that I was going to learn to speak several languages, and I would need the Latin. I asked her if she would tutor me. She said yes, and we managed to squeeze in an hour here and there.

"She fascinated me. She wasn't like the rest of the girls. She was shy, and quiet, and beautiful in a fairy-like kind of way. She had a big luxurious room all to herself in a large house just off campus. I found out that her presence at Duke was the result of a rare rebellious moment, a wish for freedom that didn't last long."

He shoved away from the mantelpiece, and came to the low table that sat before her to pour both of them a snifter of brandy. She refused hers.

He looked at her oddly, but continued. "Ann-Marie was raised in New Orleans by two maiden aunts and attended convent schools all of her sheltered life. When it came time for college, she insisted on a secular school, and so came to Duke unprepared for the realities of life. She never learned how to drive a car with any measure of safety, or cook a meal without burning herself, or pay her bills on time. She lived in a world of poetry, and flowers, and knights on white horses, and saints and angels. I found myself taking care of her, and falling in love with her at the same time. We were married right after graduation."

Lannie couldn't tell whether she felt better or worse as he told the story. She wished for a seat belt to hold her upright.

"Chip was born nine months later." A smile warmed his face, and took the terseness away from his words for a short time. "The doctors said Ann-Marie shouldn't have another child. Having him almost killed her. So we settled into a nice life. I worked twelve-hour days, and she was content to live quietly, tending to Chip, reading, and writing. I think she would have been a major poet one day. We didn't have much of a social life. Ann-Marie was happiest when she was with Chip and me."

He walked to a mullioned window to look out into the night and the forest of evergreens beyond, then came back and stood in front of her, absentmindedly twirling his brandy glass in his hand.

"They had never seen the northwest, where I grew up, so we planned a trip there the spring Chip was five. Ann-Marie hated flying, but agreed to go on our company jet. At the last minute, I had to change my plans because of a competitor's bid to take over Rutledge Timber. I insisted, over Ann-Marie's objections, that she and Chip go ahead. I would meet them in Oregon later. I let business take precedence over them. The guilt of that will never leave me."

The tortured lines on his face slacked, and he grew bleak and drawn.

"A sudden violent storm blew up over Colorado." He finished the brandy in one long swallow, as if he wanted to wash away the words that must come next. "The plane crashed. Ann-Marie was incoherent when we reached them the next day. From what we could understand and piece together, the pilot lived long enough to make a shelter for them under a wing. He gave her his revolver, showed her how to use it, and told her to watch for wolves. It had been a long, bitter winter and the wolves were starving.

"She'd broken an ankle. Chip was bruised and battered, but he took care of her all that day, scooping snow for her to quench her thirst, covering her with the pilot's jackets.

Night came, and sure enough, a family of wolves began sniffing around their camp. I don't know if they were just curious, or ravenous, but they frightened Ann-Marie to death. She scared them off with several shots, but at dawn the next morning the wolves circled closer. She had only one bullet left, and she'd lost hope of being rescued. Afraid they were going to be torn to death by the wolves, she took Chip in her arms and shot him through the temple with her last bullet."

"Oh, dear God."

Her hand flew to her mouth, and she almost retched from the shock of his words. Swamped with a sea of conflicting emotions, Lannie's stomach roiled and bubbled. Swallowing hard, she sipped water from the glass in her shaking hand.

"But it was a brave thing that she did," she managed to say.

"Yes, but unnecessary, as it turned out, which makes it even more tragic. The rescue party was close. I was only a mile away. I heard the shot." He turned away from her and took up his original stance at the fireplace, his back rigid, his head bowed. "Chip's body was still warm when I reached them. Ann-Marie hummed a lullaby as she rocked him."

"Drum, I'm so sorry."

He didn't reply, and she used the silence to attempt some sort of acceptance of this horrifying drama. Would she have had the courage to kill Gracie to save her from a torturous, appalling death? She didn't know, and prayed she would never have to make a decision like that. She smoothed her hand over the precious gift in her tummy and recoiled at the thought of destroying it for any reason. She already loved her baby desperately.

"How does Ann-Marie feel about what she did?"

He sighed. "Ann-Marie had never been emotionally stable, but she seemed fine for a few days, and then one night we found her wandering in downtown Charlotte in her nightgown. In a week's time it was clear she was losing her mind. Since then she has gone through several stages of progressive withdrawal. I have taken her all over the world looking for a cure, a doctor who might have a miraculous method of restoring her to normalcy. They've all told me the same thing. She doesn't want to get well, so she never will. She lives in a world of her own, slipping in and out of severe periods of madness. In her brief moments of clarity, she thinks Chip is still alive."

Drum took a deep breath and came to sit next to her. He took her hand in his and kissed each finger, and then the palm. He closed her fingers over his and held it tight.

"If you'll allow me, I'll try to explain my life since then."

She nodded.

"For three years I kept her at home with me, hiring nurses to watch over her, but she always escaped and placed herself in dangerous situations. Once we found her walking a train track, and another time climbing a water tower. There was only one thing that brought her peace, and that was talking of New Orleans and the elderly aunts who raised her. The aunts had died, but I took her to visit the convent down the street where she'd gone to school. She walked into the arms of the nuns, reverted to her childhood, and looked completely at peace. They have a villa next door, a small private haven where they nurse special cases, a few terminal patients, but mostly people like Ann-Marie who need psychiatric and spiritual nurturing."

He sighed, for a moment lost in his thoughts.

"She's happy there. I visit frequently. Sometimes she knows me and is fairly coherent, other times she's lost in a netherworld of horrors only she can see."

Lannie struggled to say comforting words, but was so lost in confusing emotions of her own, she thought it best not to say anything. Sorrow and empathy warred with anger at his thoughtlessness. How could he not have told her about this traumatic part of his life?

He got up and began to pace back and forth across the library, thrusting his fingers through his hair repeatedly until it stood in spikes as it did after a sweaty day's work in the carpentry shop.

"I thought at first that this would be the pattern of my life," he said. "I carried a youthful idealization of Ann-Marie in my heart, always will, I suspect. But after four years of stoic behavior, the caveman male in me found I needed female companionship, someone to talk to other than buddies, someone to be intimate with. Eventually I started seeing a few women. It seemed strange at first, but most people knew the story and, knowing that Ann-Marie could never be a wife to me again, they accepted my behavior. It's not something I'm proud of or ashamed of. It just is. And I'm terribly, terribly sorry that I didn't make all of this clear before now. I could have saved you this major embarrassment. God, I feel like hell."

He frowned, and sat down directly in front of her on the thick Georgia pine coffee table that squared the space in front of the fireplace. "When I met you, everything went out of my mind. Nothing mattered except having you, and I made the intolerable mistake of assuming you knew I was married . . . or maybe subconsciously, I was afraid to bring it up, afraid you'd run from me as fast as you could."

Remembering the child she carried, and the happy news she'd planned on giving him this evening, Lannie's anger elevated and edged.

"Drum, I'm so very sorry about Chip and . . . Ann-

Marie." Despite her empathy, she could barely get the woman's name out. "If there is anyone who understands your grief, it is me."

He took her hand in his again.

"But tell me," she continued, her tone sharp, "were you planning on just diddling around with the mountain hippie woman, and then returning to Charlotte when you were physically sated without filling me in on this most important fact of your personal life?"

His face blanched, then tightened. The muscles of his jaw clenched once, and his lips set hard against his teeth.

"No, I never, never intended to hurt you. You know me better than that, Lannie. I would never knowingly hurt you. I thought we had entered into some sort of unspoken mutual agreement to enjoy each other without hindrance, and let the rest of the world go their own way. But, as I began to understand you, things changed, and I started to wonder why you didn't ask questions about my personal life," he said, biting off each word. "When I realized that you had no knowledge of that part of my life, I also realized that this was more than a summer fling, and I decided to discuss the situation with you tonight."

"Did you think I would just continue to frolic through mountain meadows with you, screwing around at our slightest whim, feeding our lust-ridden egos whenever the selfish urge hit us?"

"No, I . . . God, forgive me." He bowed his head for a moment, but then lifted it to say softly, "I guess we carry so much of our grief and personal stories with us that we think they're imprinted on our face and body, as they are indelibly imprinted on our soul."

"Well, trust me, this story was not written on your face."

Lannie jerked her hand from his and stood up, unable to control her anger any longer. She needed to move around, before her quivering limbs and tilting stomach made her ill, and she began to pace as he had.

Her mind flew with the seriousness of the situation she found herself in, and all of its implications. The knot of anger in her stomach grew. Furious with Drum, and furious with herself, she worried about the effect her emotional reaction to this news was having on the developing fetus in her body.

The music had switched tunes and moods several times since Beezy had dropped her bomb, and now, somewhere in the background, in the hazy maze of her confusion, she heard Billie Holiday's smoky "These Foolish Things." How appropriate, she thought, how foolish I have been.

Calm down, Lannie, calm down. This is hard, God, this is hard.

She whirled to pace in the other direction, and the long sash on her dress whirled with her and caught a pipe stand sitting on an end table. She knelt to pick up the scattered pipes, her hands shaking. Does Drum smoke a pipe now, she wondered?

His warm, callused hand, capable of coaxing beautiful works of art from wood, and so talented in firing her body to fine-tuned ecstasies, closed firmly over hers.

"Leave them, Lannie." He drew her to her feet, and tipped her chin so she would have to look squarely at him. "We can get through this."

"Oh, God, Drum, I'm so angry at you, and so angry with myself that I don't know what to say." Unexpectedly, tears rushed out then, flooding her eyes, running down her cheeks, and landing on her bare shoulders. She hated them, but she couldn't stop them.

He brought her swiftly to him, wrapping his arms around her quivering body, and kissed the tears off her shoulders. "Christ, Lannie, don't cry. I can't bear it. Can't bear it that I've hurt you. And you have absolutely no reason to be angry with yourself, so get rid of that burden right now, sweetheart."

Ah, but I do have a reason, Drummond Rutledge. Because of my wanton carelessness, and your disregard for what others thought, because of our selfish actions, the most important of reasons grows in my body. And you haven't mentioned divorce, haven't even come close to the notion.

But his shoulders were broad and protecting, his firm chest supporting and safe, his arms warm and solid, and she sank into him like a lost bird finding shelter on a cold winter night.

"I have to think about all this, Drum," she said into his chest. "I have to have some time."

"I know."

"Right now I seem to be awfully tired, and I need to be alone. Do you suppose you could direct me to a guest bedroom and have someone bring my things from the jeep?"

Ten minutes later, she was safely settled in a feminine bedroom decorated in a daffodil and cornflower motif. She sat stiffly on the edge of a dainty boudoir chair and waited for Bry and the few personal supplies she'd needed for an overnight stay.

She heard Bry's ferocious bark and jumped to her feet. Bry never barked unless he was provoked or sensed something he didn't like. She ran to the door, but hesitated with the knob in her hand. She knew her face was tear ravaged, and Drum had kissed her thoroughly before he brought her to the guest room, doing serious damage to her once-elegant upswept hair.

Ordinarily, she wouldn't have cared what people

thought, or what they surmised from how she looked. But after the humiliating scene in the library, she was sure Beezy would have circulated the news that she and Drum were having an affair and that Lannie had acted like a naive fool.

She retreated to the chair again and waited nervously.

A soft knock brought her to her feet. She opened the door to find Drum holding Bry by the collar with one hand and her paper sack with the other.

"Sorry it took so long," he said. "I had to say goodbye to the last of the guests and sent Jack Edwards to the jeep for your things. Bry took umbrage at that. He wouldn't let Edwards near the jeep."

"Thank you."

He kissed her on the cheek. "Good night. We're going to be okay, Lannie, trust me."

She didn't think so.

She sat on the floor and wrapped her arms around Bry's big neck. Accustomed to the tears that flowed down her cheeks, he licked them off her face, as he had during that first year on the mountain, then waited while she emptied what remained into his coat. The tears she shed tonight were the first in a long time, and she hated them. After the tears from Gracie's death had dried up, she'd sworn she would never cry like that again, sworn that life would never throw her another curve.

And I'll be damned if it will. I'll be damned if I'll cry again. I'll lick this like I've licked everything else.

Defiantly, she wiped her face dry, straightened her shoulders, and poured herself a cup of tea from the silver pot Drum had so thoughtfully supplied. She would think of something, some way to survive this.

There was, however, one thing that she knew she had to do, someone who drew her like the earth drew the moon, someone she would visit as soon as possible. Her curiosity was an itch that had to be scratched.

Her sleep was fitful. She slipped in and out of dreams and nightmares, tossing and turning continually. Blissful dreams of Drum's arms around her were interrupted by horrid snatches of Gracie's sing-songy rhyme.

"Gracie, lacey, dancing daisy, makes her mom a happy lady."

In the middle of the night, she stiffened in horror, certain that someone whispered the chant close to her ear. Wide awake, she opened her eyes to find that she was alone. *Nerves, Lannie, nerves. Certainly not an unusual reaction after the scene in the library with Beezy and Drum. Go back to sleep.*

At five o'clock in the morning she gave up the battle. She got up, made the bed, and wrote a note to Drum.

Dear Drum,

I need time to think about what you told me last night.

Please do not come to the cabin. Please respect my wish to be left alone.

Lannie

Dressed in her old cut-offs and a thick sweatshirt to ward off the morning chill, she gathered up her lovely green cocktail suit and slipped quietly out of the lodge. Bry leaped happily in front of her, obviously elated they were leaving this strange place where they'd spent the night. He stopped short at the jeep.

"What's wrong, Bry? Squirrel raiding our chariot?" she teased.

He growled and glared at the jeep.

Darkness still covered the mountain and a misty early

morning fog hung low through the evergreens and around the lodge. But when Lannie reached the jeep, it wasn't difficult to see what had upset Bry.

A bright red ball sat in the driver's seat. A ball like the one Gracie had chased. A ball like the one in Lannie's nightmares.

TWENTY-ONE

Lannie, deep in a pile of old shoes, stopped sorting for a minute and looked around Gavin's Garret. There were no windows here in the attic, but she knew it was still light outside. As always, she had to be home before night fell.

If she hadn't promised Spence that she'd finish organizing the costumes, she'd have left long ago. In fact, she wouldn't be here at all. After the party at the lodge Saturday night, and the disastrous scene with Beezy, her inclination had been to hole up at the cabin right away, but she'd remembered her promise to Spence.

The change in Spence lately had been nothing short of miraculous. She had a strong notion that it had to do with the woman she'd caught him speaking sugary phrases to over the telephone. He was filled with energy and renewal, and the whole theater troupe had caught fire.

This was a "blue Monday" and her last day at the theater. She would miss it, but everything in her told her to run, flee, get back where it was safe.

Get back to the cabin.

The nervous recovery from Gracie's death and Tom's desertion, and the new beginnings she'd made had been dashed away, batted away hard like a baseball on an aluminum bat. Drum's betrayal had sent her back to where she felt safest. The doctor had made her promise to come for a monthly checkup, and she'd said that she would.

She threw a foul-smelling pair of shoes into the throwaway pile, and stifled a sneeze.

Next month she planned to go to Franklin to buy a new four-wheel drive. For the moment she had to concentrate on stocking supplies and canning the vegetables from her garden.

Someone ran up the steps and into the attic.

"Lannie? Lannie, where are you?"

"I'm back here, Daisy. On the far end."

Daisy soon appeared, poking her head through a rack of Revolutionary War uniforms. "Gosh, it is so spooky up here. I hate it. If I hadn't been in a hurry, I'd have waited until you came downstairs."

"Hi, darlin'. I expected you sometime today. Come to say goodbye?"

"Yes. Grandmother is parked outside waiting for me."

Lannie got to her feet and hugged her. Daisy felt like she'd grown a foot since the first time Lannie had hugged her early in the summer.

"Daisy, I'm going to miss you so much. You'll never know how much you've helped me be happy this summer."

"Not as much as you've helped me," said Daisy, grinning. "Guess what? Grandmother has given me permission to attend the North Carolina School of the Arts in Winston-Salem."

"That's wonderful. So next summer maybe you'll be ready to audition for an ingenue part."

"Well, maybe not next summer," she said shyly, "but some summer I will. Thank you so much, Lannie. You really helped me feel better about myself."

"You're welcome, darlin'. Have a good school year, and write to let me know how you're doing."

"I will. How should I address it?"

"Lannie Sullivan, General Delivery, High Falls."

Daisy hugged her, and said, "Goodbye, I love you."

"I love you, too."

Daisy left as she had come, running, and took with her any brightness or happiness Lannie had felt in the past few days. The door slammed shut behind her, and Lannie thought about going to prop it open again, but decided against it.

A movement at the other end of the long aisle where she sat stopped her sorting. She sat up straight, a quick chill chasing down her back as she remembered the stalking last month in the auditorium. The hem of a flapper dress fluttered for a moment. A mouse, she supposed, trying to calm herself. There were plenty of little creatures up here, more than she liked to think about.

You're not alone this time, Lannie. Jack Edwards had escorted her up here and given her a key he'd had made for the lock he'd installed. Kent Shaw was in the theater somewhere, too.

She glanced at her watch. The numerals were difficult to see in the dim light, but she thought it read six o'clock. Another hour here, and then she would have to leave.

Ten neat rows of shoes, boots, and other assorted footwear sat in front of her, and above were ceiling-high shelves filled with the same. They'd been cleaned, catalogued, and labeled. Romeo, Juliet, Annie, Rebecca, Auntie Mame, or Dolly, would all have proper shoes to wear. A pair of cowboy boots glared at her accusingly. She'd forgotten them in the midst of the ballet shoes. They belonged on the top shelf. She grabbed them and climbed the ladder to place them properly.

The lights went out when she was halfway down the ladder.

"Damn. I thought Jack said he'd changed all the bulbs and fixed the wiring," she muttered to herself. She reached for the light dangling close by, and gave several yanks on the string. Nothing. She twisted the bulb. No response. Of course not. Not only was this light out, all of them were out.

She'd known the moment the attic was plunged into blackness that this was not an electricity problem. The person who'd frightened her to death last month was at it again, but she reminded herself that Jack and Kent were in the building . . . but Bry wasn't here. She'd let John Lamb talk her into letting him take Bry to a children's animal petting party for the Mountain Relief League.

Taking a deep breath to settle her queasy tummy, she gripped the ladder tighter. Should she stay where she was or descend to the floor?

Her hands dug into the splintered supports of the old wooden ladder. Should she climb up or down? If she fell, the baby might suffer. But for some crazy reason, she felt safe suspended in the air. Her pursuer was beneath her somewhere. She had a height advantage.

"I don't know who you are," she called, "or why you want to torment me, but I'm not afraid, and Kent and Jack are here somewhere."

A soft laugh came from close beneath her, and fingers circled her ankle, then dropped away.

"Don't touch me again. I'll scream. Someone will come."

Another soft laugh, and the hand felt her bare knee.

She screamed, and screamed again. The shrill ache of it in her throat sounded loud in her ears, but was muffled in all the padding the costumes provided in the attic.

She scrambled up the ladder and onto the top shelf,

bumping her head on the ceiling. Though there was little head space, she found the shelf was wide enough and strong enough to support her.

She grabbed the top of the ladder, lifted it, and thrashed it around, hoping to connect the bottom rungs with her tormentor in some way, maybe get a lucky thrust into an eye, or a shoulder, anything.

Again, the soft, throaty, laugh. Such a know-it-all, superior laugh, as if he had her where he wanted her.

He ripped the ladder out of her hands, and it fell to the floor. She heard it fall on top of the neat rows of shoes, shoes flipping in all directions.

Get away, Lannie, get away. Where?

She crept along the shelf, feeling her way as she went and prayed she was headed toward the door. She screamed again, but knew it was even less effective here near the ceiling than it had been on the ladder. It was hot and dusty close to the ceiling, and the air was difficult to breathe. She coughed, sneezed, and coughed again.

Something jabbed her in the face, and she reached to shove it out of the way, but it kept jabbing. Her pursuer was following her progress and thrusting at her with a broom. The stiff straw bristles scratched her face and poked at her side.

"Stop this, just stop this." Her voice sounded tinny, and high-pitched like a frightened little girl's. She hated it, and hated the "thing" below.

She shrieked again and again, and crawled faster, with no idea where she was headed. Hatboxes, spare parts for props, musical instruments, and wired petticoats fell to the floor as she pushed them aside in her haste. The "thing" below grunted as something connected with him.

"Shit."

She'd hurt him. Good.

"You bitch." He was angry. She was trapped. Circling around the attic on a precarious perch, with a vicious predator beneath, and she knew he could get at her anytime he wanted to. He was playing with her now.

A whining sound came from the door and a frantic scratching.

Bry. Bry had come. A sob of relief broke from her.

The whining became a vicious rumble, emanating from deep in Bry's throat. A cobweb caught her face, and she swiped at it, tears mixing with the tiny spider threads.

"Bry, Bry, I'm here," she shouted. "Come and get me, Bry."

At the sound of her voice, the fragile door shook and rattled.

A voice whispered, "That fuckin' dog. How did he get loose?"

"I told you," she said. "Don't bother me again. Bry will kill you."

And Bry would.

Someone come and help Bry, please, please. She wanted to scream again, but this time when she opened her mouth she found fear had frozen her throat, and the dust and hot air wouldn't let her take a breath hearty enough to give a proper scream. She tried again. She tried to yell "help," but nothing came out.

Bry's assault on the door batted at her ears, and finally she let go with a shaky scream, and then another, stronger, and stronger.

Finally, the door fell with a bang, and she heard Bry leap into the room.

"I'm here, I'm here, Bry," she called weakly.

He barked as he jumped upwards to see her. She stretched out a hand so he could smell her and know she was okay.

"I'm fine. Just fine." He sniffed her hand then circled the attic quickly, nosing here and there, digging through clothing, and years of jumbled mess.

With huge relief, she sensed they were alone, she and Bry. Whoever had been here, was gone. How? How had they gotten past Bry? He would have torn the man apart.

Footsteps hurried up the stairs, taking two at a time, she thought.

"Miss Sullivan, you okay?" It was Kent Shaw.

Bry had disappeared, but reappeared quickly at the sound of Kent's voice.

"Yes, yes, just get me down from here."

"The light doesn't work."

"I know," she said dryly.

His flashlight went on, and the beam swept sound the attic. "Where are you?"

"Up here, Kent."

Jack Edwards had joined him now, and so had John Lamb. The three of them moved down a dim aisle toward her, lighting their way with their flashlights. With every step they took, Bry's growl grew more menacing.

"I'm up here," she said, trying to laugh, but a pitiful mew came out, a tired, frightened, pitiful little helpless mew came out, and she hated it. Hated being frightened, hated being helped, hated needing someone. "The ladder is there somewhere."

"The dog won't let us near you," said Kent, with a note of awe.

"Down, Bry. It's okay," she said, and then she fainted.

When she woke up, she lay on the sofa in the office, and Bry lay on the floor, as close as he could get, his anxious eyes never leaving her. Spencer's worried face hovered over her. A beautiful golden-haired woman Lannie had never seen before, but who seemed vaguely familiar, looked over his shoulder.

John Lamb came in, his face pinched and white. "God, Lannie. Bry broke away from me, and tore out of the barn and down Main Street like the hounds of hell were after him. He must have sensed you needed him. Thank the Lord."

She tried to sit up, but Spence, a hand on her shoulder, urged her back down.

"Rest, Lannie. We've called the doctor. He's on his way. How are you feeling?" asked Spence.

"Shaky, but okay."

"Tell me exactly what happened."

She told him, and they both related it immediately to the stalking a month ago.

"I know now that this is not some deviant passing through. This is someone who knows me, Spence."

Spencer frowned, and said, "Bry nosed his way through three crowded racks of clothes and found a closet that must have been covered up and forgotten about years ago. He scratched on the door until we opened it. It was filled with Civil War muskets, and lanterns, and looked as if someone had hidden there recently. Bottles of fresh water and cookie wrappers were on the floor. Someone waited for you up there."

The strange woman, concern creasing her forehead, said, "Dear God, who would do such a thing? Sounds like something straight out of a nineteen-thirties melodrama, my love."

"Lannie, this is Julia Jane Howard."

Of course, no wonder she looked familiar. Lannie had seen her in numerous productions when she lived in New York. Julia Jane Howard must be the reason for Spence's new surge of energy and the successful change in the last of the summer season. But her worried mind and her weary body had more important things to think about right now.

"Hello. It's an honor to meet you," she said politely, but then struggled on with what she had to say. "There is only one man I can think of who might want to scare me, but I haven't seen him here in High Falls, and I can't imagine how he would find his way into a hidden closet in the attic of the theater. Thank heavens the season is over, and the theater is closed. If it isn't Jeb Bassert, then there's a local madman on the loose and the theater isn't safe."

Spencer reached for the phone. "Let's call Drum."

She grabbed his hand, "No. I don't want Drum to know. He's in Charlotte, and he'll come charging up the mountain intent on rescuing me, and that is the last thing I want."

"My old reliable Maine common sense tells me that Drum is in love with you, Lannie. What's wrong with letting him rescue you?" asked Spence, a tender smile in his eyes.

"Yes, for heavens' sakes, dear girl, sounds terribly, deliciously romantic to me," said Julia Jane, in her throaty dramatic voice. "After all, that's just what I did. Rescued Spencer. Didn't I, darling?"

She kissed him on the top of his head. Spencer blushed three shades of pink, and said, "Yes, love of my life, you did," and reached to caress the hand Julia Jane rested on his shoulder.

Lannie hadn't the spirit to figure all this out right now, or ask questions, but she thought she remembered a husband in Julia Jane's life who lived in Hollywood. Never mind, she had just enough strength left to finish up here, and then find her way back to her retreat.

"Drum and I met at the wrong time, Spence. Sometimes fate loves a good laugh, and the bugger is certainly enjoying one now."

The older couple shook their heads, as if to say they didn't agree.

"For the moment," Lannie continued, "until I decide what to do with the rest of my life, I'm going to hide in my blessed, peaceful hidey-hole on top of the mountain."

"I'm glad there is a place that makes you feel that way. Thanks for everything, Lannie. I don't know what we would have done without you this summer. You brought light and grace to everything you did. I'm closing the playhouse tomorrow and returning to New York with Julia Jane. That's where we both belong . . . together."

Lannie could see that. They were both glowing. "Spence, tell me to mind my own business if you want, but does Julia Jane's appearance here have anything to do with those secret phone calls you've been making and the inspired energy you've injected into the cast and crew?"

He hung his head, embarrassed.

"Yep. Someday when you feel better we'll tell you how we got back together."

Julia Jane gave her a glass of water. Lannie sat up to drink it while Spencer tried to explain how he felt.

"It took Mae's death and the crumbling of the show to finally lead me to the right answers in my life." Unaccustomed to airing his personal feelings, he stopped and blushed, and probably wouldn't have continued if Julia Jane hadn't squeezed his shoulder. He mumbled on. "Love was missing in my life, Lannie. My heart was withering away, and the lack of feeling and caring leaked into my work. The passion wasn't there anymore."

"It is now, darling," said Julia Jane, nuzzling his ear.

"Yep,"mumbled Spence, grinning and blushing harder than ever.

Lannie found herself rife with envy and was ashamed of herself. She had never envied anyone, but she did now, and it was a pain she didn't like. With all the will she possessed, she convinced herself that how she felt wasn't important. She had the business of bringing a child safely into this world to occupy her, and that is what she could do and would do. Making sure her child was safe and well taken care of was something she could control with blessed assurance on her mountaintop.

Jeb welcomed the sweltering Florida night air that rushed through his open car window. The dark, smothering hotness matched his mounting mood of depraved melodrama. He'd driven through the night to get to Madison and had ridden on waves of exhilarating excitement, which had now taken on a feverish pitch.

His brain still blistered with the memory of Drum Rutledge and Lannie together. He'd watched them through the library window. He'd seen Drum kiss the back of her neck, slide his mouth across her bare shoulders, and catch the wispy tendrils of her blazing hair in his lips. He'd seen Lannie turn and slip so easily into his arms.

It had taken every ounce of willpower he possessed to control his fury. The urge to drive his fist through the glass, and strangle them both had been monumental. He should have stopped watching, left, and gone about his business because he knew Lannie would be his soon. She just didn't know it yet. She didn't know he was close by. When she did, everything would be different.

That loudmouth Bowden bitch had saved them. If she hadn't broken up their embrace, Jeb probably would have, and that would have ruined all his careful planning. He thought he had learned to control his temper, but the sight of his girl in Rutledge's arms had tested him sorely.

So much so that he hadn't been able to resist one last encounter with Lannie before his trip to Florida. His heart beat so hard it scared him when he thought of how she screamed in the attic, of the feel of her slender ankle in his hand, of the frantic frightened breaths she took when he poked the broom at her.

But he didn't have time to think about that now.

His anger at Lannie and Drum had made him press forward with his plans for Nell, and here he was, about to take care of little Nell Smather and her nosy busybody ways.

He had just turned off Interstate 10 onto a little-traveled track twenty miles west of Tallahassee, which led to an abandoned farm he had used before. With the roar of traffic behind them, Jeb listened for the thumping sound from the trunk of the car. Nell had kicked and fought like a wildcat. A hard punch to her chin had taken care of that, and he'd loaded her into the trunk of the rental car easily.

Evidently she'd recovered. When he'd stopped at a rest stop to relieve himself, she'd started kicking at the trunk lid. He'd heard the *thump-thump* when he got out of the car, and he'd had to jump back in and drive on.

Damn her. Now he was about to piss in his pants. He hated that. Pissing in his pants. He'd wet the bed until he was fifteen, and his cousins had taunted him unmercifully. They were clear of the highway now. He stopped, jerked open the door, and pissed on the ground.

He listened for the thumping. Yep. There it was, but much weaker. She wouldn't have much fight in her when he let her out. Too bad. He liked a skirt with some fight.

Minutes later he pulled up in front of a leaning wood structure with a rusting corrugated tin roof. His headlights caught the remnants of ivory-colored paint hanging in curling peels off the sides of the old farmhouse. Jeb parked in knee-high weeds near the front door, got out, and stretched.

He smiled, and his heart beat like crazy at the thought of what he was about to do. He unlocked the trunk and directed the beam of his flashlight into the interior.

Nell Smathers stared up at him, her big baby-blues chockful of fear. Every nerve end in his body tingled, alive with anticipation, and he got a hard on. She was gasping for air.

"Well, hello, Nell old chum. Time for us to continue the party. So sorry you didn't get home to rest from the last one."

He had followed her home from a bridal shower and hidden in the shadows. As she'd unloaded gifts from her car, he'd watched to make sure no one was at home, then had tapped her on the head with the police billy he always carried. Two blocks away, he'd pulled into a deserted park and transferred her to the car he'd rented with Buster's old driver's license. She'd fought him then, and he'd socked her on the chin. He'd tied her wrists and ankles, stuffed a handkerchief in her mouth, and placed her in the trunk.

Now he untied her ankles and lifted her from the trunk.

She stumbled and fell on her knees.

"Ah, come on, Nell. You need to be rested up for our party."

He jerked her to her feet and yanked the handkerchief from her mouth.

Nell coughed and choked, then gulped air like a race-horse straining for the finish line.

Breathing hard, her beautiful little breasts moving up and down like rabbits fucking, she croaked, "Who are you? What do you want with me?"

"Don't know your childhood friend, Jeb Bassert? Why, Nell, you should be ashamed of yourself. But then, you never were very nice to me, were you? It was always Lannie who smiled at me, and talked to me, if any of your crowd gave her a chance."

He was delighted. She hadn't recognized him. Good. Lannie hadn't either.

Confusion joined fear in those big round baby-blues. "You sound like Jeb, but prison couldn't age you that much."

"Ah, prison, the vacation spot Lannie sent me to. Yeah, it aged me real good. The white hair was my idea, though. Only takes a few minutes every week to bleach my roots. Get used to it, Nell, baby. It's me, and we're going to spend quality time together tonight. You'll learn to like the new way I look."

"You *are* Jeb. You are truly weird. I don't know what you've done to yourself, but it wasn't an improvement," she said spitefully.

He slapped her. "See? You just can't help yourself, can you?"

She moaned with pain, but then jerked her head upright and said, "What game are we playing, Jeb? Cops and robbers? Whatever it is, I don't like it. Untie me this minute, and let me go."

He laughed. "Oh, Nell, that's really funny. Don't you know that it's my turn? For years I watched while you and Lannie had all that fun and never invited me. In fact, it suddenly come to me that you're one of the reasons Lannie never looked at me as a boyfriend. She never laughed at me, but you did. You probably told her that dumb Jeb wasn't worth botherin' with."

"I don't know what you're talking about, Jeb. Lannie and I didn't do anything to hurt you when we were teens."

"You never let Lannie near me. She was so preoccupied with you and her other friends that she never had a chance to give Jeb the time of day. Yeah, the more I think about it, the more I have to blame you for me and Lannie never gettin' together like Jesus intended."

Nell shook her head, her short blond hair tossing furiously in the faint moonlight.

"No, Jeb, you're wrong."

"Shut up, bitch. Yeah, and I'll just bet you helped Lannie send me to prison. She would never have sent me to prison. Lannie liked me. She must have had some help from her old law partner, Miss Prissie, stuck-up Nell Smathers."

"Lannie was the state's attorney, Jeb. The state of Florida—"

"Yeah, yeah, yeah," he cut her off. "I know. They think I raped Susie Slater, and Lannie was just doin' her job. Well, I didn't rape Susie. Susie and I was just having a lil' ol' party, and things got a lil' rough. Just like you and me are going to have a lil' ol' party."

He held her by the back of the neck and pushed her toward the house. She stumbled through the dirt, gravel, and weeds, and fell to her knees again. He yanked her to her feet, onto the slanted porch, and through the sagging door.

"Why are you doing this, Jeb? I never hurt you." He heard the sob in her voice, and satisfaction glowed in him.

"Wel-l-l, there's lots of reasons. One of them is, I don't want you pokin' around tryin' to find out how I got a pardon, and then reporting everything to Lannie. I want to surprise her. The other thing is that I been wantin' you almost as much as I want Lannie, only for different reasons. I love Lannie, but I know you're a good fucker, and I been thinkin' to try some of it for a long time."

"You don't know anything about me, Jeb."

He sat her in a wooden chair and lit the candles he'd

earlier placed on the yellow Formica surface of the kitchen table.

"Ahhh, but I do, Nell, perky blond high-school cheerleader, best friend of Lannie, and Madison's bright young attorney. I know everything about you and Lannie, mostly because you were with her all the time. But, you had some fine moments of your own. See, I was in the bushes watchin' when you and Bobby Tucker fucked in his car after the prom. Hmmm, ummm, good." He grinned. "You were makin' some mighty sexy noises. I got a super jack-off just listenin'."

He held a candle close to her face and saw her lips quivering. He kissed them, sucking carefully at first, then took a gentle bite of the bottom lip. She bit him back, hard, and kicked him.

He slapped her, and blood flew from her busted lip.

"Sorry, Nell, but if you're goin' to be nasty, I'm goin' to have to tie your ankles again. Might make it more fun anyway."

She jerked away and ran for the door. He caught the back of her sundress, yanked her around, and threw her on the floor. Anchoring both ankles with one hand, he took a wire from his pocket, and twisted it around them until it bit into the skin. She was panting now, little squeaks of terror escaping from her lungs, like one of those field mice he used to catch in his traps.

"Let me go, Jeb, I promise I won't say anything to Lannie. Let me go. Please. You don't want to do this. If you hurt me, my family will find you. Jesus will punish you."

She was begging. God, how he loved it. Fancy-smancy, prissy, always-laughing Nell Smathers was begging.

He got up to get the candles, and Nell tried to roll away. He placed a foot on her chest and stared down at her. She screamed, and he slapped her again.

"Okay, so you don't want Jeb. Too bad, I think you'll like what's comin'."

His slap had stunned her. Good. He placed candles around her on the floor and lit them. Candles always made things more romantic. He knelt next to her, stuffed the cloth back in her mouth, and ripped her dress down the front.

An hour later, the candles had burned low, the wax spreading and congealing in smooth layers on the floor. He blew them out, regretful that this tryst was over. It had been special. She had given him a good fight until he tired of slapping her, and had banged her head on the floor to finish it.

He stood up, wiped the blood from his cock with his shirttail, and walked to the kitchen sink to wash his hands.

The house was still. He got a beer from the cooler he'd stored there earlier and headed for the porch, kicking aside a blue sundress on the floor as he passed. Except for the occasional chirp of a cricket or croak of a tree frog, the woods were silent.

He sat on the edge of the porch, and took his time lighting a cigarillo, inhaling the cheap sweetness of its wrapping. It smelled good in the hot muggy swamp air and chased away the mosquitoes. He leaned against the post railing to enjoy the peace of the summer night.

He would clean up the mess later.

TWENTY-TWO

Lannie stared across the street at the two-storied, plastered-brick eighteenth-century French Renaissance house. She hesitated, praying for courage.

The horrible night in the attic last week seemed like yesterday. Would it never leave her?

She should never have come to New Orleans, but she'd been flirting with the idea ever since the scene in the library at the lodge. Then later, Julia Jane and Spencer that last night in the theater, remembering the love in their faces, the peace and rightness reflected in their actions, and their happiness, had brought her to this decision, had pushed her off her mountain and given her the courage to obey her instincts.

Her quick visit to a boutique in Asheville for presentable clothes, the flight to Atlanta, and then on to New Orleans seemed all a blur.

New Orleans, though only mid-morning with a cloudless blue sky, sweltered with oppressive heat and humidity. Her new cream-colored slacks, matching silk shirt, and jade-green linen jacket clung to her damply. Due to the muggy weather or nervousness, she wondered.

She continued to waver before crossing the narrow cobbled street in the Vieux Carre, wanting to blame the heavy gardenia-scented air for closing her in and keeping her immobile.

The venerable house said it all. The walled courtyard implied "privacy please," as did most buildings in the French Quarter. This old residence, not far from the original Ursulines convent, gave an effect of withdrawal and agelessness, yet strong purpose. It said, "Approach if you are in need, and we will take you in, but do not disturb the peace within these walls."

Was she about to do that? She hoped not, but the apprehension in her chest was as thick as the air about her, and curiosity about the woman who claimed Drum's first loyalty burned so hot within her that she was ashamed. She knew that despite the guilt and shame of coming here without Drum's knowledge, her heart and soul would never rest until she finished this quest.

A man came out of the shop behind her and swept the sidewalk. She moved out of his way. "Can I help you, miss?" he asked.

"No, no I'm fine. Just admiring the old convent."

"Yes. Many come to sketch it, but the light won't be right until later this morning." He reentered his shop.

Lannie leaned against the stucco wall, not caring about the damage it might do her new jacket. A woman dressed in countless layers of colorful shawls approached with a basket filled to the brim with fresh carnations and camellias.

"A creamy camellia for the lady with the crimson hair?"

"No, I . . ." *Why not?* she thought. *Maybe it will give me courage.* "Yes, I'll take one."

Tucking the round silken bloom into the center of her French twist, she drew a shaky breath, and finally crossed the street. She walked rapidly, as if she had important business at the villa, though she didn't. An impulsive urge and compelling curiosity had brought her here, but more important were the questions she hoped would be answered.

They were expecting her. She had called earlier, saying she was a friend who wanted to visit.

She entered through the conciergerie, and followed a pathway through gardens leading to the portico. The deep windows, with their batten blue-green shutters and lacy grilled lower openings, seemed the eyes of a wise old woman who inspected her as she approached and found her wanting. Flushing with guilt, Lannie stumbled on the crushed oyster shell path and stopped to gather her equilibrium.

Drum would eventually discover she had been here. It was inevitable. Why hadn't she told him what she was going to do? Because she needed answers to questions, and she wanted to search objectively without his influence. He would have insisted on coming with her, and his very presence would have swayed any opinion she formed.

Inside, a frail, elderly nun with a sweet smile greeted her.

"Good morning, Miss Sullivan. I'm Sister Cecily. How nice of you to visit Mrs. Rutledge. She doesn't have many visitors. When she first came to us, friends came to see her occasionally, but I think they've forgotten about her now. Mr. Rutledge is here every two weeks, of course, just like clockwork."

"Of course," repeated Lannie, feeling especially traitorous at this deception. She'd told them she was an old friend.

The former convent, so courtly and fine on the outside, was massive and plain on the inside, with thick timbers overhead, and a staircase with heavy iron railings. As she followed the nun through wide, silent and serene hallways, her heels tapped hollowly on the cracked alabaster marble floor. She had an absurd urge to whisper, "Shhh, shoes, shhhh."

"Mrs. Rutledge is having one of her good days," said the nun.

"I'm glad."

They entered a corridor that seemed friendlier than the previous ones.

Green plants in porcelain urns sat against the walls, and from the rear of the villa came the aroma of chocolate baking.

Several of the doors they passed were open, and she saw beautiful beds and sitting rooms. One occupant sat reading a book by a large sunny window.

The nun finally stopped at a door that was ajar. She poked her head in, and then turned to smile at Lannie.

"Ann-Marie is sleeping, but should be awake soon. It's time for her morning snack. I don't mind if you sit with her and wait, or you may leave and come back this afternoon."

"No. I'll wait."

The nun ushered her in and indicated a wooden chair next to the bed. "You may sit there if you like. Mr. Rutledge sits there sometimes. Or there's a lovely sitting chair by the window overlooking the garden."

"Thank you."

The nun bustled away, and Lannie was left alone with Ann-Marie Rutledge.

Her first impression of the room was one of peace and safety. It was a corner room with two large windows, one looked out on a small courtyard with a fountain. In the center of the fountain an angel poured water from a pitcher. Pink bougainvillea cascaded over the walls and tumbled into the flowing water.

Sitting in front of the other window were a plump club chair and a chaise longue, both covered in cheerful polished cotton. A picturesque garden grew outside this window. Pale green clematis vines trailed hither and yon and mingled with spiking lavender nepatas and climbing lemon roses. White-painted cast-iron furniture, a settee, two chairs, and a table sat in the center of the walled-in garden.

Avoiding the figure on the bed, her eyes swept the room swiftly: shelves jammed with books, shelves with delicate china figurines, a table with silver-framed pictures, plants in lovely terra-cotta pots of different shapes and sizes.

Coolish air came from an air conditioner somewhere in the archaic villa, but hot Louisiana summers dictated more, and the high ceilinged room required the old wooden ceiling fan that whirred lazily overhead.

Heart thumping madly, Lannie finally fixed her eyes on the reason for her journey from North Carolina. She approached the intricately carved walnut bed, her knees shaking, and sank heavily into the chair next to it. With nervous irrelevance, she wondered if Drum had built the headboard. The elegant, but simple design of a tiny bird nesting on a tree branch looked like his work.

The immaculate pillow held an airy cloud of dark hair framing a fine-featured face with skin so creamy pale it seemed made of the smoothest unlined parchment. Winged eyebrows flew over dark feathery eyelashes. Ann-Marie had a heart-shaped face, with a small cleft in her pointed chin. Wisps of the angel hair blew softly in the gentle breeze of the ceiling fan. Lannie reached involuntarily to smooth errant tendrils off the delicate blue-veined temples, but jerked her hand back.

Ann-Marie Rutledge, angel-faced, vulnerable, looked almost like a child sleeping in the bed.

With trembling hand, Lannie poured herself a glass of water from the tumbler that sat on the table next to the bed. The chair by the garden window looked more comfortable, so she left the bedside and moved to sit in the plump chair. She'd planned on sitting there until Ann-Marie woke up, but jumped up and went to one of the bookcases.

I'll find a book to read. No, I should leave. I've satisfied my awful curiosity. No, I can't leave. I haven't found an answer yet, and my instincts tell me I will find answers here.

She stared at the bookcase as she vacillated between staying or leaving.

A book title jumped out at her, and she began to focus on the varied books before her. Slim volumes of poetry occupied one whole shelf. Ann-Marie's books? *A Short History of World War II, The Battle of Britain, America in the Air War,* Saint-Exupery's *Wartime Writings 1939–1944,* and others sat on one whole shelf devoted to World War II. Another shelf was filled with F. Scott Fitzgerald's work, another with Hemingway, another with all of John Grisham's books, and some quick reads by James Patterson. From what she knew of Ann-Marie this would not be her reading fare.

The next shelf was dominated by books on furniture craftsmanship.

Drum, of course. All of these books belonged to Drum. She swallowed the hard lump that formed in her throat and willed back the tears that threatened to spill from her burning eyes. She imagined him sitting in the comfy chair reading while Ann-Marie slept, a cup of coffee at his side, the room quiet and peaceful while he patiently waited.

An elaborate CD system occupied another shelf, and

a collection of jazz and classical music waited to be heard.

"Hello. You must be Chip's kindergarten teacher come to visit."

Lannie whirled around at the sound of the silvery-light voice. Ann-Marie Rutledge sat upright in her bed, her lavender eyes focused clearly on Lannie, a sweet smile on her face.

"Oh, n-no, I . . . well, yes I am. How are you?"

"A bit under the weather today, but good enough for a nice visit. Sister will be here in a minute with juice, or I'll have cook fix you some lunch. You will stay for lunch, won't you?"

"No, not today, maybe another time."

Ann-Marie reached for and shrugged into a silk-ribboned and rosebud-embroidered bed jacket that lay handy across the footboard of the bed.

"I received your note about Chip last week, Miss Champion. I'm sorry I've been late in getting back to you. We flew out to Oregon, and just returned. Chip is doing well, isn't he?"

Lannie clutched the back of the chair in front of her, hesitating, then working quickly at her reply.

"He's doing very well. He's my best student. A joy to teach. Eager to learn. He owns the stalwart athleticism of his father, yet the romantic poet nature of his mother also. He's also good with his hands, artwork, and block-building." This sounded like a child of Drum's. Would her child be similar in nature? Guilt ran rampant through Lannie, but she played her role well.

Ann-Marie's face shone with happiness. She clapped her hands like a child. "Oh, wonderful. I tell Drummond we're so fortunate and must protect ourselves from invaders."

The nun came carrying a tray with juice, a pot of tea, and molasses cookies. She helped Ann-Marie wash her face and hands, then made sure she was comfortable on the chaise longue. Lannie sat in the opposite chair.

The nun indicated a button on the wall close to Lannie, and said, "Sometimes she goes away completely or gets uncontrollable. If you should need me, just press the buzzer."

"Miss Champion," whispered Ann-Marie, "come quietly to the window and see the small daisies beneath the clematis vine. Can you hear them singing? It's a poem by Kate Dell. Listen."

"Please tell me what they say," said Lannie.

With a dreamy look of worlds beyond what ordinary mortals could see and hear, Ann-Marie recited:

This fair stem
which holds my head
to praise thee,
loves you, Lord, in all ways.
I stand in trembling ecstasy and
Pray thanks for this small flower that
I am.

"Small flowers," Ann-Marie repeated. She picked up one of the photos from the table at her side.

There is a true, pure innocence in this woman, thought Lannie with awe, which shouldn't be tampered with.

"Look," she said, and crooked her finger at Lannie, beckoning her to come closer. "This is *my* small flower. Here we are at the lodge last June. Chip loves it there. Not me, I hate it, but I'm not important. Drummond and Chip are important."

Lannie leaned close to look at the picture. Drum, leaning against the curving trunk of one of the cedars in front of the lodge, held his wife and son in his embrace. The airy fragrance of an expensive perfume she couldn't identify hovered around Ann-Marie. Lannie's throat filled again with held-back tears. Tears for herself, or for this tragic woman, or for Drum and the family he'd lost in the pull of a trigger?

Tears for all of them, she decided.

"Drummond will be home soon, and we'll dine together. Chip will be so excited to find you here. Miss Champion, do you mind if I knit while we talk?"

"Of course not."

Ann-Marie reached beneath the chaise and brought out her knitting bag.

"What are you working on?" asked Lannie.

"A winter sweater for Chip to take with him to boarding school. It's hard to believe he'll be thirteen next week, isn't it? We will miss him, but it will be heaven having Drummond to myself again."

It took a moment, but Lannie realized that Ann-Marie had jumped eight years, and had now entered another age with an imaginary Chip.

Lannie decided to agree. "I'm sure."

Ann-Marie fell silent while she knitted, her feathery cloud of dark hair sheltering her face as she worked, and Lannie sensed that she should not disturb the woman's intense concentration. She drank her tea and watched as the slim, nimble fingers worked the needles. It was then she realized that what Ann-Marie constructed was not a sweater, but a rectangular piece four feet long. The messy ball of navy-blue yarn she pulled from was kinky and looked as if it had been knitted and released many times.

She glanced up and found the woman looking at her, her brow wrinkled in a puzzle.

"Good afternoon." There was youth in her face, and her voice held the innocence of childhood. "Oh, dear, you're Auntie Clare's friend, aren't you? She'll be back shortly. She's with the caterer making plans for my engagement party tonight."

Lannie knew right away that Ann-Marie had returned to a time before she was married. Her whole demeanor had changed.

"I know it will be a lovely party."

"Yes, you must come and meet Drummond. You know, sometimes I think God sent me to North Carolina just to meet Drummond. Otherwise, I never would have gone."

Pinwheels of pain whirled dizzily through Lannie's head. She wanted to shout, "No, he's mine. You never should have met." But she knew that wasn't true, and then guilt at her relationship with Drum, and at her deception in coming here, crowded her chest like a growing mushroom. For a moment, she thought she would faint. She closed her eyes and sat upright taking deep breaths.

Ann-Marie chattered on about walking in the garden with Drum, about poetry they read together, and how gentle he was with her.

Open your eyes, Lanier Sullivan. Open your eyes to reality. It's time for you to leave here. You've found your answers.

The room had become silent, as if Lannie was the only occupant. She opened her eyes and found Ann-Marie staring at her blankly.

"Ann-Marie?"

The fragile woman, wrapped in her silk bed jacket, with yards and yards of yarn in her lap, seemed to be in a catatonic state. Not a muscle moved, and her lavender-blue eyes looked straight through Lannie, as if she didn't exist.

Lannie pressed the alarm button, and waited nervously until two nuns ran into the room.

"Oh, thank heavens," one of them said, crossing herself. "We were afraid she was having an angry time. She turns vicious then and wants to do harm to herself. But this mood she's having is nothing to worry about, Miss Sullivan. She'll come out of it in an hour or two."

"I should go, then," said Lannie. "Thank you. I enjoyed my time with her."

"Yes, she's an angel isn't she? Please come again."

"Thank you. Maybe I will." But she knew she wouldn't.

She took the delicate, creamy camellia blossom from her hair, placed it in Ann-Marie's lap and walked purposefully from the sheltered private room.

Ann-Marie and Drum Rutledge had a world of their own, and Lannie Sullivan and her child didn't belong in it.

Lannie curled up on the pillows of the plush bed in her room at the Royal Sonesta. The sounds of bustling life outside her windows on Bourbon Street were muffled by drawn satin drapes. It was lunchtime, and she should be enjoying a leisurely meal in one of New Orleans' exquisite restaurants, but neither her stomach nor her mood were receptive to the idea of rich food.

She stared at the television. She hadn't watched television in two years, but the images before her came and went without notice. Swamped with remorse over her secret trip to visit Ann-Marie Rutledge, and even more so over the decision she'd come to, she nursed her misery.

Exhausted, she fell asleep, and woke up six hours later with the evening news passing in front of her on the television.

"Good Lord."

Was that Nell's picture on the screen? She sat up and rubbed at her bleary eyes. It was Nell. What were they saying?

The photo of a laughing Nell disappeared, and the anchorwoman said, ". . . memorial service will be held tomorrow in Madison, Florida. The peaceful little town, to the east of us in the Florida panhandle, hasn't had a murder in fifty years and is trying to recover from the brutal rape and murder of the popular attorney. So far, officials have found no clues to the murderer. And in Atlanta today, Ku Klux Klan members formed a . . ."

Shock waves sent her reeling to the bathroom, where she vomited into the toilet until she had dry heaves.

Finally, emptied and shaking, she washed her face with a cold cloth.

Can't be true, she thought. *It's the tail end of a nightmare, right?*

She returned to the bedroom and reached with trembling hand for the telephone. Mausie should be home from her cousin's by now. If what Lannie had just heard, or thought she heard, on the television was true, Mausie would have come home right away. She punched in her home number.

"Sullivan residence."

"Mausie?"

"Oh, Lord, chile, we been tryin' to reach you."

Barely able to get the words out, Lannie asked, "Is what I heard on the TV true?"

"Lord love you, yes, it is. Nell is gone with Jesus."

Sickness welled in her throat again, but she fought it down.

"I'm coming right home, Mausie."

"Blessed Jesus, we need you."

"I'll make my reservations into Tallahassee. Big Billy can pick me up there."

"Yes, chile. Come fast as you can. Mausie wants to put her arms around you and keep you safe."

I wish that would do it, Mausie. I wish your arms could keep us all safe. Oh, dear, God. Nell gone? Not possible. Never. No.

TWENTY-THREE

The scent of carnations saturated the sanctuary of Saint Paul's Episcopal Church. Carnations had always been Nell's favorite flowers, a fact many people had remembered. Voluminous arrangements of the cinnamon-perfumed blooms filled every corner of the church.

Waves of nausea washed through Lannie and sloshed into her burning throat. She would never be able to stomach the sickening fragrance again.

She sat between Nell's parents. On her right, Mr. Smathers sobbed openly, and Lannie continued to supply him with tissues. On her left, Mrs. Smathers clung so close to her side that she felt the woman's body trembling. Nell-Louise Smathers sat with stoic face, her hand gripping Lannie's, her arms shaking, her bottom lip bitten until it was raw.

This isn't real, Lannie kept telling herself. This is a horrid nightmare. Any moment now, Nell will appear and tell us it was all a joke. But mischievous Nell had never told a joke or pulled a prank that would hurt anyone.

Oh, God, Nell. What happened? Who did this to you? Please tell me you didn't suffer, Nellie, girl, please.

Get real, Lannie. The sheriff had given her every gory detail. Face it. This is all true. This is happening.

Numb with shock and grief, Lannie had stayed close to the Smatherses since her arrival late last night. Big Billy had delivered her to their home, three houses away from Sullivan's Rest. She had slept in Nell's bedroom, where Nell's wedding dress hung on the closet door, its creamy, billowy whiteness haunting her throughout the night. Mausie had brought her a change of clothes and a dark dress to wear to the funeral.

Early this morning, she had slipped out to visit the sheriff, to find out what had happened. Nell had been found by hunters in an abandoned farmhouse outside the town limits. It was obvious she had been brutally raped, and then mutilated, her body too disfigured for a casket viewing. Her car, still filled with wedding gifts, had been located in a park not far from her house. So far, they hadn't a clue as to who murdered Nell.

Unaccustomed to murder investigations, the shaken county sheriff and the Madison chief of police had called in investigators from the state of Florida to assist them.

". . . and so we put to rest the soul of Eleanor Anne Smathers. Nell will always be remembered as the brightness and laughter in our lives, as the giving young attorney who cared deeply about the rights of her clients, as the loving daughter who gave her parents such joy. She goes with God now. God bless us all."

The choir hummed a reverent amen, and the minister said, "Nell's ashes will be interred privately at a later date. Ned and Nell-Louise Smathers have invited all of you to their home for lunch today."

An usher came to escort the Smathers family, and Hartley King, Nell's fiancé, who sat with them in the pew. As they traveled shakily up the aisle, Ned Smathers leaned on his brother's arm, and Lannie supported Nell-Louise by the waist. A drawn, heartbroken Hartley followed.

Lannie heard the whispers, but didn't care. She was in a fog of such misery and heartbreak that she could scarcely walk herself, much less help Nell-Louise, but Nell's parents needed her.

"My God, you're right," she heard the comment, and others as they moved up the aisle. "Who else can it be? Only one person with that glorious hair."

"Poor Lannie," someone said. "She looks all dramatic and mysterious in those big black glasses, not like herself at all."

Lannie supposed the severe black sheath she wore added to their observations, but she didn't care. The gossip had probably already begun to burn telephone lines and zip across e-mail trails. Nell's tragic death was enough fodder for ten years of scandalized speculation and intrigue in the small town, and Lannie's reappearance added an extra measure. She and her blond-haired buddy, Nell, had grown up in tandem in Madison.

"Dear Gussie, Lannie must still be recoverin' from Gracie's drowning, and Tom Ravenal leaving her, and now this."

"Wonder where she's been?"

"Why, honey, some people say she's been in North Carolina in an old cabin out in the boonies somewhere."

"About time she showed up. The judge was actin' mighty lonely before he went off to Ireland."

On hearing that snippet of conversation, Lannie felt a pang of guilt, but it soon left as the painful emotions of this day reclaimed her again.

"After all, she's not the only one who's had hard times in her life."

"Well, you're dern right about that. Did you hear Betty

Jackson has lung cancer, those two children of hers are only ten and eleven? You don't see her off on some mountain suckin' her thumb."

Lannie tuned most of it out, and tried to breathe evenly. But every breath she took brought more of the sweet carnation scent into her nose and lungs, and her stomach rebelled. Nell-Louise's arms were twitching, and her breathing was shallow. Lannie swallowed the rising bile, and squeezed her tighter.

Ahead, sitting on the aisle in a row toward the rear, a tall, broad-shouldered figure in a discriminating dark suit caught her eye. Light streaks in his dark blond hair caught a beam of sunlight coming through the open church doors.

Drum. It could only be Drum. The set of his shoulder, the slight tilt of his head. *Oh, no, God, I really don't think I can handle any more.* But, yes, this was like Drum. If he had heard about Nell, he would come. She didn't know whether to be angry or grateful.

Not even glancing his way as they passed, she managed to tune him out also. She would deal with his presence in this her personal grief later. Nell-Louise sagged against her.

"Almost there, darlin,' just a few more steps," she managed to say. They'd neared the end of the aisle. They made it out the church doors, Lannie gulped fresh air, dizzy with relief.

Small child of mine in the making, I hope you're getting through all of this okay. Hang tough for a little while longer.

At the house, uniformed waiters and waitresses circulated among the subdued crowd, offering cheese olivettes, Low Country pickled shrimp, and caviar-stuffed mushrooms for starters, with fat glasses of Bloody Marys to wash it all down.

Lannie made sure the Smatherses were safely ensconced in a corner of the spacious living room and begged them to eat something.

"I couldn't eat a thing, Lannie, darlin'," said Nell-Louise. "Please, just go and circulate. Everyone here is dyin' to talk to you. We'll sit here and receive our guests."

"Yes, please, Lanier. We'll be fine. We can talk later, after everyone is gone," said Ned Smathers. He smiled, a wan sort of helpless smile, nodded his courtly head, and took his wife's hand in his.

Nell was their only child. Lannie knew they were survivors, but the struggle to live with joy again would last until the end of their days. Lannie placed a tall glass of iced tea, the sides beaded with moisture, beside each of them, and mourners began to file by to pay their respects.

Her gaze swept the room searching for Drum, but there was no sign of him. With mixed feelings of disappointment and relief, she slipped outside onto the wide shady veranda, similar to the one at Sullivan's Rest.

They were setting up lunch beneath the spreading oak, which she and Nell had both fallen from when they were nine, Nell breaking an arm and Lannie spraining an ankle. The tables, with their starched white cloths, looked like white checkers on the manicured green lawn.

The Smatherses' guests would enjoy the typically southern meal she'd helped the Smatherses' cook plan late last night. All Nell's favorites; the tarragon shrimp and red pepper cole slaw, the boned baked ham with pecan stuffing, a creamy carrot pudding, French fried okra, and for dessert, a fresh fruit compote with whipped cream.

As weary as she was, she knew she would have to take up the slack here, to smile and be gracious, to assure longtime friends that all was not lost, that life would somehow go on without darling, irrepressible Nell. The crowd surged toward her, then seemed to acknowledge that this wasn't accepted behavior and held back, two or three of them approaching at a time.

Sobbing openly, Mary-Beth Canyon said, "Oh, Lannie, darlin', we've missed you terribly, just terribly. Honey, what are we going to do without Nell? I simply can't bear the thought."

They embraced, and Lannie tried to console her. Patting her back, she said, "There, there, Bethie, Nell wouldn't want us all broken up. Try to hold up for Nell-Louise and Ned. The best thing you can do is visit them frequently, take them out for dinner sometimes, maybe."

"Yes, yes, you are so right. Eh, Lannie, you'll be comin' home now, won't you? I know it's none of my business, I mean where you've been and all, an' I don't want to be nosy, but we sure would like to see you back in Madison."

"I know, and thank you. Right now, I'm not sure what my plans are. But don't you worry about me. You just be concerned for the Smatherses."

Bud Pheiffer, captain of their high school football team and current football coach at the same school, hugged her a bit too snugly, she thought. "Hey there, Lannie. Happy you came out of seclusion. Have dinner with me tonight?"

"Thanks, but I can't, Bud."

"By the way," he said before he left her, "they think the guy that did this has left the area. A clerk at the 7-Eleven said a guy with blood on his pants and seat stopped for cigars and beer early on the morning they found Nell. Said he headed east on I-10. The sheriff said from all indications he could gather that he believed the guy has moved on. Said generally, murderers with the hate this guy has in his heart don't hang around too long. They always have an agenda and move fast. But the women in this town should be careful anyway. You never know about these things."

Lannie vaguely recalled the sheriff telling her this, but didn't really care right now. Her grief and disbelief at the trauma outweighed everything.

The next hour was filled with similar conversations; sincere grief expressed over Nell and veiled hints and questions as to where Lannie had been, and would she return, and admonitions not to go anywhere alone because one never knew what evil lurked around the corner, even here in Madison.

At one point, Lannie felt faint and leaned against the porch column behind her.

Oh, dear God, this can't be good for the baby. Help me here, Lord.

Drum appeared suddenly, making his way politely through the crowd and heading toward her. Curious glances and whispered asides followed the handsome stranger's path through the fascinated guests. Was it really Drum? Her vision wavered, grew hazy. Was she imagining his presence? Did she need and want and love him so desperately that she conjured him up with ease? No, she'd seen him at the church. Remember, Lannie?

Fading in and out, her hands sought inconspicuously for a secure hold on the solid column supporting her back.

Mausie, who had come down the street from Sullivan's Rest to help, appeared miraculously at her side.

"Now look here, chile, you're pale as grits." She took Lannie by the elbow and sat her down in a wicker chair in a cool, quiet corner of the porch. "Lunch is bein' served. You wait right here, and I'll bring you some."

The thought of eating any of the meal she'd planned so lovingly with the Smatherses' cook, made her ill now.

"No, Mausie. Just tea, please."

Mausie gave her a second look. "Ummph. There's somethin' wrong with you besides terrible grief. I've never known you to turn down food on *any* occasion."

"I'm fine, really I am." But the porch and the people and the vines and the smiles and the tears and the scent of carnations began to swirl around and around and around, and she slipped from her chair onto the floor.

Strong arms picked her up and held her close. Drum's voice sounded concerned. Secure against his solidness, she felt his chest reverberate when he spoke to Mausie.

"I've got her, ma'am. I believe you must be Mausie. I'm Drummond Rutledge, a good friend of Lannie's. If you'll lead the way, I'd be happy to take her wherever you think best."

She woke up late that night in her own bedroom with Mausie on one side of the bed and Big Billy on the other. Big Billy cradled a shotgun in his lap.

"Was I dreaming or was Drum Rutledge at the funeral?"

"He sure was, honey, an' I don't know who he is, but he came in mighty handy at the Smatherses'. Picked you right up and brought you here," said Mausie. "He is a good friend, isn't he? I mean it's okay for him to be here?"

"Yes." *If you only knew how okay it really is.*

"Did he carry me all the way home?"

"Sure did."

"And I suppose everyone was all a twitter about that."

"Some," said Big Billy with a gentle smile. "Bud Pfeiffer wanted to do the honors, but Mr. Rutledge wouldn't hear none of it. Just gave ol' Bud a terrible look and carried you off like you was treasure from heaven."

"Oh, great! More fodder for gossip."

Lannie closed her eyes again, wishing it all away, wishing she'd never heard of the High Falls Summer Playhouse or Drum Rutledge, wishing she was still at the cabin with only Bry for company, wishing the heartache of Nell's murder was just an awful nightmare.

But she couldn't wish anything away anymore. It was

time for her to face up to the situation with Drum, and the horror of Nell's murder, but she needed time to think things out. She sighed and opened her eyes.

"Where is he now?"

"Down in the kitchen havin' some iced tea and waitin' for me to come down and say he can come up and see you."

"I'm not ready to see him, Mausie. Later, maybe. Put the gun away, Big Billy. We're not going to live in fear. Whoever murdered Nell is probably miles away from here."

"I don't think so, Lannie." He frowned. "I'm not puttin' the gun away. Someone said they saw a man looked like Jeb Bassert lurkin' in the woods last week. He was always hangin' around you like a lovesick hound dog, and he was mad as hell when you got him sent up for rapin' that white trash, Susie Slater."

"Okay." She remembered with dawning horror the man in the attic. "If it makes you happy. Nell *did* say something about Jeb being released, and she was checking on how he got a pardon. But I hardly think he'd carry a grudge for ten years."

Fat tears rolled down Mausie's dusky face. "You got other troubles besides Nell and Jeb Bassert, don't you, chile? When are you expectin' this baby?"

There was no trying to fool Mausie. She'd have to 'fess up.

"You look jest like you did when Gracie was growin' inside of you. Eyes all silvery and sparkly, but with dark circles underneath. And you are already gettin' thick at the waist."

"Please, no one is to know."

"I'm not tellin' no one, I'm jest goin' to take good care of you."

"No, I don't need babying, and I've got a murderer to track down."

"Now you listen to me, Lanier Sullivan. You're stayin' here where I can keep an eye on you," said a shocked Mausie. "Gracie's birth wasn't an easy one for you, an I 'spect this one won't be much better."

Big Billy shook his head adamantly. "No way are we goin' to let you go gallavantin' around getting into trouble. You're goin' to stay here. That's what the judge would want."

Again, she wished with all her heart that she could stay here and be cosseted or better yet run back to the mountain where she could selfishly do her own thing and not worry about hurting anyone.

Everything in her body urged her to withdraw again, run away, go where it's safe, go back to Haystack Mountain, to Bry, and the cabin. That had been her plan when she left the convent two days ago. Her acute sadness at the decision not to tell Drum about the baby had rocked her physically and emotionally. She hadn't the heart to ask him to divorce Ann-Marie, and she knew instinctively that he would do so if she told him about the baby. He would carry the guilt of desertion with him always, and she would hate that.

But her monumental anger at the person who had robbed Nell of her life shouted louder than her cowardly wish for safety, and every alarm bell that rang within her told her it was Jeb.

"Both of you stop worrying. I'm healthier than I've ever been, and, trust me, I'm not going to endanger this child's life. I just want to follow up on a few things Nell said."

Mausie frowned.

"We'll talk about this later, chile. I'll bring you up some food, and then you rest. Then we'll decide what to do." She shook her head in worry, as she walked away, and muttered under her breath, "I sure wish the judge was here.

He be the only one who could talk the livin' sense into you."

After she'd eaten Mausie's famous chicken soup and corn muffins she let her gaze wander about the bedroom. Poignant memories and love rose in her chest, and Lannie let the tears flow. Here was where she and Nell had revealed their precious secrets, and dreamed their dreams, and she remembered that she'd never had a chance to tell Nell about the baby.

"I'll find the bastard who took you away from us, Nell. I promise I'll find him," she murmured into her pillow, and drifted into an exhausted sleep with the sound of Big Billy humming "Precious Lord" outside her door.

TWENTY-FOUR

At Mausie's invitation, Drum had spent the night in one of the guest bedrooms, and now sat in the large kitchen, eating Mausie's hefty breakfast and talking with Big Billy. They sat in a sunny-yellow breakfast nook next to windows that looked out on the Sullivan's rear lawn. Thick layers of shiny, dark-green ivy climbed the outer walls of the white painted brick house. It curled around the frames of the long sash windows to peek into the kitchen.

Across the old-fashioned black-and-white tiled floor, on the other side of the square kitchen, Mausie polished a silver tea set. Drum felt her watchful gaze and wanted to reassure her that his purpose here was to help Lannie, not hurt her. Big Billy was talking. He was shaking his head in worry.

"Lannie said she's goin' to go lookin' for Nell's killer, Mr. Rutledge, and that's just too dangerous. Lannie has always been headstrong. The judge has always pretty much let her do whatever pleased her, but we're mighty worried now."

Strangely enough, it had been Lannie's elderly friend, Faye Wickfort, who had alerted him to Nell's murder. She had called him in Charlotte, her soft aristocratic southern voice trembling a bit over the phone. "I don't know that I approve of your relationship with Lannie, Mr. Rutledge, but I know she cares for you very much. She needs support and a strong hand right now."

"Yes, Mrs. Wickfort, I'm on my way right now. Thank you for calling . . . and, by the way, I hope someday you'll change your mind about me."

"Perhaps."

The Lear Jet had gotten him to Tallahassee in no time, and he'd rented a car for the one-hour drive to Madison. An inquiry at a gas station outside of town led him to the right church. At first, he'd felt like an uncomfortable intruder inserting himself into the grief of a very private community, but the moment he saw Lannie's drawn, stricken face, he knew he'd been right to come.

"I'm worried, too. Did she speak with her father?"

"Yes sir. They spoke over the phone, and he told her to do whatever she wanted, but I don't think he realizes the seriousness of the situation. Another thing that troubles us, Mr. Rutledge. Mausie and me are the only family Lannie has close by. The judge sounds like he's goin' to stay in Ireland till Christmas time, when he's bringin' his bride home, and Nell's gone now. Lannie hasn't got nobody who really cares about her lookin' out for her, 'cept us, and we are gettin' old. Besides, Lannie has always done jest exactly what she pleases, ever since her mother died."

"Do you have any idea who might have killed Nell?"

"Not really. Only real strong suspicions. Jeb Bassert's out of prison, and that's another thing Lannie didn't tell the judge when she called him." Big Billy frowned, and his soft brown eyes filled with worry. "Jeb grew up here in Madison, was always a misfit, hung around Lannie's crowd, but none of them ever gave him the time of day 'cept

Lannie. He worshipped Lannie. He used to help me clean up around the place, but more than once I found him where he wasn't s'posed to be. Found him on the porch roof spyin' on Lannie's bedroom, and I fired him."

"Why would he want to hurt Nell or Lannie?"

"When Lannie was an assistant state's attorney, she got Jeb convicted for rapin' a piece of white trash, Susie Slater. I saw the hate in his eyes when they took him away. He was screaming at Lannie, his face all screwed up ugly and evil pourin' out him of like sour alcohol. Yellin' he was innocent, and Lannie had humiliated him. He blamed her for everything. His love turned to hate, and there is nothin' more dangerous, no sir."

"You know for a fact that he has been released from prison?"

"Yes sir, he has. I asked the sheriff. He said some fancy new DNA tests proved Jeb was innocent, and the governor pardoned him. Someone said they seen him here in town, but I know him well, Mr. Rutledge, and I haven't seen hide nor hair of him."

"Is there anything to connect him with Nell?"

"Well, no, sir, not really, 'cept Lannie and Nell were always together, and Nell used to make fun of him when they were young, and after he was sent to prison Lannie went back into private practice with Nell. It's hard to tell where twisted minds go, Mr. Rutledge."

"That's true, and please, call me Drum."

"Yes, sir. All their lives, Lannie and Nell have been connected real strong. I s'pose that's why when something happens to one, we think of the other."

"Does Bassert have any woodland or mountain survival abilities?"

"Hard to tell what he learned in prison. When he was growin' up here he didn't know how to do nothin' but rake leaves, fish, chew tobacco, and spit, and he also waited tables sometimes at the country club. Why do you ask?"

"Because, unless I can convince Lannie to come to Charlotte with me, I suspect she will return to the spot she considers her safest haven. A place that's almost inaccessible."

"The judge's ol' huntin' cabin on top of the mountain?"

"Maybe." Drum saw the hurt look on Big Billy's expressive face, but he couldn't tell anyone where the cabin was or if that was where Lannie lived, not even Big Billy. "I'll speak to the sheriff and the town police this afternoon."

"Not without me, you won't," said a voice behind him. "And besides, who asked you for help? Not me. I can take care of myself, remember?"

Drum's heart galloped like a runaway horse at the sound of Lannie's sleepy voice. He turned, and at the sight of her yearned to take her into his arms, carry her back upstairs and make slow, sleepy morning love.

She stood in the kitchen door, as she must have done thousands of times through the years, pulling the tie of a worn, comfy, soft-pink chenille robe snug to her waist, and yawning. Her feet were bare and her crimson hair tumbled wildly about her shoulders.

He knew the mountain hippie woman, and he'd met the glorious, glamorous sophisticate who attended the party at his lodge only a week ago, and now, here in the home of her childhood and growing-up years probably wearing the same robe she'd worn as a teenager, was an impression of a younger Lannie. Each woman fascinated him more than the one before, and he found himself falling in love with her all over again. If he had his way, he would find it a delicious, mind-blowing habit to fall in love with her in a thousand ways always and forever.

"Come and sit, chile," said Mausie. "I'll have you some

eggs and biscuits ready in no time, and bacon, all crispy jest like you like it."

"Good morning, Sullivan," Drum said, unable to restrain the smile on his face.

"Good morning, Rutledge," she said and sat down across from him next to Big Billy. "Sorry, about my less than stellar attire this morning, but you've seen me in worse. I tried on some old jeans, but nothing seems to fit . . . ah . . . well, so . . ."

Mausie crossed the kitchen quickly, interrupting Lannie's seeming embarrassment. Embarrassment about what, he wondered. Everyone gained a few pounds now and then, and a few pounds wouldn't bother someone like Lannie whose lack of vanity had always intrigued him.

"Here, chile, you drink this coffee. Need to wake up, and be polite to your friend here."

Lannie paled and shoved the cup away from her, and Drum could have sworn she got a little green around the mouth. "Uhh, no coffee, but how about a nice cup of decaf tea?"

Mausie raised her eyebrows, "See, I tol' you, chile. You need . . ."

"Just some nice hot decaf tea will be fine," said Lannie firmly, giving Mausie an odd look.

"Right. Comin' up, chile."

Lannie threaded her hands through her tumbled hair and smiled weakly.

"Sorry, Drum. I'm not usually so inhospitable. Frankly, I'm a bit surprised you're still here. Madison is a nice little town, but you're accustomed to more action."

"Lannie Sullivan! You thank Mr. Rutledge for bringing you home yesterday," said Big Billy.

She dropped her head in her hands, then shook her

head and sat erect, shoulders back, expression set and unreadable.

"I'm sorry, Drum. I think I'm still in shock. I do thank you for rescuing me yesterday. Thank you very much for coming."

She tried to smile, but the effort was too much. The corners of her mouth fell back into place.

Mausie placed a cup of tea before her, and she raised it shakily to her lips.

He ached to take her into his arms and soothe her, tell her things would get better eventually.

"Lannie, I know you want to help find Nell's killer," he said, "but law enforcement officials can handle these things much better than we can."

"I know that, and I'm not going rushing into dangerous places, but there are questions that should be asked, and I know where to go and who to ask."

"Then let me help you. I have resources and manpower available that could make things much easier for you."

He held his breath as she studied him for a long moment. With teacup in hand, her sad gray eyes searched for unfathomable truths within him, truths that he knew even he couldn't access.

Finally, she lowered her cup to the saucer, and nodded her head.

"Yes, you're right. As much as it hurts to admit it, I can move faster with your help. After all, that's what friends are for, right, Drum?"

She smiled stiffly and stuck her hand across the table for a short shake of his hand.

"Right, Lannie." *So that's how it's going to be, is it? Friends. Just a friendly businesslike handshake, and we're buddies. Well, we'll see about that, Lannie Sullivan.*

° ° °

With great reluctance Lannie had agreed to drive to Tallahassee with Drum. She had no car of her own, and it seemed foolish to rent one when Drum's was available.

Now he watched Lannie with amazement and admiration. Here was yet again another part of her, the efficient, hardworking prosecuting attorney for Madison County. She questioned the head of the criminology lab assertively and knowledgeably.

He listened to Dr. Richard Reese answer her questions.

"We pulled Jeb Bassert's records after you called, Miss Sullivan, and after close examination, we think you may be correct. The DNA results *could* have been tampered with."

"We need to do better than that, sir. I need a definitive answer. Were they or weren't they, and if so, how were they changed, and who did it?"

Drum had led the way into the man's office and begun the questioning, but Lannie had soon taken over. Unaccustomed to playing second lead, he had at first resented her taking charge, but soon realized that she knew exactly what she was doing.

"Yes, Miss Sullivan. We're working on that right now. There's a possibility that one of our former employees was responsible."

"Fine, Dr. Reese." She glanced at her watch, and for the first time seemed uncertain of her next move. "It's five-thirty. When does the lab close?"

The man looked embarrassed. "Well, actually, Miss Sullivan, we're closed right now. Security let you in because Mr. Rutledge called the governor. But don't worry about that. My best technician said she would work overtime. However, it may take a while. Are you going to be in the area overnight?"

It was Lannie's turn to be embarrassed, and she hesitated, glancing at Drum as if not sure where to go from here. He knew her dilemma. She desperately wanted quick answers, but she hadn't planned on spending the night here, especially with Drum.

"We could return to Madison for the night, if you want to, Lannie," Drum suggested.

"No, we would be backtracking. The sheriff and the town police gave us all they could." A stubborn look settled on her face, and he knew she'd made up her mind. "We'll spend the night here, Dr. Reese. I'm accustomed to staying at the Governor's Inn, so you can reach me there. Please call at any time of the night. I want to know as soon as possible. They say these monsters are easier to track if the trail is fresh."

"Certainly, Miss Sullivan."

As they drove away, Drum said, "*I'm* accustomed to staying at the Governor's Inn, too. I hope you don't mind."

She stiffened, her back erect as she pointedly kept her eyes on the highway ahead.

"No, of course not. Although, it is the beginning of the term and parents of FSU students might have filled the hotel."

"I think that was last week, Lannie, but there are some freshmen legislators in town. In fact, I anticipated this and already reserved a suite."

"A suite? Drum, I made it clear that I thought it best if we stayed away from each other until I got things clear in my mind. If you think we're going to spend the night together, you are wrong."

"The suite was the only space available, and it has connecting doors that lock."

He smiled as he watched her body curve back into the seat with relief.

"Fine, and thank you very much for arranging to keep

the lab open until we got there . . . and thinking of the hotel accommodations."

The Governor's Inn was a gracious old hotel, small and intimate, and recently renovated with lovely antiques in an antebellum motif. Their suite overlooked a square close to the capital building. A sitting room separated the two bedrooms.

"It's nonsense for us to be here together and not dine together," said Drum before he entered his room. "Would you do me the honor, Miss Sullivan, of dining with me this evening purely on a friendly basis?"

She smiled, her sense of humor seemingly restored to some extent, and said, "It is a rather ridiculous situation, isn't it? Yes, let's have a nice dinner somewhere."

Later, ensconced in a booth in an intimate out-of-the-way Italian restaurant on the outskirts of Tallahassee, Drum couldn't believe his good fortune. Lannie sat across from him, reserved and reticent, but smiling. She'd scarcely said two words during dinner. He knew she wanted this to be a nice evening for them, but the shocks that had ripped her apart in the last ten days held her prisoner.

For a while, they talked of impersonal things, the history of Sullivan's Rest and a land purchase Drum was negotiating in California. Fifty thousand acres that he'd been wanting for years had finally been put on the market. Lannie seemed interested and caught all the nuances of the importance of the deal, which pleased him.

They had finished their pasta, and Lannie sipped her sparkling water and appraised the dim interior of the warmly welcoming place. Red-checkered tablecloths covered the tables, and in the center of each sat the essential candle stuck into an old wine bottle covered with wax drippings. The mouth-watering aroma of garlic and marinara sauce pervaded the place, and in the corner an elderly

Italian man strummed a guitar, singing, and humming softly to himself. It was late in the evening, and the place had emptied of college students. Only a few diners sat in view of the romantic candlelight.

"Delicious, delicious, delicious," she said, and let her smile momentarily widen into a broad grin. "My first real pasta in almost three years. What a treat. Thank you."

"It's a shame you don't like red wine. It was excellent, too."

The silence between them fell again.

Finally he could stand it no longer. "I can only imagine how you are hurting, Lannie. I'm not afraid or ashamed to say that I wish you'd let me hold you. I wish you would let me console you. Maybe I could kiss away the hard edges."

He reached for her hand on the table, and she let him hold it, but she shook her head at his remarks. "I know you do, Drum, and I wish that I could let you, but I have to get through this on my own. If I don't, I'll never feel strong again."

He brought her hand to his lips and kissed each finger reverently, lingering over them, covering each one with his lips, saying a small prayer to himself with each kiss. His gaze never left hers, and he saw her gray eyes turn smoky, watched the desire grow, shook with the explosive electricity pass rapidly between them.

He captured her hand now in both of his and propped his chin on his joined fists, staring at her with naked need. Tears sprang into her eyes. "Please, don't do this, Drum. My resistance is low. Don't make this any harder for me. I have decisions to make on my own. Please respect my feelings."

The waiter brought them each an espresso, and Drum released her hand.

He tried again to apologize for the monumental error

he'd made in the beginning, in not making sure that Lannie knew of his marital status.

"Lannie, I was so wrong. I hope someday you'll forgive me."

"I . . . I can't even think of that right now," she said, but her face grew pale, and he knew that she *did* think of his betrayal. "I can't think of anything but Nell and the bastard who did this. I'll sort the rest out later."

Drum knew her mind must be a jumble of conflicting emotions, some of which concerned him, some about Nell, and some about something else, he thought, something she was keeping from him.

The waiter approached again and handed Drum a portable phone. "Excuse me, Mr. Rutledge, Miss Sullivan. Your hotel has called. They have a message for you."

Drum listened carefully, then said, "Thank you, Dr. Reese. I'll tell her." He said to Lannie. "It's somewhat encouraging news. Jeb Bassert's results were switched with those of another felon serving time for armed robbery. Also, they're fairly sure the tampering was done by a part-time employee named Buster Bush. He had access to the material during the time the governor's staff was requesting a review of Bassert's records, and he's somewhat of a computer genius."

"Who is Buster Bush and why would he do such a thing?"

"My chief security man, Bob Lambert, stayed at the lab with the technician tonight. When they discovered the switch, surmised how it was done, and by whom, Jim began investigating Bush. Bush made several phone calls to Raiford prison during that time period, and Jim discovered through birth and school records that Buster Bush and Jeb Bassert are cousins."

Excitement grew in Lannie's eyes. She grasped his hand

and started to slide out of the booth, "Okay, let's find Buster Bush and talk with him. Come on, let's go."

"Wait, beautiful. Buster Bush resigned from his job in June. Said his cousin, who was his best friend, had invited him to go on several fishing trips, and he didn't know when he would be back. Bob has tried to locate him, but Buster hasn't been seen since he left the criminology lab that day."

Lannie's face fell back into an expression of restraint, patience, and resignation. "Jeb probably did away with his own cousin. Is that what you think?"

"Yes, but we have another lead. Bob has traced Jeb to Atlanta. We're going there tomorrow."

In the parking lot on the way to their car, Drum tucked Lannie's hand around his elbow. They were almost to the car when she let out a long sigh and slumped against him.

He wrapped her against him quickly. "Lannie, Lannie, are you all right?"

"Yes . . . I, ah . . . just need . . . I'm fine." She tried to pull away from him and stand on her own, but faded into him again.

"You're not fine. You're worn out. You need rest, and a lot of it, and I'm going to make sure you get it."

At the hotel, as weary and faint as she was, Lannie insisted she could get herself undressed and into bed without his help.

He paced the sitting room, waiting for a sound or anything that would indicate that she might have fainted again. Her bedroom door finally opened, and Lannie, looking like a lost and lonely waif in the flannel nightgown she'd brought from Sullivan's Rest, peeked out at him.

"Drum, I've changed my mind. I don't want to be alone tonight. Will you sleep with me?" she asked softly.

Just before she went to sleep, her head tucked snug

beneath his chin, she whispered, "Promise me we'll go to Atlanta tomorrow, no matter how tired you think I am."

"I promise, beautiful."

He held her all night long, close and safe, her breathing a lovely rhythm against his chest, her hair a silken nest to rest his cheek, his physical desire dampened for the time being as his protective nature took charge, and his complete love for her burgeoned into higher realms than he'd ever known.

Lannie stared out the window of Drum's Lear jet. She knew they were headed to Atlanta, but time and destinations and people and life weren't what they should be, or what they used to be. A hideous, noncaring storm, which foretold only an unpredictable existence, had blown her away into a strange land. She would never believe in anything again. Nothing was ever guaranteed, not goodness, not family, not love, not security.

What had happened to her life of last week, a life of the mountain, of Bry, of the cabin, of volunteering at the playhouse . . . and of loving Drum?

She loved Drum more than seemed possible, more now than a month ago, but the events of the past ten days had changed them both forever. The man she loved was married to another woman, an angelic, helpless woman whom Lannie couldn't bear to hurt. And Nell was gone. Horribly, horribly gone. Laughing, loving, best friend forever, Nell, had probably been murdered by a man *Lannie* had sent to prison.

Could she ever do anything right? Her negligence as a mother had caused Gracie's death. Her headstrong disregard of the consequences of her passion had led to a totally irrational affair with Drum, which had resulted in the baby she now carried, a baby who would probably never know his father as he should. Her dedicated prosecution of Jeb Bassert had sent him to prison and ultimately resulted in Nell's death.

On top of it all, she hadn't told Drum of her visit to see Ann-Marie in New Orleans. She should have told him last night at dinner. She should have told him before she shamelessly asked him to stay with her last night, before she selfishly fell asleep in his safe, strong arms. But she was afraid. Afraid she would see the love on his face turn to anger and to disappointment in her. She couldn't bear that right now.

Stop feeling sorry for yourself, Lanier Sullivan. You are alive. You are carrying the child of the man you love.

Drum's voice, across the aisle, intruded on her thoughts.

For a single self-indulging moment she let her gaze follow the strong line of his jaw as he spoke into the telephone, the decisive movement of his tanned hand as he jotted notes on the white paper in front of him, and the quick arch of one eyebrow as he listened to the party on the other end.

She closed her eyes in a swift agony of desire. Never, never again. *Get used to it, Lannie. You will never feel those hands again.*

He completed the call, and looked across the aisle at Lannie.

"Well, we may have something to go on." He smiled with encouragement. "I've had Bob Lambert looking for Jeb Bassert ever since Big Billy mentioned the name, and that's why we're going to Atlanta. Early in the summer a stolen car was abandoned in the parking lot of a shopping mall just outside of Atlanta. Though the car was wiped clear of prints, one small print was found on the gas cap. It was traced to Jeb Bassert. They are questioning owners and store employees in the mall right now."

"Good. How soon do we land?"

"In about fifteen minutes. Are you okay?"

"I'm just fine," she replied, and she meant it. Just knowing that something was being done about finding Nell's killer lifted her spirits.

Bob Lambert had flown ahead of them from Tallahassee and met them at the airport. He drove them to the suburban mall where the car had been found last June.

"We've talked with everyone we could find who was working the week the car was found, Drum. We've come up with only one possible lead. I figured you and Miss Sullivan would want to talk to the lady."

"Yes, we would, Bob. Thank you."

Bob pulled into a strip mall and parked in front of Connie's Curl-Up-and-Dye Beauty Shop.

Inside the shop, an elderly woman with purple curlers in her hair was getting a manicure from a gum-chewing teenager and an overweight, fortyish-looking hairdresser gave Bob a flirtatious grin as she blew out a client's hair. Connie hurried from the back of the shop, stripping off plastic gloves covered with maroon dye.

"Hello, Mr. Lambert. Back again?" she called as she came. "Thought we'd told you all we could remember, but you are always welcome, that's for sure. Brought some friends, I see."

She set a timer on the messy reception desk, dropped the gloves into a wastebasket, and nervously shoved her straw-blond bouffant hairdo into place. She smelled of dye, Charlie cologne, and cigarettes.

"Hi, Connie. Couldn't help myself. You girls are fun to be around."

She grinned, whisked off her apron, and quickly fiddled with the waistband of her tight black latex shorts, making sure her T-shirt was tucked snug.

"Well, we just love havin' you, honey. Now what can we do for you this time? Maybe your girlfriend here would like a haircut or a manicure? I wouldn't dare touch the hair color, though. Mighty pretty as it is. Wish I knew the formula for that. Someone done a right good job on her."

She grinned at Lannie. Lannie didn't know whether to be insulted or amused. She glanced at Drum and caught him struggling with suppressed laughter.

"No, thank you," said Lannie quickly, "but we could sure use your help."

"Sure, sweetie, what can we do for you?"

"Bob says you remember a man fitting this description," said Drum, and held out a picture of Jeb Bassert.

"Yeah, kinda. Only his nose was a bit different. But I remember him because he wanted his hair bleached. First place, we don't have many men in here, and second place . . . I never had a man who wanted his hair bleached white."

"Anything else you remember?" asked Lannie anxiously.

"Yeah, come to think of it, there was. He was real curious about how I done his hair. Wanted to know every step of the process, and the names of the products I used."

"Did he say why?" asked Lannie.

"Not really, 'cept I got the impression that he was going to keep his hair that way, and he would be doin' it himself, maybe."

"Can you remember what he said that made you think that?"

"Not really, 'cept he said he was going away for a long time, he was going to see his girlfriend and he wanted to surprise her with his new hair."

"How did he seem to you, I mean, how did he act? Did he seem afraid, or dumb, or nervous?"

"No, he didn't seem none of those things. Let me think

a minute." She closed her eyes, and her false eyelashes laid like black spider legs against the caked rose-colored foundation on her lined cheeks. She opened them, and said, "He was right cocky, like a little banty rooster, and he seemed smart, but he didn't talk much, and he wasn't nervous."

"Anything else?" pressed Lannie.

Connie called to her associate.

"Hey, Madge, you remember that weird guy who came in early part of June and wanted his hair bleached?"

"Yeah."

"You remember how he acted?"

"Honey, I sure do. When I was shampooing his hair, he felt me up real good, I mean, like man, he practically had his finger up my twat before I could jump away. I told him he'd better keep his hands to himself or I'd call the cops."

"Why didn't you tell me?"

"He told me he'd give me a hundred dollars if I kept my mouth shut. So, I did. You left the next day for your two weeks in Myrtle Beach, and by the time you come back I'd forgot about him."

"He abandoned his car across the street. Do you recall how he left here?" asked Drum.

"Sure. It was late afternoon. He was our last customer, an' he just walked out like anybody else," said Connie. "And like Madge said, I was gone for the next two weeks, so I didn't notice that car sittin' there all that time."

"I didn't pay it any attention because I was too damn busy while Connie was gone," called Madge, as she put the finishing touches on her client's hair. "It was Harry in the hardware store next door who finally reported it to the cops."

"Okay," said Jim, "you ladies have been very helpful. Here's my card. If you remember anything else, please give me a call. Thank you."

Outside the shop, Bob Lambert shook his head in discouragement. "Drum, my men have interrogated everyone in the mall, everyone who had contact with Bassert at Raiford, and anyone else we could think of that he might have come in contact with. No one has seen him since he was released from Raiford, except the ladies in this shop. Every airport and every seaport in the country has been flooded with his picture and no one has come up with anything."

"Keep it up, Bob. You're the best man I know for the job, and I know we'll find him."

"I know we will, too, but not as quick as you and Miss Sullivan would have liked. There's not a sign of him anywhere. It's possible he's left the country, and if that's the case, it will take a while to trace him."

Bob Lambert's cell phone rang. He unhooked it from his belt and answered the call. He looked at Drum with concern, then glanced at Lannie. He handed the phone to Drum.

Lannie watched Drum's face etch with worry as he listened. Finally, he said, "Yes, Sister, I'll be there right away."

Lannie grabbed at the last breath she took and held on to it desperately, hating the tremors that shook her entire body.

Drum said, "Bob, would you excuse us?" Bob stepped back into the shop to flirt with the women, and Drum took her hand in his. "Lannie . . . Oh, God, this is hard, and it isn't fair. I have to . . . Ann-Marie is sick. They think she has pneumonia and she refuses to go to the hospital. I have to go to New Orleans."

Everything within her grew still, frozen, chilled with dread and foreknowledge. She'd asked for this. This would always be the case. Ann-Marie would always come first, and that was as it should be.

"That's okay, Drum. I understand. I'm ready to go back to Haystack. It looks as if we can do nothing more to find Jeb until Bob digs up more information anyway."

"Go to Madison, Lannie. Be with Mausie and Big Billy. You'll be safe there."

She had told him of the night in the attic, of the horrid taunting and torturing, and the fear that she could still taste in her mouth. Now, with the murder of Nell, she could see that he was sick with worry for her.

"Jeb knows exactly how to get to me in Madison. I'll be safer at the cabin. Leave me alone, Drum. I'll keep in touch from time to time to see if you have any news of Jeb."

"If you won't go to Madison, then come with me, Lannie, please, I want you with me, I—"

She interrupted, "No. It's not right, Drum." Her heart caved in as she saw his face close and leave her out. "Just take me to the airport and I'll get a flight to Asheville. That's where I left the jeep, and Bry is in a kennel there."

She attempted a smile, and said, "I hope Ann-Marie recovers quickly. I know your presence will make a difference."

TWENTY-FIVE

Drum sat next to Ann-Marie's bed. Across from him sat Sister Cecily, her hands folded and resting quietly on the pristine sheets.

Ann-Marie's sleeping face held the peace of angels, but her fragile hands twitched restlessly, picking at the sheets, discarding and letting go of the creamy fine linen.

Drum reached to hold them in his and with steady strokes soothed them quiet, then held them in his strong ones, hoping to give the comfort she sought.

"Why do you think she does that, Sister, and what do you think she dreams of?"

"The peace in her face reflects what she has found here, I think. But with her hands, she tries to undo the horror she still hides within her. If she would only let God's love in, she would be fine," murmured the sister. "I'm just grateful she's recovering so nicely from the pneumonia. When we called you to come, we thought she would have to go to hospital. Thank you for coming quickly."

Drum sighed, his guilt and responsibility lay heavy on his heart, for his love for another woman was always there and demanding attention.

"Ann-Marie needs me, doesn't she?"

"Yes, she does, like a child needs a father. You are familiar to her, and safe and loving, as I am, and the other sisters."

He nodded, thinking about what she had just said. Except for Ann-Marie's years at college and her years married to Drum, Sister Cecily had been with her for her entire life, first as her Nanny and now as her nurse. No one knew Ann-Marie as well as Sister Cecily, not even Drum.

There was no way out of this dilemma. He'd known that from the beginning, and he should never have let himself fall in love with Lannie. But that was like telling a nun she couldn't pray, or a child he couldn't play, or nightingales they couldn't sing. Lannie was part of him, as whole and necessary as water to drink, air to breathe, food to eat, and love to make. Lannie was the beat in New Orleans jazz, the lyrics of a Gershwin song, the fragrance of a freshly picked gardenia, the laughter of playing children, the color in a Van Gogh.

Still, the future was clear to him. He would take it and be glad of it, be glad he had a dear, but broken soul like Ann-Marie to care for, be glad she had given him Chip, be glad he had the money to ensure her continued protection even if he should die.

"Drummond," said Sister Cecily. "Ann-Marie had a visitor not long ago."

"Oh, Emily Appleby probably. That's nice." Ann-Marie didn't remember her old friend, but Emily was kind enough to come two or three times a year.

"No, this woman has never visited before. A lovely woman who handled our child quite well." Sister Cecily smiled. "I think Ann-Marie went through several of her stages while Miss Sullivan was here."

Drum let go of Ann-Marie's hands, afraid he would

squeeze them in his shock. Stunned, unable to move, he stared at Sister Cecily, while a jumble of conflicting emotions bid for attention. What did this mean? At first, resentment flashed through him. How had Lannie dared enter this private world of his without even asking, and why had she not told him? But the resentment left quickly and never returned. Hope came then, soaring and restless and searching. Should he hope that Lannie wanted him in spite of Ann-Marie?

Finally, he found his voice.

"Lannie was here?" Filled now with curiosity, questions tumbled out of him. "What did she do? What did she say? What did Ann-Marie do?"

Sister Cecily told him of the visit, of Lannie pretending to be Chip's kindergarten teacher for Ann-Marie's sake, of Ann-Marie reverting to younger years, and of finally going into a catatonic state.

"Miss Sullivan seemed very affected by Ann-Marie. She had tears in her eyes when she said goodbye, and she left a lovely camellia in Ann-Marie's lap."

Yes, Lannie would do that, thought Drum.

"Does Ann-Marie remember the visit?"

"Sometimes. She asks if that pretty redheaded teacher of Chip's is coming to visit again."

Drum kissed Ann-Marie on the forehead, then walked to the window to look into her fairy garden. Water from the angel's pitcher splashed and tinkled onto the fountain and over the side into lavender bougainvillea. He rested his hand on the back of his armchair, and his eyes swept the books he'd stuffed into the wall-to-ceiling bookcase.

This isn't a bad life, he thought. *Millions of people would give an arm and a leg to have such a beautiful wife, to have my money, to have the respect I command, to come to this room and sit in holy peace for several hours.*

So why aren't you happy with it, Drummond Rutledge? he asked himself.

The answer, of course, was Lannie. Lannie wasn't in the picture. He'd only been treading the surface of life, of an existence, until he met Lannie. He gripped the plump chair until his fingers ached. He squeezed until the ache turned to pain, and zipped to his shoulder, but he held on, never letting go.

This picture, empty of Lannie, would have to do, he told himself. *I've come this far with Ann-Marie. I won't let her finish this by herself. We made vows that she doesn't remember, so I'll have to keep them for both of us.*

A frail, careworn hand covered his gripped fist. Sister Cecily's touch was warm, gentle, and reassuring. She held his fist until he relaxed, then tucked her hand back into the sleeve of her habit.

"I feel Miss Sullivan is more than a friend. Am I correct, Drummond?"

"Yes, Sister."

"Would you like to talk about it?"

"I . . . yes . . . I think I would."

"Let's be comfortable here by the window. I'll call for some tea or would you care for some chocolate?"

"Tea would be fine, Sister."

Drum sat and tried to gather his thoughts. How much should he tell this sheltered, saintly clergywoman? Would she frown with disapproval? Would she have the slightest notion of the love of a man for a woman? He didn't know, but he did trust his instincts, and they told him he could unburden his heart to Sister Cecily.

She poured tea from a fine bone china teapot into his cup, and then into her own. Patiently, she gazed out the window at the angel and the tinkling fountain as Drum searched for a way to begin. He had a feeling she would have sat there calmly from dawn until dusk until he was ready to speak. The peace of her countenance and her serene spirit illumined his own soul, and he felt safer than he had in years.

It's no wonder Ann-Marie is happy here.

Finally, he told her of the playhouse, and how he'd met Lannie, and how, through the summer, he and Lannie had fallen in love. He told her that Lannie hadn't known about Ann-Marie, and that he wasn't sure why he hadn't told her. He wasn't sure himself, he said. At first, he'd assumed she knew, but when he realized that she didn't know, he was afraid to tell her, afraid he would lose her.

When he had finished the story, Sister Cecily said nothing for a long time. She drank her tea, poured another cup for the two of them, and then spoke.

"Lannie feels you deceived her. Now she doesn't trust you, and she wants time alone to think about it. Is that correct?"

"Yes, Sister."

"What would you do if she said, 'Yes, we will live together without the blessings of God'?"

Shocked at her question, Drum had to think for a minute.

"I want to be with Lannie in any way I can be, but if I'm very honest with myself, I know that I could never let her degrade herself for me."

"So the reason you haven't dashed to spirit her off her mountain top is because this separation is not entirely her doing, but also an opportunity for you to make decisions."

"I hadn't looked at it that way, but, yes. Although I really have no choices. Ann-Marie is my wife."

"Drummond, Ann-Marie is a child. She always will be. When she recognizes you at all she sees you as good friend and maybe a romantic figure such as a young teenager might envision. I know you are trying to honor her by remaining her husband, but you're making no one happy, especially not yourself, and certainly not Ann-Marie. Ann-Marie was never suited to be a wife. I often marveled at your patience with her. Now she has gone so beyond and away from all of us that the only way we can really honor her as a human being is by loving her and keeping her safe and protected."

She offered him a plate of cookies, but he shook his head.

"In matters of the heart and soul, legalities aren't important, what others think isn't important," she continued. "God's love is all wise and all consuming. It reaches beyond the laws and rules we self-important humans have made."

She smiled. "I think He must get a big kick out of our determination that we should all march lockstep to drummers *we* have created, not He."

"Are you trying to tell me something, Sister?"

"As a bride of Christ, Drummond, I cannot advise you to go against the laws of my Church. But, in my heart of hearts, I know God treasures, nurtures, and encourages the love I sense you have for Lannie.

"God made us creatures of love, and there are a million ways to love. It is universally present, everywhere and in everything. We can accept it joyfully, or we can so fill our lives with guilt, and getting, and impossible attempts to make our lives perfect that we forget how to love." She paused, and then, a smile on her face and tears in her eyes, she said, "And that I think is the greatest sin of all, forgetting to love, not loving. I think we make God sad when we go to our grave without having used the greatest gift He has given us. Love."

"Sister, are you saying that you think it's all right for

Lannie and me to marry?" He held his breath, waiting for her answer.

"Did I say that?" She winked at him, her faded blue eyes twinkling in the late afternoon light. "If you're asking for my approval, or permission, I don't have the authority or right to give either one.

"But there are some truths that live so bright and real and honest that when you hear them, see them, and feel them you know you have touched the hem of God. I can only tell you to follow your heart, Drummond Rutledge."

"You knew such a love once, didn't you, Sister?"

"Yes, and I denied it." An expression of sadness crossed her face, so intrinsic it hurt to look at her. "But the love of Our Precious Savior has more than made up for the loss. He takes all, gives all, and is all, Drummond. Trust in Him."

A soft knock at the door drew their attention.

"Come," said Sister Cecily, her gentle smile and peaceful countenance restored.

"Sister, Mr. Rutledge has a phone call."

"Bring the portable here, Sister Antoinette."

It was Hatch Appleby. The Rutledge Timber deal in California was about to fall apart and required Drum's presence.

"Is Ann-Marie well enough for me to leave?" he asked Sister Cecily.

"Yes. Leave with a clear mind."

As he left the convent, Drum wondered if Sister Cecily's last words encompassed more than his concern for Ann-Marie.

Blood flew like wet red asterisks, marking every face and shirt close to Drum. By this time he was numb to the blows that rained on him as he pushed and elbowed his way through. He didn't feel the blow, but saw the flecks fly from his cheek, and figured it was his blood that punctuated the air. He didn't care. The harder he hit, and the harder he was hit, the better he felt.

The trip to California had been successful, and he was home in Charlotte. But he wanted to be at the lodge, he wanted to be with Lannie. He wanted Lannie here with him. Bob Lambert had found no trace of Jeb Bassert, so Drum had no excuse to contact her. He'd promised to leave her alone.

He launched himself into the pile-up, then careened down the field into a crowd of players. Someone passed him the ball, and he passed it to Hatch, who wore his usual crazy rugby grin. The ball was knocked away. They drove forward until there was open field, and they were chasing the ball again. Hatch stayed right with him, hadn't left his side since the first scrum when he had evidently sensed Drum's penchant for violence building.

Hatch was protecting him. Drum didn't want to be protected. *Leave me alone, Hatch. The more it hurts, the better I'll feel. I'm not going to kill anyone, I just feel as if I'd like to, or maybe someone will get a lucky shot on me and put me out of my misery forever.*

The gauze bandage they'd wrapped around his head earlier in the game came loose, looped over his ear, and drooped into his eyes. Impatiently, he tore it off, ripping skin and hair off the side of his head in the process, and threw it on the ground.

The score wasn't even close, but Drum didn't care. He charged harder and harder until his ears whined and buzzed, and the whole world was red and blue, and filled with grunts and shouts, and whirling heads, trees, and sky. His ferocity fired the whole team, and they poured on ten more points for an easy win over Charleston, South Carolina.

After the game, he sat silent on the chewed-up turf, finally spent. Hatch gave him a large paper cup filled with cool water. He downed it quickly and held it out for a refill.

The chairman of the annual charity match approached, the spindle heels of her white shoes sinking into the dirt and grass. He got to his feet.

"Drum, thank you again for a wonderful afternoon. I don't know what the Boys and Girls Clubs would do without this annual fund-raiser. Thank you, as always, for making the arrangements and for your mighty generous donation."

"You're welcome, Sarah Jane. I like doing it."

"Gracious. You look like you should be in the hospital emergency room. Are you all right?"

He tried to give her a reassuring smile, but his whole face ached now, and he wasn't sure how his effort looked. "I'm fine. Just need some soap and hot water."

"Well, I'm delighted to hear that, because I'm looking forward to a slow dance with you this evening at the ball." She self-consciously adjusted her fashionable Hillary Clinton straw Panama hat, and smiled winningly. "Since you've indicated you wouldn't be bringing a dinner partner, we've all been fussin' about who gets the first dance with you. I asserted chairman's rights and declared you were mine."

"I'm sorry. I won't be attending the ball this year. You must have gotten the wrong impression from my aide."

After declarations of dismay and disappointment, Sarah Jane left, waving goodbye with a white-gloved hand.

He sank to the ground again, the rush of adrenaline finally draining from his body and mind.

Hatch looked at him with a worried frown. "Look, ol' bud, you aren't going to make things any better by killing yourself on the field and not socializing with people. Ease up. Things will look better in a few weeks. You'd be amazed at the problems solved and the wounds healed by Father Time."

Drum shook his head. "Not this time, Hatch. Lannie's the best thing that ever happened to me. I knew in the beginning that I should stay away from her, but I couldn't. I've never felt anything so powerful as the pull I felt every time I looked at her. Someone would have had to bind me in chains and lock me away to keep me from her. Now I've hurt and embarrassed her, and myself and Ann-Marie."

"You know, Drum, you could divorce Ann-Marie. Lots of people wonder why you haven't."

"She's my responsibility. Divorce would be a betrayal." But Sister Cecily's words echoed in his ears. *"The greatest sin of all is not loving."*

Drum interrupted and got to his feet abruptly. "I don't want to talk about it right now, Hatch."

He walked away.

He drove directly to his office. The security guards tipped their hats and greeted him warmly. They were accustomed to his late Saturday visits. He entered the elevator to his private suite and drew a sigh of relief as the chrome cylinder rose like mercury through the tall, silent building.

There were times, like now, when he couldn't face the emptiness of the big house. The portraits of Ann-Marie, which he hadn't the heart to put away, no matter how much he'd like to, stared at him with reproach. In essence, it was really Ann-Marie's home. Every room of the low country-style house had Ann-Marie's delicate touch. It didn't feel like home to him and wasn't to his liking. It never had been, but he'd never told her that. He should have had it redecorated after he'd taken her to New

Orleans, but the thought of changing what she had created made him feel more unfaithful than sleeping with another woman.

Most painful was Chip's room. The cheerful place where Drum had told many a bedtime story remained as Chip had left it; a tee-ball pitcher in the center of a big braided rug, a few cotton shirts tossed willy-nilly, a baseball cap hanging over a post of the bed. Except for a monthly dusting, the room was never entered and the door was kept closed.

He should have sold the house long ago. It was the container of a life long-past lived, gone, but not forgotten. He had ordered an appraisal yesterday. It would go on the market next week.

The lodge was where he wanted to be. The place he'd avoided for so many years because he was afraid of the memories it would trigger, now called him to return. The rugged beauty of the mountains and the peaceful endurance of the big old log-built structure, beckoned him as never before. It was Lannie's presence there that summoned him so urgently, and it was because of Lannie that he couldn't go there.

Unlike the poignant memories of Chip and Ann-Marie, the suffering he'd caused Lannie was raw and fresh. She had made it plain that she didn't want to see him again until she'd had time to assimilate all that had happened.

Would she ever want to see him again?

He showered vigorously, imagining the hot water washing away his woes. As he dried himself with a thick white towel, he caught a glimpse of his face in the mirrored all stainless steel and aluminum spa–styled bathroom. Shocked, he stopped rubbing and took a good look. No wonder Hatch and Emily were concerned. Yes, his face was a bloody mess; his nose pushed to one side, a black eye, a gash across one cheek, and a deep abrasion above one ear. But it was the look of agony in his eyes that caught him, and the obvious loss of weight. He looked tense, haggard, and worn.

He laughed out loud when he thought of Sarah Jane's eager invitation for a dance with him at the ball. The derisive laugh bounced back and forth off the mirrored walls, mocking him.

"Lady, my dubious reputation preceded me. I'm not the dangerous, stalwart, but naughty knight you imagined you'd dance with this evening," he said out loud, and like his laugh, the bitter words echoed. "I'm simply a luckless bastard who has royally screwed up his life."

And I certainly haven't improved the lives of those I love, he thought.

Dressed in chinos and blue chambray shirt, he sat at his expansive desk and dug into the work awaiting him. This had been his routine since his return from High Falls. Work and more work. He welcomed it like lungs welcome air. He needed it to survive.

But as always, Lannie's face soon intruded. For a valiant hour, he fought her away. He worked grimly through file after file, setting his teeth until his jaws ached. Finally, when even the fragrance of her hair entered the quiet office and wouldn't leave, he gave up. He tossed his pen aside, switched off the computer, and the lights in the office, and swung his chair around to gaze out the vast glass window that overlooked the outskirts of Charlotte.

He'd picked Charlotte for the center of Rutledge Timber's enterprises because of its location; close to his timberland, not far from Atlanta, with college friends nearby, and easy connections out of the airport to New York. Now he had a corporate jet that flew him, and an office in Manhattan, but he still preferred North Carolina and the slower pace of life.

The city lights of Charlotte were behind him on the other side of the building. In front of him, in the distance, headlights from cars traveling Interstate 85 flicked briefly in the darkness and zipped away. Where to, he wondered. Were any of them on the way to the mountains? High Falls, maybe? Close by, moonbeams reflected off a lake, and the company's golf course lay dark and silent in the night.

He got up, flipped on the stereo system, poured Glenlivet to a halfway mark in his favorite crystal tumbler, and returned to his chair by the window.

Miss Bessie Smith's blues-rich voice filled the room. Her "In House Blues" matched his melancholy mood. It was a woman's song , but a song anyone could use to sit and think things over. He held the golden mellow Scotch whiskey in his mouth, savoring its richness, and allowed himself to think of Lannie.

The shadows on the walls formed silhouettes of her face, and reflections from the lake seemed the silver sparks from her misty eyes. He ached for the sound of her quick laughter and the feel of her lithe body resting against his.

This was what he did every night, and he had to stop what he knew was destructive behavior. He'd never been a drunk before, even when Chip died, and he'd never been a man who let fate push him around. He'd always taken control of his life, formed it to his satisfaction and made it work. His only failure had been Chip and Ann-Marie.

By God, he'd be damned if he'd sit around and nurse his blues with whiskey. He reached for his phone and punched in Bob Lambert's cellular number.

"Bob. Where are you?"

"Dallas, Drum. Seems like Jeb Bassert took the time to leave a number of false leads and this was one of them. He bought tickets in Orlando and Atlanta, on different days, to several different cities. We're checking them all out. So far we've discovered that he never boarded most of the flights. The ones he did board, like this one to Dallas, he deplaned before he ever got here."

"Where did the plane stop? Where did he get off?"

"New Orleans. My men have checked all over that city and the local police are working with them. So far, nothing."

"Okay, where are you off to next?"

"Seattle, then Paris."

"I'm coming with you. I can't stand sitting here doing nothing. I'll meet you in Seattle."

"Right, Boss."

TWENTY-SIX

With an exhausted, but satisfied, sigh Lannie sat on the doorstep to the cabin. She needed to rest before she made the trek to the falls to clean up.

She let the drowsy afternoon stillness sink into her. The silence of the mountain ridge on a drowsy afternoon brought her peace. It was the peace an innocent child must know or a bird who has found a draft and, wings spread, floats serenely above the cares and woes on earth below.

She could hardly believe it was the last of October. Late-afternoon sun sent long shafts through poplar trees and evergreens circling the clearing. The autumn afternoons still held moments of summer heat, but mornings and nights were chill, and felt like winter. After a long day of taking in the last of the potatoes and raking up row after row of weeds, she was filthy, and though she'd promised herself she would never go to the falls again it was the only way to come entirely clean.

Common sense overrode any reluctance to step onto Drum's land.

She hated the feeling of being surrounded by Drum's

land, hemmed in by his strength, his quick humor, his potent physical presence. She reminded herself that before she'd met Drum, she'd used a legal right-of-way through Rutledge land to get to the main highway and never gave a thought about the owner of the land through which she traveled. She owned twenty acres. That had been enough.

Had she known his timberland would bother her so much, she might not have returned to the cabin.

But where would she have gone? Only here could she find the peace she sought. At the least, she wasn't down there with flatlanders and the vileness of Jeb Bassert or with the heart-shattering Drummond Rutledge whose allegiance was to another woman, the mother of his son. The mountains, with their wild and rugged slopes, would protect her spiritually and physically.

When the thought of Drum's ownership of the surrounding acreage began to bother her, as it did at some point on most days, she had programmed herself to look at it as a bulwark, a protective wall that kept her safe, because, if Drum knew he would be fiercely protective of her and the baby.

Their child. Drum's child.

No. Don't do that. Don't relive it again.

But the door had opened, and she did relive it, marveling at the whips and curves, the highs and lows the past summer had taken. The wildness that had overtaken herself and Drum continued to stun her, as if their meeting had been inevitable, the summer had been ordained, and listed in an almanac God had made of things to do.

First on the list was lure Lannie off the mountaintop; second, bewilder her and make her doubt everything she ever believed in; and last, let her drop, plummet to the earth with a bang, shake her all up. Give her heartbreak and joy at the same time. Nell's death, and the manner of it, had been the spitting hot end of a tail wind that had whirled her around and set her down so hard she doubted if she'd ever recover.

Would God let all those things happen? Was there a God? It was getting harder and harder to believe so. Wanting to fend Him off, she squeezed her eyes shut and folded her arms over the top of her head.

"Go away, God. This is enough. I've had enough. No more."

Close the door, Lannie, close the door.

But the scent of Drum intruded and the solid feel of him, the hard, taut body, the slick smoothness of his skin stretched across his angular shoulders, the moist pool of perspiration that formed between his shoulder blades when they made love, his hands stroking the small of her back and finding the vulnerable hollow on the inside of her thighs.

Go away. Close the door.

But the sound of his laughter filtered through, hearty and delighted when they talked, soft and satisfied after they'd made love. A sob broke loose and lanced through her chest, erupting from her throat in a long moan.

She stood up and yelled, "Go away, God. Go away, Drum."

And in a softer voice, almost a whisper, she said, "Leave us alone. We're doing fine here, just fine, my baby and me."

Yes, more than anything, there was the baby. It smoothed the edges of hurt and fear and filled her with love. Gracie could never be replaced, but this child would warm her arms and her heart in its own special way.

Bry came from a foraging trip in the woods and nosed her hip. She sat back down and mistress and dog were on an eye-to-eye level.

"Have a good time, big bud? Nervous today, aren't you? Squirrels been teasing you again?" She gave the coarse hair on the top of his head a brisk rub, and kissed his black nose. "Don't worry, Bry. We're safe here."

But he poked his nose in the air and gave a long mournful howl.

"Well, I don't know what's bothering you, but I hope you're not going to howl all night long like you did when bears were nearby. Is that it? Bears? They're stockpiling right now, getting ready for winter. I suppose one of them could be in our woods." She rubbed his head again. "You'll take care of things like you always do. Just chase them away. Send them onto Rutledge land. Let them scare up food over there."

They should go to the falls now, but a purple and gold twilight drifted softly into the clearing, casting the trees and cabin into rich, mysterious, and liquid shapes and sounds. She hated to miss the show.

For the hundredth time she went over the arrangements she'd made for the baby's birth.

She'd changed doctors and now went to an obstetrician in Franklin once a month. She had also changed her mailing address to Franklin, and shopped for groceries there. In High Falls, her changing appearance would have caused great speculation. The theater people had dispersed, and were all over the country now, back where they'd started from, getting ready to spend the winter in New York, Atlanta, Miami, or Maryville, Iowa. But, of course, Beezy Bowden would get wind of her pregnancy and send the news of Lannie's and Drum's coming child all over the South, thus alerting Drum.

She wasn't stupid enough to think that Drum would never find out, but she wanted to delay his discovery as long as possible. As long as it took to make him realize that they didn't need him. She would worry about that later.

The obstetrician knew little of her living conditions, except that she lived in a remote region by herself. He wasn't happy about it, but she'd assured him she could take care of herself. He had given her vitamins to be taken every day, and instruction books and medication to use in case she started to miscarry or the baby decided to come early. He'd implored her to come into Franklin six weeks early to be sure she was near him and the hospital. She'd agreed to this.

Tomorrow was the day she would go into Franklin to pick up the new four-wheel drive she'd ordered last month. Just the thought of it gave her a sense of security. The trust fund her mother had left her and her own savings from the law practice gave her enough income to do as she wished for a long time.

The wind flipped a corner of her towel into her face and she shivered. Late afternoon shadows gathered around her, and the feathering breeze, which blew continually this high up, quickened and grew colder.

The sky had changed while she daydreamed. A storm was brewing. Thunderheads were building, and she smelled rain in the air. But she had plenty of time to get to the falls and enjoy a shower before the storm broke.

"Come on, Bry, let's go to the falls and scrub clean."

Bry loped in front of her along the evergreen-guarded path. He hadn't had any stomach upsets since they stopped going into High Falls, and Lannie had come to the sickening conclusion that she had been correct in her suspicions, someone had been poisoning him. It was difficult to imagine anyone she knew who would do such an evil senseless thing. She'd wracked her brain for days trying to come up with an answer, but could think of no one.

Could the treatment of Bry be connected with the same person who'd been haunting her?

Again she noted his nervousness. He'd grown increasingly wary the past few days. He sniffed behind every bush and darted into every break in the trees, and she began to look with trepidation into the forest, imagining all sorts of horned and long-toothed creatures staring out at her.

The path grew darker as clouds covered the once bright sun.

With the thunder of the falls beckoning, she eagerly removed her sweaty T-shirt, stripped off her dirt-caked shorts, and ran nude the last few yards to the falls entrance.

Oh, God, more than anything, thank you for the freedom.

Where else on earth could she move around naked and carefree, not worried about proprieties or people watching, and who cared anyway? Soon it would be too cold to wander around her private domain nude. People would consider her crazy, she was sure, but this was her space, her declaration of independence, her shield against all the chaos that existed off the mountain. Instead of waiting for someone else to give meaning to her life, she would make her own world and nourish her own soul. She didn't need anyone else.

She snagged her towel over a tree branch, tossed her clothes on a big rock nearby, and stepped behind the great fall of water and into the cave. Memories of Drum assaulted her like pellets from a shotgun, and she stepped quickly into the hard stream of water hoping the images of Drum, and the increasing unfamiliar and uncomfortable feelings of this night would scrub away like the soil from the garden.

She soaped vigorously and, closing her eyes, ran her hand over her body searching for signs of the gift she'd been given. Yes, there was the swelling across the lower portion of her tummy. She felt the tightness beginning, the satisfying fullness, and smiled. She smoothed her hands over her tender, burgeoning breasts and growing stomach, and willed the peaceful wisdom of the mountain to enter her body and thus the child's.

Bry barked. Startled, she dropped the soap and bent over to retrieve it. What was wrong? She stepped out of her shower for a moment and glanced around the cave. Bry usually lay in the grass near the entrance, but she saw him prowling restlessly in and out of the cave, out onto the slippery rocks near the path and then back into the cave, sniffing the air, and growling.

"Okay, okay," she shouted to him over the noise of the falls. "You must be worried about the storm, which means it's a big one. I'll hurry."

Suddenly, the vivid impression that she wasn't alone set her pulse racing. How foolish, she thought. She stepped back into the falls to shampoo her hair. Bry would know if anyone was near, and his uncommon nervousness was beginning to affect her. Was there someone out there watching her?

For a heart-stopping moment, she thought of Jeb Bassert. No. It was what happened in the theater attic that caused this fear that kept reoccurring. Stop this, Lannie. Whoever taunted and tortured her in the attic, whether it was Jeb Bassert or a complete stranger, would never find her here. Would they?

Nervously, she stepped out of the pelting water and wrung the water from her hair. Lightning crackled. She had misjudged the arrival of the storm. Bry was nowhere in sight as she left the cave entrance, grabbed the towel from the tree and rubbed herself dry.

The sky had darkened considerably. What a dramatic change from the earlier sunshine and brisk blue sky. One of the things she loved about the mountain was its swift and varied moods.

She hurried now. She didn't want to feel her way back to the cabin in complete blackness. On nights like tonight, when the star-sprinkled heavens were cloud-covered or the moon was only a sliver, darkness fell on the mountaintop with sinister murkiness that was surreal in its impenetrable depth.

Snatching up her soiled clothes, she tucked the towel around her and called for Bry. No answer.

"Bry? Where are you?" Full-blown worry gnawed at her now. Bry always came when she called. Always. Earlier she'd teased him about a bear, and there was always the possibility of cougars this far into the wild. "Bry, come."

He barked, crashing at her through underbrush ahead.

"Heavens, you had me worried there for a minute, bud. You must have had something cornered that you didn't want to leave. Let's get home before the storm breaks." She kept her voice light, but she knew he sensed her growing unease.

As they hurried along the narrow, darkening path, it was difficult for her to ignore the strong impression of eyes watching her, of someone traveling along with them. Bry's increasing skittishness didn't help.

Night creatures, she assured herself, curious about the audacity of her presence here in the dimness of dusk and the approaching storm.

They arrived at the clearing just as big drops of rain began to fall.

"Okay, Bry. What a great day we've had. The garden ready for winter and a refreshing shower at the falls. Time for a nourishing dinner. We'll have tomatoes, squash, and pole beans, and I've had corn bread warming in a corner of the fireplace since noon. For dessert, we'll have a big fat apple, maybe with peanut butter on it. No? You don't like any of those suggestions? Well, how about some of the squirrel you brought in yesterday?"

He gave a short bark of approval, and she laughed.

They entered the cabin, and Bry froze, his body quivering tautly. Alarm bells clamored in Lannie's head.

A red ball sat in the center of the planked floor.

Bry's growl deepened, guttural and threatening. Lannie grabbed the ruff of his coat and held tight for support and reassurance. Her eyes searched into the dim reaches of the cabin, but she saw no one. However, the fire, which should have been only glowing embers, had been stoked by someone—someone who expected to return soon. Flames leaped merrily, casting grotesque shadows on the once safe cabin walls.

Her thoughts raced in jumping stops and starts. This was not coincidence, or a joke, or a harmless game. Only those who loved her knew where she was. This was someone who didn't love her, and they had gone to enormous and clever effort to find her and taunt her. Jeb Bassert? How? How could he have found her here?

Leave, leave now. You're trapped here. Run. Run. Run.

"Come, Bry," she managed to get out, the strain hurting her throat.

He resisted her tug at first, but finally followed her into the black, rain-driven night.

TWENTY-SEVEN

The jeep. Go for the jeep.

Lightning split the sky. Rain rushed at her relentlessly. The wind snapped at her, pushing and pulling, and whipped away her towel. She ran naked, the rain sluicing down her body like holy water off a sinner. But she felt nothing except an enormous need to reach the jeep.

Bry leaped in front of her, turning his head again and again to check her progress and safety. She slipped and slid down the incline to the creek, didn't have time to search for the stepping stones she'd placed there years ago, and splashed in knee-high water across to the jeep parked on the other side.

Bry already sat erect in the passenger seat, his ears cocked forward. He barked at her to hurry. She slammed her bare wet feet onto the gas pedal and the clutch, and turned the key. Nothing. She turned the key again, so hard it bit into her fingers. *Please, old friend, come through for me one more time.* Nothing. Again and again, she twisted the key. The jeep was dead. A sob tore from her.

No. No crying. *Don't give in, Lannie. There's always a way.* She would not allow herself to be at anyone's mercy.

Okay. Which would be safer? Refuge in the cabin or taking a chance in the forest?

If it weren't for the storm, she would have gone into the forest and headed for Drum's place. But she would never find her way through the wet blackness. She would have to take her chances in the cabin.

She jumped out of the jeep, crossed the creek, and raced back up hill to the cabin, digging her hands and toes into the now muddy slope. Bry was right behind her. Thank God for Bry.

They reached the cabin, and she approached slowly, breathless, and afraid the intruder had returned during her mad dash to the jeep. Open to the furies of the storm, vulnerable, and at the mercy of whoever was with her here on the top of Haystack, she hesitated, and slipped into the shadows of the cabin eaves. She tried to see through the screened window, but saw nothing except her bed and the far wall.

Decide, Lannie, decide. There's still time to go into the trees.

The baby, my God, how could I forget the baby? At least the cabin would be dry, and there was food. Better for the baby than slipping and falling, and getting lost and frozen in the woods.

She turned the corner, climbed the three shallow steps with knees shaking, and opened the door slowly, expecting someone to grab her at any moment. She knew Bry would take care of whomever it was in short order, but the thought didn't make it any easier, or her any braver.

The cabin was as she had left it, quiet and undisturbed, but she felt the evil in its waiting stillness. She grabbed the red ball and threw it out into the storm, then slammed the door and worked a heavy wooden bar, which hadn't been used in many years, through the big iron latch. She latched the two windows, too.

Exhausted and terror-stricken she tried to get her breath. Her staccato gasps for air sounded loud in the stillness of the cabin, ricocheting off the walls. All she could hear was her harsh breathing and the crackling of the fire. Even the roar of the storm outside had receded. It seemed too quiet, she thought, menacing.

Bry whined and licked her hand.

"It's okay, Bry. Really it is," she said, trying to reassure herself as she soothed him. "First, I'll dry off and put some clothes on. I don't know what's coming next, but I sure don't need to catch a cold."

She found a clean towel and dropped to her knees in front of the fire. While she squeezed the water from her hair, and pulled on jeans and a red flannel shirt, her mind foraged for methods of defense. With relief she remembered the shotgun. Her eyes darted to the corner where it had rested for years.

It was gone. Her heart dropped to her feet, and her stomach lurched with sick fear. Evidently he'd spent time in the cabin and had made his plans carefully. What did he want with her? Who was he?

"We have to keep up our strength, Bry," she whispered. "We'll eat."

She gave him the squirrel she'd saved for him. The cornbread, which had rested on a warming brick in the corner of the fireplace, was gone, consumed by flames the stranger had stoked. Though the leaping flames warmed her shivering body, they were too high for cooking. Her hands trembled as she tried to eat an apple and a dry biscuit, and she admonished herself. "Don't let him defeat you. Be prepared, not cowed with fear."

The food gagged her, but she choked it down with determination.

He's out there. She could feel him. She felt him waiting, watching. The heavy latched door would keep him out for a while, unless he burned her out, which she knew instinctively he didn't want to do. He wanted contact with her, wanted to spend time with her, or he wouldn't have gone to all the trouble of tracking her here.

"We'll just wait him out, Bry. We'll hold him off. We have enough food for a few days." The words came out strained, her throat already hurting with the effort to swallow food her tummy didn't want. But talking to Bry helped. "If I have to, I'll let you out to take care of him. But Wilkie Talley is due here anytime to help me chop the winter's wood supply."

Hope soared when she thought of Wilkie. Yes, yes, he had said he would come the middle of October, and it's past that. Yes. Thinking of Wilkie made her feel better. If she could outwait the intruder, maybe he would get tired of playing his evil games and go away. *Wishful thinking, Lannie.*

The loss of the shotgun was demoralizing. She needed a weapon of some kind, if for nothing else than to shore up her self-confidence. Her gardening supplies and tools—hoe, rake, hammer, and ax—were in the small attached shed outside. The poker. It usually sat on the hearth, along with the shovel for ashes and coals. Oh, God, the poker and shovel were gone, too. The razor-sharp hunting knife she'd used to skin Bry's squirrel would have to do.

Had he found the knife? No, it was still on the hearth, partially hidden by the heavy gloves she used to extract food from the coals. It meant close contact with her tormentor, but she could handle that. She picked it up and sat down in the ladderback chair next to the fire. Holding the knife in two hands, Lannie decided this would be her command post.

"We can outlast him. Our chances will be better in the

daylight, too, Bry. We're not helpless, you and me. We'll be okay."

She hugged him to her, but his body went rigid and he howled, a long mournful sound. He pulled away from her embrace and stalked to the door, sniffing, his ears back, his ruff standing stiff. He sat down next to the door. A menacing growl came from deep in his gut as he sat alert and stiff, never taking his eyes off the barred entrance.

The menace was on the other side of the door. She hated the idea of sitting here and cringing all night long and pondered the wisdom of letting the dog out to attack the man. But what if it's more than one person? What if it's two or three people? How many could Bry take care of at one time?

Her hands gripping the knife, her eyes glued to Bry and the door, Lannie sat prepared for anything. Alert and ready, she sat deep into the night, her eyes never leaving Bry or the barred door. At some point, the roaring storm abated. The wind downgraded to an occasional lonely whistle through the pines, and an eerie wailing echoing off far canyon walls.

She felt the menace from outside creep under the door and silt through the cracks in the wall. It wove itself like a fine spider web throughout the cold cabin, spinning its sinister filaments from each corner of the cabin to the back of her chair, then over the small table where she ate. It looped through her clothes hanging on the wall and covered the beams overhead. It tried to braid a sticky band of terror around her neck, but she fought it off.

Lannie's head nodded, her chin dipped more than once, but she always jerked awake. She woke up shivering with cold. She coughed and massaged her chest. The grim web of fear had encircled, caught, and squeezed her. She heaved to catch her breath.

"Deep breathing, Lannie. Deep breathing. There's no one here except you and Bry. He wants you to panic. Stay cool." Talking to herself helped.

The fire had died and there was nothing to poke it alive again. Numb with cold, she stumbled stiffly to the bed and wrapped the quilt around herself. Her fingers ached with the cold and from her tight grip on the knife. She released the thick bladed instrument and placed it next to her on the mattress.

Bry watched every move she made, then resumed his scrutiny of the door. He hadn't moved an inch since he'd stationed himself there hours ago, quivering at attention.

The warmth of the quilt felt so good, so comforting, Lannie had trouble keeping her eyes open. But hunger, thirst, and fear kept her eyelids propped wide and dry.

She heard an early morning bird's trill. A bird singing in the darkness, heralding the coming of sunset. How beautiful, she thought. A good sign. A tiny bird knows another day will arrive and all will be well. His faith will take him through, no matter how tough his day is. Her chin drifted toward her chest, but she yanked it up.

"If you have the faith of a bird, no . . . no it's a mustard seed, if you have . . . the faith of a mustard seed . . ."

The bird's tiny, but brave, trill came again.

Stay awake, stay awake. Think, Lannie, plan. Think about what you will do when morning comes.

Her chin drifted down again. It had been a long, long, hard day: ripping out the garden, the hike to the falls and back, the dash to the jeep, the storm, not enough to eat, the fending off of the creeping, weaving ominous web . . .

I have to stay awake. I have to. I have to.

"I wish in me heart it was Sunday, drinking buttermilk all the week, whiskey on a Sunday."

Lannie's heart leaped with gladness. Her father was here. Whistling in his den.

Her eyelids, heavy with sleep, struggled to open. Then she remembered she wasn't supposed to be sleeping, and her father was in Ireland. Suddenly wide awake, she saw it was morning. The windows were still closed, but the door was ajar letting in weak, early morning light.

Bry slept on the floor near the door. The door open, Bry asleep? No. She disentangled herself from the quilt and fumbled for the knife at her side.

"Is this what you're looking for, Lannie?"

Shock hit her like a cold pocket of water in a warm lake. Her lungs heaved for air. She couldn't breathe. A man with white hair emerged from the dim corner of the cabin. Jack Edwards? He walked slowly toward her, dangling the hunting knife in his hands, and stood at the foot of her bed.

"Who are you? How did you get in?"

"Getting in was easy. Just needed this." He held up his other hand. It held a long, sliver-thin knife about two feet long, and he brandished it through the air over his head like an avenging pirate. "Used it to dislodge your latching bar."

"Who are you?" she asked again. "What do you want with me?"

"Ahhh, Lannie, I'm so disappointed you don't know me."

"Jack Edwards?" she managed to get out.

"Take a better look," he said, and grinned. "I did a damn good job of acting , didn't I?"

"I don't care who you are," she whispered. "What have you done to Bry?"

"Bry is taking a nap. He'll be fine."

"You're trespassing. Leave right now."

"Oh, I can't do that," he laughed. His laugh sounded

familiar. But it was that of a young man, not a middle-aged man. "I can't leave. You and me have needed time away from everyone for a long time, and now we're going to get it."

"I don't know what you're talking about."

"You will." He put a finger in his mouth, extracted a tiny bag of marbles from each cheek, and put them in the pocket of his denim overalls. With the removal of the bags his cheeks smoothed out, and the crease across his chin disappeared. "You and me, you know, we should have been married by now, giving the judge lots of grandbabies."

"How do you know the judge?"

"Such stupid questions, Lannie. 'Lacey Gracie, dancing daisy, makes her mom a happy lady,' " he sang, mockingly. "Mausie still sings that, you know, while she's working in the kitchen."

She wanted to slap her hands over her ears and scream, but she didn't. Poker-faced, and trying to hide hideous foreboding, she said, "If you think you're scaring me, you're not."

"Scare you? I don't want to scare you. I just want a chance to tell you that I love you, Lannie." He moved to the side of the bed and stared down at her. She stiffened with fear. He bent his head and swiftly dislodged contact lenses. The strange green eyes were now blue. "I've loved you ever since sixth grade when I wet my jeans during recess, and everyone made fun of me except you."

My God, it was Jeb Bassert. She recognized him now.

"Jeb!"

A nervous giggle jiggled out of him, but he cut it off, as if he knew it revealed a part of him she wasn't supposed to see.

"Yep, it's me."

All of a sudden everything fell into place: the red ball, Gracie's rhyme, her father's Irish ditty, the stalking in the theater. Uncertain relief filled her. After all, she'd known Jeb all her life. She knew how to handle him.

"So you're the one who's been taunting me. Not very nice of you, Jeb. You scared me to death. Now you go on out of here while I get dressed, and then I'll fix us breakfast."

He laughed, but it wasn't the laugh of the young, nerdy, earnest Jeb she heard, it was the derisive laugh of a cynical ex-con, and it held all the resentment and anger he'd accumulated throughout his poor excuse for a life.

"I don't think so, Lannie. You don't understand. I'm the king of the hill now. I'm willing to make you my queen, but first you have to apologize for accusing me of rape and sending me to prison. Then we're going to get reacquainted so you can get to know the real me. I'm a better man than I was a boy, Lannie."

He touched her hair. Her mouth dried and wanted to pucker with revulsion, but she sucked at her teeth, determined not to show any fear.

"Ahhhh, man, I been wanting to do that for a long time." She saw the nostrils of his large squashed nose quiver with excitement, and his hand trembled as he stroked her head. She froze as his hand slipped beneath her hair and caressed her neck. "See what you been missing all these years, sweetness. Jeb's going to make you real happy."

Should she humor him or fight him? She'd let it play out for a while, and then make a decision. Her skin crawled as he caressed her ear and her chin, and finally ran a thumb, which smelled like bear excrement, around her lips.

She pulled the quilt tighter around her. What was wrong with Bry? He would never have slept through all of this. *Bry, Bry, please, I need you. Oh, dear God, what has he done to Bry?*

"Bry? Come, Bry."

"I told you, the dog is sleeping. I shot him with a tranquilizer dart. He's tough though, ain't he? Damn near tore my arm off before he passed out." He indicated a rip in his sleeve and a bloody gash on his forearm. "Damned smart dog, too. I had to spread bear shit all over myself and keep down wind of him for two days, but he still knew something was around. Had to put him out, Lannie. He'd a killed me."

Lannie's chest heaved in dry gulps. She clutched the quilt even closer, hoping he wouldn't notice her panicked breathing. "You're sure he's okay?"

"Yeah, don't worry, sweetness. But keep in mind that the only reason your dog is still breathing is because he's my insurance. A hostage, you might say. I won't hurt him as long as you follow my orders. Understand?"

"Yes, I understand, but I'm sure we're going to get along just fine."

"Good. Now, are you going to apologize for sending me to prison, or are we going to sit here forever and not have any fun?"

"Sure, sure, but I'm cold, and I'm hungry. If you'll get a fire started, I'll fix us something to eat."

"Well, now, that sounds nice and cozy, and just the sort of thing I've always imagined you and me doing. But, I ain't heard no apology yet, and I'm not sure I trust you, so before we get the fire going and eat, let's make sure you don't run away from me." He sat on the side of her bed, and she shuddered at his closeness. He put his finger on his lips, as if he was thinking about how to solve this problem of trust. "First thing is this. If you run away from me, Lannie, I'll kill the dog. He's a pain in the ass anyway. Second thing is, you have to take off your clothes."

"Why?"

"I don't think you'll be running away real easy if you're bare-assed nekkid. It's cold out there this morning. About forty-five degrees, I'd say. Cold for us Floridians."

"This is all entirely unnecessary, Jeb," she said, using a brisk businesslike tone. "I'm not going to run. I look forward to discussing your case. Maybe I was wrong, but we need to talk about it first."

He reached behind himself and pulled her hunting knife from his belt. "I have my own knives, Lannie, but I like this one of yours. You handy with this, huh? Like to skin squirrels and things? The judge taught you real good, I'd bet. Well, I never had the privilege of goin' hunting with my father or learning things other kids took for granted."

He flipped the knife in the air and caught it with expert precision. "But I learned a helluva lot in prison, some things that would make you shit in your pants they're so scary. And I learned a lot this summer. Two survival camps and hanging around a community theater in Atlanta kept me pretty busy. Had to learn enough about the theater to get a job at the playhouse."

He placed his hand on her stomach and flipped the knife even higher.

"I got a high IQ, you know. Came in real handy. I'm a quick learner." He flipped the knife higher, caught it, and placed it under her chin. "Don't fool yourself, Lannie Sullivan. I spent nine years getting ready for this moment right now. Don't make the mistake of thinking I'm still that jerk of a backwater kid who had a crush on you. He couldn't have fought his way out of a paper sack. He never had the guts to take you for himself. Stood back and let all the other guys sport you around. Not this dude, Lannie."

He pressed the tip of the knife into her skin and leaned close to her, his tobacco-laden breath on her face. "So don't do any lawyer talkin' with me or school-teacherish stuff. It won't work. Don't make the mistake of thinking I won't hurt you, because I will. I don't want to, but I will."

His voice was cold, his eyes like chips of blue ice. He meant every word he said. The network of fear threading the small room drew taut and real. A fine mist of chill coated her body. She was sick to her stomach.

No! This is what he wants. Hold on. Hold on.

She forced down the bile rising in her throat, and said, "Sure, Jeb. Just don't hurt Bry."

He jerked the quilt away from her and tossed it on the floor.

"Now, stand up and take them clothes off. I already seen you naked anyway, showering at the falls and running to the jeep last night. So don't be shy."

Knees watery, stomach heaving, she stood and did as he ordered. When she was finished, he said, "Ahh, no underwear, huh? Good. Any girl of mine wouldn't be allowed to wear underwear. Now, come to the doorway so I can see you better. Light ain't too good in here, Lannie."

She walked to the open door. "Can I pet Bry?"

"Sure."

She knelt and ran a hand over the dog's still body and ached to take him in her arms. He was warm and breathing. He was still alive. Jeb hadn't lied about that.

"Get up, Lannie. Enough sniveling over that dog. Stand here where I can see you." He jerked her by the elbow. Weak early dawn sunlight came through the open door. The air was frosty, raising goosebumps on her bare skin. "Good. That's good."

A raging hunger heated his cold eyes as he looked her up and down, and she thought she was going to faint.

"Oh, baby, I been waitin' all my life to get a close gander and feel of your body. Most beautiful thing I ever saw." He undid her braid, and ran his fingers through the mass of hair hanging down her back, and ran his stubby fingers over her buttocks. "Oh, yes, yes."

"I said I'd take my clothes off, Jeb. I didn't say you could manhandle me," she said sternly, commanding her voice not to give way, and hiding the tremor of her hands.

He ignored her.

"Now, Lannie," he said, his excitement so great that his voice squeaked. "Lift all that beautiful hair up off your neck. Hold it on top of your head, like them models do in the porn magazines."

She did as he asked, but said, "This is silly, Jeb. Let's get the fire going, and eat breakfast."

"Turn around. Turn around real slow so I can get the full effect."

She turned.

"Do it again," he ordered. His tone had changed from one of lust, to one of anger.

She turned, fighting again the urge to vomit. Oh, God, she was sick, so sick.

"You're pregnant! Jesus H. Christ! You're pregnant. I knew you were fucking Rutledge, and it made me mad as hell. But I didn't think you'd let this happen." He grabbed hold of her arm and jerked her close to him, and her hair fell down over her back. "Big mistake, Lannie. I have to think about this."

She started to deny her pregnancy, but as he had told her previously, he wasn't stupid.

"Get back on the bed. You're going to stay there while I rethink this whole thing."

He shoved her onto the bed and took a thin coil of rope from his deep utility pockets. He jerked her hands over her head and tied her wrists together to the rustic twig headboard. Then he bound her ankles so tightly together that the pain was unbearable, and she couldn't control the small moan that escaped her.

"Sorry, Lannie, but you deserve any pain you're feeling. I thought you could never cause me pain again, but you just did. I don't like your bein' pregnant, Lannie, don't like it at all."

He grinned.

"I may decide to get rid of it," he said.

"Get rid of w-what?" she asked, unable to control the tremor in her voice any longer.

"The baby, of course. Can't have another man's child around."

"No, Jeb—"

He slapped her. "Shut up. I can't have you sniveling. I gotta plan, gotta think."

The blow on the side of her head made her ears ring, and her head pounded with pain, but she fought the tears gathering in her eyes, and tried to focus on outwitting him.

"Please, Jeb, let's talk abo—"

He slapped her again.

"I said, shut up!" He stuffed a cotton handkerchief into her mouth. "That should keep you quiet while I'm gone. Not that it's needed. There ain't no one within ten miles of here. But I don't want you sniveling at me the minute I get back."

He ran his hand possessively over her breasts and over her abdomen, stopping for a horrible moment on the tender rounded spot that had grown there.

"Yep, I know what I'm goin' to do. Gotta leave for a while. You be good while I'm gone. No flirting with other dudes, you hear." He laughed, a thin, malicious sort of whinny, then leaned over and kissed both her breasts.

Chillbumps erupted all over her body. The sour fluid in her throat tried to come up, but was blocked by the handkerchief, and she was afraid she would drown in her own vomit.

"Don't know how long I'll be gone. You'll be glad to see me when I get back, I bet, and we'll fix this whole mix-up. You'll be mine, and no man will ever touch you again."

TWENTY-EIGHT

Nell?"

Nell was here.

Lannie could see her, and hear her. Nell was talking to her.

Wake up, Lannie, girl. Don't let Jeb get the best of you. Wake up. You can make it through. You have to. For me and you, and that blessed child you carry.

"Nell? Nell? Where are you?"

Nell disappeared somewhere in the deep black void that Lannie swam in. Lannie groped for her. *Please come back, Nell. Help me.*

Wet and cold, she woke up shivering. She was alone. Jeb hadn't returned. How long had he been gone? She remembered struggling to stay awake through an interminable morning and afternoon. She thought it must be daybreak again. A wavering pale early dawn light filtered through the one window he'd left open. Jeb had been gone about twenty-four hours, she estimated.

Her feet were numb. The bonds around her ankles had cut off the circulation of blood. She'd lost control of her bladder sometime during the night, and now lay upon a damp, rank quilt. Tears of humiliation, weakness, and fear rolled freely over her temples, into her hair, and dampened the pillow beneath her head.

A movement caught her eye. On the floor, Bry's body twitched. Her heart leaped with hope. She couldn't see his head, but his tail jerked briefly sometimes, as though he was trying to wake up.

Thank you, God. Thank you for keeping Bry alive. Oh, if only she could speak to him, prompt him, give him some encouragement. She grunted through the sodden cloth Jeb had stuffed into her mouth, but there was no response from the dog. His large powerful form lay lifeless, and she knew fresh fear.

There's no one to help you, Lannie. You're going to have to survive by yourself. You wanted to take care of yourself. You wanted to escape the demands of relationships, of civilization, of the responsibilities expected of a civil community.

For the thousandth time she struggled against the bonds that held her to the headboard. They bit into her wrists like barbed wire. Her fingers again found the split in the rustic wood of the headboard that Wilkie Talley had sworn he would fix someday. The hickory tree's woven branches needed adhesive and new bindings of stretched dried leather.

Her restless, searching fingers had found it last night, and she had realized that the aged but sturdy shard of wood might be the answer to her prayers. Her idea of putting Jeb off until Wilkie Talley arrived had vanished quickly when Jeb talked about doing away with the baby. She had to save herself and the baby as soon as possible.

Imagining inserted coat hangers or some vile vomiting poison that would tear the fetus from her womb, her terror put her frantic fingers back to work at the wood, desperately pulling, poking, lifting, tearing fingernails and twisting her wrists until the pain made her weep again. She ignored the pain and the tears and persisted in her tugging and pulling on the wood.

The arrow-shaped segment wasn't sharp enough to sever the plastic-like cable that bound her, but she might be able to insert it into the knot to loosen it.

Bry's tail twitched again, as if in warning. The door opened and Jeb came in with his arms filled.

She stopped working at the wood sliver and closed her eyes, pretending to sleep.

Oh, God, please don't let him do anything to harm my child, please, God, please.

Too late. Too late. He was back with whatever he'd gone to get. He would kill her child, and he might as well kill her, too. She wouldn't be able to live with the knowledge that she'd been at fault for the death of a second child. If she hadn't been so know-it-all pigheaded about retreating to her mountain haven, if she hadn't been so noble about not forcing Drum to decide between her and Ann-Marie, if she hadn't been so *afraid* to be hurt again, this would never have happened.

She knew Jeb stood at the side of the bed. An astringent, drugstore type of aftershave emanated from him. She felt him staring down at her. He took her breasts in his hands, then placed his mouth over one of the nipples and bit down until she wanted to scream with agony.

"Open your eyes, Lannie. I know you're awake."

He yanked the cloth from her mouth. She coughed and tried to work up enough saliva in her parched throat to swallow.

She glared at him, and croaked, "That's not a nice way to wake up, Jeb. If you want to be my man, then you're going to have to treat me better than that."

"Ah, ha. Spitfire Lannie has returned. Good. That's one of the things I love about you."

He'd cleaned himself up. The bear excrement residue,

which had repulsed her before, had been scrubbed away. The filthy overalls had been replaced with a tan turtleneck shirt, and with immaculate jeans so new they still held a crease where they had been folded and stacked in the store. His bleached white hair was slicked back and looked as if it had been sprayed to keep it in place.

He must have driven to the cabin. He couldn't have hiked up the mountain and remained so pristine.

"I'm awfully hungry, Jeb, and thirsty," she said softly, enticingly. If she could get him involved in other tasks, he might forget about the baby for a while. "Do you suppose we could eat something? I haven't eaten anything since night before last."

"Sorry, beautiful. I'll give you a doughnut to hold you until we eat a proper breakfast together later. But we got something to do before we get onto other business, and eating can wait."

He dug a glazed doughnut from one of the sacks he'd deposited on the floor and held it to her mouth. Resisting the urge to gulp huge big bites of the light, rich, creamy, sugarness, she bit into it with ladylike bites while he held it for her.

"I'd do a lot better if you would untie me."

"Goin' to do that right now."

He loosened the rope that held her wrists to the headboard, and she prayed he wouldn't notice the shard she'd been prying at.

The urge to swing and tear at him was monumental, but he held her tightly and retied her wrists as a soon as they were free of the rustic bed.

"I left some things by the creek, Lannie. That's where we're going."

For a wild, hope-filled second, she thought he was going to untie her ankles, but he didn't. He lifted her and carried her through the cabin and out the door. Her bare skin crawled at the closeness of his stocky body. As they passed Bry, she inspected him as well as she could, but could detect nothing, not even the slight rise and fall of his chest that she'd seen yesterday.

"Is Bry still sleeping? How could one tranquilizer keep him asleep for so long?" she asked with worry.

"I poked another dose of tranquilizer down his throat. He's happy, probably dreaming of rabbits to eat. Told you I wouldn't hurt the dog as long as you behave."

"I will. I promise. You can untie me, Jeb. I promise I won't run."

"Nope. First, I gotta take care of a personal grudge against Drum Rutledge. When I finish with you, there ain't goin' be no man who wants you 'cept me. I'm goin' to make sure of that."

Oh, God. Drum, I love you. She'd fought to keep him out of her thoughts, out of her hopes, out of her fear and regrets and new knowledge of herself. How arrogant, how unfair she'd been, to keep the gift of the baby to herself.

Make conversation. Be friendly. Make this seem like a social occasion. Defuse the tension.

They started down the slope to the creek. "How did you find me, Jeb?"

"Easy. I've known where you were, and just about everything that's happened to you the last nine years. My cousin, Buster, kept me filled in on all the Madison talk of you and Gracie, and then Ravenal leaving you. Everyone knew you came to High Falls."

They had reached the creek. He shifted her in his arms and deposited her on the dewy grass next to the creek. She could read the label on the cardboard box now. Clairol Blue Bleach. She saw a large aluminum bowl, a large bottle of peroxide, and an unopened cardboard box of some sort, and assorted shopping bags. What was he planning?

He ran his fingers through her snarled hair, pulling at the knots impatiently. It hadn't been brushed since she'd rubbed it dry in front of the fire evening before last. He reached into one of his shopping bags and pulled out a large pair of scissors.

"What are you doing, Jeb?"

She caught her breath as he began to whack off her hair. It fell in blunt crimson chunks around her on the dew-soaked grass.

"Relax, Lannie. Consider yourself lucky. I was going to shave it all off, but changed my mind. Decided it would look more like mine if I cut it to just below your ears."

"Why?"

"Drum Rutledge ruined you when he got you pregnant. Now I'm going to ruin what he liked best about you so he won't want you no more. I saw the way he loved your hair with his hands when you was in his library. Made my blood boil. Well, he won't want to do that no more, and neither will no other man . . . for a while anyway."

Keep a friendly conversation alive.

"How did you know I'd be at the playhouse, and that I lived way up here on top of the mountain? You're awfully clever, Jeb."

"Again, easy. I had Buster do some research on the people you seemed to see more than others in High Falls. You'd be amazed at the secrets people have, and how easy it is to unearth them on the Internet. He found a dirty little secret about your booksellin' friend, John Lamb." *Whack. Whack.* The clack of the scissors blades sounded loud and threateningly close to her ears. "It seems that prim and proper, and so intelligent Mr. Lamb, is a dirty voyeur. He likes to spy on ladies through windows. Gets his kicks, sometimes even jacks off, while he's peekin' at someone. Got arrested about eleven years ago in Boston. They put him on probation and ordered he get counseling. Came to High Falls to start a new life."

"You've been blackmailing John Lamb, and he's been reporting to you everything he knew about what I was doing here?" asked Lannie, shocked and dumbfounded.

"Yep. Funny thing is, he seems to have been a good boy all his years in High Falls until I told him to spy on you." He laughed, and picked up the box of bleach. Horse-size goosebumps climbed atop her already raised flesh. Delay him, Lannie.

"What do you mean? I can't imagine John doing anything so repulsive."

Jeb whinnied with delight while he poured the blue powder into the bowl. "Oh, Lannie, how innocent you are about some things. The good Mr. Lamb got hooked again. Picked up where he left off years ago. I found him spying on the young girls at the theater several times and had to chase him away. Told him his job was over because I was taking care of you now."

He poured the whole bottle of peroxide into the powdered bleach and muttered to himself, "Damn, I forgot the measuring cup, but this looks about right." He swirled his concoction around and around in the bowl, then reached down and found a stick to mix it up properly. "Yep, Mr. John Lamb is in trouble again."

"What do you mean?"

"He got arrested last week for spying in Beezy Bowden's windows." He shrieked with laughter, almost doubling over at the thought of John Lamb and Beezy. "I can't imagine why he'd want to see that old bat nekked. Maybe Daisy was visiting for the weekend. Anyway, it's the big gossip of High Falls."

Suddenly, the theory she'd held about someone poisoning Bry made sense. John Lamb needed to get close to her, and he couldn't do that efficiently with Bry always there. The notion that someone she'd thought was a good friend could so betray her, could want to kill her dog, made her ill.

But any shock at the news of John Lamb was diluted by her fear of what Jeb was planning when he finished with her hair. "Why are we out here by the creek? I'm freezing."

"I know. Sorry, but that can't be helped right now. This was easier than making a mess in the cabin. I'm a very neat person, and I gotta wash your hair after a while. This seemed the easiest way. I'll warm you up real good later. Like I said . . . we got things to take care of first. Everything's got to be perfect before I make you mine."

He took a small paintbrush out of his pocket. "See, I had to buy all new supplies because I threw mine away. Wasn't no need to be doin' my roots every two weeks after I made you mine. You just hold real still, and you'll be just fine."

Monumental relief filled her as she realized he wasn't going to do anything about the baby, for the moment anyway. Who knew what crazed thoughts busied his diseased brain.

"We're going to start at the ends and work toward the roots. Don't worry, Lannie. I know what I'm doing. Been doin' it all summer."

"Doing what all summer?"

"Colorin' my hair. Now I'm goin' to change the color of your hair. The two of us are goin' to match, like bookends. You're goin' to be my white-haired gal. It'll seem funny at first, and eventually we'll let it grow back to red, but I don't want any part of you that Drum Rutledge loved, and he loved your hair. It's mine now, and I'll make it so's he don't like it anymore."

He sat down behind her, dipped the brush into his concoction, and applied it to the ends of her hair. The cold liquid ran down her already raised flesh. Her back seemed particularly bare and freezing where her long hair had previously rested. Bare and exposed now, she shivered with cold and humiliation, feeling suddenly more vulnerable than ever before.

She ached to weep, and weep and weep. Weep like she'd never wept before. But she held the tears back, her eyes throbbing with the effort.

As he worked his way closer to her scalp, it began to itch and then burn.

She hated Jeb Bassert. She hated him, and suddenly she began to wonder if she would be able to outwit his devious mind. How could you outwit thinking that had no logic or a psyche so evil? For a hideous moment, she lost hope, but heard Nell say, "No! No! Lannie. Get through this."

"Jeb, did you hurt Nell?"

"Well, now that's for me to know and for you to find out, but yeah, I had a little fun with her. She liked it."

Oh, God, oh, God.

She closed her eyes and saw Drum's precious strong face, his infectious grin, his loving navy-blue eyes, and the way the muscles of his jaw bunched when he worried. "I need you, Drum," she whispered. "Oh, please, hear me. I need you. I told myself I didn't need you or anyone, but I've always needed you, and I always will."

"Whatcha whispering about, Lannie? Ain't praying, are you? Didn't do Nell any good. Won't do you any good, either. Jesus knows we're supposed to be together."

She shivered again, unable to control any longer the reactions of her body to the cold, fear, and horror of what might happen to her and the baby here on her mountaintop.

"Ahhh, sorry about the cold, babydoll." He kissed her shoulder, then ran his tongue up and down her spine. She tried to contain her shudder of horror, but couldn't. "I'll hurry so you won't freeze. The sun will be drying everything up soon anyway."

This is okay, Lannie. This is nothing. Hair grows out. This is not important. Think of Drum and the Ferris wheel and the lights and the music and the stars.

He stood back and admired his handiwork. "Goin' to be right pretty, Lannie.

"Only one problem," Jeb muttered to himself. "Not sure how long I leave this stuff on for a redhead. I'll just have to keep an eye on it. It's already turnin' orange. Let's see . . . she said to add toner if that happens."

He dug another bottle out his sack and poured it over Lannie's hair.

"Ahh, there we go. It's turnin' a real nice white. I think I leave it on for about forty-five minutes. While we're waiting, I'll stoke up the fire for some breakfast. Sorry, but I have to leave you here. Gotta wash your hair in the creek when it's finished bleaching out."

He yanked her backwards, scraping her butt across the gravel from the creekbed and then across the ground through the rough grass and small sticks and twigs downed from the storm, and tied her to the trunk of what she had always thought of as her "towel tree." The sun shone full and bright now on the banks of the creek, and she leaned gratefully against the warmth of the tree's trunk.

While Jeb was in the cabin, doing whatever diabolical task he thought necessary, Lannie allowed herself a few tears and a prayer.

"Please, God, forgive me for being so selfish, arrogant,

and unthinking about the child I'm carrying. I give in. I need your help. Please send something, or someone, or find me an opportunity to save myself. I've been wrong about many things. If it is my time to come home to you, please take care of my father, and let Drum know how much I love him. Also, help him to find it in his heart to forgive me. Thank you. Amen."

Her scalp felt as if the Greek sun god, Helios, had hurled flaming rods into her head as he raced across the morning sky, and the sensation intensified with each passing torturous minute. She wanted to scream for Jeb to come and douse her head into the cool creek water, but she bit her lip, bit it until it bled and blood dripped off her chin and onto her collarbone, along with the dripping bleach. The bleaching mixture Jeb had concocted was too strong for her fair complexion and skin. Was it causing permanent damage? Would she be bald?

What a laugh, Lannie. What difference does it make? Her head was the last thing she needed to worry about.

Smoke puffed from the chimney, and the delicious aroma of bacon cooking over an open fire reached her.

He hurried down the slope toward her, his eyes eager, his hands twitching at his sides, and a towel thrown over his shoulder. As he drew closer, she saw his expression change to one of dismay.

"Oh, fuck," he said.

Swiftly, he untied her from the tree, then more or less dragged her to the creek, and rolled her over the bank into the water. She caught her breath at the sudden immersion into the frigid water, but welcomed the cool sensation on her abused head.

"Poor, poor Lannie. Oh, I really am sorry. I didn't mean for you to get all burned," he whined. He ducked her head into the water again, and she knew a blessed moment of relief from the fiery sensation on her scalp. "You've got blisters on your scalp and some red spots on your forehead, but I'm sure they'll go away soon. I couldn't get a prescription for ergot to get rid of the kid, so a guy is finding some for me. When I go pick up the ergot, I'll buy some salve for your skin."

Ergot? No. No. He couldn't do that.

He dunked her head in the water again and she prayed he'd just drown her, just hold her under until she blacked out and forgot everything. But she found herself gulping the cool water, swallowing, swallowing, swallowing to assuage her giant thirst.

I don't care what I look like. I don't care if I'm bald and scarred forever. I'm going to get out of this. I'm going to save myself and this gift I carry.

Jeb yanked her onto the creek bank and wrapped her in the towel he carried.

"Ergot?" she choked out as soon as she could breathe properly. "We don't need ergot, Jeb. I know you don't care about the baby, but surely, you don't want me to be in such pain."

"The guy I'm getting it from says it's still the best way to empty a woman of a baby. You'll be just fine, Lannie. Trust me."

TWENTY-NINE

Lannie closed her eyes, pretending to sleep. Her heart raced so fast she was afraid she would faint. Jeb pushed the door open, letting in the hard-bright October sunlight.

Bry growled weakly. Her heart jumped with joy. Bry was alive. "Shut up, mutt," muttered Jeb. "I should have killed you in the first place. But you've been good insurance."

She heard a thud and a mewling sound of pain from Bry. Jeb must have kicked him. She moaned, hoping to draw his attention to her and away from Bry.

The sound of his footsteps approaching the bed froze everything in her. Her heart stopped beating, the sheen of fear that painted her body wet, chilled, her pulse stilled, her stomach stopped rising and falling. She was in complete shut-down, entrapped in a camera still, flicking onward and onward forever but never changing, and occurring now in horror-struck, life-threatening realness on top of Haystack Mountain.

"Ahhh, Lannie, my sleeping princess. I missed you."

His hand traced around her navel and down into the curly mound of pubic hair. He ran his fingers through it, and she heard his breath quicken. *Oh, God, no.*

He leaned over and sucked on a nipple, his chapped lips scraping against her bare skin, then inserted a rough hurtful finger into her dry vagina. He grunted, and his saliva dropped to run down her breast and over her ribs.

Repulsed, her frozen body did a rapid emotional meltdown, and her eyes flew open. It was obvious what he had in mind and she had to stop him.

She drew her knees up and knocked his chin away from her breasts. He yelped in surprise, and grabbed her legs and held them down.

"Well, well, well. The fire-cat is awake. I think maybe I'm going to have to have some of this pussy before we get rid of the brat. Don't think I can wait any longer, Lannie. We'll do it together next time, but now I need to get rid of a big aching I've had for a long, long time."

He sucked the finger that had been inside of her and grinned his clownlike grin, his childlike teeth tiny in the cavern his blubbery lips formed. He yanked the sodden handkerchief from her mouth and kissed her. She almost vomited with disgust right into his mouth, but choked it down instead.

Okay, if this is what it takes to delay whatever he's planning to induce a miscarriage, then she could do it.

No, I can't. I can't!

She spit bile into his face, and he laughed. "I love it when you fight, Lannie. We're going to make a good pair, you and me."

He took a nipple in his mouth again, sucking hard, and inserted his thick stubby finger in and out of her. With his free hand he found his penis in the opening of his overalls and began to manipulate it. With a surge of supernatural energy, fueled by maternal protection, fury, and utter loathing Lannie yanked on the headboard, tore it loose, and smashed it over Jeb's head.

He yelled and jumped in surprise. For a moment they

were both caught in the myriad of openings in the intricate plaited structure, like two rabbits beneath the roots of a tree. But Jeb threw off the contraption and grabbed at her. Still attached to the headboard, Lannie used it awkwardly as a weapon, like some large primitive shield from the days of knights and dragons.

He pulled at the wood, and she pushed at him, finally maneuvering herself into a sitting position. With each violent shake of her unwieldy weapon, her wrists found more movement.

Jeb cursed as she sat on the side of the bed and kicked him with her bound feet and shoved at him with the headboard. His frustration mounted as he tried to reach around her shield to get to her.

Without warning, with his yank, the headboard fell free of her wrists, surprising Jeb, and there was empty space between them. Off balance, the rustic piece of furniture in his hands, Jeb stumbled backwards. If Lannie tried to stand on her bound feet, she would fall. She had to remain sitting on the side of the bed and let Jeb come to her. She still held the shard of wood in her hands. She saw now that it had a nice sharp point.

Jeb grunted in mounting frustration. He threw the headboard aside, and it landed on top of a weak Bry, who was valiantly trying to stand on all fours, with little success. Jeb reached for Lannie, and she jabbed at him with her pitiful weapon. He laughed.

"Whatcha think you're going to do with that? Give it to me."

He grabbed at the shard of wood, but she wouldn't release it. They fought, twisting, pushing, and pulling at the side of the bed. Jeb tried holding her still with one hand, and prying her fingers open with the other, but she kicked at him with her feet and bit into his shoulder.

He grunted and tried to shake her teeth away, but she bit harder, sinking her teeth deeper into the tender muscle near the shoulder blade.

Cursing and twisting to get away from her, Jeb punched her in the stomach, but her lock on his shoulder didn't allow much leverage, and the punch became more of a shove.

She brought her knees up and caught him hard on the scrotum. He yelped in pain and grabbed at her bound ankles.

Lannie loosened her hold on his shoulder, and with all her strength, swung her arms up to jam the stick into his eye. Screaming with agony, Jeb dropped her feet and reared up, reaching for her throat.

He squeezed her neck and twisted it like he was wringing the neck of a chicken. Unable to breathe, she fell back across the bed. Lannie stared into his eyes and saw herself dissolving.

Enraged, blind in one eye and bleeding profusely, Jeb held her throat in a death grip, and no amount of thrusting her knees or thrashing with her bound wrists would break his chokehold. Her head swam with gray, and then burst with spattered brightness. She wondered if this was the last color she would see, wondered if this is what Gracie saw at the last, and then she sank into a murky fog.

I'm sorry, so sorry, Drum, dear child that lives and grows beneath my heart, beloved judge, Mausie, Big Billy, I've done the best . . . I could . . . wasn't good enough . . . how foolish, how foolish . . .

Suddenly, Jeb fell on top of her. Through the deepening fog, she felt his hands give up the death grip on her throat, and she gasped for air, sucking it in like a stranded fish on a dry beach. In a whirling, swirling, sickening world of upside down, spinning ceiling, Jeb's eye dripping blood on her, and the quilt smelling of her urine, Lannie heard a growl. And through all the fear and sickness and blood and horror, she knew swift hope.

Bry. Bry had leaped on Jeb's back. The weight of both of them threatened to smother Lannie. With his feral teeth sunk deep into the back of Jeb's neck, Bry wrenched Jeb up and away from Lannie.

As she struggled to clear her head and sit upright, Jeb's cries of fright and anger rang in her ears. Finally, her head swirling and retching with sickness, she sat erect at the edge of the bed and watched Bry wrestle Jeb to the floor. Her hunting knife fell out of Jeb's belt. She slid to the floor and scooted across to pick it up.

"Good, boy, Bry," she croaked, her dry throat wracked with pain. "If you can . . . just buy me . . . a minute."

The bonds around her wrist were already loose, so it didn't take long to cut through one of them completely, just enough to snake one hand out, and then the other. She didn't have time to feel relief or joy, or anything. She went to work on the rope around her ankles, sawing back and forth savagely.

Jeb and Bry rolled around the floor, the sounds of their struggle hideous in her ears. The struggle came to an ugly end as Jeb found the knife in his boot and plunged it into Bry's belly. The dog fell limp on the floor next to Lannie.

Again, Lannie had no time for shock or anger, only action, only the monumental drive to survive. She caught Jeb as he made it to his knees, stabbing him in the side, then yanked her knife out to stab him again as near the heart as she could reach.

He oinked like a pig and landed next to Bry.

Panic set in when she realized Jeb's chest was moving up and down. He still breathed. She cut through the last of the rope in swift order, freeing her ankles. She tried to get to her feet, but they were too numb, so she crawled to the door and down the steps onto the blessed, green grass.

She crawled to the slope that led to the creek, thinking nothing had ever felt so good as the grass under her knees, the sun on her back, and the crisp pine-scented air filling her heaving lungs. She made it to the creek and slid down its bank to drink the clear pure water. Champagne had never tasted as rare, fulfilling, or invigorating.

She sat on the bank and massaged her feet and ankles until needles of feeling returned. Grief swamped her as she thought of Bry, lying up there alone and probably dead. Jeb must have bled to death by now. She had to know about Bry. She couldn't leave him alone.

She turned to climb back up the slope and saw Jeb at the top, weaving around like a strawman, blood pouring from him like the proverbial stuck pig. He lifted a shotgun, lurching dangerously as he aimed at her. He missed, but the blast shaved off the bark of a nearby tree. Incredibly, he came after her in a run, his short, stocky legs churning down the slope with determination, the gun gripped in his hand.

Suddenly, her feet found wings and she spun around, splashed through the creek, and entered the woods on the other side. When she saw Jeb's truck parked next to the defunct jeep, she veered in its direction, but knew immediately that would be a mistake. Jeb could reach the truck before she could, so she turned and plunged into the thick forest.

Jeb kept up with her, firing every now and then, but his aim was off. He crashed through the underbrush behind her, breaking off low-lying tree branches, and cursing as limbs smacked him in the face.

He gained on her. Her legs and feet were weakened by two days of inactivity and little blood flow, and her body, yearning for food and fuel, hungry and feeble, was losing its first burst of false energy.

Jeb's survival camp training kept him unerringly on her trail. How was he managing to stay on his feet? He was bleeding profusely.

She knew then that his obsession with her would keep him alive even if he were drained of blood. He would chase her until one of them was dead. Jeb Bassert would catch her eventually.

Fury drove her now, pumped her legs, swung her arms, filled her lungs. No! No! No! This wouldn't happen. If he could run her down, then she would give him a run he would never forget. If she had to die then she would run until her last breath, and she would run him until he died. Yes, she might die, but so would he.

Her long legs lifted, her knees almost hitting her chin, then reaching out for longer strides. A branch slapped across her face, and blood from a gash across her forehead dripped into her eyes. He was gaining. She could hear his gasps for air, his groans of agony as his wounds drained him of strength.

Another buckshot tore by her, and another. Something winged her shoulder and she knew she'd been hit. Tough. After what she'd been through the last few days, buckshot was minor stuff. But it hurt. It hurt like hell.

She heard him throw something into the woods. Probably the gun, out of ammunition. Well, the race was a little more even now. His heavy footsteps thumped close behind her, and his harsh breathing sounded like it was right in her ear. She leaped forward, letting the fury fuel her, remembering all the sweating nights of ballet rehearsal and the strength of her leg muscles.

Help me do this. Help me do this, God.

The lodge, dear God, where was the lodge? Had she

missed the tricky turn through the laurel brush and the tiny spring? *Please, please, I can't be lost.*

She looked frantically for a familiar sign. Finally, about twenty yards ahead sat the big boulder outside the laurel patch. Make it, Lannie, make it. Yes. There was the roof of the lodge.

Jeb saw it, too, and she heard him utter a triumphal grunt. They both knew that even if she could make it to the phone, it would be too late. He would catch her there, trap her in Drum's house.

Lannie knew there was no recourse. She could go no further. She would take her chances in the lodge.

The big sturdy structure came into full view. She skirted the back side and climbed the steps, praying all the while that the front door would be unlocked. She remembered that Wilkie Talley came to the lodge every other Wednesday and always left the door unlocked for Mrs. Chambers. Was this the right Wednesday?

She fell against the door and twisted the big knobs. Oh, God, it was locked. She pushed, put it was futile. Behind her, she heard Jeb stumble into the clearing. Where, where would a key be? Under the doormat, of course.

She found it and tried to insert it, but fumbled in her nervous haste. Cool it, Lannie. Now! It's now or never. Cool it. Get it done.

She twisted again. The door gave and she fell into the entrance hall onto her knees. Jeb was right behind her. He grabbed for her, but she stood and ran a few more steps into the huge reception room.

Jeb's hand grabbed her shoulder, and she fell to her knees again.

She jerked her shoulder out of his grasp and crawled away. The library, she thought. She could make it there.

The phone was there. She could close herself up in there, lock the door, she would be safe.

She crawled as fast as she could, Jeb right behind her.

She began to sob uncontrollably and turned her head to see him right on her heels.

He was white with fatigue and loss of blood, his eyes were out of focus, and he was covered with blood, but he grinned a hideous grin.

"Die," she hissed, "die."

"Not without you, Lannie," he exhaled softly, using precious energy with his effort to speak. But he continued. "We'll die together, with you in my arms." Sobbing harder now, Lannie reached the library.

Jeb's hand clawed at her foot, then he drew abreast of her and caught her by the neck.

The last six weeks had been a hell of a nonsensical journey across the United States, and even to Paris once, fumed Drum. He felt like a damned idiot for following all the false leads Jeb Bassert had so cleverly placed. But they couldn't afford to ignore any of them.

Returning now from New York to Asheville, North Carolina, Bob Lambert's latest phone call had given him hope, and he clung to it desperately. Bob Lambert's men had returned several times to Connie's Curl-Up-and-Dye. A client who had been in the shop when Jeb was there had returned for a haircut while the detectives were grilling Connie again. The client remembered Jeb asking her if there were any sporting goods stores or outdoor supply stores nearby. She had directed him to a wilderness survival warehouse frequented by militia groups two streets away.

Further investigation at the warehouse indicated that Jeb had bought camping equipment. The salesman said that Jeb seemed very knowledgeable about militia groups and survival training.

Bob's phone call alerting Drum to this newest information elated Drum yet put the fear of God into him. For him, it was a clear indication that Jeb was smarter than they thought he was and that Jeb had probably been in, or near the mountains for months. Jeb Bassert knew the general vicinity of where Lannie was and had been preparing a wilderness search for her all summer.

A phone call to the town police in High Falls had proved fruitless. They'd told him that they couldn't go to someone's rescue when Drum had no proof or reason to give to them. They said Lannie's cabin was outside their jurisdiction anyway and that he should call the county sheriff. The sheriff had told him the same thing. They couldn't tear out to some remote cabin at someone's whim. Drum couldn't blame them. How could he explain this compelling pressure to race to Lannie, wherever she was?

He assumed she was at the cabin, and he prayed he was right. He'd searched so long and so hard that his sense of time and what day of the week it was had left him, and he didn't care, except for any negative influence on his judgment.

He'd called ahead, and Hatch had ordered the helicopter to pick him up at the Asheville airport and fly him to High Falls. They'd landed on the ball field where his Land Rover had been delivered and waited for him.

He swore as the rugged four-wheel drive bounced across a log over the road that led to Lannie's cabin. It must have been downed during a recent storm. The road, strewn with fallen leaves, was really little more than a wide, barely discernible path that made its way through a dense forest. The trees, some orange, gold, and russet with fall colors, others already bare and skeletal, were close-fitting against the road. He splashed recklessly through several fast-running creeks that bisected the trail.

Must have been a hell of a storm, he thought. The creeks were usually mild streams wending their way gently through the mountains forests and meadows. Lannie's creek was one of the larger ones on Haystack.

He heard its rushing waters before he saw it, but his sense of relief on finally arriving at his destination was brutally dashed when he saw a strange vehicle parked next to the jeep.

No one knew how to get to the cabin except Lannie, her father, himself, and Wilkie Talley. This wasn't Wilkie Talley's truck.

Apprehension bellowed so loud inside of him that he couldn't hear. His ears pounded with the sound of his thudding heart. He waded the creek and ran up the slope. The cabin door stood wide open. He saw the blood right away, and his thudding heart stalled, then stuttered to start again.

He stiffened, and grabbed the door frame, bracing his arms for support. Bloody fingerprints marked the frame, and he knew someone else had held it for support as they'd passed through. He jerked his hands off the door and forced himself to take a deep steadying breath. The cabin smelled of blood and of stale urine and vomit. The sunlight, warm on his back, cast his long shadow into the one-room cabin, and he couldn't see what the rustic, once protective shelter held, but the silence screeched at him.

Even the birds, who usually sang freely and happily in the cheerful clearing, had been silenced by what had happened here.

Too quiet, too still, and too bloody.

He stepped in and saw that the cozy cabin was empty except for Bry's body, which lay inert on the floor near the bed. He knelt and ran his hand along the dog's ribs, trying to find a heartbeat, but found nothing. Bry dead? This huge bundle of force and energy, of innate intelligence, of fierce protectiveness, and great love for Lannie . . . dead? Lannie's last line of defense, dead.

No! Drum's whole body, his brain, and his heart yelled in protest.

His eyes took in the blood, spread in ugly splotches on the planked wooden floor like ragged patches of dull red sewn on a golden-brown quilt, and his stomach turned. Whose blood painted Lannie's haven? Lannie's?

His whole being shook with refusal and denial.

Where was she? Had she been kidnapped? There was nothing he could do here. He had to find her, and find her fast, and he needed help. He needed a telephone and cursed the fact that neither his cellular or his mobile phone in the Land Rover were any good here on the remote mountaintop.

The closest telephone was at the lodge.

He picked up Bry and slung him across his shoulders, barely noticing the weight, and ran toward the Land Rover. On the way, he now noticed what he'd missed in his frantic race up to the cabin. The green slope was speckled with what looked like dried blood. Next to the creek lay a long lock of red hair and bits and chunks of more hair were strewn about, incongruous and macabre in the yellow light of late morning. Someone had gotten a haircut, and it looked as if it was Lannie's hair. It scattered now, feathering and blowing away like wafer-thin confetti in the skipping breeze that had found its way through the canyons to Haystack's summit.

What the hell had happened here? His mind refused to even consider the possibilities.

Carefully, he deposited Bry's body in the back of the

Land Rover, then did a quick, but thorough, search of the copse of woods surrounding the clearing. It didn't take him long to determine there were no bodies close by, but two people had entered the woods on the other side of the creek. His impulse was to track them down, but he would be wasting time, and time was precious, especially since one or both of them were bleeding.

He needed help from the Mountain Rescue Team in High Falls. He ran to the Land Rover and headed toward the lodge and a telephone.

Twenty minutes later he drove into the clearing in front of the lodge and screeched to a stop when he saw the door open and a trail of blood leading up to it. He looked around. The clearing was quiet. No signs of violence here. The big front door stood ajar. He approached it with reluctance, afraid of what he would find beyond the beckoning opening.

The flagstone entrance and the great room with its mammoth fireplace were in perfect order except for pools of blood. Someone was bleeding to death. He advanced slowly through each room, finding nothing until he reached the library and heard sounds of tortured breathing.

He stepped quickly into the library and saw a man with shaggy white hair, his shirt and overalls soaked with blood, strangling an older woman.

Drum's mind refused to take in the horror of the scene, but his body leaped to untangle the two bodies. It took all of his strength to lift the man off the woman. He worked frantically to undo the man's rigid fingers from the woman's throat. Finally, he socked the man in the back and, with relief, saw the determined grip loosen. With a gush of fetid air, the man's body collapsed next to the woman, and he died.

Drum turned him over and drew back in shock. Jack Edwards. On closer look, Drum decided that it wasn't Jack Edwards, but someone who looked a lot like him. Someone younger and stronger than Jack had seemed to be. The man was very dead, whoever he was. Jeb Bassert, of course, he realized, in a clever disguise that Lannie hadn't seen through.

Where was Lannie?

The naked woman, her white hair in jagged disarray, lay face down, half on, half off his leather recliner, her knees on the floor. Her hand was stretched toward the telephone, which sat on a small desk next to the chair. She didn't seem to be breathing.

Two people dead in his house. Where was Lannie? His anguish and anxiety mounted. As he looked closer at the woman, he realized she wasn't as old as he'd thought. Her body was scratched and bruised, her head looked as if it had blistered and burned in places, and her ankles were circled with severe lacerations, but this was a young body. A beautiful young body.

Jesus! It looked like Lannie.

Gently, and filled with cold fear, he turned her over. It *was* Lannie.

He felt for a pulse in her throat. *Yes. Yes. Yes.* Faint, barely discernible, but there. She was alive, but needed immediate medical care.

Holding her chilled, bloodied hands in one of his, he grabbed the phone and called the emergency room at High Falls Community Hospital and told them he was on his way with a critical care patient. He knew he could transport her there faster than an ambulance could find its way up the mountain. Then he called the sheriff and told him about the dead man whom he thought was Jeb Bassert.

He picked Lannie up in his arms to carry her to the Land Rover and an anguished sob tore its way from soul deep within him, driving him to his knees.

This time he'd arrived in time.

He let it all come then, all the fear, all the guilt, all the confusion, all the impelling need to be with Lannie, poured out in the sobs that racked him as he held her tenderly in his arms. His tears soaked her ravaged head and dropped on her forehead like holy water.

Get hold of yourself, Rutledge. Lannie needs you. Cry later.

He ran to the Land Rover, placed her in the rear seat, fastened seat belts over her, and covered her with a blanket he kept there.

He ripped out of the clearing on two tires. He would never forget the back-twisting, rib-breaking ride down the rugged trail to the main road and the hospital with Lannie close to death in the seat behind him, and Bry dead in the cargo area.

THIRTY

Lannie woke up in a pristine white hospital room. It didn't take much smarts to figure that out, she thought, as she struggled to clear her mind. And she didn't care where she was or how she'd arrived, or what condition she was in, she was just grateful to be alive.

Tentatively, she moved her toes, then her fingers, then wiggled her legs and arms. She seemed to be all in one piece, so maybe Jeb hadn't gotten to her before she passed out. She extracted one hand from the cocoon they'd tucked her in and gingerly explored her face and head. Her head was wrapped in gauze.

"Hi, beautiful. About time you woke up. I've been hanging around for three days."

Her heart sang with joy at the sound of Drum's voice.

She turned her head and saw him standing near the window, his hands stuck in his jeans pockets, his face in shadow. It was nighttime. Behind him, outside the window, a single light shone from the parking area. A soft night light shone warmly around her solitary bed, the only brightness in the room. There were no sounds from the hushed corridors of the sleeping hospital.

Suddenly, the remnants of sharp fear returned, and she asked, "Jeb Bassert?"

"Jeb is very dead. He died in the library. He'll never bother you again. Guardian angels were with you, my Lannie."

She heard the love in his voice, and her heart sang again.

"Well, I know I'm in a hospital somewhere, but I guess I'll ask the proverbial question. Where?"

He laughed. "You're in High Falls Community Hospital. I wanted to take you to Duke, but the doctors here insisted you were fine, but you were in shock and needed a few days of recovery. I had a few doctors flown in to double-check that you were okay, and they all said tender, loving care would bring you around sooner or later, and that could be done here as well as anywhere."

"But they don't know about . . . " She stopped, then began again. "I have to tell the doctors that . . . I'm . . ."

"Pregnant?" he supplied.

"Yes."

"They know, and they told me."

She wished she could see his face. "I know I should have told you, Drum, but I was afraid."

"Afraid of what?" His tone was neutral. What was he thinking?

"Afraid you'd leave Ann-Marie because of me. Afraid you'd be sorry that you'd been forced into a decision you didn't want to make." Her voice broke. "I'm so sorry, Drum."

"Don't cry, Red." He made it to her bed in one long stride. Through her tears she saw that his face was stamped with the strain of the last few days, but his eyes held a contented glow. "And don't be sorry. You did what you thought you had to do to survive and protect our child.

Retreating helped you heal when Gracie died. But I'm here now, Red, and we'll solve our problems together from now on."

"You mean you're not angry that I didn't tell you?"

"Angry as hell for a few minutes, but then so elated that you and the baby were going to be okay that I got over it."

She broke into tears, boo-hooing like a heroine in a dumb movie.

"Hey, hey, no more of that." He sat on the side of the bed and took her in his arms. "You're here in my arms and that's where you're going to stay for the rest of our lives."

With a sigh, she nestled into his neck. "I love you, Drum Rutledge, and I want you in spite of everything. I understand about Ann-Marie, and I don't care what people think if we live together in sin."

She felt a smile puff his cheek. "Listen to me, sweetheart, and understand that I made this decision *before* I knew about the baby. I don't think we'll have to live in 'sin' as you call it. I've made many phone calls and talked to many people while you've been having your beauty sleep."

She raised her head and looked at him. "About what?" She sniffled.

He whipped a tissue from the bedside box, and said, "Blow."

She did as he said and had to smile at his paternal ordering about.

"Why were you making phone calls?" she asked again.

"I love you. You are my life. I decided while I was hunting for Jeb that I wanted you to be my wife . . . if you'll have me."

"Yes, yes," she said, and then started crying again, "but I thought you . . ."

He handed her another tissue, and laughed. "You sure

are a weepy dame tonight, Red." He folded her into his arms again.

"Stop worrying and listen to me," Drum said. "Ann-Marie lives in a wonderful world of her own. She always will. She's like a child, and she's loved and happy with the sisters in New Orleans. The Catholic church is considering my petition for annulment, but those things take a long time. I think it will happen, but even if it doesn't, I've already filed for divorce. We can be married soon as it comes through."

"But what about Ann-Marie?" she asked, remembering with a tremulous heart the delicate face with the vulnerable eyes and the feathery cloud of dark hair.

"Look at me, Lannie." He took her chin, and tilted it up so she had to meet his gaze. "Ann-Marie will always be my responsibility. When I petitioned for divorce I also filed papers asking to be appointed her guardian. If you marry me, you have to know that Ann-Marie will always be in our lives. I hope you understand that. I will visit her and hope that you will join me."

"I wouldn't have it any other way, Drum."

He kissed her then, a soft, lingering kiss on her chapped lips, and she melted inside, wanting more, but she wasn't ready. She had another question to ask, and she dreaded it.

"Drum, what happened to Bry?"

"Look on the other side of your bed."

Tucked close to her bed was a large, low cot. Bry lay there with intravenous lines connected to him, feeding him nourishing liquids and healing antibiotics. His belly was shaved, and a white bandage was wrapped around his midsection. He slept peacefully.

"Oh, Bry, my Bry." Tears fell again, and he handed her another tissue. "Is he going to be okay?"

"Yes, but it will take him a long time to heal and get his strength back. I thought he was dead when I roared into the emergency room, but I had one of the doctors examine him. He was clinging to life stubbornly, so they worked on him right here in the hospital." Drum smiled again. "I had to bribe them with a huge donation to their expansion fund, but they finally agreed to let him stay here with you instead of being transferred to the veterinary hospital."

"You're sure he's okay?"

"As soon as they put him in here with you, it's been like a miracle. He's fought to get stronger every day."

"Thank you, God, and forgive me for wondering if You were there."

"Amen," said Drum and bowed his head.

Her hands flew to the gauze turban on her head. "Oh, Drum, how bad is it? I must be so ugly. How can you love me when I look like a bald, blistery witch from hell?"

He took her hands in his and kissed them, then kissed the gauze on her head. "You will always be beautiful to me, Lannie. Someday I'll be bald, and you'll have beautiful white hair, and I'll love you more then than I do now."

"Am I going to have bald spots, Drum?"

"Maybe, for a while, but the doctors say your scalp will heal gradually, and your hair will be as glorious as it ever was."

"Honest?"

"Yep, honest."

"Who sent all the flowers?" Spots of color shone through the dim shadows.

"Spencer and Julia Jane, Beezy Bowden and Daisy, Nell's parents, the Applebys, and your father."

"You've talked with my father?"

"Sure, and Mausie and Big Billy. I told the judge everything about you and me, and about Jeb, and that you were fine. I asked him if he minded having me for a son-in-law, and he was delighted."

"Well, I guess you're going to get that twenty acres you wanted. You sure went about getting it in a roundabout way."

He roared with laughter, and a nurse came running to poke her head in the door. "Everything okay in here?"

They looked at her, grinning.

"Everything is perfect," they said.

EPILOGUE

The peace and safety she'd felt when she'd first entered this sanctuary three years ago were still here, maybe more so. Lannie's visits with Ann-Marie always brought her a great measure of tranquility.

Outside in the courtyard, lavender nepatas and climbing green clematis still spilled thither and yon over the wall and into the tinkling angel fountain.

But the books on the shelves were now a mixture, some belonging to Drum and others to Lannie. The plump, comfy armchairs in front of the windows had been recovered in serene shades of soft coral and misty greens. Fresh flowers, delivered every week, filled the creamy antique urns on the tables.

And in one corner sat a baby's high chair and a small rocking chair holding big, floppy cloth dolls.

Lannie closed the book she was reading, but kept her finger on the page so she wouldn't lose her place. Behind her, a child giggled and silvery laughter came from the bed in the center of the room. She sighed with contentment and ran a hand over her swelling tummy. This one was a boy.

"Lannie, did you know that Nell Anne can count to twenty when she uses her toes?" asked Ann-Marie. "Of course, we have to tickle the toes before they can be counted."

She turned to feast on the happy tableau behind her.

Ann-Marie sat in the middle of her big bed playing with two-year-old Nell Anne Rutledge. The bed was a jumble with picture books, dolls, and toys of all kinds. On the floor next to them sat an erect, but graying, Bry, his head cocked with interest as he watched them play.

As she watched, Ann-Marie tickled the redheaded child's toes. Lannie joined them in their laughter and was filled with gladness at the sound. She ran her hand over the narrow white streak in her otherwise red hair. The streak had grown in with the rest of her healthy hair and was her only reminder of the harrowing two-day ordeal with Jeb Bassert.

Ann-Marie hadn't aged a bit. In fact, she seemed to grow younger every year. She believed herself to be eighteen years of age, and doctors said that would always be so. Her angel-shaped face shone with happiness as she played with Lannie and Drum's child. There still were days when she went into a comatose state, but they came less often.

"Lannie, don't you think that God finds His way to us through little children, dogs, and flowers?"

"I'd never thought about it before, but I think you may be right."

"Sometimes I dream that I have a little boy named Chip, and he lets me read to him like I read to Nell Anne, and he puts his arms around me and hugs me when we finish, just like she does. It's so real. Isn't that wonderful?"

"Yes, darling, it is."

"You do love me, don't you, Lannie?"

"Yes, you know that I do, and so does Drum."

"I know. Life would be terrible without love in it."

"I think that once you've known a great love, no matter what you had to go through to find it, or to keep it, going back to a life without love would be like going back to being a caterpillar after you have put on the wings of a butterfly."

Ann-Marie hugged Nell Anne to her, and said, "Oh, I love what you just said. May I write it in one of my poems?"

"I'd be flattered if you did."

"Where is Drum?"

"He went to pick up a very important shipment of books at the bookstore. He should be here any minute."

Sister Cecily came in with Drum right behind her carrying a cardboard box.

"Hey, how are all my girls?"

Nell Anne squealed to be picked up by her daddy. He tossed her in the air and hugged her to him while Sister Cecily opened the box.

She pulled out a slim volume of poetry with a cover resembling the courtyard outside the window.

"Here it is, my child," she said to Ann-Marie. "The second edition of *Winged Shadows: Poetry from a Convent*, by Ann-Marie Rutledge."

Ann-Marie held it to her heart for long moment, then gave it to Lannie to put on the table by the window.

"I couldn't have written some of these poems without your love, my friends."

"Sure, you could have," said Lannie, but Ann-Marie had forgotten they were there, and sang a song to herself and Nell Anne.

Drum gathered Lannie into his arms. "You are love." He kissed her reverently on the forehead. "Thank you."